PRAISE

STARLIGHT CHILD

"A superb futuristic romance!"

—*Affaire de Coeur*

MOONLIGHT RHAPSODY

"Nancy Cane creates a richly detailed futuristic world sure to stimulate the reader's imagination."

—Kathleen Morgan, Author Of *Heart's Surrender*

"Scintillating and heart stopping. Ms. Cane has definitely proven herself a master of this genre."

—*Rendezvous*

"*Moonlight Rhapsody* is an action-packed, fast-paced futuristic romance....Nancy Cane has a visionary gift of writing about the future in a manner that makes it seem like it's happening today."

—*Affaire de Coeur*

CIRCLE OF LIGHT

"An extraordinary reading adventure you cannot pass up."

—*Rendezvous*

"Nancy Cane sparks your imagination and melts your heart!"

—Marilyn Campbell, Author Of *Stardust Dreams*

Love in another time, another place.

STARLIGHT DESIRE

"What did you do?" Deke cried.

Mara froze. She had no excuse for her behavior.

"You tried to read my mind!"

"I can't read thoughts," she protested. "I can only sense emotions, even when I'm in someone else's viewpoint. I...I'm not sure how it happened, but you appear to have triggered a *separation.*"

He stared at her, horrified. "What do you mean?"

Agitated, she brushed her hair off her face. "When I was younger, this sort of thing happened all the time. I had difficulty controlling my ability. But never in my adulthood have I experienced anything similar."

"Do you mean you have no control over this freakish ability? Gods, could this happen again?"

She saw his fear mixed with resentment. He stared at her as if she were some sort of monster.

"You're the only man with whom I've ever had a spontaneous *separation,* Deke. There's got to be something significant involved. Perhaps we should explore our feelings for each other."

Other *Love Spell* Books by Nancy Cane:
MOONLIGHT RHAPSODY
CIRCLE OF LIGHT

STARLIGHT CHILD

NANCY CANE

LOVE SPELL  NEW YORK CITY

LOVE SPELL®

April 1995

Published by

Dorchester Publishing Co., Inc.
276 Fifth Avenue
New York, NY 10001

Cover Art by John Ennis

Printed in the United States of America.

To my children, Paul and Sara: May you achieve your dreams and live a long life enriched by love, laughter, and health. You are the essence of my future and my love will always be with you.

With special thanks to:

Robert E. Sheridan, Anchor Scuba, Ft. Lauderdale: technical diving instructor trainer, commercial diver, and independent consultant to the diving industry.

Christine Nemeth, B. Dalton bookseller

Starlight Child

Chapter One

A woman's high-pitched screams of anguish tore through the night. The piercing cries lanced into Mara's sleep-numbed mind and awakened her. Sitting up abruptly in bed, she listened acutely. Dead silence filled the room. Her dark eyes swept the bedchamber, resting upon her modern built-in shelving unit with its holovid array, the chest of carved wooden drawers from her home planet Tyberia, and the display case with her collection of sculptures. The room's illumination had brightened automatically when she sat up, but still her heart raced and her spine chilled with fear.

Could the awful sounds have come from Hedy? An urgent need to check on her roommate propelled her out of bed, but a glimpse of the petite brunette sleeping next door reassured her that all was well. After a hasty search of the rest of the apartment, Mara concluded she'd been dreaming. Letting out a breath of relief, she grabbed a wrap from her chamber and told herself to calm down.

But the agonized cries kept reverberating in her mind as though they were real, and she couldn't dismiss the uneasy feeling that something was wrong.

Trying to shake off the remnants of her nightmare, she strode to the fabricator in the living area to conjure a warm drink, hoping it would soothe her sensitized nerves. She stood watching the alcove in the wall as her beverage materialized in a large ceramic mug. Drinking a cup of wagmint tea always calmed her when she felt tense, and it had been a particularly aggravating day at work. Maybe that was why her sleep had been disturbed.

As soon as the notion came to her, she dismissed it. She hadn't awakened because of insomnia. A woman's screams had torn her from the fabric of slumber. They had sounded as real to her as the mug felt in her hand. Although it had been synthesized from a molecular matrix, the mug was solid. She believed the sounds she'd heard were just as substantial. It couldn't have been a dream! And if not, then whose distress was so great that it had touched her in her altered state of consciousness?

She was just raising the cup to her lips when a loud chime shattered the heavy silence.

"Computer, open channel!" she said, her voice trembling. "Hello? Who is it, please?" Holding her breath, she waited for the response.

"It's Sarina," came her friend's hoarse voice, tense with anxiety. The video was off, so Mara couldn't see her face. "Can you come over?"

Her throat constricted. "It's two-thirty in the morning. What's wrong?"

"I . . . can't explain over the commlink. Oh God, Mara, what am I going to do?" Sarina's voice cracked. "Please, come quickly!"

"I'll be there." Terminating the link, she set her mug down and obtained a set of lace underwear and a plum stretch jumpsuit from the fabricator. As she pulled them on, she wondered what could have happened. Her imagination ran wild with all sorts of ominous possibilities, making her fingers quake so badly that fastening her jumpsuit required a major effort.

Sparing a brief glance at the reflector to straighten her long hair, she strode into the foyer. Her shiny black boots were where she'd left them beside the door. As she shoved her feet inside, she composed a voice message for Hedy. Normally her roommate slept as soundly as a hibernating bear, but Mara didn't want her to worry should she awaken and find herself alone.

Outside, the dark sky above the biosphere's crystal domed ceiling was studded with stars. Breathing in the cool, crisp air, she focused on determining the quickest route to Sarina's. They lived some distance from each other even though Bimordus Central was relatively compact.

Taking an airbus or a people mover meant she'd have to change vehicles along the way. It might be more expedient to walk three blocks to the transport terminal and requisition a speeder.

Making her decision, she strode at a fast pace along a paved walking path dimly lit by low footlights. Her surroundings faded into the background of her preoccupied mind. Wrinkling her brow, she wondered what could have happened to cause Sarina such anxiety.

Was her daughter ill? Seven months old, the pretty blond-haired, blue-eyed babe already showed signs of her exceptional heritage. Jallyn Diana bore the sacred sign of the circle on her palm in the same manner as her gifted mother. Although Sarina was the legendary Great Healer, Mara knew that her healing power was limited. She hoped Jallyn hadn't been stricken with a disease Sarina couldn't cure. As the child's godmother, she felt very close to her.

Moisture pricked her eyes and she sought to divert her

own concern by examining different possibilities. Perhaps Jallyn was not the cause of Sarina's trouble. Could Sarina herself have been attacked? She'd made her share of enemies while becoming the Great Healer. Briefly, Mara reviewed the story that had become nearly as familiar to her as her own history.

Sarina had been abducted from Earth by Captain Teir Reylock of the Coalition Defense League. As ordered, Teir had delivered her to the High Council on Bimordus Two for her marriage to Lord Rolf Cam'brii. Through this union, it was believed Sarina would fulfill an ancient prophecy and become the Great Healer. Mara could hardly believe that a mere two annums had passed since the horrible plague called the Farg had swept through Coalition space, followed by the dreaded Morgot conquerors. The Great Healer had been their only hope for salvation.

The Morgots had sought to stop the prophecy's fulfillment. They hired Cerrus Bdan, a Souk slave trader, to capture Sarina and Teir, who was acting as her bodyguard. When Bdan failed in his objective, he was executed. Sarina became the Great Healer when she fell in love with Teir. He was her destined mate, not Lord Cam'brii. With her newly activated power, she eradicated the Farg and helped chase the Morgots from Coalition territory.

Beside the Souks and the Morgots, who else would have reason to resent Sarina's interference in their affairs? Mara supposed former councillor Daimon could be considered a contender. The powerful statesman had been a leader of the Return to Origins faction, a secessionist movement that had gained favor during previous crises. Daimon tried to have Sarina and Lord Cam'brii assassinated to prevent their marriage from taking place, fearing the legend's fulfillment would strengthen Coalition unity. When Sarina became the Great Healer, Daimon was forced to resign in disgrace. Mara had heard that his followers were active on other worlds.

As she mulled over the alternatives, her gut feeling told her that none of these pertained to Sarina's current distress. Something else was involved here.

Sighing, she decided she'd just have to wait to learn the answers.

Twenty minutes later, she stood at the entrance to Sarina's residential tower, a spiral structure made from glittery pink stone and white marbelite. An unusual number of security personnel patrolled the well-lit perimeter.

A middle-aged man with a stern visage caught her eye as she neared the entrance. "Excuse me, can I help you?" he said, blocking her passage. He wore a nondescript khaki jacket but his stiff military posture and firm voice proclaimed his authority.

"I'm here to see Sarina Reylock." Her voice trembled, and she laced her frozen fingers together in an effort to calm herself. A stranger might not recognize anything as being different, but she'd been here before at night and had never encountered any resistance.

"You are?" The man fixed her with a piercing glare.

"Mara Hendricks."

He scanned a file on his hand-held datalink. After a moment, his face brightened, and he looked up with a smile. "Got your name right here. The Great Healer expects you. I'll let you in."

A few moments later, she entered a short foyer. To her left rose a spiral staircase. Up ahead was an atrium with a glass lift. A couple of men were running a sensing device over a portion of the floor by the stairs. Bent in concentration, they didn't bother to look up at her entrance.

Her feeling of dread deepening, she entered the lift. "Fourteen," she intoned, and the door slid shut. The conveyor began to rise. She watched the different levels pass by in a blur as the lift sped upward. By the time it reached the fourteenth floor, her knees were shaking. A pair of guards stood in front of Sarina's door, frightening her with their fierce expressions. One of them announced her arrival over the comm unit.

Inside, Sarina rushed to greet her. "Mara, I'm so glad you're here!"

After giving her a brief hug, Mara stood back, regarding her friend's tear-streaked face and disheveled appearance. Sarina's gray eyes were wide with shock. Her blond hair was in rumpled disarray, her nightclothes haphazardly covered by a crimson drape. A faint, sickly sweet odor was in the air. The casements were wide open, letting in a cool breeze that ruffled the hairs on Mara's skin.

Her stunned gaze swept the living area, lighting on a tall, bearded figure seated on a double lounger in front of a black crystalline table. Glotaj, the supreme regent, was here! And standing in front of the holovid entertainment center, studying the flashy dials, was Lt. Wren, one of Teir's crew. He was on medical leave, having been injured on a recent mission. Great suns, had something happened to Teir that they were both here? The captain was away on assignment. Why else would Glotaj and Wren have come together if not to deliver bad news?

"What's happened?" she asked, her heart thudding in her chest. "Teir, is he—" She couldn't get beyond the two words.

Sarina shook her head. "It's Jallyn. She . . . she's been kidnapped!" Sinking onto a chair, the Great Healer covered her face with her hands.

Mara's jaw dropped. "What?"

Glotaj rose from the lounger to greet her. "Mara," the older statesman said, regally inclining his head. Wings of gray fanned his temples, flanking a forehead creased with worry lines. A pair of dark, piercing eyes met hers. Without preamble, Glotaj launched into an explanation.

"Someone showed up at Sarina's door pretending to deliver a bouquet of flowers. She thought they were from Teir and opened the portal, wherein the delivery person disabled her with a noxious fume sprayer. When her life-form readings dipped, the automated sentry sent out an alarm. A security team found her out cold on the floor. We've already done a sweep of the apartment. Traces of quantum resolution activity were found in the baby's chamber."

He scowled as though that had a significance Mara didn't understand. "The other results won't be available for a few hauras yet," Glotaj continued. "The team's in the foyer. They've picked up unusual readings by the stairs."

"I saw them," Mara acknowledged. "Who do you suspect is responsible?" Her friend's look of anguish pierced her and she wavered between talking to Glotaj and rushing to Sarina's side.

"Speculation can wait," Sarina snapped, making the decision for her. "Will you do a separation, Mara? I . . . I have to know if Jallyn's all right!"

She nodded, eager to comply. As a Tyberian, she possessed extrasensory ability, but her power went beyond the norm for her people. She could actually separate her spirit from her body and jump into another person's life space. This allowed her to see what the other person saw; to experience their viewpoint as events unfolded. It was a gift she was loath to use because it had caused her an unhappy childhood, but in this case, she would do anything to help Sarina.

To ease her mind in preparation, Mara let her gaze roam the living area, artfully decorated in ivory and teal. Various ornaments collected on Sarina's travels to different planets in the galaxy were displayed. They would be meaningless to her friend if her beloved daughter was lost.

"I need an object that's touched Jallyn," she reminded Sarina gently.

"Of course." Rising, Sarina rushed from the room, returning a moment later holding a lavender woven blanket.

Mara took it from her and clutched it to her chest. Her eyes closed, and she began the inner flight along the astral plane. As she concentrated, a vibration hummed through her body, expanding outward. A buzzing noise rang in her ears. She felt herself lighten as the sound altered, changing to a rushing noise like water gushing through a narrow gorge. All at once, her essence separated from her body and floated upward. She hovered a moment, feeling as airy as a feather. It was an incredible sensation and she wanted to savor it, to remain immersed in the peace and warmth of her new state.

Unencumbered by a physical body, she could go anywhere. Freedom beckoned her. The dimensions of time and space didn't pose any restraints to her spiritual being. She still had a form of sorts, but it was different, like an energy signature of what she had been.

She focused her thoughts on the baby, on the pretty blond-haired child who'd be frightened and bewildered without its mother. She could feel its vibrations emanating from the blanket, guiding her. Almost instantly, she was with Jallyn, popping into her head.

Confusion struck her. Seeing through the baby's eyes, it was difficult to make out the view in Jallyn's perspective. She was lying on her back, squirming, her diaper wet and uncomfortable. Overhead a bright light shone in her face. When her head twisted to the side, rows of painted wooden strips obstructed her view. Beyond the slats was a curved metal wall.

Footsteps sounded. A woman's face appeared, peering at her with a frown. Jallyn saw a large set of violet eyes, a pale complexion, brown hair knotted in a low bun. As the face neared, the nose seemed to expand, threatening to jab into her. She began to cry.

"Not now!" Mara whispered to herself. She couldn't see well through the moisture in Jallyn's eyes.

Huge hands grasped her pudgy legs, raised them, removed the wet diaper. She was roughly dried and powdered, then rediapered. As Jallyn was turned onto her stomach to have her back rubbed, Mara glimpsed a small round casement set high in another metal wall. A viewport, and outside all was dark.

Having seen enough, Mara separated. Instantly, she found herself in Sarina's apartment being sucked back into her physical body.

Slowly, she opened her eyes. The feeling of weightlessness, of freedom, was gone, but the serenity she'd experienced remained. Once more encumbered by her physical being, she took a moment to adjust.

"Jallyn is lying in a crib. A woman is caring for her," she told Sarina, trying to keep the emotion from her voice.

Seated on the lounger, Sarina stared at her, wide-eyed. "Thank God someone's looking after her." Her composure shattered, and tears streamed down her face. "Jallyn . . . Oh, dear God, what am I going to do?" Her face paled, and she slumped back.

"She needs a medic," Mara said in alarm. "Let's call Hedy." With the supreme regent's permission, she gave Wren the coded signal that would trigger Hedy's bedside alarm. Her roommate, a respected physician, could be relied upon for discretion.

Reassured that Hedy was on her way, Mara obtained a sedit beverage from the fabricator and handed it to Sarina. "Drink this. It'll help." Watching her friend drain the contents, she wondered if she should conjure a restorative for herself. It might help stem the flood of tears that were perilously close to overflowing. She couldn't bear to see Sarina so upset.

"What else did you notice?" Glotaj asked.

A shudder racked her body and she struggled for control. "A viewport and a metal bulkhead."

"What?"

Mara sank onto the lounger next to Sarina. She described her additional perceptions.

"By the moons of Agus Six! That sounds like a ship." The supreme regent narrowed his eyes. "Computer, open channel. Get me the control center for Spaceport Operations." When the connection came through, he identified himself. "I want the manifest checked for all departures within the past two hauras."

"I'll get right on it, Your Excellency " said the controller in charge. "Do you wish to wait?"

"No, call me back." Abruptly, he terminated the link and turned around. "If Jallyn isn't on Bimordus Two, it will take us longer to find her, and the Elevation Ceremony is scheduled for sixty days hence. It will be disastrous if Jallyn fails to appear. We must keep this whole thing under wraps until she's found."

"I agree," Wren said in a quiet voice. He'd been listening off to the side but now walked over to join them. "If Jallyn's abduction becomes public knowledge, it will frighten the Auranians. They'll fear they are still in danger from those who would oppose them."

Glotaj nodded solemnly. "They might be deterred from revealing their legacy for another millennium. Jallyn has to be found so she can make her scheduled appearance."

Mara considered his words. The Auranians were a people of ancient descent who'd been persecuted because of their ability to mentally manipulate the aura surrounding living matter. Forced to flee their home planet of Shimera, they'd scattered among the stars, hiding their heritage to avoid further repression. Sarina's ancestors had been Auranians who'd landed on Earth. Teir was thought to be of Auranian descent as well. Ever since their joining, Auranians had been coming forward to claim their legacy. To these people, Jallyn's birth symbolized the reemergence of their race. The Elevation Ceremony had been set to recognize their right to freedom of expression, and Mara prayed Jallyn would be found in time to be there.

"Do you think Jallyn was taken because someone wants to discourage the Auranians from making a comeback?" she asked, puzzled. She didn't think the Auranians would pose a threat to anyone. Those who had come forward were learning long-forgotten skills based on Sarina's experience. They'd become healers, albeit on a more limited scale than Sarina.

"Who would be against us?" Sarina's voice rose barely above a whisper. "My people just want to live in peace." Her fingers plucked at her crimson drape, opening and closing the folds in a nervous, repetitive motion. Mara gripped Sarina's cold hand in her own to offer reassurance.

"Why would someone take Jallyn?" Sarina wailed, her face crumbling into silent tears.

"Do you think Sarina is in danger?" Mara asked Glotaj. A weight settled in the pit of her stomach at the possibility.

Glotaj shook his head. "The abductors had the perfect opportunity to harm her, but she was left untouched. No, it was Jallyn they wanted." The supreme regent paced the room, his hands folded behind his back.

Wren swept a sympathetic glance toward Sarina and Mara and she drew strength from his presence. A strong, confident male, Wren was a Polluxite who served as Teir's navigator aboard the *Valiant.* Like his captain, he ignored military convention and opted to wear leather breeches and a white shirt half open at his muscular chest.

Her gaze scanned his liquid hazel eyes and rose to his

layered eyebrows. A white streak was sandwiched between two chestnut layers darker than his head of brown hair. Combined with the rugged angles of his face, the unusual brows gave him a striking appearance.

Beside her, Sarina gave a long tremulous sigh. Mara shot her a sharp glance, wishing Hedy would hurry up and get there. She squeezed Sarina's hand, willing her to be strong. Her own heart fluttered rapidly in her chest. Jallyn . . . the poor child.

"Does Teir know?" Mara rasped.

"He's on special assignment with the *Valiant* and can't be reached," Glotaj said, facing her. "They're on orders to observe radio silence."

A cry of grief escaped Sarina's lips. The empty cup slipped from her fingers, falling onto the carpeted floor. Mara caught her by the shoulders just as she slumped to the side. "By the faith, she's passed out!" Mara exclaimed.

Wren hurried over. With his big arms, he scooped the Great Healer into his protective embrace and headed for her sleeping chamber. "She's had a terrible shock. I'll put her on her lounger until Dr. Te'larr gets here," he said, using Hedy's formal name.

Mara wiped her moist eyes with the back of her hand. An emptiness stole into her heart, partly from fear for the missing child and partly from sharing her friend's anguish. She felt powerless when events were unfolding so fast and wished there were more she could do to help.

Wren marched out of Sarina's bedchamber, his expression somber. "I think we should consider different angles," he said. "Jallyn could have been taken for reasons other than the Auranian issue." His nervousness was betrayed by the large set of muscular wings that suddenly sprouted from his back. With a grimace of annoyance, he forced them to fold and retreat. "Personally, I think it's the Morgots making another stab at Sarina," he went on. "K'darr, the Morgot leader, tried to capture her before she became the Great Healer. He could be trying to gain through the infant what he failed with her mother; that is, to twist her power to his own uses. Of course, the extent of Jallyn's ability is unknown at this stage. She may not possess the healing gift despite the sign of the circle on her palm."

"Jallyn does have the gift," Mara responded. "I've sensed it in her, and she might be capable one day of doing more than healing. The light of the aura is strong in her."

"Revenge could be a motive for either the Morgots or the Souks," Glotaj cut in, his face pensive. "They both have reason to resent Sarina's opposition to their goals."

"I doubt the Souks are involved," Wren protested. "After Lord Cam'brii's secret mission to Souk last annum, the pashas who gained power have been friendly to the Coalition."

"Where is Rolf?" she asked, knowing that Lord Cam'brii and his bride had become good friends to Sarina and Teir.

"He and Ilyssa are visiting his family on Nadira," Glotaj answered. "They know nothing about this. The fewer people who hear about it, the better." His icy blue gaze stared at her meaningfully.

"What about former Councillor Daimon? Could he be making a replay for dominance?" Mara felt compelled to discuss all the possibilities. Even though she felt something else was at stake here, the others might come up with an angle she hadn't considered.

Glotaj stroked his bearded jaw. "I don't see how stealing Sarina's baby would fit into his scheme of things. The Return to Origins faction is a secessionist group."

"I've got it!" Wren exclaimed, his eyes lighting up. "It's a ransom demand!"

"That's absurd," Mara retorted. Her head throbbed, and she rubbed at a pulsating point on her temple. "Sarina and Teir don't have a lot of credits. What would someone stand to gain? In my opinion, you're both off track. I sense there's something else here we're missing."

"Yes, we're missing Jallyn!" Glotaj cried, exasperated.

It disturbed her to see the supreme regent so flustered. Normally the elderly leader's demeanor was calm and poised, as it had been through all the crises that had afflicted the Coalition so recently. It proved how much he cared for Sarina that he felt so deeply for her and let it show.

The chime from the comm unit broke the silence.

"Computer, open channel," Glotaj thundered. "Greetings. This is Glotaj speaking."

"Spaceport Operations on-line; Controller Brecch here. I have the information you requested, Your Excellency."

"Go ahead."

"Three ships have launched within the past two hauras," Brecch's gruff voice spoke over the comm unit. "One belongs to Fromoth Trun and the Yanuran delegation. They're returning to their home planet, Yanura. Another is Gregorski's, a pilot who applied for mining rights to the Doby asteroid belt; and the third is Ambassador El'Rik's ship. He's returning to the Minx system."

"That's very helpful, Controller. Thanks for your assistance." Glotaj signed off, his brows furrowed in thought.

"I've been representing the Yanurans before the Admissions Committee," Mara mentioned. "Their departure was expected."

Glotaj nodded absently. "I'd like to have a private conversation with Adm. Daras Gog. I'm sure Sarina won't mind if I use her upstairs office."

While he was gone, the door chime rang and Hedy was admitted. Her haste in getting there was apparent in her disheveled appearance. She wore a pair of leggings and a pullover sweater, and her brown hair was fastened into a ponytail.

"Thank the stars you're here!" Mara cried, rushing to her. Quickly, she filled Hedy in on what had happened. Hedy's face paled and her lips compressed. When Mara finished, she rummaged in her bag for her medscan unit.

"I'll tend to her right away," she said, her voice quietly competent. Turning on her heels, Hedy headed into Sarina's sleeping chamber.

Wringing her hands, Mara paced anxiously in the living area. Her mind was filled with the issues they'd discussed. Had anything been left out, any item of small significance that would be relevant to the situation? A thought struck her and her heart raced. Why hadn't she thought of it before?

"Lt. Wren!" she said excitedly. Wren was at the holovid unit, scrutinizing Teir's new image crystallizer. At her summons, he glanced up. "The kidnappers knew Sarina would open her door to receive a bouquet of flowers, yet Earth isn't advanced enough to be a member of the Coalition. First contact hasn't been made. How would they know about the Earth custom of delivering flowers? It would have to be someone like me who's studied Earth's culture."

Wren raised his layered eyebrows. "Has anyone consulted you recently on the subject?"

She regarded him thoughtfully. She worked as a cultural attache for the Department of Interstellar Relations in the Diplomatic Affairs Bureau, representing new alien cultures applying for admission to the Coalition. In addition, she attended the interdisciplinary team rounds at the wellness center, offering her knowledge of alien customs as they pertained to medical care.

"I don't recall anyone mentioning the subject," she said, frowning. "Of course, anyone could use the data base in the study center." The main library on Bimordus Two had a huge directory, receiving input from over 500 worlds.

"This could be an important clue," Wren remarked, his

voice a pitch higher with excitement.

"What could?" Glotaj asked, descending the spiral staircase. When Mara explained her idea, he nodded his agreement. "You're right. On Bimordus Two, we consider it a sacrilege to snip blooms and deprive them of their short life span. The kidnappers specifically used a knowledge of Earth customs to trick Sarina. We'll have to look into this more thoroughly."

He briskly strode down the last few steps. Though dressed casually in a short tunic and trousers, his lined face, sharp gaze, and proud posture displayed his status as a member of the royal House of Raimorrda.

Teir also claimed lineage from that respected ruling family, Mara remembered. Was it possible the baby had been abducted by someone working against the Raimorrdans?

No, it couldn't be. Destroying the Elevation Ceremony would harm Auranians, not those of Raimorrdan blood. She was grasping at straws. Hanging her head, she felt discouragement wash over her.

"I notified Adm. Gog about the traces of quantum resolution activity found in the nursery," Glotaj announced, staring at a Carellian thorn vase displayed on a pedestal.

Mara followed the direction of his gaze. Pink veins highlighted the translucent white vase, and thorny prominences decorated the curved upper edge. It was one of the best pieces she'd ever created. The day when Sarina and Teir had accepted her gift with lavish praise had been one of her proudest moments.

Her eyes wandered to the holographic image of Jallyn fixed on the wall. The baby girl was gurgling with laughter, her tiny hands and feet waving with uninhibited joy as the camera had captured her. She remembered how Sarina had beamed with pride when she showed her the picture, and her eyes misted.

Pushing aside her emotions, she focused on what Glotaj had said. "What's the significance of quantum resolution activity?" she asked him, breaking the silence in the room. It was easy for them all to be lost in thought on such a sorrowful occasion.

Glotaj's mouth tightened as he moved closer to where she stood. "It means the abductors used transporter technology to escape. We've determined that there were two of them, but our scans are inconclusive for further details."

Her jaw dropped in astonishment. Transporter technology? As far as she knew, their scientists were only able to transport a roomful of objects from one location to another, but they hadn't perfected the technique enough to transfer people. Transporter technology was not related to the molecular alteration device that ran their fabricators or allowed shuttles to be disguised in different configurations.

"How is this possible?" she asked, stunned.

"There are several nonaligned species who possess technical knowledge in advance of our own," Glotaj answered, his voice grim. "The Rakkians, Fire Weavers, and Bolons come to mind."

"They should all be checked out," Wren stated, frowning. "One thing I don't understand—why the ruse with the flowers if the abductors could have gotten in using the same transporter method?"

"Apparently they arrived downstairs in the lobby. They must have been uncertain as to the location of Sarina's apartment. But once they found it and gained entry, they beamed directly out."

"Is there any way to trace the pattern to learn where they went?" she asked.

Glotaj sighed. "We don't have the instrumentation available. We do know she was taken aboard a ship. Adm. Gog is sending patrols after Boris Gregorski and Ambassador

El'Rik. The Yanuran delegation is another matter. Their situation requires a closer look, so I'm sending a special team to Yanura."

At Mara's look of puzzlement, he explained. "The Yanurans have applied for admission to the Coalition. You've been helping them with the application process, Mara, so you are more familiar with their situation. But Wren may not know the details."

He directed his attention to the Polluxite. "Fromoth Trun, the Yanuran leader, has offered a miracle age-preserving drug derived from seaweed as a trade incentive. The data seems conclusive, but the Admissions Committee requires a fuller investigation before reaching a decision."

"But the Yanurans don't need a trade incentive to enter the Coalition," Wren said, confused.

"They want immediate access to our technology instead of having to wait the usual probationary period of one annum. That can only be allowed if they're granted special trade status."

"What's their hurry?"

Glotaj shrugged. "We're not sure. That's why a closer look at their situation would help."

"If you ask me," Mara interrupted, "the Admissions Committee is looking for an excuse to deny their application! No one likes their smell and that's why I think the committee is delaying its response." The Yanurans exuded a fishy odor and she felt that prejudiced the committee against admitting the amphibian race to the Coalition. After her personal experiences with prejudice, fighting intolerance had become her passion in life. She was particularly adamant about the Yanurans. They were being discriminated against without reasonable cause.

Glotaj compressed his mouth. "I'm sending a team to Yanura regardless of your views, Mara. The mission will be to confirm the data regarding the drug Vyclor and look into Jallyn's disappearance."

"Then I'm going," she insisted. "I've been working with Fromoth Trun for the past five weeks, and I'm familiar with his habits. You won't find anyone else better acquainted with Yanuran culture."

"Agreed," Glotaj said cheerfully, as though he'd expected her to volunteer. "Lt. Wren, you'll join the group as navigator. Consider your medical leave canceled."

"A medic." She bounced on her heels excitedly. "Ask Hedy to go!"

A small smile cracked the supreme regent's face. "Very well. Lt. Ebo, a Sirisian, will serve as communications officer. He's also a qualified engineer. Adm. Gog suggested him."

"Who's in command?" Wren asked curiously.

Glotaj's smile grew broader. "Lt. Comdr. Deitan Sage will be pilot and mission leader."

"Commander Sage?" Wren's eyes widened. "He's a diving specialist in the SEARCH Force. We've worked together before."

"What's the SEARCH Force?" she asked, unfamiliar with that particular branch of the Defense League.

"SEARCH stands for Sea & Aerospace Command Detachment," Wren answered. "It's a commando unit whose operatives are trained to function in all types of environments. Comdr. Sage joined our crew last annum for a mission on Souk. We had to get two prisoners off the Isle of Spears in the Scylla Sea. He was dropped forty kilometers offshore. The commander swam to the island, did a quick recon, and laid out the laser markers to guide in the rest of us. We came in with our chutes. Luckily for us, Sage had taken out a squadron of Hortha guards that would have pinned us on the beach and wiped us out. Those beasts are nasty fellows. I don't know anyone else who could have taken them on single-handedly without leaving one of them alive to sound the alarm."

"Great," she muttered. Just what they needed: a gung-ho soldier in charge of a mission requiring diplomacy and tact. She knew the best way to deal with the Yanurans, and muscle power was not the approach of choice. Hopefully, Comdr. Sage was an intelligent man who would respect her opinions. But if he took an aggressive stance, she'd have to deal with him in the only way he might understand.

She loved a good fight, as long as the weapons were words.

Chapter Two

"Be careful, those fish squirt acid if they're handled improperly," Deitan warned through the commlink embedded in his face mask. Beyond the glimmer of his lamp, it was difficult to follow the movements of his fellow divers. The reef stretched into the inky blackness and his vision extended only as far as his light source.

Sighing with frustration, he checked his own net. A school of flatfish was entrapped inside. Being careful not to touch any with his gloved hand, he twisted the net opening around a tensile bar knot to seal it. His mouth tightened with the completion of his task. He'd much rather be exploring the reef that teemed with marine life instead of capturing fish destined for Defense League research. Flatfish could change colors to match their background. The military hoped to isolate the chemical process responsible and apply it to camouflage uniforms. No longer would it be necessary to issue desert wear for dry terrain or white parkas for frozen icelands or forest green bodysuits for verdant planets. Enhanced with a chemical color changer, a standard-issue uniform could be created to suit all types of missions. It wasn't the kind of research Deke prided himself in.

For nearly the entire span of his 35 annums, he'd been fascinated by the watery depths. Coming from the planet Eranus, where most people lived in floating cities on vast oceans, that was easy to understand. But his father, the director general, had hoped that he would pursue a different path. Having been a military hero, Jon Sage had always expected Deke to follow in his footsteps. But instead of the warriorlike sports his father preferred, Deke excelled in swimming and diving. He chose to pursue marine biology as his career. Despite his father's disappointment, Deke had coaxed Jon into sending him to the Institute for Marine Studies.

The chancellor, Samuel Ho Chin, had recognized his potential and had encouraged him to pursue the research that fascinated him. Deke had advanced rapidly and earned his doctorate. He had become keenly interested in environmental concerns when he heard that Sammy intended to retire. That was when Deke considered applying for the position. His area of study focused on deep-sea vents, but to continue his work, he needed a large grant. Securing the chancellorship would get him the required funding.

He had realized many other qualified people would be in competition for the position, and it would help if he could stand out from the crowd. Talking it over with his father, he had agreed when Jon advised him to accept a commission in the Defense League. Serving in the military would provide him with a well-rounded experience and should win him points over the academicians applying for the chancellorship.

Deke had joined the elite SEARCH force as a diving expert. He had concentrated on learning new skills and prided himself on his performance. But although he had accomplished his missions satisfactorily, the end of his two-annum term of service was rapidly approaching and he despaired of reaching his goal. Sammy's contract was due to expire in six more months, and a rival was being considered for the chancellor's position. Deke needed to do something to distinguish himself before his best career opportunity dissolved.

Glancing around the murky depths, Deke realized he wouldn't be earning any rewards here. Collecting schools of fish was child's play, a waste of his time and talent.

His eye caught on a patch of long, whitish tubes with bloodred tips glimmering in the cast of his light beyond a piece of brain coral. The ghostly cluster swayed gently in the current. Nearby, small crabs crept among a rise of rocks while an eel slithered off into a crevice.

Great stars, could those be giant tube worms?

Excited, Deke swam over. He'd never seen the eight-foot-long tube worms in the absence of hot sulfur-rich water before! Did this mean they could exist in environments other than a deep-sea vent community? Or was there something special about this reef that made the red-tipped creatures show up here?

His heart racing with the thrill of discovery, he yanked a specimen container off his weight belt. He'd just obtained a sample of ocean water when an agonized scream sounded from the commlink in his ear. He looked up in time to spot one of his colleagues sinking to the seabed in a flurry of bubbles.

Snapping the collection jar onto his belt, he took off. With the efficiency of a strong swimmer, Deke kicked his legs and thrust water out of his path with powerful arm strokes to reach his stricken comrade. One glance at the ruptured air-supply hose showed him that a flatfish had spewn its acid. Nueva was barely conscious. Deke ripped the woman's mouthpiece out and replaced it with his own. Sharing breaths, he revived her enough to get her to cooperate when he put his arm around her waist. His muscles trembling from the strain, he began to ascend toward the surface, stopping every few meters to give Nueva several intakes of air. The stress of controlling her fear was a tremendous burden. Sweat dripped inside his dive suit, and his pulse raced. The passing minutes seemed like hauras as they slowly gained on the surface.

At last they broke free. One quick glance told his crewmates what had happened.

"Get her on board," yelled Larse, the team medic. The bearded man helped haul her onto the dive platform. It wasn't easy considering her weighted gear. The weather had deteriorated and the boat was rocking violently.

A pretty redhead appeared at the rail. Carmin was a biochemist from Eranus, a lusty free spirit who was as unrestrained in bed as she was masterful over a microscope. She and Deke had gotten to know each other quite well during the voyage. An orange slicker covered her body as she glared at him through the driving rain.

"Where do you think you're going?" she hollered as he broke away from the dive platform, his head bobbing in the water.

"I've got to check something below," he called, intending to obtain a tube-worm specimen.

"No, you're not," a fierce male voice said. Comdr. Brigarde strode into view. The executive officer's large bulk was impressive even in his rain gear. His heavy dark brows furrowed in an angry line. "A message has come through from Command. You're to report to the captain's stateroom immediately."

Annoyance rippled through Deke. "What? I'm not going to leave now. I've just found something—"

"Get your ass up here," Brigarde shouted, his face reddening.

"Yes, sir!" Deke flipped onto the dive platform and removed his headgear. Rain splashed his face and cascaded down his neck as he wrestled with the rest of his equipment on the swaying deck.

Still wearing his insulated wet suit, Deke clutched the specimen container in his hand and headed for the stateroom that served as the captain's office. His thoughts raced as he wound his way through the metal-lined corridors of the ship's interior. A message had come from Command. Did that mean he was needed for a SEARCH commando operation? A wave of disappointment hit him, sharp as a knife wound. Despite the feeling that his talents could be better utilized, he didn't want to leave. He felt at home on the sea.

Reaching the captain's cabin, he identified himself on the comm unit. Capt. Manseur's gruff voice invited him to enter. Deke stepped inside, closing the door behind him. Then he turned and gave a crisp salute.

"You can dispense with the formalities, Lt. Comdr. What's that?" The captain eyed the collection jar in Deke's hand.

Deke grinned, appreciating Manseur's blunt manner. "I found tube worms by the reef, sir. This is the first time I've seen them in this type of environment. I took a water sample so I could test it for unusual properties." He ran a hand through his damp hair, wondering if he'd be allowed time in the ship's lab.

Capt. Manseur gave a curt nod. A stern military man who nonetheless possessed a keen sense of humor, he was in charge of the fleet of oceangoing research vessels that Defense League maintained on Setai IV. The world was mostly water with a few land masses, much like Eranus. Setai IV was being explored with the possibility of colonization in the near future.

Despite his research vessels' purpose, Manseur was no science scholar. He preferred fine wines, gourmet foods, and beautiful women as his hobbies. With Lt. Comdr. Sage receiving new orders, he could concentrate on getting to know that voluptuous redhead when Deke transferred off his ship. She'd had eyes just for the lean, muscled officer since he'd come aboard. It was difficult to compete with a younger man whose dark good looks seemed to appeal to every woman in sight.

"You'll have to leave your specimen for our biochemists. Here are your new orders." Unlocking a drawer in his desk, Capt. Manseur withdrew a datalink and handed it to Deke.

Deke activated the device and peered at the contents displayed on the screen. He was to report for duty at the Defense League station on Bimordus Two, the Coalition capital. He'd be taking charge of a special mission probe. A space voyage of 16 days' duration was involved.

Deke stared at the datalink in stunned silence. His missions had always utilized his diving expertise. He belonged here, working on the sea, not piloting a starship.

"I don't want to do this!" he blurted. Appalled, he glanced at the captain as though his superior officer could change his orders.

A small smile played on Manseur's mouth. "A transport vehicle is scheduled to arrive for you within the next haura, Lt. Comdr. I suggest you pack your things."

"The hell I will!"

"You wish to contact Vice-Adm. Rutta to protest your orders?"

"They're not from Rutta," Deke muttered. "Supreme Regent Glotaj is responsible."

Astonishment marched across the captain's features. "Your mission must be important."

Deke didn't care what his new task entailed. He wanted to remain on Setai IV, exploring the underwater environment he loved. Perhaps it was all a mistake. "May I have use of a secure line, sir? I wish to learn the details of this assignment."

"Permission granted. As long as you're ready when the shuttle arrives, you can stop by the comm center. I assume you keep your own personal scrambling codes?"

Deke nodded, his brows spewing droplets of water into his eyes. Blinking rapidly, he snapped a salute. "Thank you, sir. It's been a pleasure serving with you." Still clutching his specimen container, he left the captain's stateroom.

Detouring by the ship's lab, he gave his valuable water sample to one of the biochemists before heading for the comm center. The officer on duty left him alone with the flashing electronic equipment so he could make his call in private.

Glotaj came on the line right away. Deke faced the older man on the monitor screen. From the background view, he could see the supreme regent was in his office.

"Sir, I don't understand why you're giving me command of a special mission probe," Deke began. "My skills can be better utilized in undersea research."

"Your diving expertise is one of the reasons why I selected you to lead the team to Yanura, Deke."

Deke drew in a breath. He hadn't known their destination. "Yanura? Why there?"

Glotaj patiently explained the purpose of the voyage. When he was finished, Deke let out a long breath. He had reasons of his own for wanting to go to the planet, so he didn't need to be convinced. But he was still puzzled as to why Glotaj had chosen him as team leader. "Why didn't you just assign me as science officer?" he asked.

"I know your father, and he's spoken to me of your interest in the chancellorship. I thought I'd give you the chance to demonstrate your leadership skills. I've been following your career since you entered the service, Deke, and I believe you have the potential to succeed."

"Thank you, sir." Deke's voice was choked with emotion. This could be the opportunity he'd been waiting for, the chance to distinguish himself from all the other candidates applying for the chancellorship. He'd better make sure his team accomplished their mission objectives. "The shuttle is expected at any moment, and I need to prepare for departure."

Glotaj's lined face creased into a smile. "May the Light of the Aura grace your voyage. By the way, the name of the vessel you'll be taking to Yanura is the *Celeste.*" His eyes twinkled mischievously. "You'll find she's different, but that can have its advantages. Glotaj out."

As soon as the supreme regent terminated the link, Deke went to his cabin to gather his personal belongings. While automatically piling his things into a single worn case, he thought about the problems Glotaj had mentioned. He looked forward to investigating the underwater seaweed farms on Yanura. Mariculture was familiar to him from his home planet, so he knew what to expect. If the Yanurans were fooling anyone with their story about an age-preserving drug, he'd be able to detect the truth. And if the Yanurans had anything to do with Jallyn's abduction, he'd find her, too. He wouldn't let them get away with any more of their dirty tricks, not after what happened to Larikk.

His good friend and colleague, Larikk, had mysteriously disappeared on Yanura three annums ago. Deke had reason to believe foul play was involved, but the Yanurans had effectively blocked any attempts at an investigation. At the time, they were not members of the Coalition, so he couldn't pursue the case. But now that the Yanurans were applying for admissions status, they would come under Coalition provisional law.

Deke halted in his packing and clenched his fists. Before their next victim vanished, he'd expose their crimes and make them pay the consequences. Any deceit the Yanurans hoped to greet him with would be quickly and easily dispersed.

"I feel we're off on the wrong track, Hedy," Mara said. "Fromoth Trun was extremely courteous in all my encounters with him. I'm sure the Yanurans have nothing to do with Jallyn's disappearance."

"We'll find out when we get to Yanura," Hedy replied. They were home packing for the long voyage ahead. Hedy had finished stuffing her small case and had wandered into Mara's room. She sat on the lounger, examining her painted fingernails for flaws.

"I'm looking forward to seeing their planet after working so closely with Fromoth Trun. They're a most interesting species." Mara carefully placed a stack of data cards into her bag. "Did you know they are nocturnal? We'll have to adapt to their way of life. It'll be quite fascinating."

Hedy raised her green eyes, which sparkled with mischief. "I'm more excited about spending sixteen days in close quarters with that handsome Polluxite, Lt. Wren. Did you see his shoulders? By the corona, I've never met a male with a physique like that before!"

Mara rolled her eyes. "What about that Fraisirian messenger from the finance ministry? Didn't you say the same thing about him?"

Hedy shrugged. "That was last week."

"Hedy! This is a serious mission."

The petite brunette grinned. "No one said we couldn't have fun along the way."

"Lt. Wren is a member of Capt. Reylock's crew. Normally he ships out on the *Valiant*."

"So what? He's just recovered from a disrupter wound

he sustained on their last mission." She heaved a long sigh. "I wish I had been his medic."

"You're impossible." Mara snorted. "I keep telling you men are nothing but trouble, and you won't listen." Her last relationship had been a disaster. She and Pietor, an advocate in the Enforcement Bureau, had been seeing each other for seven months when he'd invited her to his home planet to meet his parents. They'd taken one look at her dark hair and olive complexion and voiced their disapproval. Mara was nothing like the albino beauties on Sonoria. How could Pietor have taken up with someone like her?

Instead of coming to her defense, Pietor had told them about her special gift. The memory of his mocking words still cut her deeply.

"Pietor wasn't worthy of you," Hedy said gently. "If he'd really loved you, he would have appreciated your unique attributes."

"I was nothing more than an exotic plaything to him. What a fool I was to believe he cared for me."

"The man was weak, Mara. He wouldn't defy his parents. Be glad he didn't marry you on Bimordus Two and then take you home. You were lucky to get rid of him when you did." Hedy poked her arm, giving her a teasing grin. "Come on, loosen up and you'll have more fun."

"I'm not going on this voyage to have fun. I intend to prove to the Admissions Committee that the Yanurans deserve an unbiased approval of their application." She threw a few cosmetics into her case despite her knowledge that the *Celeste* fabricators could supply most of what they'd need. She still preferred to bring along certain favorite items of her own.

"I wonder what Lt. Comdr. Sage will be like," Hedy mused. "I hope he's not one of those stiff protocol types."

"Wren speaks very highly of him."

"We're not in the military. He can't order us around."

Mara heard the note of defiance in her roommate's tone. "We are under his command while on this mission, Hedy."

Hedy raised her eyebrows. "Spoken like a real trooper. I can't wait to see how you react when he gives you an order!" She rose, smoothing the skirt of her minidress. "In the meantime, I'm going to get ready to meet that gorgeous Lt. Wren again!" She indicated her brown waves of shoulder-length hair. "Do you like this style or should I straighten it?"

Mara threw her hands up in mock despair. "Hedy! What am I going to do with you?"

Hedy flashed her a brilliant smile. "Try having a lighter outlook. It'll work wonders on your psyche. Say, maybe you could jump into Wren's viewpoint the next time we meet. You'll be able to sense how he feels about me."

That did it. Mara picked up a pillow and threw it at her roommate.

Hedy shrieked as she dodged the hit and ran out. Mara stood looking after her, her hands on her hips, wondering how she was going to stand hearing Hedy's ramblings about Wren for the entire trip.

Although their teasing banter was fun, Mara knew Hedy was just as worried as she was about Sarina and the baby. It seemed to be an unspoken agreement between them to focus on the political ramifications of the mission and not the personal aspects. Otherwise, thinking about Jallyn could paralyze them both with anxiety. Mara packed her last item, the baby's blanket. She'd need it to do separations to check on Jallyn's status. Her heart filled with pain as she pictured the tiny infant, so sweet and vulnerable. May the Light shine upon us, she prayed. We'll need all the help we can get.

Hedy was a competent physician and Mara knew she wouldn't be diverted by her attraction to Wren when her skills were required. Despite her passionate nature, Hedy could be quite serious when the occasion demanded it. Mara, on the other hand, was always serious. She drove herself hard and needed to be constantly busy. On this trip, as cultural attache, she'd be responsible for ensuring that the Yanurans were greeted properly, according to their customs. It was a role she looked forward to with enthusiasm. Hopefully the crew, and Lt. Comdr. Sage in particular, would be receptive to her suggestions.

Chapter Three

"Hedy, what's the problem?" Mara asked, frowning.

They'd just stepped off the moving walkway at launch bay 72 and were facing the air lock that would take them out of the protective domed section of the city. The whine of engines and roar of thrusters coming from outside hurt Mara's ears.

"I forgot something." Hedy was loaded down with bundles. She'd dashed into a few of the shops along the spaceport concourse and now paused, staring at Mara. "I've got to go back."

"Oh, for heaven's sake." Mara fumed beside her, eager to get aboard the *Celeste.*

"You can go on. I won't be long. Did you remember to call Sarina and tell her we were leaving?"

"Yes, I did. She's so disappointed that she couldn't come along."

Hedy raised an eyebrow. "Glotaj told her the reason why. She needs to be home in case the abductors contact her."

"He's right, of course. I'm just sorry I can't stay to lend her support. With Teir gone, she has no one. Glotaj won't let her share the news with anyone else."

"Stop feeling guilty about leaving her behind. You know you'd never pass up this chance to go to Yanura."

Mara smiled sheepishly. "I shouldn't feel so excited about it."

"Mara!"

"Oh, all right. Let me take some of your packages."

Hedy handed over several of her bundles. "I'll see you on board the ship!" she called, turning away.

Mara stepped inside the air lock, her arms laden. A steel door hissed shut behind her, followed by a whoosh of air that clogged her ears. Another door slid open on the opposite side. She strode out into the late-afternoon sunshine, shivering from the sudden drop in temperature.

Stopping in her tracks, she stared at the fat, cumbersome spacecraft standing on the launchpad.

"Great suns, what kind of ship is that?" she cried.

Instead of the sleek combat vessel she'd expected to find, the *Celeste* reminded her of a manatee, an Earth mammal she'd read about in her studies. Maneuverability for a ship of this size and shape had to be minimal. Although its strangely reflective black surface might provide some sort of protective camouflage, Mara judged the ship to be more suitable for hauling cargo than for taking a crew into a potentially dangerous situation.

Not that she thought they'd run into hostilities from the Yanurans. On the contrary, the amphibians were sure to welcome the Coalition team, since the visit would give them the opportunity to prove their claims about a miracle drug. Fromoth Trun had left Bimordus Two to make the necessary arrangements to receive an inspection team.

Examining the ship, she realized it made sense for them to be assigned a civilian vessel. If the crew showed up in a military ship bristling with gun ports, it would alert the Yanurans that more was at stake than a scientific expedition. Still, considering the hazards of space travel, she'd have felt better if the ship had a sleeker aerodynamic design. It didn't matter that her fears were foolish, that pirate attacks had diminished since the Souk slave runs had ended. A few obvious armaments on the ship would have reassured her.

After checking in with a security detail, she marched up the gangplank and boarded the *Celeste.* The embarkation area was located in a cargo section. Mara spotted a schematic diagram of the ship inlaid on a far wall and hastened over to learn the location of the crew's quarters. The bridge was on deck A, the engineering section on deck C. Staterooms were located on deck B, two flights up. With surprise, she noted there were six private cabins. Since the crew consisted of five members, she hoped that meant they'd each have their own space. Deck B also had a holovid lounge, a physiolab, a dining/conference facility, and other public areas that weren't labeled.

Maybe the ship's unwieldy shape had some advantages. Anxious to explore, she entered the turbolift. "Deck B," Mara commanded, and the door slid shut. Hopefully someone would have arrived who could tell her which cabin was hers. She wanted to unload Hedy's packages before taking a tour.

Silently, the lift rose, and a moment later it came to a smooth halt. The steel door opened to reveal a long, narrow corridor with soft lighting and pastel walls.

Balancing the packages in her arms, she stepped into the corridor. As she moved forward, a door to her right shot open and a tall, dark-haired man stalked out, walking directly into her.

Crying out, Mara dropped her bundles and teetered backward. His arm shot out, catching her at the waist.

"What do you think you're doing?" he snapped.

Pulled against him, she found herself staring into his face. Nearly a head taller than she, he reached a good six feet two inches in height. They were so close she could smell the musky scent of his aftershave.

"I . . . I was just getting out of the lift."

His glance drifted to her slightly parted lips. "You should watch where you're going."

"So should you!" she retorted, flustered.

Her senses flared as she regarded him, unable to move away. The man's features were angular and even, sculpted like one of her art forms. He had heavy brows, a straight nose, and a perfectly chiseled mouth. His jawline was firm with just the hint of a shadow. Imagining what it would be like to smooth her fingers over the planes of his face, her artistic persona itched to touch him. With that desire came the stirrings of something familiar deep inside her. She was all too aware of her breasts pressed against his solid chest, and her heart hammered in a rapid tempo of response.

"Ships have confined spaces," the man said in a low, suave tone. "There isn't room for tight maneuvers."

"I can see that." Her breath came short as she felt every point of contact between them.

"Try to be more careful, or we might run into each other again." His mouth curved into a grin as though it would be a pleasurable event.

Gods, when he smiled, his brown eyes warmed like melted chocolate and two adorable dimples appeared in his cheeks. Never in all of her 28 annums had she met a man as engaging as this.

"Who are you?" she demanded, barely recognizing the husky tone as her own.

His grin widened. "Lt. Comdr. Deitan Sage at your service. You can call me Deke."

He was Comdr. Sage? Her eyes widened. She'd expected him to be a stiff soldier, not a rakishly attractive devil with a smooth tongue. Warning bells rang in her mind. This voyage might be more dangerous than she'd anticipated.

"Release me!" she ordered. Struggling to free herself, she tilted her neck back and found his mouth hovering centimeters above hers.

"This could prove to be an interesting journey . . . Mara." His eyes danced as he continued to hold her without any apparent inclination to let her go.

"How do you know my name?" she asked, trying to ignore the sudden weakness in her limbs.

"I've read your dossier. I know quite a bit about you." His arm tightened. "But not as much as I'd like to know. You feel quite good in my arms."

"Commander!" Her face flushed hotly.

Someone cleared their throat behind them and Deke released her. She sprang back with a guilty expression. Hedy stood grinning at them in front of the open turbolift car. Her arms were loaded with bundles.

"Pardon me for interrupting," she cooed.

"Hedy, this is Comdr. Sage," Mara said, struggling to regain her composure. "Can you tell me which cabin is mine?" she asked him, her tone impersonal.

"Your stateroom is the third one on the left," he told her, amusement in his eyes.

The farthest from his, she noted. Flushing under his scrutiny, she stooped to pick up the bundles she'd dropped. He bent over to help, and their heads collided.

"My, you do enjoy personal contact, don't you?" he murmured, picking up the scattered packages.

Her heart somersaulted as he gave her another disarming grin. If he kept displaying those dimples, she'd be lost. "Thank you," she said, trying to tug her green shift dress into place while she took the remaining bundles from him.

"You must be the medic," Deke commented, nodding at Hedy. Dusting off his maroon and gray uniform, he straightened and squared his shoulders.

"Pleased to meet you, Commander," Hedy replied. She stepped forward, her arms full of packages.

"What is all this stuff?" he asked.

"I went shopping," Hedy gushed. "Wait until you see the terrific games I bought. We're going to have a great time. I picked up some sweet pies for a special treat, and you won't believe the bargains on music chips!"

Deke's brows drew together in a disapproving frown. "This is not a pleasure cruise, ladies. I suggest you use the next couple of hauras to stow your gear and familiarize yourselves with the ship's interior. We'll be meeting in the conference room at eighteen hundred hauras for a mission briefing. That stateroom is yours." He pointed to the closed door opposite Mara's.

With an abrupt turn, he stalked toward the hatchway at the opposite end and disappeared into another compartment.

"Wow!" Hedy exclaimed. "If this isn't a pleasure cruise, he sure has a strange way of greeting his crew. You two didn't waste any time getting acquainted."

Mara flushed. "I accidentally ran into him."

"You didn't seem eager to withdraw."

"I . . . I couldn't. I don't know what came over me."

"Uh oh, this sounds serious." Hedy strode toward their staterooms.

"The only thing that's serious is our mission," Mara said, walking beside her. For all the fun things Hedy had brought, they shouldn't lose sight of their purpose.

"I need to make sure my equipment is in order. Did you check to see if your foot pan arrived?"

Mara grimaced. She couldn't see why Hedy kept referring to her sculpting tray as a foot pan. "I figured it would be too big to fit in my cabin, so I had it delivered to the cargo bay. Do you want to take a tour with me after we're settled in? You can help me find it."

"Sure. Maybe I'll run into Lt. Wren the same way you encountered Comdr. Sage." Hedy's green eyes sparkled with mischief as her mood abruptly shifted from somber to lighthearted. It was one of the features about her that Mara admired. Dealing with pain and suffering on a daily basis, Hedy was able to walk away from her job and enjoy herself on her time off.

After unloading Hedy's packages, Mara entered her cabin and shut the door. She wished she could be as blithe about life as her friend, but one cause or another always seemed to attract her attention. This latest one with the Yanurans threatened to undermine her goals. She knew her obstinate insistence that the Yanurans be admitted to the Coalition was offensive to certain influential parties. It impeded her chances of getting promoted to the next level of service, but she wouldn't sacrifice her ideals for selfish purposes. The Yanurans were being mistreated and it was up to her to prove their sincerity, regardless of the consequences.

Yet she still felt torn about her decision. Fromoth Trun's emotions hadn't been easy to sense, and she'd relied mostly on her impressions of the Yanuran leader to form an opinion. Even Hedy had advised her to be more discriminating in her judgments, but after experiencing prejudice firsthand, Mara felt compelled to support the Yanuran cause. She was as firm in her commitment as that ruby crystalline table was rock solid.

Her gaze swept from the low table to the plush sitter upholstered in a rose and beige pattern that sat behind it. Hanging on the wall above, a painting displayed colorful geometric designs. The sharp lines failed to appeal to her artistic sense. She preferred the smooth rims and graceful curvatures of her sculptures.

Through an archway beyond, she spotted the firm double lounger that served as a bed. Her case had been placed beside it on the carpeted floor. Built-in shelves, a lighted vanity, and a fabricator alcove completed the decor. Off to one side was the entrance to a private sanitary.

Not bad, she thought, going in to use the facilities. The sanitary was roomier than on other ships, and the sonic shower was big enough for two.

With a sigh, she remembered the voyage to Antarus IV, Pietor's home planet. The ship Pietor had leased was small but comfortable. Taking advantage of the autopilot, they'd spent most of the time in their cabin. The spacious shower had been an added attraction. All had gone well until they arrived at his home world and she met his parents. She could still feel the sting of their disapproval.

Not only was her complexion dark compared to their own people, but she was . . . different. It was a label she'd suffered through her childhood, but she'd never thought to hear it from Pietor's lips. The hurt was still fresh in her mind.

Drying her wet hands on a towel, she pushed aside those painful memories for more important concerns. It had been a while since she'd last checked on Jallyn's status. Glotaj had requested that she do periodic separations to see if the baby's location had changed. Mara unpacked her case until she came to the baby's blanket. Clutching it in her hands, she sat on the lounger and closed her eyes.

The astral plane beckoned her easily. Leaving her body, she floated upward in her energy form and concentrated on receiving vibrations from the blanket. A strange sensation tugged at her, something dark and unpleasant. Disturbed, she ignored it and concentrated on Jallyn. The next moment found her inside the baby's head.

The child was sleeping. Its eyes were closed, and somnolence started to overwhelm Mara as she absorbed the infant's tranquil state. She dissolved back into the astral plane, recalling that Sarina's hands had touched the blanket. How was her friend faring? Instantly, she was zipping through nondimensional space and popping into Sarina's perspective. The Great Healer was in her residence, sitting alone by the comm unit. Her gaze kept wandering to the image of Jallyn that hung on the wall. Staring at the happy vision through tears swimming in her eyes, Sarina's heart twisted with anguish. Abruptly, Mara separated. She couldn't bear to share her friend's pain and not be able to alleviate it. Sarina would have felt better if she had been allowed to come with them, but there were no guarantees they'd find Jallyn. More than likely, the baby had been taken aboard one of the other two ships that left that day. Mara didn't believe the Yanurans were involved but realized Glotaj wanted all possibilities checked out, and rightfully so.

Back in her body, she prayed Jallyn would be recovered quickly. At least the baby appeared unharmed. She'd have to do more frequent separations in case the situation changed. How terrible for Sarina, waiting by the comm unit for the chime to sound, worried about her beloved daughter. Mara's eyes flooded with moisture.

She covered her face with her hands and was about to indulge in a bout of tension-releasing sobs when someone knocked on her door. Thinking it was Hedy, Mara called out: "Come in!"

Comdr. Sage marched inside her cabin. Taking one look at the teardrops streaking her face, his handsome visage blanched. "I'm dreadfully sorry. I didn't mean to intrude." He stepped back as though meaning to leave.

"It's all right." Mara managed a smile. "I . . . I was just thinking about Jallyn." Uncertain of how much he knew about her, she didn't mention the separation.

Standing, she appraised her visitor. His thick dark hair swept his forehead in a casually styled look. His eyes held a look of sympathy. Her gaze fell to his one-piece uniform. The fabric stretched tautly across his broad shoulders and tapered over a wide chest, trim waist, and narrow hips, disappearing into a pair of polished black boots.

Shifting restlessly, she wondered how the cabin had grown so warm without her noticing it earlier.

"I came to ask if you'd received whatever items you sent on ahead," Deke remarked, his tone light.

"Yes, my case is here, Commander. Thank you for your concern."

"I said you could call me Deke." His eyes crinkled with amusement.

"Very well . . . Deke." She felt strange using his first name, and uncomfortable when he was so near. His bulk seemed to take up half the space in her cabin. Swallowing, she tried to look anywhere but into his eyes.

"You're the alien culture specialist, but you're also a friend of Sarina and Teir's?" he asked.

"Yes, that's right."

"And the medic, is she a friend of theirs also?"

"They're just acquaintances."

"You two room together on Bimordus Two, don't you?"

"Yes." Mara smiled at him. "Hedy and I met at the conservatory where we both took exobiology. Hedy branched off into multispecies medicine, and I went into cultural studies."

"I see." Deke studied her, his expression oblique.

Mara wondered what he was thinking. It didn't take her long to find out.

"I'd like to get to know you better," he said, taking a step closer.

"What do you mean?" Unconsciously she backed away. "You read my dossier, so I assume you're aware of my professional qualifications." The backs of her legs hit the upholstered sitter and she halted.

"You know that's not what I'm talking about." A sly

grin lit his face as he sauntered directly up to her.

She took one look at his dimples and melted. Her eyes locked with his. "Sh-shouldn't we discuss our mission?" she stammered, desperately grasping on to an impersonal topic.

"We'll do that at the briefing." His gaze swept across her face and rested on her hair trailing down her back.

Noting the look in his eye, she realized he intended to make a pass at her and she wasn't sure how to respond. Her nerve endings tingled in anticipation of his touch, and her faculties whirled giddily. What would be the harm in it? He knew she was a professional. His opinion of her as a crew member shouldn't be influenced by her response.

"Don't worry," he murmured reassuringly, placing his hands on her shoulders, "we'll have plenty of time to talk business later. Let's get acquainted."

His eyes pierced hers with a seductive warmth that stole into her blood. She couldn't tear her gaze away, nor did she want to. But before she gave in to her yearnings, she sought to free her mind of lingering concerns.

"Do you think we'll succeed?" she asked. Where his fingers gripped her shoulders, heat blazed a path along her sensitized nerves.

"Succeed? At what?" He drew her closer so that their bodies touched.

Her will seemed to evaporate and she could barely speak. "Our mission to Yanura," she whispered.

"Our mission is obvious, although how we're going to face down the Yanurans in this unwieldy ship is beyond me. We'll find a way." He bent his head toward her, clearly wishing to dispense with small talk and get on with his seduction.

Her anger flared. "What do you mean by *facing down* the Yanurans?"

Deke's face folded into a frown. "Our weapons array

shows a minimal configuration. It concerns me because the amphibians are sure to cause trouble."

She twisted out of his grasp. "Why should you think that? They're eager to be accepted into the Coalition." Her eyes narrowed. "We're not planning a commando raid. Our visit to Yanura is a diplomatic affair."

"That's what the Yanurans are supposed to think, but we're searching for a missing child. We have to be prepared for any contingencies."

It infuriated her that Deke was anticipating hostilities. Why would Fromoth Trun, the Yanuran leader, spend over a month on Bimordus Two pleading his case with the Admissions Committee if he planned to harm the visiting inspection team?

"I expect the Yanurans will be glad to cooperate with our efforts," she said stiffly.

"Well, I don't." His voice rang with annoyance. "Are you so gullible that you believe those creatures? Didn't you see the preliminary survey that was done when they first mentioned joining the Coalition? Glotaj told me that hints of political unrest came to light, but the extent and nature weren't known. He wants us to find out more about it. Jallyn's disappearance might be related to whatever problems the Yanurans are having at home."

"How preposterous! I don't see any connection between the Yanurans and Jallyn."

"Oh, no?" His eyes chilled. "Fromoth Trun's vessel launched shortly after Jallyn's abduction took place. Are you denying he's a suspect when you saw for yourself that Jallyn was on a ship?"

So the commander did know about her separations. "Two other ships also left the spaceport during that time interval." She puffed out her chest. "You're just prejudiced against the Yanurans like everyone else. I thought you were selected to command this mission because of your diving expertise.

You're supposed to check out their seaweed farms and confirm the data on Vyclor."

"That's only part of our mission."

"It's the most important! As soon as you verify their claims regarding the drug, we can make a favorable recommendation to the Admissions Committee."

He shook his head. "It's not as simple as that. We still have to locate Jallyn."

"Why don't you come right out and say you believe the Yanurans are guilty of her abduction?"

"We'll find out soon enough." He gave her a smug look.

"How dare you accuse them of such a grievous crime without having any experience in their affairs!" Clenching her fists at her sides, she glared at him in righteous indignation.

"I do have experience," he said quietly, his brown eyes intense.

"How so?"

"I'll explain during the briefing."

"Fine, then you can leave now." She was disgusted with his attitude.

Deke's mouth tightened. "Very well, but this isn't over, Mara. And neither is our other . . . conversation." The innuendo was clear enough to make her flush hotly as he stalked to the door and left.

She stared after him, rage constricting her throat. Who in Zor did Comdr. Sage think he was? Judge, jury, and executioner? How dare he accuse the Yanurans of wrongdoing when he couldn't prove anything! She wondered what experience he'd had with them that made him so biased in his views. Regardless of his reasons, his attitude could be a hindrance to their mission. Briefly she considered contacting Glotaj and registering a complaint, but then she remembered Deke had been selected by the supreme regent himself. Glotaj must have thought he was the best person for the job.

It would be up to her to persuade Comdr. Sage to take a reasonable approach, she decided. Hedy was always chiding her for promoting one cause after another, but she felt compelled to defend issues she felt strongly about. Instilling tolerance in Deke was going to be an enjoyable challenge.

She hadn't always expressed her opinions so openly. As a child, she used to shy away from interpersonal encounters. Because of her special ability, her relationships usually ended in bitterness and rejection.

The people on her planet were naturally psychic, but in most cases the full range of their ability didn't develop until after puberty. Mara had manifested her innate talents much earlier. Although other Tyberian children were able to sense emotions at an early stage, it was rare for one so young to be able to travel the astral plane. Usually it took years of study for an adult to reach that level of consciousness.

Because she didn't know how to discipline herself, Mara would jump into her friends' viewpoints without warning. Her ability frightened her playmates, who were too young to understand. Under those circumstances, no one wanted to be her companion for long. Eventually it became too painful to make friends because she knew it would only lead to ridicule or rejection.

A special school existed for children like her who were specially gifted at an early age. Mara's parents sent her there so she could learn how to channel her psychic energy. They didn't realize their action only made her feel more alienated.

Applying herself to her studies so she could leave the school and enter "normal" society again, she learned how to control her separations. As an adult, she declined the opportunity to extend her powers and chose instead to study exobiology at the Science Conservatory on Gemini VII. Her own experiences gave her the motivation to specialize in cultural relations. In her opinion, the key to accepting alien cultures was in understanding them.

Comdr. Sage didn't seem to feel that way. If he approached the Yanurans with his biased attitude, he might destroy the progress she'd made with Fromoth Trun. Mara would have to convince him to view the Yanurans more objectively.

A knock sounded on her door, and Hedy's high-pitched voice called out, "Are you ready for our tour yet? I finished unpacking."

"Yes, I'm coming." A moment later, she joined Hedy in the corridor. "Comdr. Sage stopped by my cabin," she blurted, glancing up and down the narrow space to make sure no one else was around to hear.

"Oh?" Hedy's eyebrows raised.

"I can't understand his attitude toward the Yanurans. The man's mind is poisoned with prejudice."

"Why do you say that?"

They began walking toward the hatchway. "He just about accused them of being liars. He mentioned a report that hinted at political problems on Yanura and suspects Jallyn's disappearance might be related." She snorted. "I've never heard anything so absurd! Fromoth Trun assured me he had the full support of his people."

Hedy smiled. "I'll bet you gave Comdr. Sage your opinion."

"Of course I did. I won't let him get away with making false accusations!"

"Uh oh. I get the feeling the poor man doesn't know what he's in for. This is just the type of challenge you enjoy." Hedy gave her a curious glance. "Why did he stop by in the first place? Was it to discuss the Yanurans?"

Mara grimaced. "He wanted to get to know me better."

"You don't say! And how did he propose to do that?"

They crossed into a section with open hatchways leading into the other public areas. "I'll leave that to your imagination," Mara said dryly.

Hedy grinned, intending to coax the details from Mara but just then her eyes spotted *him.* "Stars, there's Lt. Wren!" she squealed.

The Polluxite was ascending a spiral staircase just ahead of the main lounge.

She rushed forward. "Hello, Lieutenant! It's good to see you again."

"Please call me Wren," the big man offered, looking down at her. "It's my pleasure, Dr. Te'larr."

"Hedy." Her gaze locked with his and for once she couldn't think of a thing to say. She was mesmerized by his clear hazel eyes.

Wren broke the spell by clearing his throat. "There's work to be done." He turned away to continue his ascent.

"Is it time for the briefing yet?" she asked, desperately trying to hold his attention. Her gaze fixed on his broad back and the vertical slits visible in his shirt. She'd never seen his wings sprout but Mara had told her about them. They sounded sexy as hell.

He glanced back at her. "Not yet. We have to leave orbit first."

Mara sauntered into view. "Hello, Lieutenant."

"Mara, good to see you."

"May we watch the launch from the main viewscreen?" she asked.

"Sure, follow me. The bridge is up here." He pointed to the round opening above his head. His gaze slid to Hedy. "After you, Dr.—Hedy."

He sounded hesitant, as though he hadn't known how her name would sound rolling off his tongue. To Hedy, it sounded like music. Winking at Mara, she put her foot on the lowest rung. By the time she'd reached Wren's perch, she had purposefully hiked her skirt up to tantalize him with a view of her thighs.

"My, what a sturdy fellow," she murmured, brushing against him as she passed.

Wren's rugged face colored as Hedy swayed her hips provocatively and stepped onto the landing above. She whipped around so that she faced Wren when he reached the top. He towered above her, being at least six inches taller than she was.

"Mistress, you're in my path," he growled.

Hedy fluttered her lashes at him. "Sorry." She stepped to the side, her eyes following his every movement as he went over to the nav console to begin his calculations.

Mara joined Hedy. Deke was already on the bridge, busy monitoring one of the computer displays. Briefly her gaze rested on his broad back before she glanced around.

"That must be Lt. Ebo, the Sirisian," she whispered to Hedy, indicating a thin humanoid by the comm panel. He had the characteristic elastic pink skin of his race along with a bald head covered by a ruby turban. As they watched, he elongated his arm to toggle a switch several meters away.

Deke finished what he was doing and turned toward them, his expression inscrutable. "I see you've decided to join us for the launch, ladies. We should be getting clearance to lift off in less than ten minutes. You may wish to position yourselves beside those safety loops on the bulkhead. Our seats are reserved for ops personnel."

"That's okay, we'll stay here," Mara said, speaking for both of them. She introduced herself and Hedy to Lt. Ebo. He acknowledged their greeting and turned back to his task.

"If you want to remain on the bridge, don't distract us from our work," Deke ordered, glowering at her.

"I was just being polite."

"Save it for later. We'll have plenty of time to talk at the briefing."

"Yes," she said, smiling sweetly, "and I can't wait to hear what you'll have to say!"

Chapter Four

"The two intruders in Sarina's apartment were Rakkians," Deke said, reporting on the findings of Glotaj's investigative team from Bimordus Two. He sat at a circular table in the dining/conference facility, a pleasant room with a large oval viewport, bright lighting, and comfortable furnishings. Mara was on his left, followed by Hedy and Wren, with Ebo on his right.

Acutely aware of Mara's presence, he tried to display disinterest toward her for the sake of his crew. It wasn't easy when his gaze kept sliding in her direction. He'd never seen a woman so stunningly beautiful. His fingers ached to thread through her long glossy hair. Straight and thick, it cascaded to her waist like an onyx waterfall. Her dark eyes reminded him of the fathomless ocean depths, full of secrets he yearned to explore. She was more exotic than any sea creature and more alluring than any siren. Tamping down his arousal, Deke forced his attention back to the subject at hand.

"The Rakkians were identified as Pruet and Joro, assassins who hire out their services to the highest bidders," he continued. "Glotaj is having his team check into their recent activities in order to determine their current employer." Drumming his fingers on the table, he wished they had more conclusive information.

Mara glanced in his direction and his gaze slammed into hers. Her face flamed with color as their eyes locked and held. He smiled sardonically at her and she quickly averted her eyes.

"Forgive me, sir, but can you fill me in on what happened on Bimordus Two?" Ebo asked, drawing Deke's attention. Elongating his arm, the Sirisian reached to the fabricator to conjure himself a drink. After listening to Deke explain the ramifications of Jallyn's disappearance, Ebo nodded his turbaned head. "This is a complicated issue."

Folding his hands on the table, Deke leaned forward. "We have no idea why Jallyn was taken. No demands have been made, so we can only hope she's being kept alive for whatever purpose the abductors have in mind."

"Jallyn is being cared for as though her welfare is important," Mara said. "I would guess that means her return is anticipated."

"Maybe she'll be released after the Elevation Ceremony!" Hedy exclaimed hopefully.

Deke shook his head. He didn't believe the child's recovery would be that simple. "The abductors have the advantage over us. The longer Jallyn is missing, the more desperate we'll become. When they do make their demands known, we'll be more likely to accede to them. She has to be kept alive so proof of her well-being can be demonstrated."

"Regarding the two henchmen who abducted her, perhaps they're already on another job and could be tracked that way," Mara offered.

"Joro and Pruet haven't surfaced," Deke said in a curt tone. "Glotaj believes they're still with the child."

Silence fell over the room, broken by Wren. "Mara, tell them your theory about Earth customs."

Mara's eyes brightened. "Whoever sent Joro and Pruet knew about Sarina being from Earth," she announced. "On Sarina's homeworld, it is a popular courting custom to send cut flowers to a lover. The assassins approached Sarina offering a bouquet they said was from Capt. Reylock."

"Glotaj had the investigative team check the records at the study center, but no one downloaded files on Earth customs within the past six months other than Capt. Reylock himself," Deke said.

"And before that?" Wren asked, stroking his jaw.

"The findings were insignificant."

"Am I correct in assuming the Yanurans are not aware of our mission in this regard?" Ebo queried.

Deke nodded. "The Yanuran delegation departed at the same time as the two other ships that left Spaceport following Jallyn's abduction. League patrols have been sent after Gregorski's ship and Ambassador El'Rik's. We're responsible for the Yanurans. The Admissions Committee planned to send a science team there anyway, which worked in our favor."

Ebo elongated his neck to peer closely at Deke. "So while we're posing as this science team, in actuality we'll be searching for clues to the missing child's location?"

Deke's brows drew together. "We are the science team, Lieutenant. Part of our job is to check into the Yanuran claims about a miracle age-preserving drug."

"Comdr. Sage is a diving specialist," Wren contributed, hunching his broad shoulders. "Since the Yanuran drug is derived from seaweed, the Yanurans have agreed to let us inspect their underwater farms as proof of their claims. The commander was selected to lead the mission because of his expertise in that field. He's superbly qualified."

Deke squinted his eyes in thought. Wren had made an important point about Deke's background, and he should approach this assignment as though it were a SEARCH operation. Then they'd be prepared for any contingencies that might arise.

"We'll break for evening nourishment and then adjourn to the ordnance room," he said. "I'll need to do a weapons assessment on each one of you."

"Weapons assessment?" Mara asked. "What for?"

Deke turned his full attention on her, watching her moisten her lips with the tip of her tongue. It was an unconscious gesture on her part, but it aroused him. Angry at himself for being distracted, he made his tone of voice harsher than he intended.

"You need to be proficient in the use of tactical armaments," he told her, knowing she'd be riled. "Each one of us must be prepared."

"Prepared for what? Are you expecting the Yanurans to fire upon us?"

"You never know. I wouldn't put it past them to lure us to the surface and cause an unexpected accident."

"Don't be absurd. Fromoth Trun and his people will be trying to impress us so we'll recommend their acceptance to the Admissions Committee."

"The Yanurans are deceitful liars. You can't trust anything they say."

Mara knocked back her chair as she rose. "If you approach them with that attitude, you'll destroy the rapport I've established with Fromoth Trun. You'll ruin everything we're trying to accomplish!" Her fists clenched at her sides, she shook with fury.

"Perhaps I should share what I know about them," Deke said quietly.

"Indeed you should, Commander." Her voice dripped with disdain.

"Sit down and I'll explain."

Mara sank to her seat and folded her hands in her lap.

"Computer," Deke called, "access records for Larikk, stardates 352.7 through 352.9."

"Acknowledged," droned an impersonal female voice.

"Display the first visual recording."

Deke's eyes focused on the holographic image sprouting from the center of the white marbelite table. Larikk, bearded and slim, ware a loose tunic and trousers. A wide grin lit his face as he began speaking.

"Deke, how ya doing? I just got my first samples and they look good. I couldn't wait to share this with you. The region is tropical, with trees so high you wouldn't believe it. The vegetation is thick and abundant with wildlife. I'm lucky the Yanurans allowed me to come."

He stroked his beard. "I don't think they've even touched the surface of what's possible here. My initial analysis of the algae confirms what they've said. I've sent a specimen home to the lab but I wanted you to know how well it's going since you were the one who inspired me to come. I'll keep you posted." His image flickered and dissolved.

Deke looked at the curious faces ringing him and explained. "Larikk and I grew up together on Eranus. His father was Dr. Ventry Muir, who discovered the relationship between hydrogen uptake and blue silico amoeba."

His audience stared at him with blank expressions. "Larikk was researching a vaccine against Turtle Ravage," he went on. "It's a disease that afflicts a species of marine turtles on our planet. Preliminary studies showed that an algae from Yanura appeared to prevent the contagion. Larikk applied for permission to travel to the planet to collect samples."

"And the Yanurans agreed?" Wren asked, raising his layered eyebrows. "I thought they were closed to offworlders before this annum."

"That's not true," Mara said, the annoyance in her voice obvious. "All of you need to understand something before we arrive at their planet. The Yanurans consist of several different races. Fromoth Trun represents the Croags, the largest populace. They've always favored increased contact with other worlds, but before now they hadn't applied for admission to the Coalition. They're using the drug Vyclor as a bargaining chip to obtain special trade status. I'm not sure why they waited until now to submit their application, but I think it had to do with refining the drug so it was ready for the intergalactic marketplace.

"The Worts make up the other major faction on Yanura. They're tree-dwelling cousins of the Croags who prefer to maintain close ties to home and are suspicious of strangers. I don't know much about them, so most of my information is based on knowledge of the Croags."

"You mean the Worts may not favor membership in the Coalition?" Deke asked, incredulous.

"I'm not certain how they feel."

"How can the Admissions Committee even consider admitting half a planet to the Coalition?"

"The Croags make up nearly three-quarters of the inhabitants."

"So what?" Deke ran his fingers through his hair. "Every world that has joined the Coalition has been united. Their unity indicates that they've resolved certain political and social issues and are ready to become part of a larger community. Now you're saying that these differing factions on Yanura have opposing opinions?"

"I didn't exactly say that," Mara countered, but a trace of uncertainty hung in her voice.

"Glotaj told me there were hints of political unrest on

Yanura, but it may be more serious than we thought. We'll have to talk to a representative of the Worts when we're there. If major political differences exist between the various factions, it could be cause to reject Fromoth Trun's application. In the meantime, we're getting off track. I want you to hear this last communique from Larikk."

Deke called up another entry from the computer and Larikk's image reappeared. The bearded man kept casting furtive glances over his shoulder as he spoke.

"You wouldn't believe what I've discovered, Deke. I don't want to say anything yet because I need to gather more data, but this could prove to be a windfall." His eyes narrowed. "The Yanurans want to keep it all for themselves, but I think they'll be interested if I clue them in to the broader possibilities. We could make a fortune. The only deterrent is—" His voice garbled. "If . . . if I don't return, you'll know it wasn't an accident. Larikk out."

Deke surveyed his crewmates. "Larikk never did return home. His death was ruled an accidental drowning, but his body was never found. I applied for a travel entry to Yanura but it was denied. Even when I showed his message to the Department of Justice authorities, they said it was circumstantial and didn't prove anything."

"They're right," Mara agreed.

"You heard Larikk. The Yanurans must have found out he knew their secrets and they killed him. This might have something to do with the miracle drug we've been sent to investigate."

"Larikk could have been referring to anything," Mara insisted.

"He went after that vaccine at my encouragement, and I won't have his death hanging over my head. If the Yanurans are guilty, they'll pay for it."

"Your attitude is unreasonable. You'll be looking for things to be wrong."

"After what Larikk said, you're not suspicious?" Deke asked. He couldn't believe her naivete.

"I'm willing to be open-minded. You don't know what secret Larikk discovered, nor can you be certain the Yanurans harmed him. You're making assumptions that may color your viewpoint, to our detriment." She gestured at the others, who were listening with rapt attention. "If you offend Fromoth Trun, he'll revoke our travel entry. We'll fail in the search for Jallyn, and you'll have lost any chance you might have to learn what Larikk discovered. The Admissions Committee will merely send another science team in our place."

And he'd fail to win the appointment to the chancellorship, Deke reminded himself. Ruefully, he regarded her. "As our protocol expert, I'll expect you to suggest the best approach."

"We should be able to check into Larikk's disappearance as long as we're discreet. I don't see the harm in making a few inquiries," Wren interjected.

Deke nodded, grateful for the Polluxite's support. "Let's break for evening nourishment; then we'll reassemble for the weaponry evaluation in the ordnance room."

Land's sake! Mara thought. Deke was still insisting on that absurdity. With an annoyed frown, she got up and took her place in line for the fabricator, aware that he stood behind her. The hairs on her nape rose in response. Surely he was staring at her in irritation. He must resent her meddling presence, but she was here to ensure that the Yanurans were treated with respect. She didn't mind if Deke checked into Larikk's activities as long as their mission wasn't jeopardized. Obviously Wren thought Larikk's disappearance was worth investigating, and maybe it would lead to something significant in regard to their own assignment. Her job was to make certain the Yanurans were given a fair evaluation.

Thinking over their earlier discussion, she admitted the relationship between the Croags and the Worts was unclear to her. Fromoth Trun had insisted the Worts' interests were being met and they wouldn't object to membership in the Coalition. She hoped to meet with a Wort representative herself to confirm his words. Regardless of what Deke might think, she wasn't a complete fool. She understood the rationale for requesting proof of their claims.

She obtained her plate of food and headed back to the table. Hedy was munching on a meal of pasta and salad. Mara couldn't wait to bite into her juicy steak, mashed red tuber, and calyp greens. She'd always had a big appetite and was starving. As she bit into a soft roll, she eyed the foodstuffs chosen by the others. They certainly were a varied lot. Wren was bending over a plate of berries and nuts, while Ebo forked a gooey pink substance into his stretchy mouth.

On her left, Deke sat down, resting his plate on the table. A fishy odor assailed her nostrils. Annums of training had taught her to swallow her distaste and maintain her cool when she ate in alien company. Dining with different cultures was part of her job.

Hedy wasn't so subtle. "What is that stuff?" she asked, wrinkling her nose.

Deke responded with enthusiasm. "This is brown algae chowder, raw placar fish, and seaweed pudding," he said, pointing to each in its turn. "Want to try some?" He offered her a quivering moist white cube covered with a slimy translucent substance.

"No, thanks." Hedy grimaced and turned back to her own meal.

"You should fit in well with the Yanurans," Mara murmured unable to resist the dig. "They smell like your food."

For a moment he didn't answer and she was afraid she'd

gone too far. Then his mouth curved in a devilish grin. "If you like alien cultures so much, how about trying an iced jelly? It's a popular beverage on Eranus. I'd be happy to conjure you one."

Her curiosity got the better of her. "What is it?"

"A combination of water, slab sugar, rose concentrate, grass jelly, and crushed ice." His eyes glittered as he waited for her response.

"Grass jelly?"

"A black jelly made from seaweed. Want to try it?"

Mara was never one to turn down a challenge. "Fine," she said, sounding braver than she felt. Her eyes followed him as he rose and went to the fabricator. He certainly cut a dashing figure in his uniform. Watching him made her wonder about his background. He'd said he was from Eranus, but what kind of life had he led there? Had he always been interested in a military career?

By the time he returned with a tall frosted glass, she'd resolved to delve into his history. It would help her deal with him more effectively if she understood his origins.

One taste of the drink was enough to scatter her thoughts. The black liquid tasted like iodine. Trying not to gag, she managed to swallow the first sip. "Delightful," she murmured.

"I can see you relish the taste," Deke remarked, grinning.

With her mouth puckered from the tartness, she was unable to cast a witty retort. Bending her head, she hid her discomfort by raising a forkful of warm, soft tuber to her lips. The food had a sweet, buttery-rich flavor that thankfully erased the bitterness of the drink. As she swallowed, her ears picked up Hedy's high-pitched voice.

"How do you survive on such meager fare?" her friend was asking Wren. "You have such a powerful physique. Your nutritional requirements must be enormous."

Wren concentrated on his food, his brows drawn together as he hunched over his plate. Mara was amused to notice the flush that crept up his face. "I drink Cal six times a day," he said. At Hedy's puzzled expression, he explained. "It's a high-protein, calcium-rich beverage that supplies most of what I need."

"Most of what you need? And what else do you require for satisfaction, Lt. Wren?"

The innuendo in her tone was clear. Mara hid a smile, listening for Wren's response. The big man stuttered and gave a noncommittal reply. Mara returned her attention to her meal. Deciding she was still hungry, she obtained a large slice of kiraberry fruit pie for dessert.

As soon as they'd cleared the table, Deke ordered everyone to the physiolab.

"I haven't digested my food yet," Hedy grumbled. "Is this going to involve anything physical?"

"Come on," Mara urged her. "Wren's going. Maybe he'll unfold his wings for you."

"Ooh!" Hedy trilled, quickening her pace.

They passed by the holovid lounge, a study center, a medical facility, and finally came to the physiolab near the end of the corridor. Inside the gleaming white room with mirrored walls was an array of exercise equipment. At the far end was a set of double tempered-glass doors that led into another section.

"This way," Deke said, guiding them through the exercise area.

The next compartment, an ordnance room, was brightly lit and empty except for a wide cabinet set into one wall. Deke strode to the cabinet, punched in a code on a touchpad, and the closure swung open. Inside was an assortment of weaponry.

"Targets!" he commanded, and the far wall lit with moving images.

Mara spent a grueling haura struggling with the unfamiliar equipment. She was too proud to ask for assistance, so she fumbled along, dismayed when she missed the dancing targets by meters. But her roommate was not so reticent, using her feminine wiles to manipulate Wren into showing her how to fire the laser rifles, personal shooters, and other weaponry. The brunette cooed and shimmied when the big Polluxite reached his arms around her to teach her the proper stance.

"Mara . . . Dr. Te'larr . . . I'm going to assign you practice time in here," Deke said, frowning. "You must become proficient in each of these weapons before we reach Yanura."

"That's absurd," Mara retorted, facing him with her hands on her hips. "I have no intention of setting foot on that planet bearing arms!"

Deke drew her aside and spoke in a low tone so the others wouldn't hear. "You'll obey my orders or I'll have you confined to your quarters. You will not be included in the landing party, either. Understand?"

She looked at his furious expression, tightened her jaw, and gave him a mocking salute. "Aye, sir."

"By the stars, it's for your own protection," he cried, enraged.

"I can take care of myself." In truth, she couldn't. Instead of taking self-defense courses, she spent her free time on Bimordus Two teaching the various folk dances of the alien cultures she represented. Learning the native dances was a joyful type of exercise. Her classes at the main physiolab facility were popular. She grinned, imagining Deke performing some of the more intricate steps.

"This is not a laughing matter," Deke snapped.

"I thoroughly agree."

Compressing his mouth, Deke turned his attention to the others. "Listen up, everybody." Heads turned in his direction. "Tomorrow, we'll meet in the conference room at ten hundred hauras for a tactical discussion. I want you ladies to put in an haura each in here first." He pointed to Hedy. "You can start at eight hundred hauras. Mara, you'll go after her."

"Eight hundred hauras!" Hedy squealed. "I sleep later than that!"

"I'm usually up early. I'll trade with you," Mara offered.

"Need I remind you women that this is not a pleasure cruise?" His eyes traveled over her and Hedy sizing them up. "You'd better put in time in the exercise area, too. Your arm muscles need strengthening in case you have to lift one of those heavy blaster carbines."

"I'm damned if I'll be forced to do workouts every day," Mara muttered, feeling his suggestion was preposterous.

Deke's expression hardened. "You're under my command on this ship. Do you wish to receive disciplinary action for insubordination?"

She glared at him, unable to think of a suitable retort. He'd already threatened to confine her to her quarters if she disobeyed. As mission leader, his position was inviolable. She, on the other hand, could be considered an unnecessary inconvenience. Even Hedy, as medic, was more of an essential crew member than she was as a protocol expert.

"No, sir," she mumbled in reply, vowing to find another way to defy him.

Deke gave a curt nod. "Dismissed," he barked. After securing the ordnance locker, he turned on his heel and marched out.

Mara fell into step beside Hedy in the corridor. "Will you come to the cargo bay with me? I want to see if my sculpting tray arrived."

"Sure." Hedy glanced at her. "You know, I'm beginning to be sorry I came along."

"Why is that?"

"Weapons training . . . exercises . . . this is turning out to be more of a Defense League operation than a diplomatic visit. I thought it would be exciting to visit a new planet, but the commander is making me nervous. I have no desire to get caught in a hostile situation. My specialty is multispecies medicine, not trauma."

Mara halted, catching her by the elbow. "There won't be any hostile situation if Comdr. Sage follows my advice."

"He seems rather hardheaded."

"No kidding. The man believes the Yanurans are guilty of murdering his friend, and that conclusion is based on a single garbled communication. If you ask me, he dislikes the Yanurans and is willing to believe anything nasty about them."

They resumed their pace, heading for the turbolift at the far end of the corridor past the crew quarters. "I'd hate for Fromoth Trun to be offended by an indiscretion on his part. The Yanuran leader will tell us to leave before we accomplish any of our objectives," Mara said worriedly.

"What are you going to do?" Hedy brushed a strand of glossy brown hair off her face.

"I'll have to learn more about our commanding officer," she said determinedly. "It'll help me figure out how to deal with him."

Suddenly a door popped open and Comdr. Sage stepped out, clutching a pack of data cards. Mara hadn't realized they'd reached his cabin. Hedy slithered past, leaving Mara facing him in the narrowed space.

Their eyes caught and held. "I seem to keep bumping into you," Deke drawled, sounding not at all displeased. His mouth lifted in a smile.

Mara felt a responsive rush of heat. "We're on our way to the cargo deck. I . . . I needed to check on some supplies I had sent to the ship." She tried to get around him but his bulk seemed to stretch across the whole of the confined space. As though to purposely block her passage, he closed the distance between them. Another maneuver brought him into direct bodily contact. Mara drew in a sharp breath as her breasts and thighs pressed against his solid form with agonizing awareness. Behind them, she heard Hedy give a meaningful cough, but Deke didn't budge.

"You're in my way," she rasped breathlessly.

"No, you're in *my* way." He gave her that devilish grin again, showing his dimples.

Her knees buckled. Her blood warmed. Every nerve ending in her body sizzled. Her face flaming, she ducked and shot around him and kept on going until the turbolift door slid shut behind her.

"Whew!" She slumped against the rear wall, closing her eyes in relief.

"I think he likes you," Hedy said, her tone amused.

Mara straightened up, glaring at her. "Don't be ridiculous. He thinks I'm as annoying as a dougger gnat."

"Then he must like being annoyed, because he sure tries hard to get you riled."

"The only thing hard about him is his . . . you know. And I don't mean his head!"

Hedy giggled. "I wish I could get Wren to feel that way about me."

Rolling her eyes in mock despair, Mara strode into the immense cargo bay. The area was strewn with crates, machinery, and canvas-covered equipment, most of it bolted to the deck.

"How in Zor am I supposed to find my supplies?" she cried.

"You start searching at that end," Hedy suggested. "I'll look over here."

Ten minutes later, Mara found her stash hidden behind a crate of spare circuitry. "Here it is!" The items were fastened onto a minilevitator unit. Picking up a small hand control, she activated the lifting device and guided her load into an open area.

Kneeling down, she examined the rectangular sculpting tray, the sacks of Carellian clay and Cr'ssian soota mud, and the coloring modules. She picked up her carving splatter, feeling its satisfying weight in her palm.

"I can't imagine why you brought this stuff on board," Hedy remonstrated. "If Comdr. Sage finds you in here stomping in that muck, he'll assign you to clean out the connector conduits. You saw how he reacted when I mentioned bringing games and music chips with me."

"Why should he care what we do in our spare time? It's not as though we're regular members of the crew. We're civilians."

Hedy snorted. "That's not what you said back in our apartment when we were packing. You distinctly told me that we come under his orders on this mission."

"Only as it pertains to our jobs. He has no right to command us otherwise."

"Let me hear you tell the good commander that. You'll find yourself recruited into the Defense League before you turn around."

"Don't be ridiculous. Comdr. Sage hasn't the slightest interest in what we do in our leisure time." As she put her sculpting items away, Mara wondered about the truth of her statement. She had the feeling Deke would be concerned with everything his crew did, and for some reason, she found that oddly reassuring.

Chapter Five

The next morning, Mara was lingering over a cup of wagmint tea when Deke stormed into the mess hall.

"What are you doing in here?" he asked, his tone ominously quiet. He tapped the chronometer strapped to his wrist. "It's fifteen minutes past oh-eight-hundred. You're late for your weapons practice."

"Am I?" She raised her eyebrow.

"We're on a tight schedule. Dr. Te'larr is due at the range in less than an haura, then we're meeting in here with the rest of the crew for another briefing. You can't afford to waste everyone's time."

"Oh, I doubt Hedy will be up before ten. She's a late sleeper."

Deke's face darkened. "Don't either of you take this mission seriously?"

She met his gaze solemnly. It wasn't easy when he was towering above her and she had to twist her neck to look up. "Of course we do, Commander, but our viewpoint is different. As we see it, our visit to Yanura is a diplomatic engagement. I don't believe Jallyn's disappearance has anything to do with the Yanurans. Their flight plan was filed long before the abduction took place, so I feel military preparations are unnecessary."

She stood to face him, smoothing the sides of her forest green belted tunic. Black leggings and short, polished boots completed her ensemble. Wishing to appear professional, she'd twisted her hair into a sleek braid. She glanced briefly at the snug fit of Deke's maroon and gray uniform. Despite herself, she felt her pulse quicken at his proximity.

Deke's gaze, bold and arrogant, raked her body. "What about Larikk, huh? He was onto something and got killed as a result."

Planting her hands on her hips, she retorted, "You don't know what happened to Larikk, and even if someone did harm him, you have no right to blame an entire race. You're just prejudiced against the Yanurans like everyone else."

"How can I be biased against them? I've never met one before."

"You've probably heard talk about them." She compressed her lips. "Throughout history, people have been prejudiced against races they've never encountered. When you get to know them, you see they have feelings and problems just like anyone else. They become individuals, not a faceless entity. It's easier to hate someone when you don't know him personally."

An impish gleam entered Deke's eyes. "The Yanurans have frog faces."

Mara stomped her foot in frustration, then realized he was grinning at her. By the Light, he was purposefully goading her. Well, she'd take the opportunity to teach him a thing or two! "Do you know how many different species we have in the Coalition? Over five hundred worlds, and every one has contributed something valuable to the galactic community.

Take the Gomins, for example. They may look weird with their segmented bodies, roving eye, and wavy antennae, but their music has brought pleasure to billions of people."

"The Gomins have nothing to do with our situation." Deke's gaze roamed over her face and hair. "I'm responsible for the safety of this crew. My prime concern is that we're able to defend ourselves if the need arises. To that end, we'll practice our fighting skills. You never know when a situation may turn ugly."

The man had a one-track mind, Mara concluded. Fuming in frustration, she tried another tactic. "You're approaching this mission as though it's a commando operation. We should be discussing protocol and customs instead."

"Which is the purpose of our briefing this morning," he conceded. "I want you to tell us what to expect from the Yanurans and how we should greet them." He paced forward until he was a hairbreadth away from her. A whiff of masculine cologne drifted toward her, tantalizing her with its spicy scent. "I'm not being unreasonable, Mara. You have to understand my responsibility in this matter."

Gazing into his intense brown eyes, her resolve faltered. As mission leader, Deke was responsible for the safety of the crew. But did that mean he had to prepare them for a battle that might never occur? She turned away, but he caught her by the arm.

"Where are you going?" he demanded.

"To my cabin."

"You're due in the ordnance room."

"Land's sake! Why do you persist in that absurdity?"

His grasp on her arm tightened. "I thought I made it clear that you must be able to defend yourself. If you choose not to follow my orders, I'll have you confined to your cabin for the duration of this voyage."

She glanced at the rage smoldering in his eyes and had no doubt he'd follow through on his threat. "Very well," she snapped, "but who's going to teach me? I can't open the locker myself and I have no idea what to do."

Deke looked at her consideringly. "Wren has agreed to play instructor for your friend. I suppose I could teach you. Ebo and Wren are on the bridge, so I have some time available."

Mara had an instant vision of Deke standing with his arms around her as Wren had held Hedy during the previous weapons practice. "Er, I hate to inconvenience you," she murmured.

Deke's lips curved in a wicked grin. "It'll be my pleasure, Mistress Hendricks. Please, after you." Releasing her, he made a sweeping gesture toward the hatchway.

She preceded him down the corridor, aware of his eyes on her back . . . or more likely, on her swaying derriere. The man was an enigma. One moment he acted the stern commander and the next he was flirting with her. How was she to respond? Was he so strict because he cared about her? He'd admitted feeling a deep sense of responsibility for his crew, so his insistence on their proficiency in weaponry was a genuine concern to him. But how did he feel toward her otherwise?

She had no doubt he'd make a move on her in the ordnance room. It was too good an opportunity for a man like him to pass up when he'd have a valid reason for putting his hands on her. Her skin tingled in anticipation of his touch. But did she mean anything more to him than another conquest?

Until she found out, she decided she wouldn't respond. If he wanted to ensure her skill with weaponry, that was all he'd get!

Walking behind her, Deke saw the stubborn tilt of her chin as defiance of his orders. Surely Mara understood the need to be prepared for all contingencies? It wasn't bias against the Yanurans that made him extra cautious.

He expected any crew member under his command to be able to function as part of a team. His expectations weren't unreasonable; at least he didn't think so. Mara kept accusing him of being prejudiced, but he was just doing his job. Conversely, she considered defending the Yanurans to be her personal task. In a way, that was a form of reverse bias. She couldn't see beyond her own nose that those people should be held under suspicion. Her dedication to her ideals was admirable but misguided.

Although his purpose was to teach her how to defend herself, Deke couldn't help anticipating how it would feel to envelop her soft body in his . . . tutorial embrace. But when it came time to show her how to hold a blaster carbine, he found himself picturing her in a confrontation with a murderous Yanuran. As a result, he delivered his instructions in a stiff manner and ended up being overly critical of her performance. Annoyed with himself, he felt doubly remorseful at Mara's obvious relief that the session was over.

"Are you leaving?" she asked pointedly, her tone as cool as her eyes.

"I'll meet you here tomorrow morning. Be on time," Deke ordered, resolving to be more agreeable during the next round. He exited, nearly colliding with Hedy in the exercise area.

"Is he here yet?" Hedy trilled, breezing into the ordnance room. Her green eyes swept the empty range.

"Who?" Mara asked, rubbing her aching arms. Her muscles were unaccustomed to the workout. Maybe some strengthening exercises would be useful after all.

"Lt. Wren. He kindly agreed to be my instructor."

"Comdr. Sage gave me a lesson," Mara said wryly. "I hope you have a more enjoyable session with Wren. I'll see you both at the briefing. Right now, I'm heading for the study center to see what's on file regarding the

Yanurans." After his curt manner this morning, she fully expected Deke to give her a hard time at the briefing. She wanted to review all the available information to refresh her mind so her arguments would be well grounded.

Heavy footfalls announced Wren's arrival. Mara turned to greet him with a friendly smile. "Good morning, Lieutenant."

The big man was dressed in a standard uniform, probably at Deke's urging. Mara knew he didn't wear one on board the *Valiant.* His chest was even broader than Deke's, but then he had his huge wings folded into his back. His hair was carefully slicked off his wide forehead and she caught a whiff of a masculine musk scent. After acknowledging her greeting, Wren turned to Hedy. Mara was amused to see a dark flush suffuse his rugged features.

"Dr. Te'larr." He gave a slight bow.

"I told you to call me Hedy." She linked her arm into his, winking over her shoulder at Mara. "I'm looking forward to your instructions. I'm sure there's so-o-o many things you can teach me."

His color deepening, Wren sputtered a noncommittal reply.

Mara left, grinning to herself. Hedy could come on strong when a man appealed to her. Some males were put off by it, but if anything, Hedy's assertiveness seemed to encourage Wren. Mara had never asked him why he was still single, but now she wondered. Could it be that shyness lurked beneath his powerful exterior? He might need someone like Hedy to snag him. If that were the case, they'd be well suited for each other.

A wave of envy hit her, surprising her with its intensity. Don't be jealous, she told herself. After Pietor, she hadn't sought a relationship with another man. She was afraid of being rejected again and for the same reason Pietor's parents had refused to accept her: there was that "weird psychic stuff" she performed, to use Pietor's hurtful words.

Hedy thought she was being oversensitive, that it was Pietor's fault for not defending her, but Mara had faced prejudice before and feared it was always something she'd encounter. Hedy and Sarina were among the few who regarded her ability as a special quality and she was grateful for their friendship, but she doubted she'd ever find a man who would be so tolerant.

Having thought of Sarina, she realized she should have checked on her friend when she'd done her latest separation. Earlier that morning, Jallyn had been awake, still aboard the ship. Relieved to find the baby's status unchanged, Mara had returned from her astral journey, discarding the sense of unease that had accompanied the experience. She'd forgotten to check on Sarina and now felt guilty. Yesterday, Sarina had been sitting alone by her comm unit with no one to provide support. Mara wished she could be with her but it wasn't possible. She hoped the other crew members besides Hedy viewed Mara's current role as being important to their mission. It was hard to tell Deke's opinion. She wasn't sure if he respected her position or if he viewed her presence on the team as a necessary annoyance. So far he seemed more interested in teasing her than in soliciting her professional advice. Or maybe that was how he normally reacted to an attractive woman.

Glotaj had mentioned Deke was single when they were discussing the mission in Sarina's apartment. Now Mara found herself wondering why a man with the commander's good looks had never taken a mate. Perhaps he preferred to play the field and avoid commitments. In that case, he wasn't coming on to her because he genuinely liked her. She was merely another conquest, and it wouldn't be wise to get involved with him because it would only lead to another hurtful rejection.

She entered the study center, taking a seat at one of the

computer consoles. Using voice-activated commands, she requested data on Yanura. The upcoming briefing would give her the opportunity to show the commander she was worth her mettle. Unfortunately, the material offered nothing new. She'd been hoping to find information about the Worts that would verify Fromoth Trun's claims.

An haura later, she joined the other crew members in the dining/conference facility. Wren, sitting next to Hedy, gave a report on their navigational status, and Ebo rattled off a series of calculations from the bridge. When he was finished, Deke turned to Mara.

"Okay, tell us about the Yanurans."

He sat on her right as before, and again his nearness disconcerted her. His quiet air of authority was evident in his erect posture and firm jawline. Mara moistened her lips, trying to focus her thoughts on the subject under discussion and not on the man beside her. Despite her determination not to get involved with him, she couldn't deny the way her heart hammered in his presence.

"Since the Croags make up the majority of the population on Yanura, they're the group I'm going to describe," she began, folding her hands on the table. "They have smooth, moist green skin, broad flat skulls, and prominent eyes. They're cold-blooded, meaning their body temperature varies with their surroundings. They use their skin to breathe and also to lose or absorb water. As cold-blooded organisms with porous skin, they need to respond quickly to external changes in temperature. To maintain a stable environment, the Croags live underground in a network of burrows. There it's moist and shady, protecting them from the heat of the sun and from losing moisture on the surface.

"Because they don't need to eat frequently to maintain their body temperature, the Croags eat one meal a day. Their diet consists of insects, worms, aquacultured fish, a variety of farm-grown small animals, and fruits and vegetables. Their senses are highly developed, including their taste buds, so they can be finicky eaters. Besides the five senses we all share, the Croags can detect ultraviolet and infrared light."

Deke held up a hand. "This is all very fascinating, but I want to know what to expect on a person-to-person level."

Mara gave a small smile. "Very well. The standard greeting is to touch the fingers of your right hand to your forehead and give a short bow, saying *Rogi Kwantro.*"

"What does that mean?" Wren asked, shifting restlessly. His glance slid sideways to Hedy.

"May your source of water be plentiful," Mara quoted, steepling her hands on the table. "It's also polite to say the words as you are parting company from a Yanuran. Make sure you use your right hand in both instances. Performing the gesture with the left one implies a vulgar insult."

"Tell us about Fromoth Trun as an individual," Deke said.

Mara thought a moment. "Fromoth Trun is courteous almost to the point of obsequiousness. His style of dress is formal, his mannerisms elaborate. He enjoys the attentions of his staff."

"Vain?"

She raised an eyebrow. "Definitely so."

"What else?" Deke leaned forward.

"He's the elected leader of his people, the Croags. His most powerful aide is Lixier Bryn, who was left in charge while he was on Bimordus Two. Fromoth Trun seemed anxious to return home."

"Why? Doesn't he trust Lixier Bryn?"

Mara shrugged. "I wouldn't know. His entourage appeared devoted to him. The two females on his staff, the ministers of commerce and finance, raved about his accomplishments. I suspect, however, that the Yanurans are flatterers. They hide their true feelings under a veneer of rosy polish."

"What's the status of females in their society?" Lt. Ebo inquired. Sirisians, Mara knew, cherished the gentler sex on their planet. Possessing a more delicate constitution, Sirisian females rarely worked outside the home.

"They're considered equals," she replied. "Yanurans mate once a year." That drew startled looks from around the table. "They don't cohabitate as we know it. When a female is bearing young, she may move in with her mate for the four-month period. After giving birth, she can choose to remain or go back to her own burrow."

"But don't they raise their offspring together?" Ebo asked.

"They don't have family units. In Croag society, the community is more important than the individual. Males and females work together on an equal basis. The young are raised separately, in their own section of burrows, I presume. As adults, they can bunk with whomever they choose. Communal living is the norm."

"Didn't you say they are nocturnal?" Hedy put in.

"Yes, that's right. Their workplaces are aboveground. There's less danger of their skin drying out when the bright sun isn't shining overhead. We want to stage our arrival for early morning, when their workday is ending."

Silence fell over the group.

Finally, Deke spoke. "It's important that we assess the political situation on the planet. For all we know, the Worts might be vehemently opposed to joining the Coalition. You've only heard what Fromoth Trun has told you, Mara, and that's the Croag viewpoint. Political instability would give us a valid reason to recommend a rejection of their application to the Admissions Committee."

"That's all you care about, isn't it?" Mara cried, affronted.

"You're just looking for ways to discredit the Yanurans."

"And you're so blinded by gullibility you won't look beyond what you want to believe." His eyes flashed at her. "We need to do more than verify the existence of their miracle age-preserving drug."

"That's all the Admissions Committee requires!"

"No, it's not. Glotaj mentioned the political situation. You've been ignoring it because it doesn't suit your views of the Yanurans. Well, I don't intend to do a half-assed job while we're there."

"He's right," Wren cut in. "We should assess the entire situation, and maybe we'll learn more about what happened to Larikk."

"We have to look for Jallyn!" Mara reminded them.

"If she's on the planet, we'll locate her," Deke said, his tone ominously quiet.

Mara got the hint and bit her lip, her emotions in a turmoil. Damn the man! How could he condemn the Yanurans without even meeting them? Was she the only person concerned about giving them a fair evaluation?

"I've made up a duty roster." Deke handed out data cards. "You're each assigned times on the firing range and in the exercise lab. Watches on the bridge are posted. Our next group session will involve a holographic view of the Croag capital, Revitt Lake City. We'll review the terrain and begin a series of tactical simulations. Dismissed."

Fitting her data card into her pocket link, Mara noticed that she had nothing planned until 1430 hauras, when she was assigned an haura of exercises in the physiolab. She exited beside Hedy.

"I don't like the way the commander orders us around," Mara said, gritting her teeth. "Glotaj assigned the wrong man to be in charge of this mission. Deke is looking for trouble."

Hedy gave her a sharp glance. "You're upset because

you believe he isn't listening to you. The man is not discounting your advice. On the contrary, he's using it to take a sensible approach. You're too defensive where the Yanurans are concerned."

"I am not defensive! I'm upholding their rights. No one seems to care about treating them fairly!"

"Deke wants to make sure all angles are covered. That's a reasonable attitude. It's his responsibility if anything goes wrong."

"Nothing will go wrong unless he blunders and offends Fromoth Trun."

"Wren has a free haura after he checks his nav instruments on the bridge. He's agreed to join me in the holovid lounge to show me a presentation on his home planet," Hedy said, her tone light.

"He likes you, Hedy." Mara's voice softened.

Hedy giggled. "I hope so!"

"I'm heading for the cargo bay to start a new sculpture."

"Going to work off your angst? What about your nemesis?" She waggled her eyebrows.

"Comdr. Sage?" Mara frowned. "I'm sure his duties will keep him occupied."

"Too bad."

"Hedy!" Mara gave her a friendly jab, then left her at the open hatchway to the holovid lounge.

Mara was ankle deep in a kneading phase, her thoughts on her report at the briefing, wondering if she'd left out any important information.

"What in Zor are you doing?" cried a deeply resonant voice.

Startled, she glanced around. Deke stood watching her, a look of amusement on his darkly handsome visage. Her pulse quickened at the sight of him.

"I'm creating a sculpture." Following the direction of his gaze, she peered down at her legs. She'd rolled up her leggings to midthigh. Her bare feet were covered in clay, and flecks of mud splattered her naked calves. Flushing with embarrassment, she realized how grimy she must look.

"You're stomping on muck in a giant tray," he said in a disbelieving tone. "What kind of sculpture is that?"

She wiggled her toes in the wet, gooey slime. "It's Cr'ssian soota mud that needs to be worked before shaping. The clay hardens into a translucent material. This is the best method even though it's crude. Besides, I like the feel of wet clay on my feet and stomping on it helps me to relax."

"Oh?" He sidled closer, his eyes on her face. "I wasn't aware you were feeling tense."

Warmth flooded her face. "Ah, don't you have work to do on the bridge?"

"Ebo is on duty. I thought I'd ask if you wanted assistance with your exercises later."

His expression didn't reveal his thoughts, and she wondered why he had made the offer. Was it a peacemaking gesture? She pounded her feet, her toes squishing in the delightfully cool muck. If she accepted, it would provide her with another opportunity to discuss the Yanurans with him.

"All right," she agreed, hoping it was the right decision.

His gaze locked with hers. "I'll be looking forward to it." As his eyes trailed to her bosom, she felt her nipples tighten in response. Suddenly she knew what kind of exercises he had in mind. "Until then," he said, quirking an eyebrow. His words hanging in the air like a seductive promise, he pivoted and left.

Mara resumed her stomping with renewed vigor. She hammered her feet so hard they were burning when she finally finished. Scooping the sticky clay onto her sculpting circle, she worked quickly, molding it into a recognizable form. The heavy lipped cup would harden into a translucent crystalline piece, delicately veined in red.

Brushing her hands off on her work apron, she stepped back to view her art. The edges were curved to perfection. Just as she molded the clay, she'd like to sway Deke Sage to her viewpoint. Justified or not, his suspicion of the Yanurans rankled her. The exercise session should afford her the opportunity to discuss the situation with him further.

Putting away her supplies, Mara realized how much she was looking forward to their next encounter.

Sitting in the holovid lounge, Hedy sidled closer to Wren on the wide double lounger. A three-dimensional holovid of his home planet, Pollux, was playing in full color in the center of the room. An attractive female strolled through each scenic wonder, describing it as though the viewer were actually there.

Watching the female guide made Hedy wonder about Wren. Did he have someone back home? What had made him decide to join the Defense League? What was his family like?

She was aware of his tense posture as he sat as far away from her as possible. His shyness appealed to her. She'd never met a man before who hadn't fallen madly in love with her. Wren wasn't responding in that way and it piqued her interest. Getting him to relax in her presence was her first objective. Learning more about him was the second goal she hoped to accomplish. Then, perhaps, she could ask him to unfold his wings. Just the thought of them sprouting behind his broad back sent delicious chills up and down her spine.

"I'd love to see your world," she told him, careful to keep her voice demure.

He risked a quick glance in her direction. "I haven't been home in annums," he said gruffly.

"Your family must miss you."

"I doubt it. They were glad when I left."

The words were spoken with such bitterness that Hedy was shocked. "Why do you say that?"

Wren clasped his hands together. "It's the truth, that's all."

Feeling she'd touched upon a raw nerve, she let it pass even though her curiosity was dying for satisfaction. "Tell me more about your planet. What's that area?" She pointed to the holovid where the female was showing them a scene of high vertical cliffs overlooking a vast ocean. Children were jumping off, their wings sprouting as they soared into open space.

Wren took a moment before he answered. "Those are the Cliffs of Courage. Once you master them, you are elevated to the status of adult on our world. A ritual ceremony is attached. Everyone takes the plunge at age sixteen."

"It must have been one of the highlights of your life," she remarked, beaming widely as she imagined him jumping off the cliff's edge.

His face darkened. "I never took the test."

"What?" Her smile faded.

"Computer, cancel program." The holovid abruptly closed and the room brightened. Wren rose and began pacing. "There's something you should know about me, Hedy Te'larr. I have a disability, and it prevents me from ever . . . from taking a mate."

She stared at him, dumbfounded. He appeared healthy, virile. "What are you talking about?"

His expression echoed annums of pain. "I can't fly," he murmured, his voice so low she had to strain her ears to hear.

"You can't . . . oh, for Zor's sake!" She got up and rushed to his side. "What does that have to do with taking a mate?"

"To post marriage banns on Pollux, one must be of adult status. That privilege wasn't granted me. Any female who allied herself with my household would suffer the stigma of my shame. We would not be able to consummate our union."

"You mean physically or legally?"

"In my mind, they are as one."

Hedy paused. Did that mean he'd never been with a woman? What a terrible burden to bear! An insane impulse to wrap her arms around him and offer comfort overwhelmed her.

"A woman in love with you wouldn't care if you could fly or not," she stated vehemently.

"On my world, a female would not set the two apart."

"Why would she have to be from your world?"

"Who else would show interest in me? I must mate with one of my own species in order to produce viable offspring," he answered, seemingly shocked by her suggestion.

"That's not necessarily the case. You're basically humanoid, which means you share the same genetic basis as many other races. Look at Sarina and Teir. She's from Earth; he's a Vilaran. It hasn't stopped them from sharing a life together."

He shook his head. "Even if that is so, I haven't earned the right to join with a female."

"Exactly what is the cause of your problem?" She gazed up into his troubled hazel eyes, feeling small next to his height. She wished she could offer him a measure of comfort, but Wren seemed adamant in his self-denial.

He flushed uncomfortably. "I went through a battery of physical tests and they showed nothing wrong."

She reached out and grasped his cold hand. "What happened then?"

"My parents had me see mental therapists. It was a difficult time. I . . . lost my friends."

"Is that why you joined the Defense League?"

He answered with a miserable nod. "I had to get away. It was necessary to spare my parents the shame of always making excuses for me."

"I'm so sorry." Holding on to his hand, she moved closer until their bodies touched. Her head tilted back and she raised herself on tiptoe. With her other hand, she encircled his neck and pulled his head down. "Kiss me," she whispered against his mouth.

"No, I—"

"I know you want to." She'd seen the expression in his eyes. "Don't be afraid. Consider it a token of our friendship. We can be friends, can't we?"

With a groan, Wren swept her into his arms and pressed his mouth to hers. She reveled in the feel of his lips plundering hers, his desperate hunger evident in the urgency of his movements. She wondered how much experience he'd actually had with women, but it didn't matter. She'd take whatever he offered. Clutching her fingers in his hair, she couldn't help the small sound of pleasure that escaped her lips.

Abruptly, he released her and sprang back. "Forgive me," he apologized, an expression of self-loathing on his face. "I am forgetting myself."

"You need to forget yourself, Wren. Your problem is of no concern to me. I want to know you as a man."

"A whole man I am not, according to my kind."

"Well, I'm not a Polluxite."

He sucked in a breath. "You make this hard, *petula.*"

That had sounded suspiciously like a term of endearment. Maybe she was making some headway after all.

Wren glanced at his chronometer. "I have bridge duty in ten minutes. I regret this session must end."

"Do you really? I think you're glad to get away from me." His tormented expression snagged her heart. "I don't believe you understand," she reiterated. "I said your problem doesn't matter to me."

"It matters to me, Doctor. That's what counts." He turned his broad back to her.

"Wren, wait!" But by the time the words passed her lips, he was gone.

Hedy rushed out into the corridor, through the hatchway into the crew quarters, and knocked on Mara's door. She entered at her friend's invitation. Mara had apparently just come out of the sonic shower. She'd changed into a rust-colored tunic and black leggings and was braiding her dampened hair.

"Wren kissed me, but he won't have anything more to do with me!" Hedy blurted out, sinking onto the lounger in the sitting area. She proceeded to tell Mara about their encounter. "I'd like to run my own medical tests on him. I can't understand why no cause for his problem was found."

"Could it be psychosomatic?"

"There's always that possibility. He said he'd seen mental therapists. Apparently they couldn't do anything for him. He regards himself as half a man."

"From the way you said he kissed you, it sounds as though he's fully functional where it counts!" Mara finished tying off her braid.

"So what? His cultural taboos remain an obstacle between us. He may be able to perform, but he won't."

"You really like him, don't you?" Mara said, staring at her.

She shrugged, her eyes downcast.

"You've just got to keep working on him," Mara insisted. "If he responded to you so strongly, he must feel a similar attraction."

"Suns, men are difficult, aren't they?" When Mara didn't reply, she gazed at her curiously. "Did you run into Comdr. Sage again?"

Mara nodded, averting her eyes. "I'd started a sculpture. Deke caught me with my feet in the clay."

Hedy's mood brightened as she pictured the scene. "I'll bet he was entertained!"

Reluctantly, Mara recounted their conversation.

"So he's going to assist you with your exercises? That should be exciting."

"I can use the time to convince him to view the Yanurans more objectively," Mara answered.

"Sure, whatever you say." She smiled, thinking Mara and Deke would discuss more than the Yanurans. "I'll talk to you later. I need to check out the medical facilities."

The appointed haura for Mara's stint in the physiolab approached, but when she arrived, Deke was nowhere in sight. Wondering if he'd been detained on the bridge, she paged the command center. Wren, who was on duty, suggested she try his cabin or the study center.

She found him in the study center, peering at a monitor screen, an intent expression on his face. Her greeting startled him.

"Sorry," he said, a sheepish grin creasing his face when she told him the time. "When I concentrate, I tend to forget everything else."

"What are you viewing?" Curious to see what had drawn his attention, she meandered inside the softly lit area and squinted at his screen. A series of mathematical equations met her puzzled gaze.

"I'm catching up on the latest computations for ionic charges of undersea coppenium in relation to water temperature fluctuations."

"Oh, I see." She couldn't begin to guess why he was interested in that topic. "You, uh, read this sort of stuff often?"

"I need to keep up with what's current." He switched

off the computer and rose, stretching. "I could use a few exercises myself about now."

She swallowed hard. In her mind's eye, she pictured his sinewy body streaked with sweat, his muscles bulging as he lifted weights. The image unnerved her. Would he touch her, show her how to use the equipment? How could she abide being that close to him when already her heart was thudding so hard her temples throbbed?

Moistening her lips, she followed him out into the corridor. By the time they reached the physiolab, she could barely breathe. As long as he didn't smile at her and show his dimples, she would be safe.

Wouldn't she?

Chapter Six

Mara stared at Deke as he removed his boots and began peeling off the fastening strip on the side of his uniform. The air in the exercise room was cool but heat coursed through her veins as she watched him, too unsettled to move.

"W-What are you doing?" she stuttered, afraid to guess.

"Getting changed. I've got on my activity shorts under this uniform." He grinned at her, his eyes twinkling. "It won't bother you if I disrobe, will it?"

"Of course not!"

But her bravado dissolved into embarrassment, especially when Deke took a long time stripping off his uniform. She figured he was deliberately taunting her and when he finally stood before her in his gray knit shorts, her gut clenched in reaction. His broad shoulders and arms rippled with muscled strength. Swirls of dark hair guarded his chest in sensual patterns that made her want to tangle her fingers in them. Her gaze roamed down to his tight hip-hugging shorts and sturdy hair-covered legs.

"You finished?" Deke asked gently.

Horrified, her eyes flew to his. His face held a bemused expression. She stammered for a response but ended up staring at him as he closed the distance between them. With his bare chest directly in front of her, he halted.

"Ready for the first move?" he said, his voice a low masculine rumble.

"F-First move?" She moistened her lips, dismayed when his gaze intently followed her tongue.

"We need to warm up our muscles with a few stretching exercises," he said with a crooked grin. "Stretch your arms out and copy what I'm doing."

Her eyes fixated on his bulging biceps as he demonstrated the exercise in front of her. His head held high, his arms stretched wide, he began flexing and extending his sinewy forearms.

By the Light! This was sweet torture. To be near the man was difficult enough. To be alone with him, forced to observe his virile body half-naked and performing tests of muscular prowess, was an agonizing test of her willpower. As a coil of desire rose within her, she told herself that his interest was purely superficial, that he'd selected her because she was a convenient target aboard ship. After the voyage was over, he'd be off to the next port and the next attractive female.

To get her mind off him, she strode to an exercise machine that didn't look too difficult. But when she attempted to use the pulley contraption, it wouldn't budge.

"You haven't got that right," Deke said, following her. Positioning himself up against her back, he leaned forward and covered her hands with his. His warm breath caressed her nape as he showed her how to move.

"Do it this way," he murmured against her ear.

She sucked in a sharp breath, barely aware of his

instructions as her body responded to his powerful chest pressed against her back. It took all her concentration to focus on the lesson and not on him. When at last he directed his attention to another machine, she drew a breath of relief.

For a while they worked separately, Deke using the rowing device with a holovid screen showing a lake scene and Mara manipulating the machines to fortify her arms. It aroused her just to see his muscles gleaming with sweat. His masculine essence pervaded the room, making it difficult for her to block out his presence even when she tried to think of something else. If only her body wasn't so responsive to his nearness. Nothing could come out of a relationship with the man, and yet she couldn't deny the effect he had on her.

Finally Deke called for a rest.

Mara was astounded he wasn't short of breath after 45 minutes of steady exercise. She felt drained, as though she'd just run a marathon and finished in last place.

"Your clothing is too heavy for this type of workout," he said, giving her a disarming grin. "Next time I suggest you don suitable athletic attire."

She stared at his dimples and swallowed. The exercise had felt good after all, and she appreciated Deke's forcing her into it. It wouldn't do to sit around the ship for two weeks growing soft. "A dance suit would be more comfortable," she agreed, feeling a satisfying soreness begin to seep into her limbs.

"A dance suit?"

"I teach folk-dance classes on Bimordus Two. I'm accustomed to wearing dance suits."

"What kind of classes?"

"You know, native dances from the various groups who make up the Coalition. I find the expressive movements help me to understand the cultural nuances of the different peoples."

"Is that so? Show me one."

"I don't know that I—"

"Folk dancing is not a very vigorous form of exercise," he drawled. "No wonder your body needs conditioning."

Her mouth tightened. "Move away."

He retreated, giving her space, and she dipped and swirled in the Twirl Dance of the Nagarina Watch.

"I believe there's a more intricate pattern involving a duet," he said, sauntering forward when she had finished her simple demonstration. "I know a few steps myself. Computer, play the first movement of Mach's symphony."

As the melodious music filled the room, Mara swallowed a sudden lump in her throat. What had she gotten herself into this time? Deke's eyes gleamed expectantly as he approached her, a devilish grin on his face. Rooted to where she stood, she could only stare at him and try to ignore the wild thumping of her heart.

He walked behind her, and put his arms around her shoulders and gently drew her against his chest.

"Lean back," he commanded.

She obliged, knowing she would regret this. But she'd never done the duet before, having had a dearth of male partners on Bimordus Two. Part of her was curious to see how it was done.

"We move our bodies like this," he said.

His hips began a slow rhythmic gyration. Swaying behind her, he clutched her closer so that she bumped against him with each rocking motion. She gritted her teeth, feeling each contact like a jolt of electricity. When his fingers slid up her arms, tickling her skin, she shivered with delight. His warm breath fanned her temple as he whispered into her ear.

"This is my kind of exercise," he murmured, his low, sensual tone rumbling along her nerve endings like smooth velvet.

Shivers ran up and down her spine as his hands purposefully brushed against the sides of her breasts while caressing her arms. Pleasurable sensations roiled inside her, and closing her eyes, she tilted her neck back, craving more. Her nipples ached with need and it was all she could to do suppress the moan that rose to her lips. His hands slid to her hips, guiding them against his own in an erotic rolling movement that made her breath come short. When he began nibbling at the skin behind her ear, she gasped.

"I think we should practice this every day," he crooned, his voice husky.

Her nerves screamed with sensitivity. Unable to stop herself, she twisted around to face him. Still held in his embrace, she gazed up into his blazing eyes and licked her lips.

Holding her, he pressed his midsection against her belly, sliding himself along her length in the sensual rhythm of the dance. She tilted her head back, closed her eyes and parted her lips. She felt his breath on her mouth—

"Bridge to Comdr. Sage," Wren's voice boomed on the comm unit.

Instantly Deke sprang back. "Go ahead," he barked.

Mara's eyes whipped open, her mind alert.

"Incoming message from Supreme Regent Glotaj, sir. High priority."

"I'll take it in the conference room. Sage out."

He traced a tender line along her cheek with his forefinger. "Too bad about the interruption," he said gently. "We'll continue this later."

"Yes. I mean, no!" Her face flushed hotly. "Don't think . . . I didn't mean—"

"I know you didn't." He smiled. "It's the way things are meant to be, Mara. You'll see. By the end of this voyage, we'll—"

"We'll have accomplished our mission." She drew herself

upright, ashamed of her wanton behavior. Where was her professionalism, her pride? "I think we're losing sight of our purpose. We have to agree on an approach to the Yanurans. We're not on this trip to . . . to indulge ourselves! You clearly informed me and Hedy that this wasn't a pleasure cruise."

"Exactly. If we perform a few more dances like this one, it may soften my attitude toward Fromoth Trun and the Croags," he taunted.

"How dare you make light of the situation!" Rage engulfed her. Her hands on her hips, she regarded him coolly. "Now you're the one who's not being serious about this mission, Commander."

He grinned. "I'm perfectly serious, Mara, about you." Grabbing his uniform and boots, he winked at her and left.

"Ooh, I hate that man!" She clenched her fists in frustration. And yet, as she watched his broad back recede, a strange feeling of loss struck her. Could it be that she was getting used to his irritating company?

By the Light, she hoped not. The man was too damn attractive for her peace of mind. Shaking her head, she conjured a towel from the fabricator and wiped her brow. He'd made her sweat all right, and it hadn't been from the exercise. It had been from the closeness of his body, the hot whoosh of his breath on her temple. Suddenly her pulse was racing again and she threw the towel down in disgust. *Watch yourself, Mara. You don't want to get involved with a man like him. He's interested in a shipboard fling, nothing else.*

Yet as she headed for her cabin, she wondered how long she'd be able to resist.

Deke gritted his teeth as he listened to Glotaj's urgent pleas for haste. The supreme regent's face was projected onto the far wall in the conference facility. Cameras picked up his own image and sent it along subspace frequencies to the Coalition capitol building where Glotaj spoke from his office in the Great Hall.

"Our patrols caught up with the other two vessels," Glotaj was saying. "Gregorski's and Ambassador El'rik's ships were clean. That leaves you, Deke. The Yanurans are our best lead. We're not finding anything else on Bimordus Two."

"What about those two assassins, Joro and Pruet?" He hunched forward, his elbows on the table, his hands clasped.

"A dead end. They've covered their tracks well." A pause. "It's up to you, Commander. Increase speed so you arrive at the Yanuran system within twelve days at the most."

"But sir—" They were already going at warp six.

"It's imperative we have Jallyn back before the Elevation Ceremony. Report to me upon your arrival. Glotaj out." His image vanished.

Compressing his lips, Deke stalked out and climbed the companionway to the bridge. Wren and Ebo were on duty. Briefly, Deke told them the gist of the conversation. "Increase speed to warp eight," he told Ebo. In addition to monitoring communications, the Sirisian was responsible for the engineering console. "Let's hope this vessel can handle it."

"The *Celeste* is well built," Ebo said. "She might not look like much, but she's got power." He carried out the order. With a mild shudder, the ship responded.

Deke faced the forward viewscreen. The black emptiness of space greeted him, its velvety void punctuated by myriads of gleaming stars that showed as pinpricks of light. The vast darkness reminded him of the murky ocean depths which he considered his true home. Undersea, diverse life-forms thrived in the cold, dark water. Here, in the distant reaches of interstellar space, complex molecules drifted, the basic building blocks of life itself. This was where it all started, and in the oceans, living matter had formed from these molecules, developing and differentiating along the evolutionary scale. Each world evolved from its particular mix of atmosphere, temperature, gravity, and base elements available to support life. The diversity never failed to amaze him.

At the comm station, Ebo elongated his arm, stretching it across the room to flick a switch on a distant circuit board. The Sirisian was an example of a different evolutionary path from his own, Deke mused. On Ebo's home planet, the element dianine was common, and it accounted for their elastic body structure.

Wren was hunched over his nav instruments. His wings were the result of an evolutionary progress from a breed of avians.

Were the Yanurans so unusual, then? Their ancestors were froglike amphibians. Didn't they deserve the same respect as other species? Deke frowned, debating the point with himself. He knew what Mara would say. She'd give them the benefit of the doubt. But Larikk's communique couldn't be discarded. The Yanurans had done something to him and covered their tracks. Deke was justified in suspecting them of deceit. It wasn't prejudice, no matter what Mara said. He merely sought the truth. And if she weren't so absurdly naive, she'd see the logic of his argument.

By the stars, that woman had the power to irritate and arouse him at the same time. He would have kissed her if they hadn't been interrupted by the message from the bridge. He wanted her, and every day he was in her company, his desire increased. It would drive him crazy if he couldn't lie with her soon. Her roommate was attractive, but too small for his taste. Mara, with her smooth olive complexion and lithe, graceful body, was the one who appealed to him. Deke couldn't recall the last time he'd been so strongly attracted to a woman. Was it more than physical lust that drew him? Her beauty was unquestionable but she was also intelligent, feisty, talented, and dedicated to her ideals. But so were many other women. What was it about her that was different?

"Commander?" Wren's voice sounded alarmed.

Instantly alert, he shifted his attention. "Yes, Lieutenant, what is it?"

Wren's layered eyebrows furrowed into a frown as he hunched over his instruments. "Sensors are picking up subspace distortions. I've never seen anything like this, sir. They appear to be high-energy particles directly ahead."

"Change course ninety degrees to port," he ordered, squinting at the viewscreen. He didn't notice anything unusual.

Ebo keyed in the sequence and the ship changed direction.

"Try doing a wide-pattern sensor sweep," Deke suggested to Wren.

"Aye, sir." The Polluxite grunted. "I'm still getting weird readouts. This entire region is pocketed with subspace distortions. I'll divert power from the quantum matrix array. That might help us fine-tune these images."

"Slow to sublight speed." Deke lowered himself into the central command chair, wishing he were as familiar with space anomalies as he was with deep-sea phenomena.

"Oncoming wave dead ahead!" Wren cried out. "Collision course!"

Before Deke could sound the alarm, a crashing impact hit the ship. The deck jerked beneath him, and Deke was flung out of his chair. He landed on the solid deck with a sharp pain in his hip. Something blew up in a shower of sparks off to the side. Wren shouted but Deke couldn't see him for the smoke that billowed in the air. Coughing, he rolled to get away from the searing heat as automatic sensors initiated fire control measures over the burning console. Another jarring impact hit and he covered his head with his arms as debris rained down from above.

"Reverse thrusters!" he yelled, hoping Ebo could carry out the command. Scraping himself along the floor, he pulled himself upright and sagged into his chair. Ebo was in place, having put on his safety restraint at Wren's first warning. But where was Wren?

"By the faith, Wren's been hurt!" he yelled, seeing the Polluxite's boots sticking out from behind a heavy metal ceiling grating that had crashed to the floor. He rushed over, alarmed to find the big man unconscious, stretched out on his back. Blood was oozing from a puncture wound on his neck where apparently he'd been struck by the sharp-edged grating. Wren's face was uncommonly pale.

"Medic to the bridge!" Deke called out, a comm channel already having been opened by Ebo, who was communicating with the other crew members.

"Dr. Te'larr is trapped in the turbolift," the Sirisian said, dashing over with a first-aid kit.

"What in Zor hit us?" He coughed from the acrid odor in the air. The fire control unit had shut off, having served its purpose. Grabbing a fuser from the first-aid kit, he stanched the flow of blood from Wren's wound.

"Analysis showed the distortions to be caused by a series of density waves," Ebo explained, his pink face puckered with anxiety. "When one collided with us, the ship was momentarily charged as though we'd come into contact with live circuitry. It shorted out the lift actuators and some of our other systems."

"Life support?"

"Functioning on all decks." Ebo's mouth stretched in a

grimace. "We have sublight power but the warp generators are off-line."

Deke uttered an oath. "Have you heard from Mara?"

"Internal sensors indicate she's in her cabin, but communications from B deck are out."

Deke was torn between tending to Wren and checking on Mara. But Wren's condition was more urgent. The Polluxite was still unconscious. "I'll manage here. You can work on retrieving Dr. Te'larr from the turbolift. Have her meet me in sick bay."

"Aye, sir." Ebo disappeared down the companionway, heading for the engineering section.

Deke peered at the disarray around the bridge. Couplings were hanging loose; panels were dislodged; the charred fragments of the burnt console still smelled of smoke. There was little chance of finding a minilevitator unit. He'd have to carry Wren.

Grunting from the effort, he hoisted the big man into his strong arms. He didn't want to fling Wren over his shoulder; it might aggravate his neck wound. Now he saw what had been hidden before: another gash on the rear of the Polluxite's head. That must be the one that had knocked him unconscious, he thought. Staggering, he bore his burden toward the companionway.

Proceeding slowly, he managed to make his way down the spiral stairs to the lower deck. His head was bent, so he didn't know someone was ahead until he heard the gasp.

"Wren's hurt!" Mara cried.

Glancing up, Deke noted her hair had tumbled loose, tumbling over her shoulders. Her wide onyx eyes expressed her terror.

"Are you all right?" he asked, concerned.

"I was in my cabin when the . . . when we were hit. I grabbed hold of a safety loop. I was just coming to the bridge to see what was going on. Where's Hedy?"

"She's stuck in the turbolift." He headed down the corridor, Mara following at his heels. "Ebo is working on getting her out. The bridge sustained damage and the warp generators are off-line."

"What's wrong with Wren?" She trailed him into the medical facility, helping him to ease the big Polluxite onto a diagnostic bed. Deke's muscles bulged with the strain of lowering the man gently onto the firm mattress.

"He needs your friend," Deke answered grimly.

"I'm here!" Hedy's voice trilled from the hatchway. She took one step inside and her face drained of color. "Great suns, what happened?" Rushing over, she jabbed at a control panel on the wall beside the bed, initiating diagnostic procedures. "He's got a concussion," she said, interpreting the sensory readouts. "That's easy enough to fix, but what's this?" She peered closely at his neck, her wavy brown hair falling across her face. "There's a fragment of something lodged in his flesh."

"He was hit by a metal grating," Deke explained, frowning. How long would Wren be incapacitated? Their crew was already minimal. He couldn't afford to lose anyone.

Hedy took a cylindrical instrument and rolled Wren to his side. Passing the tool over the gash at the back of his head, she mended the wound.

Flat on his back again, Wren stirred to consciousness. "What . . . ?" he muttered as his eyes gradually opened.

"You were struck by a metal grating," Deke explained. "Lie still. Dr. Te'larr is tending you."

"I'm going to have to remove this fragment," she said, pointing to his neck, where blood had begun oozing again. "I'm afraid the location isn't very good. The piece is lodged close to your carotid artery."

"What does that mean?" Wren's words were forced and Deke saw him wince in pain as he turned his head.

"You'll have to remain in sick bay until I'm certain

the arterial wall has strengthened. A rupture could prove fatal." Hedy glanced up. "I'm going to need a surgical assistant."

"I'll help," Mara offered.

"If you don't need me, I'll be heading back to the bridge," Deke said, shooting Mara a quick glance. She reacted well in an emergency, able to function and not become unnerved by her fear. For the first time, he felt glad she'd come aboard the *Celeste* as a member of his crew. It wasn't her physical attributes that brought him to that conclusion. Working at the wellness center, Hedy was accustomed to emergencies. Mara was a diplomat who rarely found herself in dangerous situations. He admired her ability to muster her strength and offer her assistance. Deke hadn't even realized he'd been questioning her usefulness until now and the revelation astounded him.

Resolving to listen more seriously to her advice once the current crisis was past, he marched out.

As soon as Deke left, Hedy prepped Wren, murmuring words of reassurance as she applied the anesthetic that would let him sleep through the operation. It didn't take long. The fragment came out easily with her laser scalpel, but repairing the resultant weakness in the arterial wall took longer.

"He'll have to remain still while this area strengthens," she told Mara, finished at last. She stripped off her surgical gloves and obtained a final readout of his vital signs. The Polluxite was asleep, his face peaceful. "I'll stay with him."

Mara nodded. "If you need a break, call me. Is there anything else I can do?"

"No, I don't think so. I've got everything under control." She smiled at Mara, grateful for her help.

"I'm going to the cargo bay to see if my sculpture has been damaged. I put it in a microshield, so I hope it's all right. Shall I stop by your cabin in case your things got dislodged in the collision? I can straighten up for you since you're stuck in here."

"I'd appreciate that."

After watching her leave, Hedy turned to stroke Wren's forehead. It pained her to see him lying so helpless.

Two hauras later, she finished organizing the sick bay supplies and testing the emergency equipment. Satisfied that all was in order, she produced a cool fruit beverage on the fabricator and approached Wren. He'd been awake for 15 minutes and his vital signs were stable.

"Have a drink," she offered, bending and aiming a straw at his mouth.

"I'm not a helpless baby!" he said, scowling.

"You're flat on your back, Lieutenant. You are also under orders as long as you're my patient. Now drink. You need the fluid to replace lost blood." When she saw the obstinate set of his mouth, she warned, "If you don't cooperate, I'll have to start an IV."

Her threat produced results. Reluctantly, he parted his lips and she inserted the straw. Apparently he was thirsty, because he sucked the drink dry in no time.

"Thank you," he said, staring at the ceiling.

She straightened, tossing the empty container into a disposer. "You'd better stop with this stoic act, Wren. You need me."

His blazing eyes swung to meet hers. "Allow me to rise and I'll manage by myself."

"Oh, no." She wagged her finger at him. "We can't put any pressure on that blood vessel wall. And your concussion is healed but you may still have occasional bouts of dizziness over the next few days. This is the best place for you. Now I'm going to run a few more tests." She flipped a few switches on a console behind him.

"What for?" he demanded, his tone gruff.

"Er, I need to stimulate neurological function to make certain your synaptic junctions are aligned." She averted her gaze, not wanting him to realize the true purpose of the tests. She had wanted to investigate the physical basis for his disability and now the opportunity had dropped into her eager hands. She wasn't about to let it pass.

Wren grumbled but lay still while she performed a series of intricate diagnostic procedures. He'd been right; she was unable to discover any physical cause for his inability to fly. He was as normal as any burly Polluxite male.

Wren's stentorian throat-clearing drew her attention. "What is it?" she asked, hastening to his bedside.

His face flushed an uncomfortable shade of beet red. "I, uh, am not comfortable."

"Oh, I'm so sorry. Can I adjust your headrest? Or are you too warm? What can I do for you?" she gushed, fluttering over him like a mother hen.

"I am feeling tension," he said, acutely embarrassed.

"Tension?" She wrinkled her forehead. "What do you—" Her face flooded with heat. "Of course. I should have thought of it. You need a few moments with the sanitation vacuum. I'll just close the privacy curtain and step aside. . . ."

"No, it's not that." His fists clenched and unclenched by his side.

Puzzled as to his need, her gaze swept over his massive body. He'd complained of a tense feeling, yet he didn't have to void. What else could be bothering him?

"You've got to help me!" The words slipped from his mouth in a moan. "The pressure is building up. I'm afraid I'm going to burst."

Her eyes widened. "Oh, I see." Her gaze slid to his groin. "You want me to help relieve the tension? Well, that kind of service usually isn't in my sphere of duties, but I suppose I could manage just for you." Giggling, she sat beside him and slid a hand along his leg, thinking how much she was going to enjoy this. Maybe she could prolong his stay in sick bay.

Wren jerked away. "No! Great Power, that's not what I meant!"

"Suns, Wren, will you speak your mind?" She sprang up, covering her embarrassment with an irritated tone of voice.

"It's my back. I . . . I need to spread my wings every six hauras. The pressure's been rising and I'm afraid they're going to sprout." He squeezed his eyes shut in pain.

"Good heavens! Luckily this bed is equipped with a turnaround. I can lock your neck in a brace and flip you onto your stomach on this lower surface. But you've got to stay absolutely still."

"Do it!" he grunted.

It took her five minutes to manipulate the contraption. Wren's panting breaths and reddened complexion alarmed her. As soon as he'd landed on his stomach, a giant set of wings erupted from his back through the slits in his uniform.

"By the moons of Agus Six!" She exclaimed, staring in rapture at the quivering feathered appendages. "Can I touch them?" Reaching out a trembling hand, she remembered his condition and asked, "Sorry, are you all right?"

"Much better," he gasped, limp with exhaustion.

"Do . . . do you mind if I see what they feel like? I mean, they're wonderful. I've never seen anything so incredibly"—*sexy* was what she wanted to say—"large," she finished feebly.

The tips of her fingers caressed the edge of one huge wing. The feathers were soft, like fluffy down, layer after layer on a strong muscular frame. "Oh," she moaned, "this is wild!" Sinking onto the bed, she closed her eyes and reveled in the feel of his feathered wings. Her hands traced the outlines of the meshed barbs and tickled along the vanes, stroking the junctions, sinew, and coverts. She'd never thought she could get such a charge out of feeling a man's wings, but this was almost better than an orgasm.

"Dr. Te'larr!" Wren rasped.

His anguished tone brought her to her senses. Her head snapped up and she glanced at him, her face warm. "We must change your position. There's too much pressure on that blood vessel wall this way. Are you ready?"

He pinched his face and his wings collapsed, disappearing into the slits in his broad back. He was quiet while she used the contraption to return him to his supine position. His body secure, she sat next to him and began stroking his chest. "You really turn me on, Wren. Gods, I've never felt so hot for a man before. Why don't you let me pleasure you?"

"No!"

"Have you ever done it?" she asked gently. "From what you'd said, I wasn't sure—"

"Hedy," he groaned, using her given name, "it is not my right to enjoy a woman's attention. Please, leave me alone!"

"Who said it isn't your right? Just because you didn't jump off those cliffs on your home planet doesn't mean you can't function as a man. You're perfectly normal that I can see."

He glowered at her. "I am not normal according to my race. You waste your time with me."

It wasn't working, she thought in dismay. She'd hoped to convince him that being with a woman from another world might be acceptable, but his mind-set against mating was so strong he refused to yield even when his own body responded. She'd never wanted anyone as much as she wanted Wren, yet she despaired of softening his heart.

"Very well," she said, afraid of turning him against her. She rose and straightened her shoulders, assuming her professional demeanor. After checking his vital signs, she proceeded to the computer console to run an analysis of the data she'd obtained earlier. It wasn't easy to concentrate with Wren in the room. Hearing him breathe a long sigh, she ran her fingers through her hair in frustration.

It was going to be a torturously long interval for them both while he was confined to sick bay.

Chapter Seven

Emergency procedures were still in effect eight hauras later when Mara entered the conference room. Deke had called for another briefing. Hedy and Ebo were already in attendance. As she took her seat, Mara was concerned as she noted Deke's drawn face and slumped posture. She was aware he'd taken over Wren's duties as well as his own.

"Dr. Te'larr, please report on Wren's condition," Deke ordered, pushing himself upright in his chair.

"Wren's vital signs are stable," the medic said quietly. "His neck wound is healing satisfactorily. I see no signs of complications from the concussion."

"That's good to hear." Deke surveyed each of his crew members. "I spoke with Glotaj. The Defense League patrols didn't find anything significant on the other two ships that left Spaceport after Jallyn's abduction. That means we're it. We have to find Jallyn on Yanura!"

"We're not even certain the Yanurans took her," Mara cautioned, wishing the infant were on the planet so they could rescue her. She still found it hard to believe Fromoth Trun might have had a hand in the baby's abduction but wanted more than anything to find Jallyn.

"Did you bring the baby's blanket as I requested? I'd like you to do another separation while we're all present." Deke's voice was unusually kind, as though he knew she needed reassurance. Surprised by his sensitivity, she smiled warmly at him and felt a tug at her heart when he smiled back.

Tearing her gaze away, Mara held up the lavender cloth in her hand to show the others. Clutching it to her chest, she closed her eyes and let her consciousness soar. She emptied her mind, focusing her thoughts on Jallyn. Her awareness drifted and floated from her body, hovering in the air while she tried to get a fix on Jallyn's vibrations.

Something yanked at her, a force so murky her senses couldn't penetrate it. She resisted, but the magnetic pull was too strong. Gaunt, shadowy tentacles curled around her astral body, binding her and tugging her toward a place she didn't want to visit. Mara had felt these tendrils of darkness before and they'd gotten stronger with each separation. She couldn't begin to guess where they came from, nor did she want to know.

Stop! She screamed in her mind as a kaleidoscope of sensations overwhelmed her. She thought fiercely of Jallyn, clinging in her mind's eye to the child's fragile image. Jallyn needs me, she told herself. I have to go to Jallyn.

And then suddenly she was inside Jallyn's head, safe from whatever evil had been seducing her. Shivering within her astral body, Mara turned her attention outward. The scene was the same. Jallyn was still aboard a ship. Wherever she was headed, it must be on a long voyage like theirs.

Eager to return to her physical being, Mara separated and then gave her report in a toneless voice, omitting any mention of the dark cloud that had threatened to envelop her. A feeling of dread lingered, chilling her blood.

"Are you all right?" Deke asked, his face etched with concern.

"I'm fine." She clamped her lips shut, closing out any further inquiries. Without having anything definite to say, she didn't want to elaborate on the experience. Maybe it was the result of her own anxiety over Jallyn's safety.

Deke's steady gaze fixed on her and Mara glanced away. From his expression, she could tell he knew something was wrong. Hopefully he wouldn't probe further.

To her relief, Deke's attention switched to the Sirisian. "How long before we're up to speed?" he asked Ebo, his tone solemn.

"The warp coils need another five hauras to recharge." Ebo's elastic pink face sagged with fatigue.

"We're losing valuable time." With an exasperated sigh, Deke plowed his fingers through his hair. "At least the spaceport at Revitt Lake City has adequate repair facilities. Are you sure you can fix the aft sensors with a new set of sequencers?"

Ebo nodded. "Almost everything else is operational. We shouldn't have any trouble." He paused. "I discovered something important while running a check on hull integrity. Apparently, the exterior coating on the ship can absorb certain radiation bands, making us impervious to sensor scans. If another ship were to scan our area of space, they'd detect nothing unless we were within visual range."

Deke's eyebrow raised. "Would that work for a planetary defense perimeter?"

Ebo nodded his turbaned head. "The function requires an energy expenditure. It's one of the commands programmed into the defense network."

"In other words, we have a cloaking device?"

"Aye, sir."

"I have the feeling we'll be needing it in the near future.

Good work, Ebo." Deke looked at Hedy. "Dr. Te'larr, when do you estimate Lt. Wren will be ready for duty?"

Hedy played nervously with a lock of her hair. "Another twenty-six hauras should do it, Commander."

"Are you sure he'll be all right?"

Hedy smiled wanly. "That depends on what you mean. He slept well through the night. This morning, he's been as quiet as a kougra. It's difficult to tell what he's feeling when he won't admit to discomfort. The poor man hates being confined and having me wait on him."

Mara gave her a sympathetic glance. She'd stopped by sick bay late last night, offering to relieve Hedy. Hedy had confided her lack of progress with the big Polluxite. Wren wouldn't speak except in monosyllables and acted acutely embarrassed by Hedy's efforts to assist him. Mara hadn't known what to suggest other than for Hedy to keep trying to break through his stubborn shell. Eventually he might become more responsive.

"Lt. Ebo, it's your watch on the bridge," Deke said. "Doctor, you may return to sick bay. Keep me posted as to Wren's progress."

Mara watched uneasily as the other two crew members filed out. Did Deke have something special in mind for her to do?

"Well, Mara?"

She cast him a quick glance, noting his bemusement. "Well, what?"

"Aren't you going to offer any advice? That is your job, isn't it? Offering advice?"

Her lips compressed. "I'll do what I can to help, since Wren is out of commission. Assign me a task, Commander."

"I'm glad you're so amenable. This is only our first crisis. We have no idea what will be waiting for us when we reach the Yanuran system."

His eyes gleamed mischievously and she realized he was baiting her. Straightening her shoulders, she glared back at him, meeting his challenge. "Have you forgotten? The Yanurans will be trying to impress us so they can win approval for their membership application!"

"Will they be trying to impress us when we uncover their secrets? Or will they prevent us from exposing them?" He leaned toward her, lowering his voice. "Our resources are limited. There's only five of us, and you women are poorly prepared for subversive operations. I have to worry about your safety instead of accomplishing our goals."

Great suns, Deke hadn't even realized that concern for Mara's safety was what had prompted him to be so harsh regarding physical training. He'd considered it his duty as commander to ensure the fitness of his crew, but he really feared for Mara and her friend. And now the words had slipped from his mouth like water from a faucet.

Stricken by his admission, he passed a hand over his face. He was tired from working too many hauras without a break. He'd only meant to flirt with Mara to brighten her mood. Something had disturbed her during her separation, and since she wouldn't talk about it, Deke had hoped to get her mind off of it. Now look what he'd done.

"You need to rest," she chided him.

"I can't afford the time. I have to get back to work." Shoving his chair aside, he rose, his face flushed as though he were aggravated by their discussion.

"Let me get you a meal, then. When did you last eat?"

"Who knows? I don't have time to eat, either."

Mara watched him go with an irritated snort. The man was as stubborn as a Tyberian rorsh. At the fabricator, she conjured him an iced jelly and laverbread cakes, then as an afterthought, got Ebo one of his favorite food items as well. Producing a tray, she proceeded to carry the meals to the bridge.

"Breakfast, gentlemen," she called out cheerfully. Deke was manning the helm and Ebo was frowning over the communications board. Both men looked up at her entrance.

"Mara!" Deke's tone expressed his annoyance.

"I brought you an iced jelly," she said tantalizingly, holding up the carafe. "And some laverbread cakes." Laverbread—seaweed mixed with oatmeal—was a versatile food that could be prepared using various methods. Curious about the foods Deke ate, Mara had looked them up in the food selection data base.

Striding forward, Deke grasped the carafe, his fingers brushing hers. Her skin flamed from the contact and she glanced at Ebo, hoping the Sirisian wouldn't notice how the commander unnerved her.

"Thanks," Deke said gruffly. His look of warm regard made her knees turn to gelatin.

"You've been working too hard. This will help you feel better. Lt. Ebo, I brought something for you also."

Ebo took his meal, then resumed his position. Taking the tray from her hands, Deke hesitated to move aside. He stood as firmly as a tree trunk, rooted to the spot, his heavy-lidded gaze focused directly on her. She wished it were possible to sense his emotions, but she couldn't read him.

Her glance drifted to the unruly lock of hair that tumbled across his forehead. Unable to stop herself, she reached forward to brush it gently off his brow.

His eyes darkened ominously. "Mara—"

"Forgive me." She sprang back, afraid she'd offended him. He'd warned her once before not to distract him on the bridge. "I mustn't keep you from your job."

"Wait!" he called as she turned away. "Er, perhaps you'd like to help Lt. Ebo monitor communications. You're skilled in linguistics, aren't you? Ebo can explain what needs to be done. That'll free him to work on the repairs."

Eager to perform a useful function, she hastened to the comm panel, where Ebo instructed her. She took over monitoring the subspace radio, relieving Ebo until Wren was ready to return to duty.

As she bent over the comm panel, she could feel Deke's eyes boring into her back. His nearness made it difficult for her to concentrate.

It touched her that he'd admitted to being concerned for her safety. She understood now that he wasn't being unreasonable by ordering her and Hedy to engage in weapons training. He genuinely cared about their well-being. That softened her attitude toward him, and she began to wonder why he'd joined the Defense League. As soon as she had some free time, she'd check into his background.

Ebo repaired the generator coils and they were able to achieve warp speed. Over the next few days, Mara's separations showed the baby's status to be unchanged. When the baby's environment altered, they would be able to pinpoint target locations within a certain radius. The Yanurans were due to arrive home a full two days before the *Celeste* reached their planet. If Jallyn's surroundings switched before Fromoth Trun touched his homeworld, it would confirm Mara's belief that the Yanurans were not responsible for her abduction. As they got closer to their goal, she strengthened her arguments in support of the Yanurans.

"I'm sure their contribution to the Coalition will be meaningful," she said to Deke one day. "Look at some of our other member species. The Winnows gave us new theories in subspacial geometry; the Crimerans are famous as chemists; the Risivs produce specially crafted jewelry prized throughout the Coalition. Every member has contributed something significant. If Fromoth Trun is telling the truth about having an age-preserving drug, it could help billions."

"We'll find out soon enough." Deke's face creased into a smile, and he snaked his hand across the dining table to clasp hers. They were alone in the conference facility, and Mara's pulse rate soared. "Have you always been so vehement in your beliefs?" he asked.

She stiffened, withdrawing her hand from his grasp. "Of course. And I believe the Yanurans should receive the same fair evaluation as anyone else. You don't seem to share that notion. I think your mind is already made up about them."

Sighing, Deke pushed back his chair and rose. "This discussion is becoming old. You're the one who refuses to view them objectively."

"I am not!" Incensed by his misjudgment of her, she followed him into the study center. The man spent every spare moment there, perusing obscure scientific reports on oceanography. Mara couldn't correlate the serious scholar with the decisive commander and yearned to learn more about him.

"Deke, what did you do before you joined the Defense League?" she asked, sliding into the seat next to his. A blank computer screen faced her.

He gave her a quick glance from under his thick brows. "I worked at one of the research centers on Eranus," he said enigmatically.

"Really? In what capacity?"

"It's irrelevant to our current mission." He turned his attention to his studies, effectively dismissing the subject.

Mara tried a few more inquiries but got nowhere. Refusing to give up, she waited until Deke left before calling up the data base on Eranus. Her eyes widened when she read the information on her screen. *Dr.* Sage was an esteemed marine biologist who was being considered for the chancellorship at the Institute for Marine Studies!

Unable to contain her curiosity, she turned off her

computer and rushed to the crew quarters, where she knocked on Deke's door.

"Who is it?" he called in his rich, deep voice.

"Mara. I have to talk to you!"

"Come in."

She entered and stopped just inside the door. He'd apparently been resting between duty watches because he was lounging on his sitter without any shirt or shoes. His hair was askew and she thought he looked devastatingly handsome sprawled in such a relaxed pose. The strains of a symphony played in the background.

She cleared her throat. "I . . . I just happened to call up the files on Eranus. I had no idea you were such a renowned scientist. Why didn't you tell me?"

Swinging his long legs off the sitter, he stood to face her. "I felt it unnecessary for anyone to know what I do outside of the Defense League."

"But you're too modest!" Forcing herself not to stare at his massive chest with its dark swirls of hair, she fixed her gaze on his intense brown eyes. "I'd love to hear more about your work."

"Computer, secure door." After the portal had shut, Deke sauntered forward, stopping directly in front of her. "Why are you so interested in what I do?"

She moistened her lips, acutely aware that they were alone in his cabin. Had coming here been a mistake?

"I, er . . ." She didn't want to reveal the extent of her interest. He might take it the wrong way.

"Despite our discussions, you still insist on suspecting the Yanurans of murdering your friend," she stated instead. "They deserve better treatment. I'm afraid you will be biased in your report to the Admissions Committee. I was looking for something in your background that would indicate why you persist in your prejudice."

"Larikk disappeared on their *maug* planet! Isn't that

enough?" His expression darkened. "You've no faith in me, have you? You can't believe I'll act with good judgment despite my suspicions, and you're too naive to admit I might be justified in feeling the way I do.

"You want to learn more about me?" he asked. "Very well, I'll show you what you want to know!"

Ignoring her gasp of protest, he snagged her by the shoulders, pulled her close, and lowered his head. She felt the press of his mouth on hers and her first impulse was to push him away. Placing her hands on his brawny chest, she splayed her fingers and murmured a sound of protest that sounded weak even to her own ears. As her fingers tangled in his hair, he drew in a sharp breath. Hearing the sound, her excitement rocketed. She felt her inner self being pulled closer to him by a compelling magnetism that was impossible to resist. Closing her eyes, she leaned into him, enjoying the feel of his strong arms around her and the sensation of security his embrace provided.

His mouth moved urgently, demandingly over hers. He tightened his arms around her, and she swayed closer to him. He plundered her mouth with the hunger of a starving man, and barely able to breathe, she lost herself in a heady spiral of sensations. The savagery of his kiss dissolved any of her resistance that might have lingered. Hadn't Deke hinted this was where their relationship was leading? She hadn't wanted to succumb to his suave approach, but there was nothing urbane about the way he was kissing her now. She could tell by the frantic motions of his lips on hers that he was soaring on a hazy cloud of desire.

As his mouth gentled and he began tiny nibbling movements, she murmured her pleasure. She fit perfectly into the hard angles of his body as she tilted her neck back, changing the angle of the kiss. Taking advantage, his tongue thrust into her mouth, probing and teasing until she met it with her own hesitant explorations. His masculine scent pervaded her senses and stirred her rising desire. Unable to stop herself, she snaked her arms around him, letting her fingers explore his broad back, his muscles, his skin. Heat sizzled her blood, and she longed to touch him everywhere.

"Mara," he murmured, gracing her face with tiny kisses across her cheeks and the bridge of her nose, then back to her mouth. His hands roved over her back, his movements urgent. As though she were the most cherished woman alive, he rested a hand on the back of her head and gently cradled her while he deepened the kiss.

She moaned as his tongue entered her mouth, and when his hips rocked against her, a strong jolt jarred her senses and her faculties tumbled in riotous confusion. She felt his arms around her and her own soft body melting in his embrace; she felt the sweetness of her mouth as he tasted her and the crush of her breasts against his chest. It was almost as though she were in his viewpoint, sharing his experience.

By the stars, she'd entered his essence! She *was* in his viewpoint, experiencing his sensations as he kissed her! She was so astounded that she could hardly breathe. After a moment, she realized here was a golden opportunity to learn how he truly felt about her. She'd never taken advantage of anyone before but was unable to resist the temptation. She'd jumped into his life space inadvertently. It shouldn't cause any harm if she explored further.

She reached out, delving deeper into his psyche. Layers of consciousness peeled away under her strong spiritual probe. Beneath the surface, Deke was a sensitive man who cared deeply about many different issues. She'd already glimpsed his concern over Wren's welfare, his insistence that she and Hedy learn how to defend themselves because he cared about their safety. But she hadn't understood his regret over Larikk's death. In some manner, Deke felt responsible and his guilt motivated him to seek the truth. Her surprise at this insight propelled her upward into the lighter planes of his existence.

Her eyes snapped open at the same instant that Deke jumped back, abruptly releasing her, severing their spiritual link.

"What did you do?" he cried, enraged.

Mara froze, at a loss for words. She had no excuse for her behavior.

"You tried to read my mind!"

"I can't read thoughts," she protested. "I can only sense emotions, even when I'm in someone else's viewpoint. I . . . I'm not sure how it happened, but you appear to have triggered a separation."

He stared at her, horrified. "What do you mean?"

Agitated, she brushed her hair off her face. "When I was younger, this sort of thing happened all the time. I had difficulty controlling my ability. But never in my adulthood have I experienced anything similar, not even with Pietor." Her heart sank at the incredulous look on his face.

"Who in Zor is Pietor?" he demanded.

"My former fiance. His parents didn't approve of me. Instead of defending me, he agreed with them and . . . and said hurtful things behind my back."

Deke raked trembling fingers through his hair. "I can understand why! You lack control over your freakish ability. Gods, does that mean this could happen again?"

She saw his fear mixed with resentment. He stared at her as if she were some sort of monster.

"You're the only man with whom I've ever had a spontaneous separation, Deke. There's got to be something significant involved. Perhaps we should explore our feelings for each other."

"I only meant to take you to bed," Deke snapped, stepping back as though putting physical distance between them could prevent another occurrence.

"You can leave now," he told her, his eyes cold. "And that's an order."

After she stormed out, Deke let loose every expletive in his store of known alien languages. What had he unleashed by his interest in her? All he'd wanted was to bed the woman, but Mara had come dangerously close to stealing his identity! So what if her lips tasted like honey and her hair felt as fine as gossamer silk? Physical desires could be satisfied by any woman. He didn't need one who could invade his psyche without warning and stimulate emotions he didn't want to feel. Her ability frightened him.

So why couldn't he erase her lovely image from his mind?

Mara worked herself into a frenzy as she stomped her bare feet in a tray of mushy clay. She had to do something to wipe away the memory of Deke's lips on hers, the remembrance of how good it had felt to be wrapped in his strong embrace. Pounding vigorously, she contemplated the words he'd thrown at her. It was clear he feared her, and rightfully so. She'd violated her own ethical code by willfully piercing his layers of consciousness. This was the first time she'd ever used her ability in that manner and the ease of it frightened her.

Stricken with guilt and remorse, she wondered how she could approach Deke when he regarded her with such revulsion. She had to make him see their experience was meaningful. It had never happened with any of the men she'd dated.

Pietor had scorned her unusual gift and he hadn't even experienced it firsthand, as Deke had. She'd merely told him about it. She'd been devastated when she overheard him disparaging her to his parents. Would Deke tell the other crew members? Mortified at the idea, she hoped he'd have the decency to keep what happened to himself.

Hedy would understand, but Wren and Ebo might regard her differently, and she hated being considered different.

By the Light, what should she do? Stepping from her sculpting tray, she wiped off her feet and put away the supplies. An overwhelming need to share her burden made her hasten to Hedy's cabin. Knocking loudly on the door, she heard strains of music from within.

Hedy swung the door open and the noise blared. "Mara, I was just thinking about you! Want to play one of the games I brought along?"

"No, I need to talk. Can you turn that down?"

"Sure." Hedy complied, then swung around to face her. She wore an amber tunic and black trousers with the Coalition insignia embroidered over her left breast. It was the standard-issue uniform for medical personnel on Bimordus Two.

Without waiting for an invitation, Mara shut the door and strode to Hedy's lounger. She sank onto the softly upholstered surface and covered her face with her hands.

"What's the matter?" Hedy cried.

"I . . . I went to Deke's cabin to ask him about his work on Eranus and he . . . and we . . ." In a stumbling tone, Mara related the tale. "He probably hates me, Hedy." Depressed, she hung her head, her hands clasped in her lap.

"Nonsense, he got frightened. You'd be scared if someone popped into your head and you weren't expecting it. He knows you have this ability."

"But I used it wrongly, Hedy. I shouldn't have tried to delve deeper. I wanted to know how he felt about me."

"Why?" Hedy perched herself on the edge of an armchair, facing her.

Mara considered her response. Physically, she couldn't deny how strongly Deke's virile good looks appealed to her. She liked the way his thick chestnut hair swept across his forehead, how his dark eyes gleamed with amusement whenever he challenged her to a duel of words. Their encounters were always stimulating. She'd never met a man as intelligent or charming, or as irritatingly obstinate as Dr. Deitan Sage.

"I like him," she said simply, "and I wanted to know if he felt the same toward me. I felt there might be more than a sexual attraction between us."

Hedy's expression brightened. "Obviously he's attracted to you or he wouldn't have kissed you. I think you should tell him how you feel."

"He won't listen." She stood up and began pacing. "I tried to tell him this was the first time I'd had such an experience, but it didn't matter. He threw me out."

"But you're right; the two of you being together must have caused the separation." Hedy's eyes flashed indignantly. "If Comdr. Sage had any common sense, he'd realize that. In my opinion, there's no excuse for the way he treated you."

She hung her head. "But I'm guilty, Hedy. I took advantage of the situation. I probed more deeply than I should have. I knew of the terrible guilt he feels about Larikk."

"You didn't mean any harm." Hedy squared her shoulders. "If he won't listen to you, I'll talk to him. Wait here!"

Hedy stalked out before Mara had a chance to stop her.

Chapter Eight

Deke was in the study center trying to forget about Mara when Hedy stormed in.

"Here you are!" she cried, grabbing a chair and sitting astride it.

He looked up from his computer and regarded her warily. "What is it?"

"Do you realize how badly you've hurt Mara?" Hedy proclaimed. "Your behavior was insufferably rude."

Deke studied her flashing eyes and the determined tilt of her chin. Despite her somewhat frivolous nature, the medic could be quite serious when the occasion demanded it. "I don't see that it's any concern of yours," he replied in an icy tone.

"You're wrong." Hedy pouted. "Mara is particularly sensitive about her being different, and you just called her ability freakish! How do you think that made her feel?"

"How do you think I felt when she invaded my mind?" he retorted.

"It happened spontaneously. Didn't she tell you this was the first time that's ever happened in her adult life?"

"She should exercise better control over her ability!"

"Usually she can, Commander." Letting out an exasperated sigh, Hedy twisted around to sit properly in her chair. She leveled her steady gaze on him. "Mara had a difficult time growing up. Did she ever tell you her history?"

"No, and I don't see that it's relevant." He didn't want to hear this. He didn't want to know what motivated Mara or why she acted the way she did. It might make him sympathize with her and he couldn't afford to feel that way. He needed to maintain a barrier between them so she wouldn't jump into his head again. Just the idea of what she'd done made him tremble with anger and fear.

He rose, intending to head for the bridge, but Hedy charged in front of him, blocking his path. "You're going to listen to me!" she declared, her petite body standing between him and the hatchway.

"Move out of my way, Doctor."

Ignoring his order, Hedy said, "Mara exhibited her talent at an earlier age than most people on her world. She's from Tyberia, you know. Psychic ability is inherent in their race, but it usually takes annums of training to reach her level. Mara's parents sent her to a special school. Other children her age made fun of her and she was always lonely. She's still lonely, Commander. Her difference eats at her and after the fiasco with Pietor, she feels she'll never find happiness."

He swallowed uncomfortably. "So what? It's not my problem."

"Isn't it? Mara seems to feel you triggered her separation."

"That's absurd. She just lost control over her ability." His rage deepened. "She violated my privacy, Doctor. Things . . . feelings . . . I didn't want to remember came to the surface. She caused me pain with her intrusion and I won't let that happen again. Now unless you want to be physically removed from my path, I suggest you get out of the way."

Hedy's chin tilted stubbornly. Grunting with disgust, he lifted her by the waist as though she were a sack of feathers and put her down, none too gently, off to his side. As he stalked out, he shot her a last warning: "This isn't your affair, Doctor. Keep out of it or I'll confine you to your cabin."

Cursing under his breath, he strode toward the companionway leading to the bridge. What did he care if Mara's life had been unhappy? It wasn't his responsibility. Nor was the separation his fault, as both women seemed to imply. All right, so he kissed her. Could the physical contact between them have triggered the event? It hadn't occurred between Mara and Pietor, according to what she'd said. So why him?

He shrugged. It didn't matter why or how it had happened. The only way to prevent another occurrence was to keep away from her.

The thought that he was causing her grief tugged at his heart but he pushed it aside, angry with himself for even considering the idea. She was the one who'd caused him pain, damn it! He stomped up the spiral stairway to the bridge, bottling his feelings for her just as he'd suppressed his emotions over Larikk's disappearance.

Mara waited anxiously in Hedy's cabin for her friend to return. She sat on the sitter, wringing her hands. By the Light, she should never have let Hedy go! What was she saying to Deke? Whatever Hedy did, it would only make matters worse.

At least Hedy was willing to come to her defense. Mara couldn't say that about anyone else she knew except for

Sarina. Hedy and Sarina were true friends, the only ones who shared their honest feelings with her. Thank the stars for their friendship. Moisture seeped from her eyes as she felt a depth of gratitude. Still, she yearned for closeness with another person. It wasn't that she needed a man. She just craved the intimacy of a loving relationship.

It was a goal she'd never reach. Pietor had mocked her and Deke was repulsed by her. Tears streaked her face and ran down her cheeks. No one would ever want her!

Her sobs had reached loud proportions when Hedy burst inside. "Great suns, Mara, stop that at once! That man isn't worth crying over." She handed her a box of tissues and waited until she'd blown her nose.

"What . . . what happened?" Mara asked, sniffling.

"He's a stubborn son of a belleek. I told him you were sensitive about your ability and normally you had full control over it. He had to have been the influence that caused the separation. Deke didn't care. He told me to mind my own business or I'd be confined to quarters!"

"That sounds like him," she said bitterly.

"What are you going to do? We've got seven more days until we reach Yanura. You can't avoid him the whole time."

She lifted her chin. "I'm not going to avoid him. Despite his lousy treatment of me, I do believe the man feels . . . felt . . . something for me more than carnal lust. That's why the separation occurred. He doesn't realize it yet, and now he certainly wouldn't admit it. But when he thinks about it, maybe he'll understand that something significant occurred between us."

Yet as the days passed, Deke managed to avoid her, or at least to avoid being alone with her. Mara never had a chance to discuss the situation with him. Whenever they were in the same room, he maintained a careful distance, as though afraid the slightest contact might make her jump into his head. She sensed he was clearly terrified of what might happen if she entered his mind again. She wanted to explain to him that she had probed his emotions only because she wanted to learn how he felt about her. She also wanted to tell him that if she inadvertently entered his head again, she would never try to explore his feelings without his cooperation and that they could explore the new sensations together. But she never was alone with him and she couldn't discuss it in front of the other crew members. At least Deke didn't treat her like a pariah in front of them. He was coolly civil to both her and Hedy, and they were the only ones who noticed the change in his behavior.

Deke was beginning to relax, reassured that no further occurrences with Mara were going to take place, when he was summoned by an urgent call from Glotaj. Receiving the message privately in the conference room, he opened a scrambled channel.

"Aye, sir?" he said, facing the elder statesman on the monitor screen.

"Greetings, Deke. How are the repairs on the ship proceeding?"

"Very well, sir. We're maintaining speed and most of the systems are back on-line. I'm hoping to complete the mechanical repairs on Yanura."

"They've been alerted and will have a maintenance crew available." Glotaj paused, his expression darkening. "I just got a call from an investigator in the Justice Department. It seems an old case has been reopened. Would you know anyone named Larikk who disappeared on Yanura three annums ago?"

He sucked in a breath. "Of course. I filed the initial complaint. A preliminary investigation was done but nothing significant turned up. We couldn't proceed because Yanura didn't fall under Coalition jurisdiction."

"Well, it does now. Since the Yanurans have applied for admissions status, they'll be judged by our laws. The Justice Department is interested in what happened to Larikk."

"The Yanurans claimed he drowned, sir. His body was never produced."

"Apparently Larikk vanished in the Alterland, which is Wort territory. You understand what that means?"

"Aye, sir." A muscle spasm rippled his jaw. "We need to talk to the Worts. I was planning on meeting with them anyway to assess their views on Coalition membership."

"Find out what happened to Larikk. It could be significant."

Glotaj's mouth moved but Deke didn't hear what he was saying. It sounded like a jumble of voices in his head. He shook himself. What was wrong with his hearing?

Hello, Deke.

Great suns! It was Mara! His eyes widened and his jaw dropped. She was in his head again. Had she just spoken to him? No, it wasn't distinct words he'd heard. It was a feeling that she was there.

Get out! he implored, trying to concentrate on what Glotaj was saying.

" . . . imperative you find out if these rumors are true," the supreme regent concluded. "If they are, the situation is graver than we'd thought. Contact me as soon as you reach Yanura. Glotaj out."

Blast, he'd missed what Glotaj had said. And all because of Mara! She'd invaded his mind again, interfering in a sensitive communication. Did this mean he wasn't safe from her no matter where he was? Could she leap into his consciousness at any time, any place?

He ran a shaky hand over his face. At least he felt whole again. She'd left him as swiftly as she'd entered his essence. Had she heard the conversation with Glotaj?

Rage at her intrusion sent chills cascading through his body and he rose, intending to have it out with her once and for all. She just had to get her ability under control. He couldn't live like this, never knowing when she was going to invade him.

Asking the ship's computer for a fix on her life signs, he headed toward her cabin. Balling his hand into a fist, he pounded on her door, oblivious to the noise he caused. Mara's sweet voice bade him to enter. She sat on the armchair in her sitting room, her hands folded in her lap. Her expression told him she might have been expecting him.

"I'm glad you came, Deke. I've been wanting to talk to you in private. Please close the door and take a seat."

"You've got a helluva nerve to sit there calmly after what just happened." He threw the door shut and marched in front of her, narrowing his eyes. His glance scanned her, from her loose raven hair cascading down her back to her silken wrap to her delicate bare feet. What in Zor was that thing she was wearing? The crimson and gold drape barely covered her. Against his will, he felt his loins stirring as her perfumed scent drifted toward him.

"You don't need to be frightened of me," she said calmly.

"I am not frightened! You invaded my mind again. I was involved in a confidential communication and you violated my privacy. How can you account for this reprehensible action?"

She shook her head, long strands of her hair falling forward against her face. "I cannot explain the phenomenon other than that you must be influencing its occurrence. I've been hoping for an opportunity like this so we can discuss it." Her dark eyes pleaded with him to understand. "This has never happened to me before. Somehow you keep pulling me into your higher plane of existence."

"You're accusing me?" he asked scornfully. "You're the one who lacks control."

"No, Deke. Whatever is happening between us is the cause. The first time, I . . . I took advantage to try to find out how you felt about me. I apologize for that and promise it won't happen again. Perhaps we should explore the sensation if we come together again and see where it takes us."

Panic swept him. "I don't want to see anything! This is not a scientific experiment! You're fooling with my mind."

It had been difficult enough for him to assert his independence through his youth, and that struggle still affected his life. His father, Director General of Eranus, was so powerful that Deke had always stood in his shadow until he chose to pursue marine biology. His mother, Palomar, belonged to a wealthy clan who owned a giant cosmetic company. His own sense of pride made him refuse to accept her family's money to fund his research. He'd made a name for himself through his own efforts and he would get a grant to provide the necessary funding. He wouldn't be dependent upon his mother or anyone. Nor would he subjugate his identity to Mara.

He studied her solemnly. By the stars, he didn't want to fear her. She looked alluringly feminine and he'd rather twist his fingers through her long shiny hair. What if she was right? If this had never happened to her before, maybe he did have something to do with it. In any event, they couldn't go on accusing each other. They were members of a team, and they had to work together when they reached Yanura. But could he trust her to keep out of his head while he was involved in delicate negotiations with Fromoth Trun?

He hadn't been treating her very well in the interim. What was happening between them must be just as confusing to her as it was to him. He had to look at it from a scientific viewpoint. Wasn't his purpose to explore unknown phenomena?

Not when it threatened to undermine his privacy! A cold chill washed over him but it was quickly replaced by a surge of heat when Mara shifted her position and the slit in her garment exposed her smooth leg. By the stars, she still had the power to arouse him despite his apprehension over her psychic ability. Never mind those erotic dreams he kept having of her. Those were fantasies his subconscious kept tormenting him with. But this was real, and her presence initiated a response he couldn't control.

"I have news regarding Jallyn," Mara stated.

"Why didn't you say so before?"

"You weren't ready to listen."

"So what is it?"

She stood and began pacing, her tight skirt clinging to her hips. His gaze focused on her firm derriere as she walked away from him.

As though sensing his interest, she changed direction, turning toward him. He perused her smooth skin, her wide almond-shaped eyes, and her pink lips. He remembered how her mouth had tasted under his, and he longed to pull her lithe body into his arms. Her drape was fastened diagonally over one shoulder, leaving the other free. How easy it would be to undo the ties and drop the fabric to the floor.

"She's been moved to a windowless room," Mara said, distracting him from his imaginary foreplay. "I can't tell if she's on a ship or on land, but I don't sense the vibrations of movement. I think her captors have reached their destination."

"I'll notify Defense League Command. This should give us more definitive information regarding possible destinations."

Mara's large eyes filled with moisture. "What if Jallyn

isn't on Yanura? I can't bear the thought of going home to Sarina without her."

Despite his resolve not to get close to her, his heart twisted inside him. She appeared so fragile and forlorn, like a lost child. Recalling what Hedy had said about her unhappy youth, he felt a surge of sympathy. Unable to stop himself, he stepped forward and rested a hand on her bare shoulder.

"We're doing everything we can," he murmured softly.

"It's not enough!"

Perceiving she was perilously close to tears, he pulled her to him, groaning inwardly as her body heat penetrated his uniform. Her floral perfume stimulated his senses. Nuzzling his face in her hair, he relished the softness of the silken strands. "Mara," he whispered hoarsely, "don't do this to me. I can't get near you without wanting you."

She sniffled, raising her face to his with such a pathetic expression that he dipped his head and kissed her without any thought to the possible consequences. Her arms folded around his neck, pulling his head down closer. Feeling the urgent movements of her lips under his and the warmth of her breath compelled him to tighten his arms around her. What had begun as a comforting embrace turned into a passionate, soul-searing kiss that neither of them could stop.

Deke knew it the instant she invaded his life space, but this time he didn't push her away. He let her linger, waiting to see if he could trust her not to probe deeper. When his hand sought her breast, he sensed her joy and wonder as she shared his incredible delight. It heightened his own arousal so that his breath came in short, labored bursts. Losing control, he mashed his lips against hers and crushed her breast under his hand. They weren't close enough. He wanted to be part of her just as she was already a part of him.

He drew his head back to regard her. Her mouth was soft and swollen from his kiss, her expression dreamy. Her soft, lush body felt heavenly in his arms. "This is my kind of experiment after all," he said in a husky tone. "Let's see how far we can go with it."

Mara's consciousness surfaced to reality with a jolt. While he'd been avoiding her, she had longed for the teasing glimmer to return to his eyes; for his disarming grin to light his face when he glanced at her. She hadn't even realized how much she missed their sparring encounters over the Yanurans or their exercise sessions until she was bereft of his presence. Now it felt as though she'd just received a dose of ice water over her head.

"Is that all this is to you, a game?" she asked, wriggling free of his embrace. "Now that you're not afraid of me, you're trying to get me into your bed?"

"Why not?" he said flippantly. "Think of it as a unique way to experience the joys of coupling." His voice lowered. "I shared your reactions to my touch, Mara. That drove me wild. I want more, don't you?"

Disappointment washed over her like a frothing surf. What he felt for her was purely physical. She must have been wrong to think she meant anything else to him. "Get out of here," she snapped, fuming at his insensitivity.

When he left, she wondered if his callousness was meant to chase her away. For a brief moment, Deke had been caring and tender, offering his strength when she'd needed it. She remembered other instances of kindness that showed his true nature but were quickly concealed. Her initial probe had revealed him to be a sensitive man. If only she could lessen his fear of her ability, he might share more of himself with her.

Thinking it over, she decided to try an intellectual approach. Deke had seemed pleased the first time she'd asked about his scientific career. She could use that avenue to open a dialogue between them. Maybe he just needed time to accept his feelings for her and to trust her.

She had her chance later in the study center. Deke was reviewing Yanuran flora and fauna when she walked in and dropped into a seat beside him.

"I didn't know you were interested in alien plant life," she stated, smiling benignly.

"It pays to be prepared," he replied, staring at his screen.

"Prepared for what?"

Sighing, he switched off his monitor and whirled to face her. "Survival skills. It is necessary to become familiar with the terrain, vegetation, and various forms of wildlife of the target planet when you're going on a mission like ours."

"Is there wildlife on Yanura?" Ashamed to admit it, she realized she knew little about the planet other than the cultural practices of its amphibian inhabitants.

"Yes," he answered, a look of surprise on his face, as though he'd expected her to argue with him and was taken off guard by her mild inquiry. "There are animals both large and small, and a wide variety of plant life. Some we've seen on other worlds, so it won't seem so different."

"How do you like this type of work compared to your research back on Eranus?"

Dashing a hand through his thick hair, he grimaced. "I prefer being near the sea. At least on Yanura, I'll have a chance to inspect their mariculture farms. I miss the ocean when I'm away from it for long."

"Why did you join the Defense League?" Her glance strayed to the lock of dark hair that had fallen across his forehead. Everything about him appealed to her: his intense eyes, charming dimples, and virile physique. He radiated a masculine mystique, and she couldn't help it if her pulse quickened in his presence. Remembering that she was supposed to take an intellectual approach, she lowered her gaze demurely to her lap.

Briefly, Deke told her about needing a grant to continue his research on deep-sea vents and how he was competing for the chancellorship. "That's why succeeding at this mission is so important to me. I have to show Glotaj and the selection committee that I can handle a leadership position."

It touched Mara that he'd confided so much in her. She suspected no one else among his crew knew his term of service was temporary, and she wouldn't violate his trust by informing them. "I appreciate your telling me this, Deke. It helps me to understand you better."

He leaned forward in his chair, and his closeness warmed her. "What about you, Mara? Why are you so adamant in your insistence that the Yanurans get fair treatment? Are you that way with all your clients?"

"Of course! Everyone deserves to be treated with respect."

"Hedy said you had a difficult upbringing. Is that why you chose a career in diplomacy, to ensure that other people receive the respect you never got?"

His insight made her squirm in her seat. Brushing back a stray wisp of her hair, she said: "Since you put it so succinctly, the answer is yes. Despite all our technological achievements, prejudice still exists in many parts of the galaxy. We can't achieve true harmony until all races respect each other."

"That's an admirable but immense undertaking for one person to accomplish."

"People like you make it difficult. You're biased against the Yanurans before you even meet them."

Deke rolled his eyes. "Here we go again."

Instantly she felt contrite. "I'm sorry. I didn't mean to

start that topic again. Tell me about your oceanographic research."

He smiled, his expression so bright it pierced her heart like a ray of sunshine. "Want to hear about the giant tube worms I found on Setai Four?"

Beyond describing his research, Deke wouldn't let Mara get closer to him emotionally as the days passed.

"There're better ways to get to know each other," he told her one afternoon when they were in the exercise lab. His body sweaty from exertion, and wearing only tight shorts, he approached her. His dark gaze swept to the exposed cleavage of her dance suit and a wolfish gleam shimmered in his eyes.

Her heart hammered as she stopped her exercise machine. "I thought you were afraid to touch me, Deke. It might trigger another separation."

"I liked the sensation the last time it happened." He spoke in a husky rumble, his eyes locked on hers.

"Is that all you care about, the thrill we can get from sharing our physical responses?"

"Sure," he said, giving her a disarming grin. "We could give each other great pleasure, Mara." He stepped closer so that the heat from his body stole into her blood. Reaching out, he tickled her upper arm with practiced fingers.

Angrily, she shrugged him off. "Forget it. I don't use my ability in that manner."

And over the next few days, Deke continued his attempts to coax Mara into his bed. She resented his attitude and wouldn't let him touch her. She knew he regarded her as another conquest and wanted to use her ability to heighten his own physical pleasure, and she wouldn't accept him as a sexual partner without meaning more to him than that.

* * *

Torn between wanting Mara and his fear of intimacy with her, Deke was alarmed that he eagerly sought her company. She was a good listener, and he enjoyed relating stories of his scientific discoveries. By listening quietly and avoiding arguments, she insinuated herself into his psyche without even jumping into his head.

You can bed her without wedding her, Deke told himself jokingly as he left his cabin. Sharing her sensations when kissing her was a wild experience. It heightened his own delight tenfold. And if a kiss gave such pleasure, what would their joining do? Every time the woman was near, his heart started pounding and his loins stirred into frustrated arousal. He'd be willing to have her essence enter his body just for sex. Why wouldn't she agree?

As he headed toward the bridge, he spotted her in the holovid lounge, watching a video on Anthrobie folk dances. She was relaxing on the lounger, the hem of her long full skirt folded about her ankles. Her low-necklined white top afforded him a tantalizing view of her unbound breasts. At his entrance, she looked up and he was pleased to notice that her expression brightened.

"Taking a break, Commander?"

He sauntered inside. "I could ask you the same thing. How come you're not studying up on the Yanurans or working on a sculpture?"

Mara glanced at his dimples, at his even, white smile, and at the lock of hair that curled enticingly on his forehead. Her knees turned rubbery as she scrambled for a response.

"I, uh, decided to have a rest," she murmured as he approached. Her eyes swept to his broad chest and his tight-fitting uniform.

Deke dropped down on the seat beside her, leaning back as though it were the most natural thing in the world for his thigh to be touching her at hip level. In a fluid movement, his arm stretched across the back of the lounger, his fingers dangling just beyond her shoulder. If she took a deep breath, he'd be touching her.

Before she could protest, he began caressing her arm, sending titillating ripples through her.

"D-Don't," she stammered, wanting to close her eyes and savor the delicious sensations.

"Why not?" he murmured. "It feels good, doesn't it?"

"Dear heaven, yes, but—" She sucked in a sharp breath as his hands brushed her breast.

"You're so lovely. Why don't you relax and enjoy this? Computer, secure door."

"Now wait a minute, I didn't say it was all right," she huffed, aware that her tone sounded weak. His fingers moved to her cleavage, teasing her into heightened arousal. Her nipples ached for his touch as a warm flood of tension arose inside her.

What would be the harm in letting him kiss her? It didn't mean she'd have to hop into bed with him. One kiss, just to see if the same thing happened as the last time.

Telling herself it would be acceptable, she turned toward him, giving in to her rising desire. But as soon as he touched his lips to hers, her resolutions faded. Her body reacted as though it had a mind of its own. Closing her eyes, she wrapped her arms around his neck, pulling his head down closer. He tasted of spice and sea salt. The mixture left her reeling with passion. She kissed him back with demanding urgency, running her hands along the broad planes of his back and raking her fingers through his thick hair.

Blissful sensations coursed through him as he felt her hands stroking his back. Deke tightened his embrace, crushing her mouth under his. She was so lovely, so different from the other women he'd met. She reminded him of a ship on a calm sea: steady and reliable, running a straight course to a set goal. You could always count on her and she'd get you through the roughest waters. He'd been with plenty of women, but most of them were shallow, wanting to use him because of his father's power or his mother's money. None of them ran as deep as Mara. That was how he wanted to be with her: buried deep inside her, rocking to the rhythm of the timeless sea.

He felt her enter his life space and wondered why it had taken so long, but it didn't matter. He could feel how her limbs melted while her blood surged with fire. Her mouth parted and he plunged his tongue inside, exploring her the way he'd search the ocean, probing and thrusting into every fissure. Her nipples ached with wanting, so he brought his fingers into play on her breasts, his own arousal soaring from her excitement.

Mara hadn't known how wonderful touching a woman's breasts could feel to a man. When Deke slipped his hand inside the upper fold of her blouse and stroked her bare flesh, she made a low sound in her throat. It was both an expression of sublime pleasure and a verbalization of his delight. He moaned her name, tearing his mouth from her lips to lavish her face with kisses. She gasped as he rotated his hips atop her, pressing his bulging manhood against her mound.

"Mara, I want you," he murmured.

She knew he was lost in the mind-boggling sensations coming from their inflamed flesh. It was like being caught in a whirlpool. He couldn't resist her, and when she entered the swirling eddy of passion and spun around with him, spiraling deeper and deeper into the dark waters, she felt his control snap.

She felt his barriers loosen and effortlessly floated with him. She was in her body and out of it, merged with Deke. When he sensed her need, he pushed down the top of her blouse and exposed her breasts. Scooting downward, he sucked a nipple into his mouth and swirled his tongue around it.

"By the Light!" She exclaimed, stabs of ecstasy shooting through her. Maybe if she allowed him to satisfy the flame burning inside her, she'd gain his trust. He'd see there was nothing to fear from her.

She knew the instant he was aware of her yielding to him and felt his joy as well as a sense of triumph surged inside him. At that moment her essence flew into her body almost immediately. She pushed him off and sat up, yanking her blouse into place.

"I'm not just another conquest, Deke Sage! I won't be treated that way."

He regarded her with a wary expression. "You were enjoying it, Mara. Why deny what we both want?"

"We want different things. I need the intimacy of a caring relationship, but you won't accept me as anything but a warm body in your bed."

"That's partly true." He stroked her arm, sliding his nimble fingers up and down her skin and causing goose bumps to rise on her flesh. "I've never felt anything before similar to what I feel with you. It's not enough to hold you in my arms and kiss you. I want to slide into you, to share what you're experiencing when I'm tight inside you."

His low rumbling tone caressed her with silken smoothness, his words conjuring an image that tempted her beyond reason. "And if we did make love, would you just walk away afterward? Is that all it means to you—another new experience to enjoy?" She thrust shaky fingers through her hair. Disheveled, it hung in clumps over her shoulders and down her back. "You just want to use me to enhance your own pleasure."

He stood, straightening his uniform. "We could have great sex together, Mara, but you're mistaken if you think it could ever mean more than that. I'd never attach myself to a woman who can invade my mind without warning. I value my privacy too much. If you can accept my limits, we'll get along fine."

"Your limits! What about mine? Don't you even care about me?"

His eyes softened. "I do care for you, and under other circumstances, I'd probably— But there's no use talking about that. We can't have it any other way."

She tried to hide her pain, but her distress was too great. Lowering her head, she hoped he wouldn't notice the moisture wetting her lashes.

"Think about it, Mara. Hopefully you'll understand my viewpoint. If you decide to take what I can offer, let me know. I'll be waiting."

She stared after him as he marched out. Was this to be her fate in life, always to be alienated from those she cared about the most? Her parents had cast her aside as a child by sending her to a special school. Now Deke was telling her she was good enough to join him in bed but she wasn't acceptable for any other kind of relationship. Would she never be treated as a normal person?

Despair washed over her, dragging her down into the dark depths of depression. Crying wouldn't help, she thought as her lower lip quivered. She'd gotten through this before and she would now. Besides, Hedy might have some useful advice.

Struggling to her feet, she turned toward the door.

Chapter Nine

"I'm not the best person to offer advice," Hedy said, her green eyes shining with sympathy. "I haven't had much luck with Wren."

"At least he wants you, even if his cultural taboos forbid him from acting on it." They were in sick bay, where Hedy was calibrating her instruments. Mara sat on an office chair while her friend moved about the room, her figure sleek in her regulation uniform.

"I told you before I think Deke likes you. He's just afraid of your ability."

"Not anymore. He wants to use me to heighten his sexual pleasure."

Hedy glared at her. "Do you really believe that's all he wants? You have to give him time to adjust."

"To what? The idea that I can invade his privacy without warning? The realization that his feelings would be always vulnerable to exposure if he accepts me? He said I hurt him, Hedy. What if it happens again? How can I expect him to sacrifice his solitude for me?"

Hedy walked closer, halting directly in front of her. "You know, Mara, maybe you should examine how you feel about yourself."

She stiffened. "What do you mean?"

"You talk as though you're unworthy of a man's esteem. This ability is not unique to you, remember? Other Tyberians share the same gift."

"After annums of training."

"So what? Why can't you consider this another form of cultural diversity? You're so appreciative of alien cultures, why not show some respect for your own?"

She rose abruptly. "Thanks for listening, Hedy. I've got to go."

Feeling guilty about her hasty departure, Mara hesitated in the corridor. Hedy's insights had been astute. On Tyberia, she'd be considered highly gifted but not abnormal. Was it her own perception that made her regard herself as different?

Deciding she needed to speak with someone from home, she entered the empty conference room and opened a commlink to Tyberia. She asked to speak to Master Keenan at her former school. He'd been her last teacher, and even though she hadn't availed herself of the opportunity to advance in her studies, she respected his opinions.

His wizened face sprang onto the far wall as a holographic image. "Mara, such a pleasure! How are you?" he articulated in the refined voice she remembered so well.

"I'm fine, thank you, Master Keenan." She frowned. "No, I'm not. I seek guidance."

"Ah." His dark eyes pierced hers as though they were actually in the same room. "Speak your mind, child."

Sitting at the table, she folded her hands in front of her. In halting tones, she related her problems with Deke.

"Have you been practicing your meditation, Mara?"

"No, I . . . I haven't wanted to stretch my powers."

"Hmm. I remember you left the seminary before you'd completed your term."

She squirmed uncomfortably. "I didn't like being considered different from my friends."

"On our world you would be revered for your accomplishments."

"Only as an adult! When I was younger, none of my friends understood. They made fun of me."

"I don't think you ever understood how fortunate you are."

She compressed her lips. "I just don't see it that way."

"That's the crux of your problem, *karima.*" The master's face grew thoughtful. "This attraction between you and Comdr. Sage must be powerful. When a man and woman forge a romantic relationship, cords grow out of the chakras to bind them. These cords exist on all levels of the auric field. Before you even approach each other physically, your higher energy fields are interacting to see if you're compatible. If you had continued with your studies, you'd be able to see the energy moving between you."

"What are you saying?"

Master Keenan's eyes took on a distant glaze. "Connections already exist between you and Comdr. Sage. That's why you keep being drawn to him. If you could perceive it, you'd see the arcs of rose-colored light extending from his heart chakra to yours. You must meditate to expand your consciousness. Perceiving the human energy fields takes practice, Mara. You should apply yourself to your studies. Accept the Light that flows around us and through us. Open your channels and let the universal life force infuse you with wisdom."

Mara listened to his words, stunned. According to the master, she and Deke were already bonded on the higher spiritual planes. In order to strengthen the ties between them on the lower physical and emotional levels, she had to open herself to the Light which permeated the universe. But she couldn't do that unless she embraced that part of herself she'd always tried to deny.

A flash of lightning exploded in her head. Of course! She'd never liked that part of herself that was different. And if she couldn't love herself, how could she expect anyone else to accept her? Her channels needed to be opened before the Light would bathe her with its brilliance.

Master Keenan smiled benignly at her as though he knew what was going on inside her head. Perhaps he could read her aura on another plane, one not bound by time or space.

"Thank you," she said simply. "I should have listened to you long ago."

"You weren't ready, child. Listen to your inner self. Once you let go of your limited ego, your awareness will expand to the higher bodies. You'll be able to perceive what this man truly feels for you."

"I sensed that he cared for me, but then I believed him when he said he wanted to use me."

"Because you didn't believe in yourself. You'll see things differently now."

"I hope so, Master. My gratitude is everlasting."

"May the Light shine upon you, *karima.*"

They signed off and Mara sat as still as a statue, Master Keenan's words reverberating throughout her being. It was true she'd never fully accepted herself. She tried hard to appear normal and suppressed that part of herself that made her special. Her difference should be celebrated, not condemned.

For the first time in her life, she appreciated the ability which her fellow Tyberians regarded as normal. Because her psychic power had exhibited itself at such an early age, she hadn't integrated it into her self-image in a positive manner. Now she had a sudden urge to learn more, to experience the higher sensory perceptions of which she was capable. Meditation was the key. Did she remember the incantations?

Hastening to her cabin, she lowered the lighting and reclined on her double lounger in the sleeping chamber. Closing her eyes, she focused her thoughts on the repetitive chants learned from her childhood, the goal being to loosen her fixed reality, to feel the fluid world of radiating energy that surrounded and permeated her.

Her thoughts drifted to her early schooling when she'd spent hauras by the lake outside the seminary, sitting quietly. She'd practiced blending in with her surroundings as she'd been taught. At those quiet times, she'd been able to perceive things beyond the normal human range of perception. It had been an incredible experience but it frightened her because she wasn't mature enough to understand.

Now she felt overwhelmed with regret that she'd wasted so many annums. She could travel the astral plane, but that was only the fourth auric level, the bridge between the physical and spiritual layers. She'd never been able to go beyond that. It was necessary to sensitize herself to the higher frequencies in order to perceive them.

The universe is a whole, she told herself. I am part of the whole. I am connected to all living beings and to all matter, real and ethereal. I am like the Light, a luminous body, transcending the limits of time and space.

Opening her eyes, she brought her palms up, holding her hands so that the tips of her fingers were facing each other. With a plain white wall in the background, she relaxed her gaze, staring at the space between her fingertips. Light blue lines rippled between her hands. She moved her hands apart, then brought them together, feeling the buildup of energy.

These were very basic exercises, allowing her to perceive her own aura on its lower levels.

She set herself a new goal, which she would try to achieve at the next crew briefing.

Subtly fixing her gaze on Deke when they were all assembled for the day's briefing, Mara examined the space at the top of his head. Relaxing her mind, she opened herself to the Light. Soon a pulsating layer became visible, centimeters from his skin. The pulsations formed a wavelike motion down his body. The auric layer was a light blue color which brightened closer to his body, with streamers coming from his fingertips and the top of his head.

As she continued her meditations, her perception increased and she was able to see the rose-colored light that surrounded Deke when he looked at her. Master Keenan was right, she thought with joy. He does care for me. Rose was the light of love.

She realized it was up to her to strengthen the cords that bound them. How do I proceed? She wondered. Deke still thinks we can enjoy great sex together, but that's all it is to him. How can I make him recognize that there's more?

Master Keenan had said Deke's higher auric layers were constantly interacting with hers. It had to be the reason why he triggered her separations. Perhaps if she joined with him on the physical plane, acceptance would follow on an emotional level. Sooner or later, Deke would understand they were meant for each other.

She smiled to herself, eager to put her thoughts into action. She'd wanted Deke from the first moment they'd met, and now there was no further reason to deny herself the pleasure.

Deke wondered about Mara's strange behavior. Sitting beside her at the conference table during a tactical crew briefing, his eyes kept sliding in her direction. Every time he looked at her, she gave him a secretive smile. He felt irritated that she could still distract him without invading his psyche but was intrigued nonetheless. Was that an invitation he glimpsed in her eyes? How could it be, after the crude way he'd behaved toward her? Mara wasn't the type who could shrug it off when told she was fine as a playmate but off-limits for marriage. She was unlike Carmin, who enjoyed brief encounters confined to the bedroom.

Was that all he wanted from Mara? Yes! he told himself vehemently. It didn't matter if she was intelligent, beautiful, and talented. He couldn't risk being linked with someone like her.

Guilt assailed him. He was contributing to her constant stream of rejections. First her parents had sent her away, then Pietor had scorned her. Now he'd added to her grief by refusing to consider her for a serious relationship. Where was the fairness she so strongly espoused? No wonder she vigorously defended other people's rights. She'd never been treated fairly herself. Was he being honest in not giving her a chance?

But she invades my mind, he rationalized. She can distract me at a critical moment, intrude during a private conversation, expose feelings I don't want to acknowledge. She gives no warning before entering my essence. How can I exist with the fear that this could happen at any time, any place?

Yet you're the only man who has ever experienced this with her, another voice replied in his head. Is she correct in assuming a bond already exists between us?

Confused by the tumult of emotions inside him, Deke sought solace in physical exercise and study. When he wasn't reading the latest scientific dissertations, he worked out in the physiolab in preparation for the coming mission.

The day before they were due to arrive at Yanura, he was vigorously exercising on the rowing machine when Mara breezed in, wearing a skimpy aquamarine outfit that clung to her curves like a wet swimsuit. Her lush raven hair cascaded down her back like strands of lustrous glass. He glanced at her appreciatively, taking in her long shapely legs, before fixing his eyes on her face as she strode toward him.

"Here you are!" she said with a musical lilt. "I was hoping to catch you alone."

Her brilliant smile nearly took his breath away. He leapt up from the machine, switched it off, and grabbed for his towel. "I was just leaving."

"But I have something to show you!" Her wide dark eyes implored him to stay. She sashayed closer, the seductive sway of her hips tantalizing him beyond reason.

He let his gaze stray to her deep cleavage. Her dance outfit was low-cut and the creamy swell of her bosom overflowed from its scooped neckline. A coil of desire sprang up within him, charging him with a tension he wished he could deny.

"What is it?" he asked, dropping the towel onto a chair.

"I've learned the steps to a new dance. I was hoping you would partner me." Her gaze meaningfully roamed over his body clad in a pair of snug activity shorts. "Come," she said invitingly, holding out her hand. "Want to give it a try?"

With the scent of her perfume drifting toward him, his arousal increased. Grasping her slender hand in his, he hesitated, curious to see what she would do next. He felt like a shooter primed for action, just waiting for her signal to explode.

"Computer, begin playing 'Starlight Enchantment.' " Musical strains filled the area. "Lower lighting." As the lights dimmed, she stepped closer. "You need to put your right arm around me."

He encircled her waist and at her murmured instructions, they began a slow slide. His body rubbed against hers as he dipped her to one side. Just the feel of her lush softness made a groan slip from his lips.

"Perhaps we should retire to a more private setting," he suggested in a husky tone, feeling his heart pound in his chest. Sweat beaded his brow. He couldn't get this near to her without wanting to thrust inside her and become one with her.

"Your cabin or mine?" she whispered, her eyes glowing happily.

"Mine. Then we won't run the risk of having your good friend, the doctor, interrupt us."

"I believe she's busy in sick bay with Wren."

"The lieutenant requires a number of examinations since his accident," he remarked wryly. Twirling her around, he brought her up against his body. "Is this the type of move you had in mind?" he said, bringing his mouth to hover centimeters above hers.

"Yes, it is."

Reading her expression, his heart soared with joy. She was willing to join with him, to march with him in the rhythm of the ages. Their future together didn't matter. She was his for now.

He crushed his mouth down on hers, his movements urgent and demanding. It was a quick kiss because he couldn't wait to ravish her. She tasted as sweet as honey wine and as soft as a rose petal. Raising his head, he gazed at her.

"Let's go," he rasped, not even sparing a moment to grab his shirt and shoes. He led her out into the corridor and toward the crew's quarters, where they entered his cabin.

He headed straight for the sleeping chamber, giving orders to the computer along the way. The lights dimmed and melodious music began playing in the background.

Inside, he turned to her with a grin.

"I'm glad you've made this decision, Mara. I've been going crazy with wanting you."

She sauntered nearer, closing the distance between them. "I want you, too. Didn't you once tell me this would happen before the voyage was over? We're meant to be together, Deke. The cords that bind us are strong."

He brushed his finger across her lips. "Too much talking," he admonished, slipping the sleeves of her leotard off her shoulders. He dipped his head to kiss her swanlike neck, pleased when she tilted her chin to allow him better access. Her responsiveness increased his desire and pummeled his senses.

"Wait," she said, stepping back.

In a graceful sweeping movement, she removed her dance outfit. He gasped as she stood before him naked, her nipples peaked. With a low groan, he splayed his hands on her breasts. As she closed her eyes, he felt a strange sensation in his mind. She was there, her reactions mingling with his. He felt her delight as he stroked her nipples with his thumbs. "Great stars!" he exclaimed as his own body responded to her aroused state.

Sharing his viewpoint, Mara felt the engorgement between his thighs and moaned with need. Was it her passion or his that needed abating? She couldn't tell. Her hands grasped at his activity shorts, pulling them down. He cast them aside and drew her into his embrace. Naked, they collapsed onto the wide lounger that served as a bed. His mouth sought hers and they kissed greedily, urgently, their bodies pressed together. Now that she'd lowered her barriers, she couldn't get enough of him. Her body, soft and pliant, molded to his heated form in a frenzy of desire.

"We're going too fast." He raised himself off her, his heavy-lidded gaze raking her body stretched out on the lounger. "Gods, you're gorgeous. I could stare at you all day." He reached out and cupped the mound of hair that guarded her feminine secrets.

She moaned as his fingers explored her sensitive folds of flesh. "Please," she pleaded, writhing as his practiced strokes aroused her passion to new heights.

"This feels so good," he murmured, watching her face as he deepened the caress. "I can't believe I'm sharing this with you." He kept his hand in place as he lowered his mouth to hers.

She thought she'd explode as she felt his lean, muscled body rock against her. She turned into him, lifting his hand out of the way and wrapping her arms around him. As she pressed her breasts flat against his chest, her fingers splayed across his back. She traced the rippled muscles under his taut skin, outlined his massive shoulders, tickled his spine, and cupped his buttocks. Every time he murmured his pleasure, she shared his delight. Mingling with his essence, she experienced the bombardment to his senses, the surge of raw masculine power that tensed his muscles, the mind-numbing effects of his arousal. And she also felt his bliss at sharing her own passionate reactions.

Expanding her consciousness, she perceived the flow of rose-colored light arcing between them, and her heart swelled with joy. If only he could see it, she thought. But she still sensed fear within him and was careful to limit her visitation. This was enough for now. Once she gained his trust, their bonds would strengthen and all remaining barriers between them would be broken.

She shifted her position so that he lay atop her. Groaning, he plundered her mouth with renewed vigor, his hands kneading her breasts. Her lofty thoughts were lost as she gave in to the delightful sensations coursing through her. The ache between her thighs grew to unbearable proportions with the twinges coming from her nipples and she spread her legs, relishing the feel of his hard bulge pushing against her.

His breathing was ragged as he glanced at her.

"By the stars, Mara, I can't hold out much longer!"

"Then do it now," she urged, rubbing against him.

He surged forward with a powerful thrust, entering her so completely she thought she'd die from ecstasy. She felt full with his swollen manhood and at the same time experienced the throbbing tightness that encased him. His name burst from her lips as she clutched at his hair.

Slowly he began rocking against her and she sensed his concern that he shouldn't hurt her. A surge of tenderness overwhelmed her as she twisted her legs around him to heighten his pleasure. For a brief moment, she glimpsed his true feelings for her: deep admiration, intense desire, and a sensitivity that surprised her. But then it was gone as lust dissolved all reason from her mind. His mouth clamped onto hers as he penetrated deeper. Primal grunts emerged from his throat as he slid back and forth, driving her wild with need. Tension spiraled within her as she felt his dam about to burst. One more plunge and she cried out at the same time that Deke reached his climax. Spasms shook her body and she felt nothing but the sublime pleasure centered between her legs.

Panting, her body sweaty, she lay sprawled on the lounger bed, drained of energy. Her eyes still closed, she heard Deke's heavy breathing beside her. Their link had broken. She was back inside her own head, but it was just as well. She couldn't have tolerated such intense feelings for long.

"Are you all right?" he asked.

"I've never been better. That was an incredible experience." Blinking open her eyes, she glanced at him. He rested on his back, a lazy smile curling his mouth as he gazed at her with warm brown eyes.

"I knew it would be good between us, but incredible doesn't even begin to describe what I felt," he said. "You have a very special gift."

She raised herself, leaning on her elbow. Her hair hung down partially covering her breasts but she felt no need for modesty. It seemed natural that they should be together. "I'm glad you feel that way, because now our relationship can proceed along its destined path. There won't be any more barriers between us."

His eyes narrowed. "Wait a minute. I'm not saying I want anything to come of this. It's okay for us to enjoy sex together but that's all."

She drew in a sharp breath. "Am I hearing you right? You don't want to have anything to do with me other than sex? How can you say that after the intimacy we've just shared? You've seen I can bring you pleasure!"

He sat up abruptly. "You can also bring me pain. You didn't this time but that doesn't mean it won't happen again. I don't want to tie myself to someone who can disrupt my life so easily."

She froze at his words. She'd thought he would realize how precious their relationship was once they made love. She hadn't done anything to harm him, had she? So why didn't he trust her?

Snatching her leotard, she dressed herself with trembling fingers. "I'm not sorry we did this, Deke, but I do regret your attitude. You're denying what I've sensed deep within you. We *will* be together, and I don't mean just in bed! And until you realize that, I hope I haunt your dreams." With those taunting words hanging in the air, she left.

Deke stared after her, wondering if she meant she'd invade his mind to torment him for his callous attitude. He couldn't help it. Sex with her was wonderful, but who needed a woman who would rip away his sense of self? Yet she hadn't done that, had she? Coming together with her had only enhanced his feelings, not subjugated them. So why was he still so frightened of her ability?

Perhaps because she couldn't control it. If it could be

limited to sex, there wouldn't be any problem. But since he never knew when or where she might distract him, he remained wary of her. He wished they didn't have this problem. As though she'd put a curse on him, his dreams that night were filled with her erotic image, and he yearned to take her in his arms and kiss away her sadness.

But his doubts the next morning couldn't be dispelled so readily, especially not when they were about to meet the Yanurans.

Frustrated, he confided in Wren as the two of them were checking through the supplies in the cargo bay, making preparations for the landing party. Ebo was on the bridge, monitoring their approach into the Yanuran system.

"You're attracted to Dr. Te'larr, aren't you?" Deke asked bluntly, loading his diving equipment onto a minilevitator unit.

The Polluxite glanced up from the survival packs he was readying. "Hedy is an appealing female, sir."

"Have you bedded her yet?"

Wren's face reddened. "I . . . I haven't earned that privilege, Commander."

"Earned it? What do you mean?" As Wren proceeded to tell him in an embarrassed tone, Deke's astonishment grew. "You're kidding! The woman is practically throwing herself at you, and you won't have her? You must be crazy!" He shook his head, unable to believe Wren's obstinacy but admiring his tenacity to his beliefs.

"I've seen the way you look at her friend," Wren said slyly.

"My problem is different." And Deke proceeded to explain.

"If I were in a position to accept such an offering, I would not hesitate, Commander. You should consider yourself a lucky man."

"Lucky! I wish I'd never met the woman!" Annoyed, he tossed the remainder of his supplies onto the platform. Obviously he and Wren couldn't communicate on the topic when their reasoning differed so greatly. Wren desired a lasting relationship with Hedy but denied himself because of cultural taboos. Deke wanted to be with Mara just for the sexual pleasures they could give each other. Was his attitude selfish? Of course it was! But what else was he to do? Lucky, indeed! He'd been cursed from the first moment he'd met the woman. Now he couldn't get her out of his mind when she wasn't even in there with her essence! Regardless of how she went about it, she continued to torment him.

Running his fingers through his hair, he decided he'd concentrate on his work. They were due to land on Yanura in five hauras. The preparations should take up most of his time, and Mara was busy helping Ebo with communications. He'd thought it would be appropriate if she made the initial contact as they approached the planet. Fromoth Trun already knew her and it would aid their cause if he expected nothing out of the ordinary from their visit.

Chapter Ten

Fromoth Trun beat his fist against his chest and bowed deeply in front of Mara. "*Rogi Kwantro,*" he muttered in a gravelly tone.

"*Rogi Kwantro,*" she repeated, imitating his gesture. She wore a shimmering emerald sarong embroidered with silver threads, her hair held back from her face by a jeweled headband. The gown represented the Tyberian style of formalwear, which she thought appropriate for greeting Fromoth Trun, especially when he'd invited the crew of the *Celeste* to a banquet in their honor. It had been worth it to dress up just to see Deke's reaction. His eyes had fired when he caught sight of her in the cargo bay before disembarkation, but he hadn't said a word with Hedy and Wren present.

As he stood beside her, she glanced at him. He looked tall and dashing in the standard dress uniform of the SEARCH force: a maroon and gray jacket with gold braid indicating his rank, dark gray pants, and shiny black boots.

His expression impassive, he fidgeted uncomfortably while Fromoth Trun rattled off endless flowery salutations. Mara had been surprised by the way Deke had pleasantly greeted the Yanuran leader, bowing graciously and remembering to utter the proper words. Each new aspect of his personality was like a leaf unfolding, and the fresh angles fascinated her. If only she knew how to gain his trust.

Forcing herself to pay attention to Fromoth Trun, she smiled politely. Wren and Hedy stood just behind her and Deke, completing their field team.

Deke wondered how Mara could appear so relaxed when there were so many questions to ask. If Fromoth Trun would stop spewing his meaningless compliments, they might get down to business. Was Jallyn here? When would he be allowed to view the seaweed farms? What had happened to Larikk?

The Yanuran leader wasn't in any hurry, Deke thought wryly. Fromoth Trun flaunted his state of office, wearing a gaudy satin robe of bright orange and red embellished with glistening cords of gold. It made his moist green skin look pale by comparison. His amber eyes bulged in a hairless, flat skull, the horizontal pupils giving him a look of cunning. Situated behind each eye were large round disks, his eardrums. With his broad head, tall heavy body, and lavish attire, he appeared a caricature rather than a leader, but he had charisma, and the animated gestures that accompanied his speech showed he had a flair for drama as well.

The fishy odor the Yanurans emitted didn't bother him since he was used to the fragrance of the sea, but Deke heard Hedy cough behind him and stifled a grin. His gaze drifted beyond the Yanuran leader to a group of aides clustered off to the side. Most of the males wore belted waistcoats in topaz or rust colors and breeches in dark brown. The females, larger in stature, wore colorful dresses with full skirts and bonnets covering their heads.

At his side, Mara stood regally, draped in her seductive sarong like a nymph come to tempt him. He tried to ignore the warmth radiating from her, the urge to draw her into his embrace. It was likely she wouldn't let him touch her again after what had transpired yesterday in his cabin, and that possibility disturbed him. Hadn't he told the woman he'd wait for her to come to him on his terms? When she approached him in the physiolab, he thought she'd agreed. Yet she was still insisting their relationship meant more than a fantastic interlude of great sex.

An annoyed frown creased his face. Here he was, thinking of Mara again when he should be concentrating on their mission. Forcing his thoughts away from her, he returned his attention to the Yanuran leader.

"I am pleased you will be accepting our hospitality," Fromoth Trun was saying. "Commander, do you wish to retrieve any items of a personal nature from your ship?"

"Huh?"

Mara nudged him, smiling sweetly. "Fromoth Trun is so kind to offer us a place to stay during our visit. I'm sure our needs will be amply met by his capable staff."

Deke stared at her. "A place to stay! But we'll be—"

"Thrilled to see your charming city," Mara crooned.

Deke clamped his mouth shut, angry that she'd accepted an invitation without his permission. He'd planned for them to stay on the *Celeste*. How did this happen? Blast, he must have missed part of the conversation when he was thinking of her. Was he to be constantly distracted by this woman?

Fromoth Trun gestured toward the *Celeste,* which rested on a launchpad behind them. They were still in the space-port, having been met by the welcome party immediately upon arrival.

"Are you certain your other team member won't join us,

Commander? Our service crew will be repairing the damage to your ship while you visit our illustrious capital city."

"No, thanks," Deke said, shoving his hands into his jacket pockets. "Ebo will stay aboard." The Sirisian was assigned to maintain security and monitor communications. In an emergency, he could initiate launch procedures.

Fromoth Trun spoke briskly into a personal communicator device strapped to his wrist. "Lixier Bryn, is the reception center ready for our guests?"

"Preparations are complete," a female voice answered.

"Good. We make for the feast." Glancing up, he smiled at them, a cunning grin that gave the impression of a predator about to snatch his prey. "This way, if it pleases you." He waved his arm in an imperious manner.

Outside, the warm humid air sang with the buzz of insects and the cries of birds. Before them spread a lake, its slate gray surface pricked with slivers of silver as dawn broke the horizon. A crimson glow lit the sky, the rising sun radiating warmth and vaporizing the dew. Off the lake rose a fine mist that shimmered just above the water's surface.

"It's lovely!" Mara exclaimed, stopping to admire the view.

Fromoth Trun beamed at her. "Beyond those trees is the business center of Revitt Lake City. Our workday has just ended, mistress. You timed your arrival well."

She inclined her head in acknowledgment. "And your residential sector?"

He pointed to the left. "See those pavilions? They are the gatehouses to our underground network. Come, we must descend before the sun makes high. We work in our factories during the night, then retire below during the heat of the day. I'm glad you assented to being our guests. All that you require shall be provided. Your comfort is our prime concern."

Deke cast a glance in her direction, still annoyed by her

presumptuousness yet fully aware that they couldn't afford to offend Fromoth Trun by refusing his hospitality. They had too much to accomplish to risk an abrupt departure. Besides searching for Jallyn, verifying the claims of a miracle drug, and assessing the situation with the Worts, he had to learn what happened to Larikk.

An armed security detail took up position at their flanks as they headed for the living quarters. Deke wondered at their watchful stance. Who or what were they watching for?

"Why are these troops here?" he asked Fromoth Trun, his eyes narrowed suspiciously.

The Yanuran leader grinned broadly. "Consider it an honor guard, Comdr. Sage." Then he marched ahead, precluding any further discussion.

As they were led into one of the pavilions, a mechanized device scanned them for weapons. Mara had reminded Deke that this was supposed to be a scientific expedition and diplomatic visit, so ostensibly he was unarmed. He had nodded his agreement, secreting a twist blade on his person when she wasn't looking. Created specifically for the SEARCH force, it was impervious to sensor scans and wouldn't be detected unless he was frisked. Earlier, he'd stuck a couple of gas grenades wrapped in silverscreen into Hedy's medical kit, knowing she'd bring her own supplies along. He wasn't leaving anything to chance.

A vertical lift shaft took them deep into the underground city of burrows. Deke glanced around, noting their route as they wound through a maze of tunnels. Fromoth Trun explained that the light was meager because his species could see in the dark. In consideration of his guests, he raised the illumination provided by sconced flamelights. As the levels declined, the air grew cooler.

Mara gave a sudden shudder and Deke realized she must be chilled. Surprised that she hadn't brought a wrap, he resisted the temptation to put his arm around her. It wouldn't do to show Fromoth Trun that he cared for her. The Croag's sly mannerisms made him suspicious. Or maybe he was already suspicious and read signs that weren't really there. Could Mara have been correct in saying he'd be looking for things to be wrong? If so, why were armed troops posted at regular intervals? And where were the youngsters? All the Croags they encountered were adults.

"Where are your children?" he asked Fromoth Trun, increasing his pace to stride beside the leader.

Mara had been wondering the same thing. An eerie feeling crept over her as they got further along the winding tunnels. She had hopelessly lost her sense of direction but not her sense of unease. She strained her ears to hear Fromoth Trun's reply.

"Our young are raised in a separate community," he replied, blinking while he swallowed. His skin shade darkened, and she remembered that an exterior color change occurred in Yanurans in response to temperature, light, moisture, or mood. Was he lying? Somehow she sensed there was more to his words than he let on. Or was it just the damp coldness that had caused the deeper hue?

She didn't get the chance to inquire further because they arrived at the reception center. Unlike the entrances to the private burrows they'd passed, this was one of the public areas and the foyer was large enough to contain a receptionist's desk and wide, upholstered couches.

"Let us make dinner," Fromoth Trun invited them, leading the group into a huge cathedrallike cavern set with long rows of tables and chairs. The place was decorated lavishly with brightly colored tapestries, potted trees, and elegant table settings.

Mara shivered, wishing for the warmth of a fireplace. She'd dressed for a subtropical climate, not realizing that while it might be appropriate for the surface, down here it was cooler. Her bones were chilled from the dampness.

"Excuse me," Deke said, addressing Fromoth Trun, "have you a wrap for the lady? I wouldn't want my crew member to take a chill." He gave her a dazzling smile.

"Indeed, we would not want Mistress Mara to catch a distemper," Fromoth Trun agreed, casting a speculative look in their direction. Turning to one of his aides, he muttered a few words in an unfamiliar dialect. "Zenith Krim will get you a cover. Mara, please take this seat next to me. Commander, you may be seated opposite."

Fromoth Trun nodded at Deke as he took his seat. "Your concern for your crew does you justice, Commander. A healthy staff works more efficiently."

Luckily Fromoth Trun had interpreted his thoughtfulness as a leadership strength, Deke thought with relief. He wouldn't want the Yanuran leader to get the upper hand by recognizing there was more to his and Mara's relationship than a professional one.

What did I just say? He was taken aback by his own words. More to their relationship? Of course, he meant a sexual liaison, but the thought still nagged him.

The Yanuran smiled evenly. "We aim to keep our people happy, yes?"

"Certainly." Discomfited by the leader's interested stare, Deke glanced around the room. Hedy and Wren were placed further down the table. He noticed that Wren stuck to Hedy's side like glue. The big Polluxite might deny his desire for the petite doctor, but his protective instincts were in full swing. Wren leaned over to listen when she chattered something into his ear. Hedy giggled nervously, and Wren's big hand crept across the table to cover hers.

Surrounded by so many frogfaces, Deke wondered how he could turn the conversation toward their mission objectives. He glanced at Mara, admiring her placid countenance. She appeared entirely at ease in this strange setting among alien hosts. It wasn't like back home at the institute, where the mixed alien races were scientists who shared a common purpose. Nor was this similar to his usual commando mission. He was leader of a science team but they had subversive goals. He couldn't help feeling slightly out of his element and realized with gratitude that Mara's presence brought him peace of mind.

"Lixier Bryn, may I acquaint you with our honored guests?" Fromoth Trun said. "This is my chief aide," he told Deke and Mara.

The Yanuran female who'd been bustling about fixing the seating arrangements strode over and Mara's eyebrows lifted in surprise. Over her rose-colored dress, Lixier Bryn wore a sash studded with gold firestones, indicating a high badge of office. As Mara uttered the standard greeting, she wondered at the female's relationship with Fromoth Trun. One of the reasons why the Admissions Committee suspected dissention might split the ranks of the Croags was because the Yanuran leader had been so anxious to return home. Perhaps it wasn't distrust of his chief aide that spurred him. Maybe Fromoth Trun was eager to return to a burrow mate.

In most cases, male and female Yanurans did not cohabitate. They followed the mating call once an annum, amplexus—or the mating embrace—lasting for several days. After the females bore the young several months later, they had no reason to stay together. Mates usually differed from season to season, although she supposed if a couple had a particular affinity for each other they might mate more than once and even decide to reside together.

"There's someone we'd like you to meet," Lixier Bryn said, smiling amiably. Her teeth shone whitely against her muddy green complexion. "Lixier Maal, please present yourself."

An elder Yanuran shuffled toward them, his skin as fragile and thin as paper. "Comdr. Sage, Mistress Hendricks, view the evidence of Vyclor, our miracle drug. I am one hundred and four annums old!"

Mara's jaw dropped. Truly, the Yanuran seemed vastly older than the others.

Deke rose from his seat. "What's your normal life span?"

"Before Vyclor, it used to be forty," the elder rasped. "Now we can last upward to one hundred fifty." He cackled, a dry, mirthless laughter. "I hope to make it a few more annums!"

"Can Dr. Te'larr do a medical scan? Just for confirmation purposes, you understand." At the elder's nod of approval, Deke gestured to Hedy.

She lifted her medscan unit out of her pack. Activating it as she walked over, she scanned Lixier Maal. "His molecular pattern is consistent with advanced age for a Yanuran," Hedy stated, astonishment crossing her features.

A muscle worked on the side of Deke's jaw. "Fascinating," he murmured. "When am I going to see the seaweed beds and production process?"

Fromoth Trun rose to face him, his robe swishing at his feet. "This evening we'll run you out to the mariculture farms. I understand you're a diver, Commander?"

"Yes, and I'll need to get my gear off the *Celeste*."

"That can be arranged."

The dinner proceeded as Fromoth Trun introduced the rest of his staff. Mara envied Deke's aplomb as he tackled the platters of squirming worms, snails, and flapping fish placed in front of them. Lixier Bryn urged him to try some of the delicacies presented in their honor and he eagerly took a heaping forkful from a dish of freshwater eels. He grinned at her as she watched him down one of the wriggling tubular creatures. Her stomach heaved, but her training pulled her through, and she managed to eat a tiny bite herself. Thankfully there were berries and greens available as side dishes.

Further down the table, Hedy whispered into Wren's ear. From the look on his face, Wren was trying hard to stifle a smile. Mara caught her friend's eye and signaled for her to engage one of the Yanurans in conversation.

Hoping to gain information, she turned to Fromoth Trun and began discussing the political situation. "I'd like to meet a Wort representative," she told him, reaching for her glass of water and taking a drink. Yanurans didn't imbibe other beverages and rarely drank at all since their skin absorbed moisture from the air. The water was a courtesy to her and the other crew members.

Fromoth Trun blinked as he swallowed a squiggling worm. "I'm afraid that is not possible, mistress. We have few lines of communication open to our tree-dwelling cousins."

"And why is that?" she smiled sweetly, hoping to put him off guard with a show of innocence.

The Yanuran leader leaned back. "The Worts prefer the company of their own kind."

"How do they feel about joining the Coalition? The alliance would bring visitors here. An exchange of cultural values would be inevitable."

"They have no objections to membership in the Coalition."

"I'd like to talk to them," Deke said loudly from across the table. He'd terminated his conversation with Lixier Bryn to listen to theirs. "How come I don't see any Worts here? Aren't they represented in your government?"

"We constitute the elected officials," Fromoth Trun declared, his skin mottling as he gestured to his ministers and aides. "If the Worts wish to participate in policy-making decisions, they can join the political process. I'm afraid they prefer isolation to involvement."

"I lost a friend in the Alterland where they reside. Larikk was a biologist from Eranus sent here to research a vaccine. Do you recall the case?"

"I have a vague recollection. If your friend vanished in the Alterland, I cannot help you," Fromoth Trun said, flicking his sticky pink tongue out to catch a fly. Blinking, he swallowed the captured insect.

"Can we visit there?" Deke persisted.

"I don't think that would be wise. I cannot guarantee your safety if you leave the city."

"Why not? And why are there armed guards everywhere?"

Fromoth Trun frowned. "You are our honored guests. We must ensure your protection."

"Protection from what . . . or whom?"

Standing abruptly, the Yanuran leader tugged at his robe. "Lixier Bryn will show you to your quarters. Our sleep period begins now. The lighting will be lowered in the corridors, so I suggest you use the opportunity to rest. This evening I'll be happy to show you the seaweed farms, Commander. Your colleagues might like to visit our business center and textile factories. *Rogi Kwantro.*" He beat his fist on his chest and bowed.

Fifteen minutes later, they were shown into a suite of rooms on a lower level. "This is our best accommodation," Lixier Bryn said, her tawny eyes friendly. "I hope such distinguished personages as yourselves will find our lodgings comfortable. Is there anything else you require?" She stood in the doorway, her hands folded in front of her.

Deke marched inside, scanning the space. "No, thanks. Someone will come for us later?"

"At eighteen hundred hauras, Coalition standard time." Lixier Bryn turned to Hedy. "I am not ready to retire yet, Doctor. Would you like to see our medical facility? It's in another section of the burrows."

"I'd be delighted!" Hedy smiled at Wren invitingly. "Lieutenant, would you care to accompany me?"

"It would be my pleasure." Casting a knowing glance at Deke, he stalked ahead into the maze of tunnels.

"Mara and I will remain here," Deke said to the aide. *"Rogi Kwantro."*

He closed the heavy carved wooden door after Lixier Bryn and the others had left. When he turned, Mara was already surveying the arrangements.

"We've got two sleeping chambers with private sanitaries and a shared sitting room," she said.

Deke peered into one bedroom and then the next. Each held two lounger beds, an armoire, and a computer desk. Spotlights in varying colors converged on the molded blastbrick walls, softening the decor.

"Hedy and I can take this one," Mara remarked, strolling inside one of the sleeping chambers.

He sauntered in after her, hooking his thumbs into his belt and leaning against the doorjamb. "I'll be happy to share with you. Hedy can stay with Wren. Knowing your friend, she'd probably prefer that arrangement."

Her face flooded with heat as she caught a glimpse of his expression. "Don't get any ideas just because we're alone. I'm not going to bed with you again until you change your attitude."

Deke's mouth curved in a lazy grin as he approached her. "Look, you must be tense after that banquet. I promise not to do anything you don't want me to do, but how about if I massage your neck? It'll help you to relax."

She couldn't resist when those sexy dimples creased

his cheeks. His brown hair curled enticingly onto his forehead, and his eyes captured hers so temptingly that she wanted to melt. As he stepped in front of her, she felt her pulse quicken from his nearness. In her mind's eye, she imagined the arcs of rose-colored light charging between them.

"All right," she agreed, moistening her lips. She'd make sure his hands didn't wander, although the notion of them doing just that made her skin tingle in anticipation.

Deftly he moved behind her and placed his large, strong hands on her long neck. He applied the perfect amount of pressure to relax muscles she hadn't known were tense, and as his hands glided to her shoulders, she closed her eyes to absorb the pleasure more fully. Her body swayed as he kneaded her knotted muscles into pliant relaxation.

"That feels so good," she murmured, shivering with delight as his fingers danced lightly up and down her bare arms.

"This is a lovely dress," he rasped, his hot breath close to her ear. "I like the way it fits your luscious body."

His seductively low tone thrummed along her nerve endings, setting them on fire. Dear heaven, she wanted him again, and she didn't care about their future. Now was all that mattered.

She made a small sound of pleasure as his hands slid toward the front of her sarong and grazed her thighs. He pressed his body against her from behind, and through the fabric of their clothes she could feel his arousal. She leaned back into the hard angles of his body, sighing with contentment.

His hand smoothed the fabric of her sarong up along her thighs and across her belly, coming to rest on her breasts.

Her rapid breathing told him she wanted more, because he began to caress her. Her nipples peaked and hardened and she cried out with need. At once his hand was inside her sarong, cupping her bare flesh. She thought she'd faint from ecstasy.

"Deke, I want you," she murmured huskily.

"I know." Gently turning her around, he slowly slipped the sarong off her one shoulder where it was fastened and pushed it down, baring her breasts. "Gods, you're so beautiful, I just can't get enough of you." And he sank to his knees before she could protest, enclosing his mouth around one of her nipples.

As he began suckling, she felt incredible twinges shoot to her groin. She moaned, clutching at his hair as he ministered to her other breast. When both her nipples were erect, he grinned devilishly and slowly, lowered her sarong, exposing her abdomen. Then he drew it down to the floor. Her thin pair of lace panties remained.

"Don't move," he said, standing to quickly dispose of his own clothing. Then he sank to his knees again in front of her, grasping her buttocks and pulling her closer. When he buried his face in her triangle of hair, she cried out.

In a quick, practiced movement, he had her panties off. "Relax," he crooned as his tongue flicked across her sensitive nub.

Suddenly she realized she was in his viewpoint, feeling his sublime pleasure as he sniffed her feminine scent and stroked her secret places with his tongue. His engorged manhood grew even more swollen as their reactions mingled and he shared her sensations.

"I can't wait," he whispered huskily, gazing at her with glittering eyes. "You're driving me wild."

Raising himself, he guided her to the lounger. She

stretched out, spreading her legs. In an instant he was atop her, plunging inside her.

Her head lolled back as she gave herself to the marvelous throbbing tension within and without. She didn't recognize whose viewpoint she was experiencing. Her perceptions dimmed and became centered on the pressure building inside her . . . in his manhood . . . and suddenly she exploded in a cataclysmic release. When it was over, she realized Deke was collapsed on top of her, his weight pressing against her.

You're still in my mind, he thought, sensing her contentment. *That was wonderful.* Then he remembered she couldn't read thoughts so he squeezed his eyes shut, concentrating on what he was feeling. Happiness . . . fulfillment . . . security. Were those his feelings or hers? It didn't matter. A calm serenity took hold of him and he sighed, resting his head on her breasts.

"Deke, get off," she said, breaking the spell and the separation. "You're too heavy."

Reluctantly, he rolled off. "I suppose we should get dressed before Hedy and Wren return, unless you agree to be my roommate?" he offered teasingly, raising himself on his elbow to gaze into her soft, warm eyes.

"No, thanks. Getting dressed is a good idea." But she didn't move, and sighed deeply.

"What is it?"

"I wish you would trust me, Deke. See how good this is for us? You don't need to be afraid of me."

"I'll admit you're not like any other woman I've known, but I can't give you what you want. You're asking for a commitment and I won't make one."

Her eyes saddened. "You don't realize what you're throwing away."

"We've been through this before." Rising, he reached for his clothes.

"Give us a chance. That's all I'm asking."

"No." With jerky movements, he yanked on his jacket and pants.

"Then I'm sorry for you, truly I am. You cannot accept what you're feeling inside."

"I know what I'm feeling and it's called lust. If you think there's anything else involved, you're mistaken." And without another glance in her direction, he snatched up his boots and stalked out.

Chapter Eleven

"Ebo, what's the status on the ship?" Deke barked into his datalink, holding the palm-size device in his hand.

The Sirisian's voice rang out loud and clear. "Repairs are proceeding rapidly, Commander. We should be finished with the major tasks by tonight."

"Keep your eye on the maintenance personnel."

"Is anything amiss?"

Deke grimaced. "I can't put my finger on it, but I don't trust these people. I may have you take the *Celeste* into orbit once she's shipshape."

"I'll keep the channels open, sir. Ebo out."

Replacing his datalink in his jacket pocket, Deke paced the carpeted sitting room floor. Mara still hadn't emerged from her bedroom and he wondered what she was doing in there. Just thinking of her stirred his blood and turned his loins to fire. It wasn't enough to be with her once. He needed her again, and it distressed him how desperate that need was becoming.

He hated to admit he was getting used to sharing her reactions during their lovemaking. He couldn't imagine what it would be like without that added enhancement. Even now, he felt hollow without her essence inside him, and that was more disturbing than his physical need for her. Mara drove him to distraction, and he didn't know how to deal with the situation.

It would be so much simpler if she accepted his limits and stopped badgering him about their relationship. He'd always avoided serious-minded women in the past, but then on Eranus, no one had really been interested in him for himself other than for his good looks. His father's power or his mother's wealth had been the main attraction. Knowing he was being used, he became accustomed to playing the field, figuring he might as well enjoy himself. Even after he joined the Defense League, the females he allied himself with were more concerned with having a good time. He supposed he'd never thought about his future, about settling down and having a family. Becoming chancellor at the institute was his immediate goal, but someday he might seek a mate, and he hoped she'd be as lovely and special as Mara.

Special? Wait a minute. Aren't you forgetting what she can do? He shook himself, attempting to break her hold on his thoughts, but she remained in his mind, tormenting him.

He tried to look at it from her viewpoint. Didn't Mara hope the man of her dreams would appreciate her, perhaps even embrace that part of her that was unique? Her inner desires weren't much different than his. She sought acceptance, albeit for her own reasons. Like her, if he ever chose a mate, he would select someone who appreciated his worth. And Mara was the first woman who cared for him in that way.

A wave of compassion struck him as he viewed her

with new understanding. Should he deny her the same consideration he sought for himself? In dismissing her regard, was he throwing away the chance of a lifetime?

No! Sex is all I want from her! He couldn't tolerate having someone intrude on his consciousness at any other time. Her psychic ability might make her an exceptional woman but he couldn't live with that kind of tension.

A door chime announced the return of Hedy and Wren and he cast aside his musings. The duo barged in with exclamations of what they'd seen. Hearing them, Mara entered the sitting room and joined in the conversation.

"What do we do now?" Hedy asked, brushing back her glossy brown curls from her face. She appeared breathless and excited. The medical facilities had surpassed her expectations. "It's only ten o'clock," she said with dismay, glancing at the chronometer strapped to her wrist.

Deke realized they weren't used to sleeping during the day. Even though they'd tried to adjust their cycle on the ship, they still weren't ready to assume a nocturnal life-style.

Wren stomped about the sitting area, restless. Suddenly his wings sprouted. "Sorry," he muttered. "I need the stretch."

Hedy drew in a sharp breath, while Mara's eyes rounded with astonishment. She stared at Wren, undisguised admiration in her expression.

Deke, following the direction of Mara's gaze, felt an unaccountable surge of jealousy. He disliked the feeling and tried to dismiss it by telling himself Mara didn't belong to him. Annoyed nonetheless, he gave her a glowering look that she totally ignored.

"By the stars, Wren, how exquisite!" Hedy exclaimed, rushing forward to admire his display. She stroked his primary feathers, caressing the length of his fluffy vanes.

A violent shudder racked Wren. "Stop that!" he said, his rugged features flushing.

"You're so magnificent! I can't help wanting to touch you."

"Doctor! Will you please restrain yourself?" He glanced at Mara, embarrassed.

Hedy shrugged. "She knows how I feel about you. Why won't you admit it, Wren? You like me, too."

He turned away and his wings collapsed into his back. "Excuse me, I wish to retire. Commander, which sleeping chamber is ours?"

Deke winked at Mara. "You can share with Hedy. Mara and I would like to stay together."

Mara and Wren both cried out protests. Laughing, Deke showed Wren which room was theirs.

"Now just a minute, you can't run away from me!" Hedy called as Wren stalked in the direction indicated. She dashed after him and shut the door.

"Poor Wren," he said, grinning broadly.

"Hedy really likes him," Mara commented, tucking her long hair behind her ears. "I think Wren reciprocates her feelings but he's too stubborn to admit it."

"He has his reasons."

"They're foolish. Hedy could make him happy. He's hung up over cultural taboos that don't apply to her."

He strode in front of her, disappointed she'd changed out of her sarong into a utilitarian dark red and black jumpsuit. "You're the alien cultural specialist, Mara. I'm surprised to hear you talk that way. Wren is upholding his beliefs."

"His integrity is admirable," she said sarcastically. Wearily, she glanced around the small space. "Is there anything to eat in here?"

"You didn't satisfy your hunger at the feast?" he asked, hoping his tone told her he'd be happy to satisfy her in other ways.

"I don't care for live seafood the way you do," she replied coolly.

He raised his eyebrows but let her remark pass. "There is a cooler drawer with a bowl of fruit and a carafe of water."

Just then a feminine giggle came from the closed sleeping chamber.

"Hedy!" bellowed Wren's voice before he yanked open the door and strode into the sitting room, a wild-eyed look on his face. "You have to get that female out of here!"

"Why, Wren?" he asked mildly.

The Polluxite's eyes bulged and he choked, unable to respond in his agitation. Hedy, following him, planted her hands on her hips and glared at the hapless Wren.

"All right," Deke said, taking pity on him, "everyone take a seat. We have to determine our objectives for this evening."

By the time the appointed haura for their guided tour arrived, they'd agreed to split up. Deke would go with the Yanurans to view the underwater seaweed farms. Mara would remain aboard the dive boat as his backup, while Hedy and Wren scouted the city. They'd meet back in their suite to compare notes later.

Outside on the surface, the sun was making a blazing crimson descent on the horizon. As fingers of shadows crept over the land, the warm, humid air began to cool. A sweet, fruity fragrance kissed the gentle breeze that wafted across Mara's skin, caressing her flesh. Goosebumps rose on her arms as her excitement grew. Ever since her move to Bimordus Two and her job in the diplomatic corps, she'd aimed toward an ambassadorship, hoping to be the first to step upon alien soil and study a new culture in its own habitat. This was the next best thing, being a visitor on a planet that had hosted few offworlders. Feeling refreshed after a nap and a light meal courteously delivered to their room, she couldn't wait to explore.

"Where are we heading?" she asked, surveying the lake and the rounded red domes of Revitt Lake City beyond.

"We're going to the transport center." Fromoth Trun took the lead along a winding brick path, his heavy robe of office swaying at his feet. He fixed an amiable smile on his face as a squad of armed soldiers took up position on their flanks. Soon they came to a section of the lake with a dock. Several boatlike contraptions floated on the water's surface, bobbing up and down on the current.

"Lt. Wren," Fromoth Trun said, turning to the Polluxite who stood scowling next to Hedy, "if you and the doctor will be so kind as to accompany Lixier Quyp, he'll be delighted to show you our furniture and textile factories and highlights of the city center. Comdr. Sage, I'll be honored to personally escort you and Mistress Mara to the *Celeste.* After you obtain your diving equipment, we'll head for Port Octaine, where a launch will take us out to sea."

"Thank you," Deke said politely, casting Wren a meaningful glance.

Wren gave a brief nod of acknowledgment. "We're using water transport to reach the city?" he inquired, raising his layered eyebrows.

Fromoth Trun smiled broadly. "I believe you'll find this means of transportation to be an extraordinary experience."

Lixier Quyp showed Wren and Hedy how to board. The vehicle had a flat base, and Wren looked askance at the floor. The green bottom quivered when he stepped on it, increasing his unease. A harness arrangement provided seats for four and a driver up front. After he and Hedy had strapped in behind their guide, the driver lifted the reins. Blowing out the air sac at his throat, the Yanuran gave a long, loud croak and the vehicle rose straight in the air.

"Great suns!" he cried in alarm, gripping a security bar that had lowered at their laps. He'd expected them to propel across the water, not soar into the sky. Hedy, seated beside him, clutched his arm as Deke and Mara grew smaller and smaller below.

"Wh-what is this?" he gasped.

The driver gave a short series of croaks and the vehicle veered toward the domes of the city.

Sitting in front, Lixier Quyp glanced back at them, his eyes crinkling with amusement. "We call them marouches," he said with a smile. "We used to eat the creatures until Mavis Kwin designed a way to put them to use. They provide transportation and we protect them from predators. Of course, for long-range transport we maintain a fleet of winged pods."

Wren trembled and his breath came in short, shallow gasps. The wind whipped at them, tumbling Hedy's hair about her face and fluffing out her blousy top.

"What's the matter?" she cried, and the marouche turned at a 90-degree angle, tossing them sideways.

Wren clamped his lips together and didn't speak. He was too terrified. The height was fearful and he dared not look down. Squeezing his eyes shut, he gripped the security rod with white knuckles and prayed desperately.

"Wren, talk to me!" Hedy urged. "Wren, what's the matter?" she hissed.

He pried an eye open. "Are we there yet?"

"Almost. Tell me what's wrong!"

He shook his head, shutting his eyes again until they'd descended and come to a complete stop. Shaking, he exited the craft after Hedy. "I hope we find another way to get back," he muttered to himself.

"Whatever is wrong with you?" Hedy took his arm, waiting with him while Lixier Quyp instructed the driver.

Wren worked himself loose from her grasp. "I felt a

wave of dizziness, but I'm all right now, Doctor. It must have been a residual effect from my neck wound."

Her face lit with concern. "Good heavens!" She swung her medpack across her chest. "I'd better run a diagnostic."

His hand stopped her. "No! I'm fine now."

"Stubborn fool!" she mumbled. Smiling gamely, Hedy linked her arm through his so he couldn't let go. "Let's get a move on. I'm eager to explore!" She fluttered her long silken eyelashes at him. "Aren't you?"

From the way she was rubbing her leg against his thigh, Wren could tell the city wasn't all she wanted to explore.

"Hedy!" he said through gritted teeth. "Please, control yourself in public!"

"Oooh!" she trilled. "Does that mean I can do anything I want when we're alone?"

His face flushed, but luckily Lixier Quyp was ready to commence their tour before he got himself into trouble with a retort. One of these days he'd give that little vixen what she deserved, and then—

What was he saying? Wren caught himself and muttered an oath. Dr. Te'larr was off-limits, as was any other female, because of his disability. Had he forgotten that? But it wasn't any other female that concerned him. It was Hedy. Her name resounded through his mind like fairy dust, replete with golden sparkles and magical effects. Hedy. The sound swept him away into an enchanted state where he was a whole man who could devote hauras to making love to her. Why did he feel such an affinity for this female? Was it because she'd accepted him, regardless of his inadequacy? He didn't deserve someone as special as her.

Wren marched behind Lixier Quyp, his booted heels crunching into the gravel path underfoot. Hedy kept pace beside him, silent as though she knew he needed time to think. Or was she discouraged, depressed by his rejection?

He didn't want to hurt her. Glancing sideways, he studied the perfection of her profile, the glossy tint of her hair, the soft pout of her lips. When her gaze, hot with desire, met his, his heart leapt into his throat. *Bareem,* he thought in his native tongue, she had such power over him. Just a glance from her made his blood burst into flame. He should distance himself from her, and yet he couldn't bear to cast her away. So instead Wren drew her closer. Against his better judgment, he wrapped his arm around her slender shoulders and pressed her near until her body heat penetrated his layers of clothing to warm his heart. He wanted to flap his wings in contentment but restrained himself, reigning in his raging desires, cooling his ardor until his emotions were once again under control.

Lixier Quyp held a whispered conference with an armed trooper waiting to escort them. Wren noted the uniformed security personnel patrolling the city streets and he pulled Hedy closer to his side as his eyes, alert and watchful, scanned their path ahead.

Deke wondered if Wren had secreted any weapons on his person as he foraged aboard the *Celeste* for supplies. While Fromoth Trun waited outside in the spaceport, Deke collected his diving equipment and a bag of personal belongings before stopping at Wren's cabin to grab a few requested items. He hesitated before a crossbow type of armament strung from a hook on the wall. Too bad he couldn't take that for his navigator, but they still had to pass muster by the monitor guarding the residential pavilions in order to return to the burrows.

He had been puzzled by the number of armed escorts surrounding him and Mara on their way here. An honor guard was one thing, but this evening the grounds bristled with military police. Were they in some kind of danger of which they were unaware? Why else would such heavy security measures be required? Fromoth Trun had been particularly tight-lipped, preferring to parry Deke's questions with meaningless compliments. Irritated, he had been glad for the respite aboard the *Celeste*.

Aware that Mara was busy in her own cabin, he hastened to the bridge to consult with Ebo.

"The major repairs are completed," the Sirisian told him, taking a break from monitoring the systems controls.

"Have you been able to tap into surface communications?"

Ebo bobbed his bald head under his ruby red turban. "I'm picking up some interesting chatter but nothing significant. Any leads on Jallyn?"

"We haven't seen any children around, which is definitely strange, but supposedly they have their own living quarters. Mara and I are going to view the underwater seaweed farms from here. Wren and Hedy have already left for a tour of the city. We'll compare notes later. Fromoth Trun is courteous but I don't trust him. We're escorted everywhere by armed guards. It's damned odd."

"Take caution, sir."

"Maintain your vigilance and keep our commlink open."

He rounded up Mara after hiding a few last-minute items among his stash of diving supplies.

"Are you ready?" he asked, approaching her in the open doorway to her cabin.

"I guess so." She straightened up from packing her bag and frowned at him, her eyes expressing concern. "I just don't have a good feeling about all this."

"What do you mean?"

"I did another separation using Jallyn's blanket. Something dark is out there, Deke." She shivered violently. "Whatever it is, it frightens me."

She was just confirming his own sense of unease. "Can you elaborate?" he asked, frowning.

Mournfully, she shook her head. "No, I can't. The feeling gets stronger each time I'm with Jallyn."

"We've got to find her soon! Let's not waste any more time." He gestured for her to depart.

Mara stepped closer, her wide vulnerable eyes seducing him into passivity. With the subdued lighting behind her, she looked the image of loveliness with her thick shiny hair streaming over her slim shoulders.

"Deke, there's something I have to say before we leave. We might not have another chance, and I need to tell you. I-I'm sorry if I've been pressuring you. I shouldn't expect you to feel the same way as I do. You're not used to—"

"Hush." He put a finger to her lips, silencing her. "This is not the time or place to talk about our problems. We have an important job to do today. I want to think about you when my mind is clear." And he lowered his head and kissed her, intending it to be just a brief touch of his lips to hers. When her soft mouth yielded under his, he groaned low in his throat and pulled her closer, unable to stop his urgent movements. His need for her was too great. As his tongue thrust inside her parted lips, he forcibly reminded himself that they didn't have time for personal indulgences.

With an effort of will, he released her. "Later," he promised, gently stroking her cheek. She would have let him have his way with her, he realized, feeling a rush of tenderness. Later, he'd pleasure her and return the offering.

Saying a final farewell to Ebo, they left to rejoin the Yanurans. A short while later, their marouche landed at a marina by the ocean. Out on the water, a ribbon of light made the border between sea and sky barely discernible. The distinction rapidly faded along with the sunlight. A stiff, briny breeze blew off the water, and Deke sniffed it gratefully. He'd missed the salt-laden scent of the sea.

Port Octaine was a bustling center of activity, and the

main work shift had just begun. Yanurans were scurrying about, intent on their tasks. Bright spotlights illuminated the area, casting long shadows and lighting up the sky in garish hues.

As instructed, Deke began loading his equipment onto a launch. The marina was lined with seagoing vessels, and he noticed their boat was a useful size, with an interior cabin. "What's in those big storage tanks?" he asked, curious about the port's usage.

"Fuel," said Fromoth Trun, his eyes darting about nervously. His padded fingertips plucked at the folds of his robe. "Let's go, Commander. The wind is favorable." He signaled to the crew of frogfaces to assist Deke.

Deke would have liked to prowl around the port but was eager to do his dive. It had been too long since he'd been underwater and he craved a taste of the sea. Grabbing Mara's hand, he strode up the ramp onto the launch after the crew finished hauling his gear on board.

Fromoth Trun gave the order to cast off and they were on their way, zipping across the waves at high speed. Deke reviewed the dive plan with the hired guide, a pudgy-faced fellow named Porvir Cash. When he finished, Deke watched Mara wet her lips as she stood on deck gripping the railing, her eyes squinting from the wind and salt air. Darkness enveloped them like an inky cloud and she shuddered violently.

"Are you all right?" he whispered.

Mara turned toward him, her long jet hair blowing in the breeze. Her wide eyes gleamed with reflected light as she regarded him solemnly. "I'm worried about you," she said, her tone low and sensual.

Desire rippled through him like a wave. "Are you?" he asked, keeping his tone light.

She swept her hand toward the open ocean. "You'll be down there alone. Who knows what may happen?"

"I won't be alone. Cash will be with me, and you'll be up here, making sure the boat is waiting. Anyway, I'm used to night dives." Unable to keep his distance from her, he moved closer until his thighs pressed against hers, the breeze wafting her feminine scent around him.

"I appreciate your concern," he said, placing his hands on her hips. The rolling motion of the boat rocked him against her. His gaze focused on her mouth, soft and ripe for the taking.

"Get away," she said, a warning gleam in her eye.

He saw the rapid pulse throbbing in her throat and grinned. "I know you want me. Say it, Mara."

"Conceited oaf. You're the one who can't keep his hands off me." Glancing over his shoulder, Mara stiffened. "Fromoth Trun is watching us."

Cursing under his breath, Deke wheeled around, striding to the minilevitator that held his equipment. He was letting her distract him again when his mind should be on his job. His movements brusque, he began preparing for the dive.

Mara observed him a moment before turning back to the railing. She gazed out at the black void, the deck swaying as they sped across the swells. Her stomach lurched as a high crest jarred the hull. This was Deke's element. He loved the sea. In contrast, Tyberia had large forested continents. She'd rarely seen the ocean when she was young. What was it like to grow up on a water planet where the populace lived in floating cities? She recalled the conversations with Deke on the *Celeste* about his work at the research institute on Eranus. He'd paid a stiff price to sacrifice two annums of his life in order to pursue his goal of becoming chancellor. She should admire his dedication, and yet it bothered her that his single-minded devotion didn't include her. She was losing her heart to this man and he wouldn't admit any feelings of reciprocation. How long would she have to wait? Was Master Keenan wrong?

No, you've seen the rose-colored light. Deke just couldn't accept what she had to offer. She'd given him her body. What else would it take to make him realize their spiritual link was something to treasure?

Sighing, she turned away to weave unsteadily toward the enclosed cabin.

Chapter Twelve

Bracing his legs on the heaving deck of the launch, Deke knelt to retrieve the neoprene wet suit he'd brought from the *Celeste.* Stripped down to his swim trunks, he felt the chill of the night air on his skin. A thrill of excitement raced through him as he went through the familiar motions of suiting up for a dive. He couldn't wait to explore the underwater environment on Yanura. Being away from his home on Eranus distressed his system, and he yearned for the watery depths that were part of his soul. Besides, the scientist inside him hoped for new discoveries below.

The snug-fitting wet suit and hood warmed his blood as he reached for his buoyancy compensator jacket, regulator, and cylinder system. The vest fastened with a series of front clips. After adjusting his equipment, he secured on his wrist a waterproof dive computer that performed multiple tasks: decompression tables, compass, and chronometer. When he wore it on land, it also served as a backup communicator for his datalink. The instrument had one additional protective function that had been designed on Eranus, but Deke hoped he wouldn't have to use it.

Cash signaled to him and he nodded, strapping on his full face mask. The mask attached to the regulator which connected to his tanks. It left him air space to speak into a built-in communication device, and he could breathe freely from the air mixture in the tanks. A knife, underwater lights, and a dive slate for taking notes completed his ensemble. The last items to go on were his heavyweight belt and fins.

"Commander? Can you hear me?" Cash's voice croaked in his ear. The amphibian had strapped on a mask that would enable them to communicate. Being able to breathe underwater with his blood-rich gills, he didn't need dive gear. His slimy, moist skin, webbed feet, and natural ability would aid him.

"Won't the cold water bother you?" he asked, eyeing Cash's meager swim trunks. Even though they were amphibians, the Yanurans were cold-blooded creatures, meaning they were sensitive to exterior temperature changes.

Cash's tawny eyes gleamed with amusement. "Our species has adapted to a cold saltwater environment. Are you ready?"

Deke gave a thumbs-up signal before remembering he was among aliens. He hoped they didn't consider the gesture to be an insult.

Cash nodded brusquely and led him to an interior cabin where a moon pool was designed in the bottom, allowing for ease of entry into the sea. Deke rolled through the rounded hole into the water and sank into the welcome liquidity. A wave of exhilaration charged through him as he turned and began kicking in Cash's direction. He easily matched his guide's progress as they headed downward.

Seaweed fronds reached up toward the surface like a layer of spikes. Merl was the Yanuran name for this variety, and according to what Fromoth Trun had told him, it didn't grow anywhere else. Like kelp beds on other worlds, the undulating masses of merl characterized shallow waters of the temperate zone. It required strong light and a rocky bottom for anchorage. The thick fronds offered shelter to numerous colorful fish, crustaceans, and sea urchins.

As Deke descended the murky depths, he was careful not to get entangled in the 100-foot-high greenish fronds as he circled around them.

"They grow as fast as a foot a day," said Cash, pointing out the gas-filled bladders that kept the fronds afloat. "This water is cool and rich in nutrients, factors necessary to the growth of merl. Here you see one of our largest submarine forests. Yanura has many others, and we've discovered a wide variety of uses for the plants."

He pointed to a tall, supple stalk. "The stipes carry sugar alcohols, the product of photosynthesis, from the upper blades, which are exposed to sunlight, to the dimmer sections below. The merl are secured to the rocks at the bottom by branched holdfasts."

Deke gave a wide berth to a sea otter that swam past and slowed his progress so he could linger in the watery environment. This was where he belonged. It almost didn't matter what world or region. He loved exploring the mysterious depths. At the bottom, he spied colorful strawberry anemones, sponges, and hardy fungus corals. The holdfasts which attached the merl to the underlying rocks teemed with clams, snails, brittle stars, and crabs. He drifted upward toward the middle range of the forest, observing a bright orange garibaldis patrolling its territory. Knowing the eight-inch-long fish would defend its turf, he veered away, marveling at the expanse of the forest. In the tallest canopy, the fronds hosted epiphytic algae and animals such as hydroids, cnidarians, and bryozoans. The marine life was as diverse as the species found in a rain forest on land and just as fascinating.

"You say these things can grow a foot a day?" he asked, propelling himself toward Cash.

The Yanuran grunted his acknowledgment, his bulging eyes luminous in the light from Deke's lamp. "They grow upward to a hundred feet each season."

"How are they harvested?"

"Trained workers cut the most mature stalks, leaving enough to fill the next season, although we've successfully replanted forests in other parts of the planet. I'm a ranger," he explained. "My job is to protect the environment."

Kicking his legs to maintain buoyancy, Deke gazed at him thoughtfully. On Eranus, his mother's family's huge cosmetic company, Drylon, had no such scruples. A by-product of kelp was an important ingredient in their secret formulas. To harvest the kelp, strands and streamers several hundred feet long were cut underwater by automated machinery that simultaneously carried the harvest aboard barges. Since the reproductive parts of the plants were not preserved, entire beds were destroyed. Drylon didn't care if the marine life that depended on the submarine forest was ravaged as well. They could always replant the crop. As director general, his father Jon granted Drylon special privileges, a concession made in return for his wife's wealth. Deke disdained his father's compromise. One of the reasons why he wouldn't accept funding from his mother's family was because of their disregard for ecology. He'd been involved in lobbying for stricter environmental controls before leaving Eranus and intended to resume his efforts when he returned.

Eranus had been colonized because the original inhabitants had poisoned their world with toxins. Strict antipollution measures were in effect as a result, but Drylon's powerful influence had permitted practices that Deke considered unethical. If he became chancellor, he'd see that marine life was better protected. It made achieving the position all the more important to him.

Suffused with passion for his projects, he didn't realize immediately that Mara was with him. He sensed her presence and frowned with annoyance. Not now! Her warmth and caring took him by surprise as he felt her steadfast support for his goals. Bewildered by the emotions she engendered in him, he lost sight of Porvir Cash. Glancing around, he realized with panic that he'd strayed from their last position and had no idea where he was. Anger struck him as he blamed Mara for the distraction. Her hurt departure didn't faze him. Where in Zor was his guide?

"Commander!" said a familiar voice in his ear.

Whirling around, he felt a rush of relief as he saw Cash swimming in his direction. As he waited for the Yanuran to catch up, he spied something that reflected brightly in his halogen light. Curious, Deke aimed his lamp downward to get a closer look. A strange outcropping of white rocks met his gaze. Kicking vigorously, he followed a ridge several meters long and noticed more of the white rocks, jagged and gleaming in the unnatural light.

"What are these? They're strewn all over this area."

Cash appeared in front of him, his large eyes glittering. "It's a mineral conglomerate. The nutrients in this water are rich and diverse. They're replenished seasonally by upswellings of colder water laden with organic matter and by mineral runoff from the land. So much food is available that marine species show up here that thrive nowhere else. Same goes for those rocks. Careful, an eel is just behind you."

Deke stilled his movements while the creature swam past. A young harbor seal weaved its way through the cool merl stipes, its whiskers white in his underwater light.

"I see another rocky ridge over there," he pointed out.

"How far out does that one go?" He swam over, intrigued by the surreal beauty of the white rocks nestled at the base of the green merl stalks.

The Yanuran motioned that it was time to begin their ascent. "The forest stretches for several kilometers. We couldn't possibly tour the entire area."

"What causes these markings?" He peered closer, examining the flaws in the rock face. It almost appeared as though someone had chipped away at it with a tool.

"Come, we're running short on time," Cash said, ignoring his question. "We must make toward the surface."

"What happens to the merl after it's harvested?" Deke asked as they swam back toward the undulating masses of merl.

"A company called Seabase Pharmaceuticals produces medicinal products from the merl and other marine resources. Their ongoing research aims to discover new therapeutic uses for the diverse forms of undersea life. Vyclor got its start many annums ago when early tribes brewed a tea from the dried fronds and noticed it prolonged their youthfulness."

Deke swung around to face him. "What about Turtle Ravage? My friend was researching a vaccine here when he disappeared. Did your laboratories ever complete the study?"

Cash shrugged. "You'll be going to Seabase Pharm's plant from here. You can ask your questions there. Follow me."

Deke had no option but to comply, ascending slowly and stopping at the intervals prescribed by his dive computer. Cash brought them up directly under the moon pool.

Mara could tell from the excitement flushing his face that Deke had been impressed by the sights underwater. She waited impatiently inside the boat's cabin while he stripped off his heavy equipment. When he stood dripping wet in his swim trunks, she handed him a towel supplied by one of the boat's crew. The engines coughed into life and the launch picked up speed.

Gripping the back of a chair bolted to the deck, she stared at his chest, his curly hair glistening with water that ran in rivulets down his taut abdomen and into the banded waistline of his trunks. Aware that Cash and the others were involved in a consultation outside, she wished they could prolong their moment of privacy. She wanted to feast her eyes on him as long as possible.

"How about drying my back?" he said airily, tossing her the towel and turning around.

She swallowed convulsively. Gods, his shoulders were so broad! She dried him off quickly, dismayed at how easily her heartbeat raced and her fingers trembled from the contact.

"What did you see down there?" she asked, barely recognizing the husky tone as her own. She was trying to get her mind off his rippling muscles and bronzed skin but all she wanted to do was to caress the broad planes of his back. It took her full willpower not run her fingers through his damp hair, down his supple neck, and along his wide shoulders.

"We'll talk after I get dressed," he said curtly.

Bending over, Deke reached for his knit shirt and pants, having opted to wear more leisurely clothes than his uniform for the outing. His position gave her a sublime view of his tight derriere perfectly outlined by the clinging wet swim trunks.

Her eyes widened as he began to strip off his swim trunks. Choking, she whirled around so her back was to him. Her ears picked up every sound he made as he pulled on his clothes.

"You did it again," he said quietly.

Pivoting, she stared at him. He hadn't sounded pleased.

Fully dressed, he glared at her, a hostile gleam in his eyes.

"What do you mean?" Fearful of his response, she moistened her lips.

"You invaded my mind. I lost my sense of direction."

"I-I'm sorry. All of a sudden I was in your viewpoint. You were excited about something. Deke, I think strong emotion might be the trigger for these separations."

"So what does that mean? I shouldn't feel anything? I got isolated from my guide in a strange ocean. I could have drifted miles away from the boat."

"Please forgive me, Deke. It's not my fault."

Ignoring her pleading tone, he tersely related his findings. "I'd like to know more about those rocks. Their appearance was distinctive, and one section looked as though a chunk had been removed. Maybe we'll learn more at the pharmaceutical plant." Striding to the door, he yanked it open and walked onto the deck, precluding any further discussion.

She gazed after him, dismayed by his stern disapproval. She'd hoped to share his excitement, and instead he'd made her feel like an item tossed in a disposer. Why couldn't he understand she had no control over these events? Slumping her shoulders, she despaired of ever gaining his true affection.

When they reached land, Lixier Bryn met them with a skimcraft, whisking them to the factory in the enclosed mechanized vehicle.

"You come from a water planet yourself, Commander," said Fromoth Trun, who sat in the rear seat with Deke. They were approaching the main entrance, a brightly lit avenue lined with tall, shady trees. "What related industries does your world support?"

Deke glanced around with curiosity. Seabase Pharmaceuticals owned a vast complex of buildings designed as interlocking diamond-shaped structures. Illuminated against the darkness of the night sky, the triangular walls shone with a brilliant golden glow.

"Undersea mining and mariculture are our two main industries," he responded. "Of course, we have our renowned research facility, the Institute for Marine Studies."

"Ah, yes. I heard that you are competing for the chancellorship."

Deke gave him a sharp glance. The Yanuran had a wily expression on his frog face.

"Everyone knows your father is Jon Sage, the director general of Eranus," Fromoth Trun continued smoothly. "And your mother's family owns a majority share of Drylon. I understand Drylon uses an extract from processed kelp by-products in their secret formulas."

"So?"

"It might be expedient for us to arrange an exchange of scientific data," the Yanuran leader offered, licking his lips expectantly.

"I'm not authorized by the Eranus government. I'm only here as a representative of the Coalition." He kept his tone deceptively mild as he pondered the reasoning behind his host's words. Did Fromoth Trun hope to learn the ingredients for Drylon's popular line of cosmetics? The Yanurans weren't in that type of business, as far as he knew. Why else would Fromoth Trun mention the topic?

"It's something to consider when you become chancellor," Fromoth Trun advised, casting him a sly look.

He liked his use of the word *when.* "We'll see," he said noncommittally.

Listening from the front seat, Mara twisted her head to gaze at Deke. "I didn't realize your family was part of the Drylon dynasty," she said, arching her eyebrow. It might have been mentioned when she was examining the data on

Eranus, but she'd been so impressed by Deke's credentials that she hadn't paid much attention to anything else. Now her curiosity was piqued. Every female she knew used at least one of Drylon's skin-care products.

"I prefer not to discuss the subject," Deke said, giving her a cold stare.

Compressing her lips, she faced forward. It was going to be difficult to continue their mission if he distrusted her. She couldn't help what occurred during his dive. Didn't the man realize she'd been just as surprised? He wasn't being fair to blame her, but then who said he was fair about anything? She reminded herself of his opinion of the Yanurans. Moisture pricked her eyes and she blinked furiously, hating herself for caring so much, and hating Deke for his bigoted attitudes which included her.

Dismounting from the vehicle beside a set of massive steel doors, they were met by a bevy of officials.

"Allow me to introduce Cozen Jaak, the president of Seabase Pharmaceuticals," Fromoth Trun said, a wide smile on his face.

"*Rogi Kwantro,*" Deke said, remembering the gesture.

They proceeded on a tour of the plant. Cozen Jaak, an elder Yanuran, explained how their researchers gathered plants and animals that showed disease-fighting potential, testing them subsequently for potency, toxic side effects, and other necessary information.

"We've had particular success lately with sea whips and their anti-inflammatory properties," the president said.

"We have a similar program on Eranus," Deke commented, pacing down a corridor beside the official. Fromoth Trun and Mara followed behind with a small entourage. "Our research ships are equipped with advanced laboratory facilities. If our biochemists find a plant with medicinal promise, a quantity will be harvested and sent to the institute. Those plants that demonstrate unique properties are purified and analyzed, followed by more testing."

After passing preliminary tests in the laboratory, Deke explained, *in vivo* trials were initiated, wherein the new drug compound was pitted against a specific disease in a human or animal patient. Initially, these drugs could only be obtained from plant extracts, but now the chemical structures were identified so the drugs could be produced synthetically.

"We don't have as extensive a production facility as you do," Deke added. "Our main thrust is on basic research."

Fromoth Trun, drawing up beside him, grinned broadly. "That is why you should consider my offer, Commander. Our worlds could benefit from an exchange of information."

"Medical research is only one of our efforts, Your Honor. We have departments in geology, biochemistry, microbiology, and other disciplines. Our researchers pursue a wide variety of studies."

The Yanuran leader pursed his lips as he gazed at Deke thoughtfully. "Who provides your funding?"

"We're supported by a foundation, but most of our people obtain their own research grants."

"And you, Commander? What is your particular interest?"

"Deep-sea vents." His eyes fired with enthusiasm. "What a rich source of life! The possibilities are endless for new discoveries."

"I see." The Yanuran narrowed his eyes. "I suppose your family supports you in your efforts."

Suddenly Deke realized he was revealing too much about himself. His vulnerabilities would become evident . . . unless Fromoth Trun already possessed information about him and was just sounding him out. He liked that notion even less.

"Where is the Vyclor processed?" he asked, switching subjects.

"Right here," Cozen Jaak answered, taking him by the elbow and propelling him ahead of the others. "Vyclor had its origins in herbal medicine," the president explained, guiding Deke and the rest of their party through a series of immaculate laboratory facilities. White-robed workers were intently occupied over long tables laden with delicate scientific instruments.

"Vyclor is given to everyone routinely beginning at age twenty," Cozen Jaak said after they'd toured several other sections and retired to a conference room. Deke and Mara had been offered cool fruit drinks and a snack of sweet grain wafers, which they'd eagerly accepted. They were seated around a rectangular table, discussing their findings.

Dr. Parannus, head of the science section, elaborated. "Once several dosages have been ingested, the drug cannot be discontinued without painful withdrawal symptoms, including the possibility of death. This is due to the altered metabolic state of the recipient. In other words, once started, the drug must be continued for life."

Dr. Parannus was a large Yanuran with a broad, flat-topped skull and an enormous belly. Obviously he ate more than one meal a day, Mara thought to herself as she observed him. The Yanuran helped himself to some of the wafers intended for the guests and crunched into them noisily.

She'd remained relatively quiet, her mood depressed because of Deke's coldness toward her. The late haura was also making her feel ill. Despite their preparations aboard the *Celeste,* she wasn't used to staying up all night. "You mean Vyclor is addictive?" she asked in horror, becoming more alert.

Dr. Parannus tilted his head. "Not in the usual sense of the word. It's more like a thyroid medication that some humans must take in order to maintain metabolic stability."

"But your people don't need Vyclor for health reasons," she protested.

"Our average life span was forty annums before Vyclor was initiated. Most of us consider taking Vyclor to be worth the risks in order to extend our life span. Think of it, Mistress Mara! We can live to be one hundred and fifty!" the scientist exclaimed.

"What about side effects?" She'd never seen the data on Vyclor but assumed Deke already possessed this information.

"Unfortunately, sterility is an unavoidable side effect of Vyclor. Those of us who want children breed at the first few mating seasons before the critical dosage is reached."

Across the table, Deke nodded his head. "A lot of people I know would feel the same way. They'd jump at the chance to extend their life span regardless of the risks involved."

He was right, she thought, and the Yanurans would make a killing in profits if Vyclor were put on the intergalactic marketplace. Cozen Jaak had described how the white crystal rocks Deke had noticed underwater provided the basis for a compound necessary to Vyclor production. The compound was combined with an organic matrix obtained from the merl to produce the drug. Yanura grew the only known source of merl. Even if they licensed drug production to other companies, the Yanurans would still have to be paid for the raw materials. Their potential for gaining wealth if the Coalition granted them approval was incredible.

"What about your toxicity trials? Did you run them on other species?" she asked.

Dr. Parannus nodded. "We had no trouble obtaining volunteers. As Comdr. Sage saw from his preliminary review of our data, Vyclor appears to be safe for humanoids."

Deke still wasn't satisfied their data was complete. "The merl," he broke in. "Porvir Cash told me it's harvested by hand. Where do you house the workers and how is the merl transported to the surface?" He might be able to apply some of their methods to his home planet.

Dr. Parannus's skin darkened. "It's all handled offshore. Here, Commander, I've prepared this data card for you to take with you. You may review these additional studies on Vyclor in the comfort of your room. I assume you brought your own datalink?"

"Of course," Deke said, wondering why Mara was waggling her eyebrows at him. Was she alerting him to something the fellow had said?

As he reached for the data card outstretched in Dr. Parannus's hand, a server knocked against him, spilling fruit juice down the front of his shirt and pants. The data card slipped from his wet fingers onto the floor.

"Sorry!" exclaimed the flustered frogface. Bending with his back to Deke and the head of the science section, the slim server swooped up the fallen object from the ground.

"Give me that, you fool!" Dr. Parannus yelled, snatching it from his hand and giving it to Deke. "Look what you've done!" he berated the hapless worker.

Deke glanced down at the spreading stain on his clothes. "It's all right. I brought some other outfits with me." Aware that the Yanurans didn't use fabricators, he'd stuffed a few shirts and pants into his bag. His uniform was reserved for state dinners.

"Forgive me," the server said, hovering about him nervously. "How may I make amends? My name is Delain Crug."

"Dr. Crug?" Cozen Jaak inquired, a look of puzzlement on his elderly face. "What are you doing in here? You belong in the chemistry division."

Delain Crug wrung his hands together. "I requested the post, sir. It is not often we have the honor of greeting such illustrious visitors."

"Get back to your laboratory," Cozen Jaak ordered, his skin mottling from anger.

"I don't understand," Fromoth Trun muttered after the male shuffled out.

Cozen Jaak turned to Dr. Parannus. "Did you know about this?"

The scientist shrugged. "No, sir. I'm not responsible for personnel in his department."

"Check him out anyway. There's no reason why he should have been allowed in here. We'd better schedule a review of security procedures."

Fromoth Trun, squirming in his seat, turned to Deke and gave him a smooth crocodile smile. "Shall we go, Commander? I have a few more places to show you before we retire for the morning."

"Sure."

Eager to review the Vyclor data, Deke was dismayed they weren't returning to the burrows right away. They had to put up with another few hauras of touring the drug production facilities, then taking the skimcraft to view some bland industrial sights and public edifices. Mara kept yawning, reminding him they'd slept little since arriving here. Finally, after a particularly long and boring dinner in their honor given by the City Science Council, they returned to the underground complex with dawn just three hauras away.

"I wonder why Wren and Hedy aren't back," Mara said once they were alone.

She didn't even retreat to her room to loosen her hair from its braid. Her face was pale against the raven locks that tumbled down, wavy from the confinement. But the surge of tenderness Deke experienced in gazing at her beauty was quickly squelched by her next words.

"Well, are you ready to recommend Yanura for Coalition membership?" she asked.

He whipped his fingers through his thick hair. "Why should I?"

"Everything we've seen today confirms Fromoth Trun's claims about Vyclor."

"So what? We've got a lot more to accomplish yet while we're here."

"Why can't you accept what you saw at face value?" she argued, brushing a strand of hair off her face with stiff fingers. "Fromoth Trun has been very accommodating. He's offered us his gracious hospitality. If you'd never heard Larikk's message, would you still be so suspicious?"

"Why did you send a signal to me during our conversation?" he countered, suddenly remembering.

Mara's cheeks colored. "Dr. Parannus's skin darkened during your discussion. I sensed he was being deceptive."

"You see?" Deke cried triumphantly. "Fromoth Trun showed us what he wanted us to observe." He let the silence between them lengthen, stunned by Mara's naivete. Didn't she notice the sly looks the Yanuran leader exchanged with his entourage? Didn't she realize Fromoth Trun and his cohorts were concealing something? And she was the one who accused him of being opinionated! Deke shook his head, admitting to himself that Mara was unlike any other woman he knew. Her convictions were strong and she stuck to them like a barnacle to a boat hull. Stubborn little fool. Her view was tinted by her own personal bias which she refused to acknowledge.

"When are you going to stop being so trusting, Mara?" he asked in a gentle tone. "These people have secrets. We know that from what happened to Larikk."

"What did happen to him? You still don't know for certain." She pursed her lips, her eyes skeptical. "Jallyn can't be on Yanura. The Croags haven't any reason to want her. As for the Worts, Fromoth Trun said they had no objections to Coalition membership."

"I intend to check that out for myself, and while I'm at it, look for clues to what happened to Larikk." Kicking off his boots, he sank onto the wide sitter. "I'm not totally satisfied with what we learned today."

"Why not?" Mara seated herself in a chair opposite him and pushed her feet out of her low-heeled shoes.

"Fromoth Trun was asking me too many personal questions. My family connections and personal goals have nothing to do with our mission." Rubbing his eyes, he thought over what he'd discovered. "No one really told us how the harvested merl reaches the production facility. The seaweed is cut by hand, so they don't have automated equipment. And then there was the matter of the security breach. That fellow, Delain Crug, wasn't supposed to be waiting on us. I gathered he's one of their chemists."

"I don't understand the significance of that incident," Mara admitted, massaging her temples.

"Neither do I. Maybe we'll be able to think better after we get some rest."

"How come Hedy and Wren haven't returned?" A worried frown creased her forehead.

He shrugged, rising. "They have their datalinks. They can contact us if there's any problem."

"Deke, wait!" Standing, she held out her hand to stop him. "We need to talk . . . about us."

He snorted. "What's there to say?" Even though she'd sensed deceptiveness on the part of the Yanuran scientist, she still refused to suspect the Yanurans of duplicity.

"It wasn't my intention to distract you during your dive. The separation just happened."

So she wasn't addressing the Yanuran issue. He noted the distress in her large, onyx eyes and the drawn lines of her face, and part of him softened. "Fine," he said gruffly, "I won't blame you. Good night, or good morning, whichever it is."

She sashayed closer until she stood directly in front of him and he could smell the sea scent in her hair. "Don't I get a good-night kiss?"

His eyes lowered to her mouth, full and inviting, and he felt his loins stirring. "Mara, I can't just kiss you and leave it at that. Please don't do this to me. Hedy and Wren might return at any moment."

She radiated a smile of pure feminine power. "I'm willing to take the chance." And her hands roamed to the fastening on her jumpsuit. As he watched in fascination, she undid it until the fabric gaped down her front, revealing her lacy undergarments beneath.

He succumbed to her irresistible lure as his body surged with desire. "All right," he gritted, already anticipating her essence flowing into him, charging him with her own sexual energy. His arousal quickened and he swooped her up into his arms, carrying her to the sleeping chamber he shared with Wren. Despite his intent not to get involved with her, he couldn't resist the magnetic pull of her attraction. Cursing under his breath at his own weakness, he laid her on the bed and stripped off his clothes.

Chapter Thirteen

Mara was in a deep slumber when someone banged against her lounger bed and cursed, waking her. Her lids flew open and she regarded Hedy through bleary eyes. Her roommate was struggling to get undressed. The clothes she wore were soiled and torn.

Mara's consciousness gradually surfaced. After her fast and furious lovemaking with Deke, they'd each retired to their own rooms. She had no idea of the time or whether it was still night or day outside.

"What happened to you?" she asked Hedy, her tongue feeling like cotton.

After pulling on a knee-length nightshirt, Hedy gazed at her with horror-stricken eyes. "We were touring a museum when a bomb went off. It was horrible! Smoke billowed everywhere. Windows smashed and masonry tumbled from the ceiling. A group of female docents were killed." Hedy sniffled, a lone tear running down her cheek.

Sinking onto the bed, she went on in a rush of words. "When we made our way through the debris to the exit, gunmen were on the street, firing at us. We couldn't get out."

"Gunmen!" Mara sat bolt upright.

Hedy's shoulders shook in a delayed reaction. "An army unit engaged the terrorists and eventually we were able to leave."

"Why didn't you notify us?"

"Wren didn't want to worry you."

"For land's sake!" Exasperated, she rose to get dressed. Glancing at her chronometer, she saw several hauras had passed and it was nearing eleven o'clock in the morning. She'd had all the sleep she needed for the moment.

Her eyes fell compassionately on Hedy. "You'd better go to bed. I'll see that Deke hears about this."

"Wren is probably telling him now." Hedy's eyes misted. "He was so wonderful, Mara. He held me the whole time."

Mara went to her and gave her a supportive hug. "He cares for you, Hedy. At least he lets it show, even if he doesn't . . . if he won't . . . you know."

Hedy brushed past to use the sanitary. "Something weird is going on here, Mara. After today, I'm more willing to agree with Deke's suspicious nature."

"Yes," she said, compressing her lips, "and we're going to get to the bottom of it."

Deke was furious after Wren finished relating the sequence of events. "Those sons of a belleek! I knew they were hiding something. Terrorists! We'll find out what's going on."

Stalking to the communicator in the living area, he demanded an audience with Fromoth Trun. Without sparing a glance in the reflector, he hastened out into the corridor, his hair askew, his shirt loosely tucked into his pants.

Mara hustled after him. "I'm coming with you."

Fromoth Trun, a look of displeasure on his face, greeted them in the anteroom of his private quarters. His fingers played nervously with his voluminous robe. "It was an unfortunate incident," he said in a mild tone.

"Who were those gunmen? Did they set the bomb? And why have we been followed all over by security personnel?" Deke demanded. "Did you anticipate an incident like this one?"

Fromoth Trun's face crumbled. "It is with deep regret that I inform you of our situation. Our tree-dwelling cousins, the Worts, have been causing trouble. We've been involved in a border dispute. They've been extending their tree roots, destroying our burrows in outlying districts. With their terrorist tactics, they are trying to coerce us into granting them rights to more land."

He gave Deke one of his characteristic sly smiles. "It's a domestic matter, Commander, one that can be easily resolved once we have access to Coalition resources. We need to perform a satellite survey in order for our boundaries to be objectively defined. I'm sure the Worts would honor the results as would my people. Considering the urgency of the situation, I implore you to send an immediate message to the Admissions Committee recommending approval of our application."

Deke wasn't fully satisfied with Fromoth Trun's response. Would people involved in a simple border dispute resort to terrorism? Of course, wars had been fought for less, he reminded himself. But why would the Coalition team be targeted? He felt certain the terrorists had singled out Hedy and Wren, being aware of their itinerary. If both sides wanted an objective ruling over their boundaries, wouldn't the Worts support Coalition membership? Attacking the visitors would ensure their rejection, not acceptance. It didn't make sense.

He shook his head. "I insist on talking to the Worts myself to confirm your claims. Besides, I still need to discuss Larikk with them. He vanished in the Alterland, which is their habitat." And there was still the matter of locating Jallyn. Speaking of which, Mara hadn't done a separation lately to see if the child's status had changed. He'd have to ask her to do so once they were back in their suite.

"It is impossible to arrange for such a meeting!" Fromoth Trun blustered.

Mara had been listening quietly off to the side. Now she stepped forward. "The Admissions Committee would look favorably upon our report if we attended a conference with the Worts," she offered, smiling sweetly. "I'm sure you could arrange something amiable to all parties."

Fromoth Trun flicked out his tongue to catch a darting insect. Blinking, he swallowed his prey. "The Worts do not like to consort with outsiders. I told you they prefer to keep to themselves."

"We'll go to them," Deke persisted.

"It's a fearsome route through the jungle to reach the Alterland."

"So get us a good guide."

Deke's obstinance must have convinced the Yanuran leader his options were limited. "Very well," he said grudgingly, "I'll see what I can do, but making the necessary arrangements will take time."

"Make it soon," Deke warned him. "In the meantime, what's on our schedule for tonight?"

"You're to attend a concert at the Grand Amphitheater."

Deke suppressed a grimace. These diplomatic functions were a waste of time. "Fine," he muttered, taking Mara's elbow and guiding her to the door. "I'll expect you to set a meeting with the Worts by then."

Outside the door, Mara shivered. "I sensed hostile feelings in him, Deke."

"I'm not surprised."

Deke waited until they were back in their suite before asking her to perform a separation. "Do it quietly, here in the living area so we don't awaken Hedy or Wren."

Mara slipped into her room to retrieve the infant's blanket. In the living area, she sat on the lounger while Deke perched on the edge of an opposite chair. Closing her eyes, she began her trip along the astral plane.

Darkness enveloped her, drew her outward like a shadow being sucked into the great void by a cosmic vacuum. Her essence transcended the limits of time and space until she floated, lighter than air. Deke's aura was clearly visible from this vantage point. His cords of energy radiated toward her, attracting her like a magnet. How tempting it would be to go to him, to merge her psyche with his. But she had a job to do and it didn't involve personal desires. Focusing her mind, she visualized Jallyn with her delicate features, smooth skin, and tiny hands and feet. Again, as before, an unpleasant force tugged at her expanded consciousness.

What is it? she asked herself, wondering if she should pursue the source but too afraid. It was strong, yanking at her spiritual body, and it seemed to hover near Jallyn. She entered Jallyn's life space with a sense of relief.

The baby was lying on her back in a crib. High stone walls met her gaze. This is different, Mara thought. She hadn't been here before. A casement high up on a wall showed trees outside. As she mentally checked over the baby's well-being, a face came into view. A frogface!

Her shock was so forceful that she was nearly tossed out of Jallyn's essence. With an effort of will, she remained. This frogface was different than the ones she'd met so far on

Yanura. It was brownish, ugly, covered with raised bumps. As Jallyn stared up at it, the frogface bared its teeth in a malevolent grin.

You! she thought. This person was the source of evil she'd been experiencing. And he hovered directly over Jallyn! Her breath caught in her ethereal throat as she waited to see what he would do, but a voice distracted him. He turned and disappeared from Jallyn's viewpoint. She could hear several people arguing in the background; then all was quiet. Left alone, Jallyn gurgled playfully in her crib.

Shaken, Mara separated and returned to her own body. Her mind was so turned inward that she didn't hear Deke calling her until he shook her by the shoulder to get her attention.

"Mara, snap out of it!"

She stared at him. "Jallyn's in danger, Deke. There's someone with her who wants to do her harm. He's a Yanuran but different. His skin is brown and covered with bumps." Her eyes widened. "It's a Wort!" she realized, thunderstruck.

"That does it," Deke growled. "They must have Jallyn. We're going to visit them with or without Fromoth Trun's approval. I'll give him until this evening to make the plans."

She couldn't believe it. So the Yanurans did have Jallyn, although she'd bet Fromoth Trun had no knowledge of this . . . or did he? How could Jallyn have been brought here if not on his ship? That would mean Fromoth Trun was acting in collusion with the Worts, but from what he'd said, they were opposing factions because of their border conflict. And what about the terrorist attack that had been aimed against the Coalition team members? Fromoth Trun would undermine his goal to join the Coalition if he were involved. Unless it was a staged attack to make them think the Worts and Croags were at odds. Unless everything he'd told them were lies.

Thoughts jumbled in her mind. What could Fromoth Trun possibly hope to gain by such a scheme?

"I . . . I need to get out of here," she said, feeling the confines of their quarters. "Can we get some fresh air?"

"I was going to check that data card Dr. Parannus gave me," Deke said, "but you look like you need a change of scenery. I believe we passed a beach on the way to the pharmaceutical plant. Let's see if we can get transport there. I'll examine the data later."

Fromoth Trun, annoyed at having his rest disturbed again, gave Deke a curt reply. "If you wish to go for a swim, Commander, our lake is close by."

"I don't care to swim in a lake. Mara and I wish to walk along the beach. We need some fresh air and exercise." Out in the open, they could talk without worrying about anyone overhearing their conversation. What a fool he'd been. Distracted by Mara's company, he'd forgotten rule number one about being in foreign territory: Check for listening devices. He'd have Wren run a security diagnostic later. It would be illuminating if their suite were bugged.

Giving a long sigh, the Yanuran agreed. "You'll be dropped off. It's too hot and sunny for any of our people to remain with you. We'll monitor the area through long-range sensors. Oh, and a word of warning—don't turn your back on the sea."

"What's that supposed to mean?"

"We call it the fire coast. You'll find out why. If you're thirsty, try the seagrapes."

Deke could almost picture the Yanuran grinning as he signed off. Puzzled, he wondered what Fromoth Trun's veiled hints had meant, but he was too eager for a dip in the ocean to care. "I don't suppose you brought a swimsuit?"

he asked Mara, glancing at her attire. All worries evaporated from his mind at the idea of returning to the sea environment he loved.

Her large almond eyes met his in challenge. "I didn't expect to indulge in frivolous activities during our visit, Commander."

His eyes crinkled with amusement. "It doesn't matter," he said, allowing his gaze to leisurely travel her length. "I'm sure we can improvise."

An haura later they found themselves alone on a sandy stretch of beach. Mara gazed at the clear, sparkling water and was glad for the respite from their problems. Danger might lurk on the horizon, but for now they could enjoy the peace and serenity before them. The calm before the storm, she thought, wishing she could relax. Fromoth Trun's words made her uneasy.

"Want some ray-block lotion?" Deke offered after rummaging in the knapsack he'd brought. He'd laid out a blanket provided by the Yanurans and erected a shade awning secured by four sturdy poles. Stripped to his swim trunks, he stood before her in his bronzed masculine glory.

"Don't you use sun film?" She kept her gaze purposefully averted.

"We use lotion on Eranus. It's one of Drylon's most popular products," he admitted in a grudging tone.

She leveled her direct gaze on him. "Why do you always speak of Drylon with such bitterness?"

"I don't agree with their policies."

"Such as?"

Deke flopped onto the blanket and began applying the lotion to his arms. She couldn't help following his movements as he smoothed the cream over his bulging biceps. Moistening her lips, she wondered why her mouth had suddenly gone dry.

"Drylon doesn't care about preserving the environment," he said, squinting up at her.

Her shadow fell over him and she moved in order to see him better. That was a mistake. Now he was rubbing the lotion on his muscled thighs. She swallowed hard, dismayed when an answering heat rose within her. Gods, his swim trunks stretched taut across his hips!

"Do you want me to put some on your back?" she foolishly offered. Not that he needed it. His broad back was so tanned he couldn't possibly burn. But there were the harmful ultraviolet rays to screen out, and Yanura didn't maintain a protective shield.

"Sure," he accepted, grinning broadly. Flipping onto his stomach, he closed his eyes and rested his head on his hands.

She knelt beside him, squeezing a line of lotion onto her palm. Just his nearness made her breath quicken and her pulse thrum with excitement. "Uh, tell me more about Drylon," she said in an attempt to remain impersonal.

Seemingly in a relaxed mood, Deke responded readily. "Drylon uses brutal techniques to reap the kelp on Eranus." Briefly he told her about the automated harvesters. "They replant the crop without caring about the other organisms that are dependant upon the kelp forest for food and shelter. In my opinion, it's a tragic situation that can be avoided, and their practices violate our antipollution credo. I've been lobbying for stricter regulations but don't have enough clout to fight them. If I win the chancellorship, I can gather the necessary support to address the issue from a stronger vantage point."

"Where does your mother fit into this scenario?"

Deke paused. "Along with her family, Palomar is involved in the administrative aspects of the company. All she cares about is raising profits."

"I can see where you two would clash."

"I won't take credits from her, not that she's offered. She's aware that I'll oppose her if I become chancellor."

"What about your father, the director general?"

"He'll do whatever Palomar says. She's got him twisted around her proverbial little finger. There's not much love in their marriage, Mara. She married him for the concessions he could give the company. He took her as a mate for the wealth he needed to back his position. They're a perfect match. Both are users."

"Is that why you've never married, because you're afraid of getting into a similar situation?"

"No." He sat up, facing her. "The women on Eranus chased after me because of my influential parents. I never met anyone who cared about me as an individual."

His words captured her heart, because they were exactly what she felt about herself. No one appreciated her uniqueness. As she raised her eyes to meet Deke's gaze, she was startled by the tenderness in his expression.

"I never met anyone who cared until you came along," he amended quietly.

"You care about me, too, Deke. I know it."

"Maybe . . . but you frighten me with your ability. I could have gotten separated from my guide yesterday. It's dangerous for me to be linked to you."

"I left as soon as I sensed your unreasonable anger. At least I can control my departures."

"Yes, but when are you going to zip into my psyche again? I can't stand not knowing what to expect!"

She noticed his tormented expression. "Yet you want me, don't you? You enjoy our mingling when we make love."

"What's even more frightening for me is how much I like being close to you." He reached out and tentatively traced a line down her arm. "Your skin, your scent, everything about you drives me wild."

She tried to ignore the sensations of pleasure coursing

through her at his light touch. “So why won’t you yield, Deke? I know you have strong feelings for me. Let them out.”

“I can show you how I feel. Let me make love to you!”

She understood. She tempted him and yet he was still terrified of her. Maintaining control was necessary to his ego and he was put off by her ability to jump into his head without warning. Or perhaps he equated sharing his feelings with losing his identity. The only way he knew how to express himself without becoming too vulnerable was through sex.

Discouraged by their lack of progress, she began to rise, but his hand on her arm stilled her.

“I’m sorry,” he blurted, his brown eyes pleading.

Patience and understanding, she figured. Those are what he needs the most. The loneliness in him reached out to her, drawing her into his embrace. Despite his fear of her, he yearned for the closeness they could share. And that admission brought her hope. It meant he’d taken another step in her direction. Through her expanded consciousness, she could see his channels opening. If only she wouldn’t slam them shut by her unexpected visitations. Yes, she thought as he pressed his mouth to hers, let him show me how much he cares in this manner, the only way he knows how for now. Later, maybe he’d come to accept her gift and cherish it.

The gentle lapping of the waves and cries of birds faded into the background as she yielded to his embrace. The shade provided by the overhead awning made their position comfortable, and the soft carpet of sand beneath seduced her to relax.

Closing her eyes, Mara imagined herself drowning in his kiss. His tongue plunged into her mouth, sending twirling sensations of delight coursing through her veins. Their arms entwined around each other, clutching tightly. Then suddenly he released her, and she looked up to gaze at him questioningly.

"Let's go for a swim," Deke whispered, smiling.

Her eyes lit on his sexy dimples. When he smiled at her like that, she'd do anything he asked. "I haven't a swimsuit."

"No problem." And he began unfastening her dress.

"What are you doing?" she cried in surprise.

His brown eyes gazed into hers intently. "Did I ever tell you about my private island on Eranus, the place I go to when I need to be alone?" At her negative response, he went on: "There's a beautiful beach with the most powdery amber sand you ever saw. I like to go swimming . . . in the nude."

Her dress gaped open and he drew the sleeves off her arms, his eyes fixed on her exposed shoulders. Her heart thumped wildly. Now that she knew what he intended, she couldn't suppress her excitement. She wet her lips in eager anticipation of his next move.

"You have such lovely skin," he murmured.

"Thanks to Drylon's moisturizers."

"No." He put a finger to her lips. "You'd be perfect without Drylon's products."

Feeling strangely light-headed, she sucked his finger into her mouth. "Umm, you taste good. Like that spicy fragrance in the air." Raising her head, she sniffed. "What is it that smells so wonderful?"

Now Deke was sniffing, too. "I don't know." He followed his nose to a short, squat bush laden with small purplish fruits. "Are these the seagrapes Fromoth Trun mentioned?"

She came up next to him. "I guess so. They're all over the beach. Do you think they're safe to eat?"

Deke pulled his datalink out of his knapsack and ran a

quick scan. "They're edible. I am terribly thirsty all of a sudden." After replacing his instrument, he plucked a cluster of grapes off a branch and plopped them into his mouth. His eyes lit up as he chewed the morsels. "Delicious!"

She tried a few. They were sweet, warm, and juicy. Before the two of them realized it, they'd picked the bush clean. She stood facing Deke as a warm flush crept from her toes up along her legs to her torso and neck. "I'm hot," she wheezed, feeling her skin burning. She could barely breathe from the intense heat.

Deke's face reddened. "Me too. I've got to cool off!" Turning toward the sea, he dashed toward the water.

"Wait for me!" Mara tore off the rest of her clothes and charged in after him. It wasn't until she watched him swim his laps and return toward her that she realized her fervor wasn't satisfied. The burning was for him!

The feverish look in his eyes told her he felt the same. "Mara—"

"I know." She fell into his arms, laughing as the salt water sprayed onto her face. The warm sea enveloped them, caressing them as they embraced. Beneath their feet, the furrowed sand was soft, and occasional schools of tiny fish swam by, but neither one paid any attention. All Mara knew was the pressure of Deke's lips on hers and the feel of her breasts pressed against his bare chest.

Her breasts! She was naked! But even as the thought entered her mind, she dismissed it as being irrelevant. Of course she was naked. It was necessary if she was to join with her man, to unite with him in the rhythm of the ages, the rhythm reflected in the undulating sea. And so it was they came together in a writhing seizure of passion.

Her eyes closed, she reveled in the aftermath of love, her aura still partially associated with Deke's. It was a wondrous feeling as they rocked together in the gentle waves, their limbs entangled and their minds sharing a warm feeling of satiation. On her lips the taste of sea salt lingered. She wanted never to let go, to part from Deke, or to leave the comfort of the water even when the waves grew rougher and began lifting them off their toes.

She sensed Deke's fear before separating from him. Snapping her eyes open, she stared in the direction of his shocked gaze.

"What in Zor is that?" he cried.

A slate gray cloud bank was rolling in, its edges sharply delineated against the bright blue sky. Similar to a fog, it obliterated the sunlight, darkening the sky as it expanded. As they watched in awe, the clouds became agitated, roiling and churning like plumes of volcanic ash.

"Let's get under the shelter," Deke urged, taking her elbow and propelling her toward shore. An orange glow exploded in the sky as the clouds ignited and the fire spread toward the horizon. The water reacted with a violent boiling motion just as she and Deke reached the beach and dashed under their meager cover. The phenomenon lasted about an haura, during which time they sat transfixed. Mara pulled on her clothes after the warm air dried her body, and finally, the cloud lightened and dissolved and the sea returned to its former calm.

"Whew!" Deke exclaimed, wiping his brow with the back of his hand. "Now I know what Fromoth Trun meant by calling this the fire coast. I wonder how often that happens."

Her eyes widened. "Why did he let us come here? He knew it was dangerous!"

His steady brown gaze turned to her. "He did warn us, remember?"

She let her glance flit over the sand, over the shells and stones and bits of seaweed that had been tossed onto the beach by the cataclysm. After a moment's silence, she smiled at Deke. "That fire was nothing compared to the one that consumed me after I ate those grapes. Do you think Fromoth Trun knew the effect eating them would have on us?"

"Undoubtedly," he said. "It's time to go back," he added curtly, activating the signal that would bring transportation. "I hope Hedy and Wren have had enough of a rest. We've got work to do."

After a long and satisfying slumber, Hedy awoke to a strange sound coming from outside her closed bedroom door. Sitting up and groggily rubbing her eyes, she listened carefully. There it was again! Whoosh—whoosh—whoosh!

Charging out of bed, she spared a moment in the sanitary to do her ablutions before throwing open her door. Still in her nightshirt, she gaped at Wren, who was pacing the living area, his magnificent wings extended at his back. Apparently he was exercising them, and the noise she'd heard was his huge wingspread cutting through the air.

"What are you doing?" she cried, rushing forward.

Wren halted abruptly, his face coloring. "I, uh, couldn't sleep any longer."

"Let me look at you!" Reaching out, she was disappointed when Wren pinched his face, folding his wings back inside his shirt slits. Suns! She'd have liked to caress his incredible feathers, to run her fingers through the stiff vanes and stroke the length of them. It was almost as good as stroking his manhood, maybe even better. Now that was a titillating idea. A small smile played on her mouth as she imagined herself performing that other activity.

"How do you feel, Doctor?" Wren asked politely, deliberately walking away from her and taking a seat on the lounger.

She spotted an opportunity and bounced down beside

him. "I'm still upset about the bombing," she moaned dramatically, widening her eyes in remembered horror. "All those injured people, and I couldn't do anything to help them!" She still felt bad about her helplessness in the situation and shocked that it had happened at all. Wren didn't have to know that her reaction was exaggerated.

"It appears Comdr. Sage was wise to prepare us for unexpected contingencies," Wren remarked, his voice gruff.

He was trying terribly hard not to look at her, she thought bemusedly. She inched closer and smoothed down her nightshirt along her leg. The lure worked. Wren gave a quick glance in her direction and then stiffened his spine.

"I'm frightened, Wren," she went on, playing her role for all it was worth. "What if we're attacked again? I don't feel safe on this planet!"

Signs of an inner struggle distorted his expression. Finally he snaked his hand over to rest on her thigh. "I'll see you come to no harm, Hedy."

His words were so low she had to strain to hear them. With a stifled groan, he pulled her into his arms and buried his face in her hair. "Hedy, I couldn't bear it if anything happened to you."

Her heart soared with joy. He'd admitted his need for her! Raising her face, she said, "Kiss me, Wren. Make me yours!"

With a wild cry, he crushed her against his chest and hugged her tight. His hazel eyes glittering, he slowly lowered his head, letting his mouth ravage hers with a desperate urgency. She felt like sobbing with happiness. Wrapping her arms around him, she felt she'd never get close enough to the man she loved.

Yes, it was love she felt for him! A tumult of emotions shook her as their mouths engaged in a passionate frenzy of activity. Dear heaven, she loved him! Tears welled up uncontrollably and trickled down her cheeks. He tasted them and made a low sound in his throat before deepening the kiss. Hedy hadn't even known he could take her to such heights and she yearned to go further, to be carried away with him on the winds of delight, to fly with him to the pinnacle of passion.

But would he go with her? Still being unable to fly, would he yield to his passionate need for her?

The door to their suite swung open and Wren sprang away from her, flushing guiltily as Deke and Mara strode in looking somewhat disheveled. They took in the situation at a glance and grinned, sharing a knowing look with each other which infuriated her.

"Why couldn't you have waited until later?" Hedy snapped irritably. Now she'd never know how far Wren would have gone.

"We gave you sufficient time to rest," Deke drawled, glancing over her attire, "although it appears you decided to use the time in a more interesting pursuit."

"You can be damned annoying, do you know that?" She stood and straightened her nightshirt, not feeling in the least embarrassed by her lack of proper dress.

Deke's grin widened. "I have been told that by someone else you know." His teasing glance turned to Mara.

Mara rolled her eyes. "I thought you had work to do."

"That's right. I want to check over that data given to me by Dr. Parannus. Wren, any new developments?" At his navigator's negative shake of the head, Deke filled him in on their earlier conversation with Fromoth Trun. "After you run a security diagnostic, take an inventory of our equipment," he ordered before heading for their room.

"Aye, sir." Wren stretched to his full height. Without looking at Hedy or Mara, he stalked after Deke.

She glared at Mara. "You sure have lousy timing."

Mara cocked her head. "How so?"

"You saw what we were doing. I just about had Wren

ready to fall into bed with me when you two barged in. Now I'll never know if he'd have done it or not."

"Sorry!" But Mara was grinning as she headed for their sleeping chamber.

Deke wasn't grinning two hauras later when he stormed from his room. "Everybody listen! We need to have an emergency conference."

He herded them into the living area. When they were seated and attentive, he showed them the data card given to him by Dr. Parannus. Wren had run his security diagnostic and it showed the suite was clean of listening devices, so Deke didn't have to worry about their conversation being overheard.

"This information about Vyclor validates everything we've been told," he said. "Apparently the drug works as an antioxidant, counteracting a harmful free-radical by-product called protein carbonyl that is thought to contribute to the aging process. Toxicity trials have accounted for variant responses in different species, which was one of my concerns. Depending upon the population, rates of drug metabolism can vary widely. Usually a response is influenced by genetic factors, structural variations in the binding receptor sites on the body, and environmental factors such as diet. But in Vyclor's case, all oxygen-dependent species should be able to metabolize the drug properly."

He paused for dramatic effect, eyeing each one of his crew members in turn. "It seems logical and conclusive, doesn't it? If it weren't for something unusual that I noticed, I'd probably have been satisfied. However, two items are included that obviously don't belong, nor can I explain how they got inserted into the data card. A location is pinpointed and a close-up shot shows . . . dead bodies."

"Dead bodies!" Mara exclaimed, leaning forward.

"They look like Worts but I can't be certain. They're piled

outside some sort of industrial facility. Since the coordinates are given, I'd like to check it out, but I don't believe we should let Fromoth Trun in on what we're about to do. I have a feeling he doesn't know about this information, and neither does Dr. Parannus. The evidence must have been added for our benefit."

Mara's eyes widened. "Remember that Delain Crug fellow? He conveniently knocked the data card from your hand when he spilled that drink on you. When he leaned down to retrieve the card, he could have done a switch."

Wren spoke up from his perch on the edge of a chair. "What do you think it signifies?"

Deke shrugged. "I haven't a clue. We could go back to the Seabase Pharm plant on some excuse and try to find Delain Crug, but if he's involved it would put him at risk. I'd rather go directly to this location. Here's what I propose."

After relating his plan, Deke contacted Ebo on the ship and relayed his instructions. A short time later, a call came in from Fromoth Trun's secretary.

"We've received notification from Defense League Command that they've received a distress call from the Regaluch system. The *Celeste* is the closest ship, Commander. You have orders to trace the distress signal."

"I see." Deke forced a note of disappointment into his voice. "I'm sorry to disrupt Fromoth Trun's schedule."

"We'll be expecting you to return as soon as you complete your task."

"Very well. Have you alerted spacedock to get ready for a launch?"

"I will make preparations at once."

Deke grinned. "We'll be back sooner than you think," he muttered after shutting off the commlink. Turning to his comrades, he signaled for them to move out. "Pack your bags. We're going to see some action for a change!"

Chapter Fourteen

"I can put her down over there," Deke suggested, piloting the shuttlecraft toward a small hammock, one of the few patches of higher ground dotting the swampy landscape. "We can't get any closer to the coordinates than that or we'll risk being seen on visual."

Seated beside him in the copilot's chair, Wren nodded grimly. They shot past a field of tall brown saw grass and veered toward a clearing just before the brush thickened. In the distance could be seen the tall stacks from the industrial complex that was their destination.

Reconfiguring their vessel to resemble a boat instead of a large bird of prey using the built-in molecular alteration program, Deke brought them to a shuddering halt on a strip of land bordered by a large canal, a dirt road, and a forest of evergreens whose trees possessed spindly white trunks. In the night, they must look like ghostly wraiths rising from the swamp, he thought. Right now, the shadows cast by the trees looked cool and inviting. The air was thick with humidity as they emerged into the bright sunlight. He glanced at the murky water in the canal. It was covered with green vegetation and hardly a ripple showed.

They'd stayed on the *Celeste* through the night, planning to arrive during daylight when fewer people would be around. No one was in sight and that suited Deke fine. He frowned, wondering how they were going to reach their target location. To the south, brown grasses stretched off in an endless flat expanse broken only by scattered bushes or trees. Water glistened throughout the grassy plain. It was shallow, but the grasses that grew out of it were tall with sharp edges. Toward the north reached a swampland forest crisscrossed by a network of waterways. Either way, they couldn't go on foot.

He eyed his crew members. Fully outfitted for a commando operation, they all wore dark cloaks to disguise their humanoid forms. His gaze inadvertently settled on Mara's slim figure, and a warm, appreciative glow fired his insides as he watched her. She moved with the grace of a dancer, and his loins hardened remembering their sensual duets in the physiolab. It hadn't been an easy decision to bring her along. He'd wrestled with himself over her assignment. He needed Ebo and Wren as members of the landing party, and Hedy was essential as medic. Dare he trust Mara not to get into trouble if she were left alone on the ship? In the end, he'd decided she should come along. Her pleas weren't what had persuaded him. He realized he couldn't bear to be apart from her for any length of time. His growing need for her frightened him, but he couldn't deny it any longer. He wanted her at his side regardless of the risk to his mental solitude. Was Mara bewitching him by ingratiating herself into his psyche, or was he just tired of being alone?

Bewildered by the emotions she aroused in him, he shook his thoughts away and scanned the terrain.

"We'll follow that road," he said, pointing. Signaling for

the others to move out single-file behind him, he set the pace down the dirt trail. The brush on either side was thick with silver-branched bushes, red-leafed trees, squat palms, and white-trunked evergreens. A sausage tree intrigued him with its oblong-shaped fruits hanging down from vinelike branches. From his review of Yanura's plant life, he knew they were edible.

He couldn't see what was around the next bend but a pungent aroma hit him as they approached the curve in the trail. Yielding to his inner sense of caution, he halted and motioned for Ebo. The Sirisian joined him and elongated his neck to peer around the corner.

"It's a fueling station," Ebo whispered, his turbaned head covered by his cowl.

A fueling station, here in the middle of nowhere? Maybe this part of the swamp was a popular convergence, Deke thought with a note of alarm. As they neared the wood structure, he pulled the hood further over his head to shadow his features and hunched his posture to mimic the Yanurans. A rustling noise from behind told him his crew were doing the same. Around the back of the shop and curving along its right side ran a slough on which were docked several strange-looking conveyances, boats of an unfamiliar configuration. Yellow water lilies and grass grew out of the shallow water whose stillness was broken by an occasional ripple as a fish jumped or a reptilian creature slid off the bank into the water. A gentle breeze blew, caressing the hairs on his forearms. Unnerved by the stillness, he approached the station with trepidation.

About 15 minutes later, they emerged from the station and headed toward the dock. Putting Mara's linguistic expertise to use, he'd hired one of the airboats without—he hoped—arousing any suspicions. The scruffy Croag who ran the station hadn't even given him a second look after being offered a generous payment. He'd even given directions, leaving Deke the impression that new workers must come through here fairly often.

Deke was the first to climb into the flat-bottomed boat with its bright blue meraninum hull rising out of the water. In the front, a protective clear windshield curved upward, shielding the rows of black plasticine benches behind it. From the flat deck behind the passenger seats rose the supports of another seat that towered over the rest. This was the pilot's chair. Behind it, at the rear of the vehicle, was secured a powerful engine which drove a gigantic propellor blade captured in a metal frame that supported the pilot's chair.

"I'll drive," Deke said, indicating the others should get into the passenger seats in front. With a grunt, he climbed onto the elevated driver's seat and donned the goggles and earphones provided by the station owner. Scanning the controls, he located the starter button and jabbed at it with his forefinger. With a cough and a sputter, the powerful engine roared into life, drowning out all other sounds. Great! he thought. We'll be heard for kilometers. So much for a stealthy approach to their target.

Wren threw off the mooring lines, then jumped into the boat after the others. He took a seat next to Hedy, snaking his hand in her direction. Deke noticed Mara cast an envious glance their way and felt a surge of anger, knowing she wished he would act toward her in a similar manner. Damn the woman. She constantly distracted him!

Clenching his jaw, he gripped the throttle and carefully eased the stick forward. The twin air rudders shifted and the boat moved ahead. Now all he had to do was navigate the maze of waterways to reach their destination.

Turning at a broad sideslip, he increased speed, shooting down a narrow waterway bordered by tall grasses. Wind whipped at his face as the vibration from the motor shuddered through his body. He felt like whooping with exhilaration. What a ride! He couldn't see his crew's reaction; their backs were to him. They bumped over a mound of black muck and his seat rose, then fell again as the boat skimmed over the water at high speed. A flock of white long-necked birds took flight at the noise but his attention was diverted by the hammock rapidly approaching after a series of turns. He cut off the motor and sideslipped the airboat into a slough beside a wooden dock. A couple of other boats that were moored there bobbed in the current. He felt the rush of silence as the noise of the engine stopped abruptly and the vibrations ceased. Removing his earphones and goggles, he scanned the area from his high vantage point.

An oasis of tall palms, flowering bushes, and fruit-laden trees met his gaze. But the idyllic scene was marred by the sulphuric odor in the air. Wrinkling his nose, he descended from his perch. An orange-beaked bird stood feeding in the shallow water, seemingly undisturbed by the intrusion.

At least no one was there to greet them, he thought gratefully as he mustered his team. As they started down a winding dirt trail, they could see the towering stacks from the industrial complex over the tops of the vegetation. He kept his hand ready to grasp his weapon. Sweat dripped inside the silvery skinsuit he wore under his cloak. The silver suits, impervious to sensor scans, were standard-issue uniform for sensitive missions. They were hot as Zor on a day like this but would make them invisible to radar. All of his team members wore one, and glancing back, he saw they looked as flushed and uncomfortable as he felt.

A huge fence loomed in front with a guardhouse at a gated entrance. He drew his group to a halt just before they were spotted. Hastening back into the shelter of the brush, he conferred with his crewmates in hushed tones.

A few moments later, Mara sauntered toward the gatehouse. Gone was her cloak. With her long raven hair loosened from its braid, her seductive walk, and the skinsuit that clung to her curves, she appeared a vision of loveliness. But would the Yanuran on guard be impressed by the human female? Deke bit his lower lip as he watched from behind a tall tree, his weapon poised.

Because she wasn't visible on their sensor scans, Mara had to call out to get the guard's attention. Two Yanurans, not one, appeared in the guardhouse archway. Hopefully they were the only ones, Deke thought as he readied his finger on the trigger. Pop—pop! The guards went down without a sound. At his nod, Wren and Ebo went to work on the gate, first jamming the electronic alarm circuitry, then disengaging the locking mechanism. The gate swung open silently.

Swiftly they entered the grounds of the complex. On the left was the guardhouse, on the right a small, nondescript building. Before them stretched a city in itself: gravel roads connecting numerous structures that confused Deke with their varying shapes. All of the buildings had an unfinished look to them, as though they were temporary. Most were constructed of cinder block or corrugated metal with a small sprinkling of brick. Each building was numbered. They were interconnected by a series of large white pipes. The piping had joints where it took 90-degree turns and consisted of varying diameters. Some of the pipelines were supported by metal superstructures. All of the buildings had outdoor stairwells wrapped around the exterior for fire escape. The landscape was dotted by spherical constructs that were separate from the larger buildings. They struck a chord in him, something he'd seen before, but he couldn't recall what they signified.

Checking out the first building on their right, he was surprised to see it held a bin with safety glasses, one with rubbery overshoes, and row after row of hanging coveralls. He appraised the room then gazed at his crew questioningly.

"What do you think?" he asked, raising his eyebrows.

"This must be a dressing room for the workers," Mara responded quietly. "We should put on these outfits. They're loose enough that they'll fit over our cloaks. It'll help if we're dressed like everyone else."

He nodded curtly. "Wren, you'll stay with the women. Wait here and make sure no other guards come around to impede our exit. Ebo, you'll come with me."

Properly suited up and hotter than ever, Deke and Ebo moved out. Each new location brought with it a new smell, none of them pleasant. Deke felt like gagging half the time but suppressed his discomfort. The cylindrical storage tanks were painted white to reflect the heat, and each one had a metal staircase running up its side. The spherical ones stood apart like outcasts and he wondered at their purpose. Scouting the grounds, they blended in easily with the similarly dressed workers scurrying about in their coveralls, rubber overshoes, and thick safety glasses.

A water treatment plant, recycling center, and the bimanthium crystal–powered generator told Deke the facility was self-sufficient. But what was produced here? He still didn't understand, although something nagged at him, telling him he'd seen buildings like this before. Outside each larger cluster of buildings was a small upright structure painted in bright yellow. He entered one, curious as to its use. Inside were sinks and shower spigots.

Showers? Rubber shoes? Coveralls and safety glasses?

It's a chemical plant! Halting in shocked surprise, Deke wondered what kind of chemicals were produced. Fertilizers? Industrial chemicals? Something to do with their pharmaceutical industry? He had seen similar buildings at one of Drylon's production facilities, but the extent of safety precautions here went well beyond the bounds for everyday chemicals. Dangerous chemicals? Yes, that would explain it. These booths must be emergency showers and the sinks were for eye washing. The spherical constructs that stood apart from the others housed the nastier products.

Great suns! A sinking feeling took hold of him as he watched the Croags scurry about outside. What could they possibly be up to? In his mind's eye, he saw those dead bodies that were pictured on the data card. Were they from here?

Another site brought another puzzle piece into play. At the opposite end from where they'd entered was a small airfield. Leading to it was a set of tracks, and on the tracks sat several rolling platforms. The platforms contained torpedo-shaped cylinders with an ominous red symbol painted on the sides of each.

"I'd like to take one of those with us," Deke muttered to Ebo from the shadow of a building.

"They're too big, sir," the Sirisian replied, his face red from the heat.

"I know. We'd need to obtain a minilevitator."

"How about checking out one of the larger buildings instead? We might find some answers there."

"Yes, let's do that." He selected a rectangular structure with a tall stack on one side. They were just approaching a casement to check for an easy means of entrance when a harsh voice stopped them from behind.

"Halt! Your identification?"

Turning slowly, Deke and Ebo faced a pair of mean-looking guards who held shooters aimed at their chests. Deke exchanged glances with Ebo, giving an imperceptible nod.

Mara bit her nails with anxiety. Why were Deke and Ebo taking so long to return? She'd taken to counting the ants crawling past on the dry ground in order not to worry, but she couldn't help feeling concerned when the minutes ticked by and there was no sign of them. If only she could do a willful separation to check on Deke's well-being, but she didn't possess any of his belongings and hadn't yet reached the point of being able to direct their spiritual contact. She found herself wishing one of their spontaneous occurrences would happen, but it didn't. Agonized, she turned to Wren.

"Maybe you should go after them," she suggested, pushing a stray wisp of her hair from her face. She'd rebraided it and twisted it up on top of her head.

Wren stood squinting in the sunlight, peering in the direction they'd gone. "Be patient. The commander will return when he is ready," he said confidently.

She grimaced. She didn't like this mission. Being an open, honest person, she liked to deal with people without reservations, and the deceit they'd used on Fromoth Trun bothered her. What if Deke were caught? How would he explain their presence here? Then again, what was this place, and why had someone tipped them off to it by inserting the coordinates on that data card Deke had been given?

She shook her head, too worried to think clearly. Leaning against the hot stucco exterior of the wardrobe building, she wallowed in the anxiety that clouded her mind. I should meditate, she told herself. I wouldn't feel the heat so badly in this ridiculous coverall and it would take my mind off Deke's absence. But she couldn't concentrate. Her gaze fixed on the path Deke and Ebo had taken where it rounded a curve and became lost to view.

Footsteps thudded in their direction and she squared her shoulders. By the stars, were another pair of guards coming to take over the watch? Alarmed, she glanced at Wren. His posture remained rigid as he stood motionless, listening.

Her heart leapt with relief as Deke and Ebo tore around the bend. Dust flew up at their heels. Their faces were red and sweaty and their expressions were edged with desperation.

"Move it!" Deke shouted. "They're right behind us."

Encumbered by her weighty outfit, Mara dashed through the gate with the others and ran down the path toward the dock. At least the rubber soles made for easy running. As soon as they reached the airboat, Wren threw off the mooring lines while Deke climbed onto the pilot's seat. He jabbed at the starter button and the engine roared into life just as a loud claxon began clanging, announcing their presence.

"We can't let them catch us," Deke hollered.

Mara barely heard him as she flung herself onto a seat. She and Hedy helped divest each other of their coveralls as Deke pushed the throttle and they eased along the slough. Soon they were skipping along at high speed and appeared to be in the clear until another airboat intersected them at a perpendicular canal. Laser fire zinged past her ear. Shrieking, she crouched in the bottom with Hedy while Wren and Ebo returned fire. She hoped Deke knew where he was going. The waterways were shallow and could be hazardous at this speed to a pilot unfamiliar with them.

Glancing toward the rear to see how Deke was doing, she noted his grim face. He'd managed to don goggles and earphones but she could tell by the set of his mouth and his taut posture how critical he considered their situation. If he got hit, or the propellor was impaired, they'd be in big trouble. She didn't care to contemplate a trek through the muck with the Yanurans in pursuit, nor could she even bear to think about Deke being wounded.

Her eyes widened with sudden realization. Why were they being pursued by armed Croags in airboats? Craning her neck, she raised questioning eyes to Deke, wondering what he and Ebo had discovered. It could be nothing more significant than industrial secrets at the plant that were being guarded, but those dead bodies implied something more sinister.

Her breath caught in her throat as a sizzling beam of red light shot past, melting the edge of the boat where it hit. With a snarl, Wren fired back and a rapid volley ensued. Deke swerved as they reached a narrow river bordered by tall grasses. Cobwebs brushed Mara's face as she tried to peer over the edge, but whenever she rose, the vibrations made her teeter. Other waterways cut off from this one.

Deke revved the engine and veered left, away from another airboat that had joined the pursuit and was heading straight at them. They hit a pile of muck and she grabbed at Hedy as the boat rose under them and then fell with a jarring thud. Without losing speed, the boat flew toward a forested section of the swamp where twisted white shapes rose out of the dark water. Her teeth rattled from the engine's vibration and she clenched them tightly, but it didn't help. She felt as if her bones were being shaken loose.

Hedy poked her arm. "Mara!" she screamed, her green eyes wide with fright. "Is that where we're heading?"

The swamp's dismal depths loomed ahead. Moss dripped from overhanging tree branches, and fallen logs and other debris carpeted the higher patches of ground. Suns, she thought fearfully, surely Deke won't drive us into that obstacle-ridden lagoon? As they neared it, she could see tall cone-shaped stumps sticking out of the murky brown water.

They veered right, and Mara swallowed hard, wondering if Deke knew where he was going. They had to lose those Yanurans. As she crouched on the deck, clutching at Hedy with both hands, her thoughts raced. What was produced in that foul-smelling factory so closely guarded in the middle of a swamp? It couldn't be a waste treatment site so far away from civilization. How about a normal industrial process that smelled so bad no one wanted it near their homes? But that didn't seem likely either considering the tight security.

The ghostly swamp flashed by on their left. She risked another glance back at Deke. His face was abnormally white, his lips pressed tightly together. She felt an uncontrollable urge to merge with him and offer her strength but knew it would break his concentration, even if she could manage the separation without holding on to an item that belonged to him. It would be wonderful if she could control the happenings, she thought wistfully. Then he wouldn't have to be afraid of her, and she could offer solace when needed. But under these circumstances she wouldn't disrupt his thoughts. Those woody growths permeated the swamp and he had to pay attention to their route.

Her ears caught Wren's whoop of exultation and she snapped her head around. One of the boats pursuing them had hit something in the water and flipped over! The Yanurans were floundering in the shallow water; then they were lost to view.

Deke raced the boat toward a dark green spot indicating higher ground. Behind them, a second boat followed but at a distance. As they approached the small island, he slowed their speed until they could make out other patches of thick tropical vegetation that dotted the landscape. When they rounded a jagged shoreline, Deke cut the engine and slipped the airboat into a small cove. The vibrations ceased abruptly along with the deafening roar.

"We'll wait here," Deke said, having taken off his earphones. "It's too far to circle around these hammocks. We'd waste too much fuel. Wait until that other boat comes into view, then fire at its propellor," he told Wren and Ebo.

They settled in to wait. Mara and Hedy slumped into the seats while the men prepared to do battle. They removed their coveralls and rubber galoshes, having long since discarded the protective glasses.

"Where are we?" she asked, mildly interested. Their location didn't matter as much as getting rid of their pursuers, but if they succeeded, then what? Were they lost?

Deke shrugged. "We'll worry about that when the time comes," he said, confirming her fears.

She gazed over the edge of the boat. At the water's surface, tall reeds and cattails swayed in the breeze. A turtle sat motionless on a slime-covered rock. The vegetation shaded them, providing a cooling breeze as a light wind rustled through the leaves. Gnarled tree roots, broad leaves of tropical plants, and tangles of vines formed a dense, impenetrable wall. A sweet floral scent drifted towards her and she sniffed at it, grateful to get rid of the unpleasant odors from the industrial plant.

"What was that place?" she asked, turning to Deke. His face was uplifted, his eyes scanning the watery expanse.

"We'll discuss it later," he replied, his voice terse.

She feasted her eyes on him. Seated high above them, he appeared powerful with his tall, muscled body, broad chest, and militant posture. He didn't look anything like the sensitive science scholar she knew him to be inside. This is the warrior, she realized grudgingly. This is the soldier who'd snuffed out all the Hortha guards on that mission with Wren to the planet Souk. This is the SEARCH force leader in charge of our mission. She should have listened to him, should have heeded his advice regarding the Yanurans. Now look at their predicament. They hadn't accomplished any of their objectives other than learning more about the Vyclor process and even that might be a scam.

Hearing a low drone coming from behind, she turned around.

"Get ready," Deke ordered. When the drone grew into a roar, he put on his goggles and earphones. The other airboat thundered past. Deke pressed the starter button, kicking the engine into life. He whipped the boat out of the cove and into a shallow lake. They saw the other boat up ahead, skimming over the tall saw grass. Deke revved the engine and they shot forward down the river, stalking the other boat. The deck rose under them as they sped over the grass.

Wren took aim and fired. His laser bolt hit home, knocking the other boat's propellor off balance. As she peered over the edge, she noticed with relief that the Yanurans' boat was settling into the grassy marsh. Deke careened down another slough to avoid them. Several turns later, he slowed their speed, finally reaching a halt. Cutting the engine, he removed his earphones. Tall vegetation lining the canal obscured their view on either side.

"Uh, Wren, can you get a fix on our shuttle?"

She didn't like that sheepish look on his face. "Deke, don't you have any idea where we are?"

He shook his head, his eyes on the big Polluxite. Wren had moved to sit beside Hedy, his large hand grasping her smaller one in his lap. Now he released her, standing on the flat deck. Hedy gasped as his wings sprouted from his back.

"Sorry," Wren said, his face reddening. "I just have to stretch! Just a minute, sir, and I'll verify our location."

"How?" Hedy asked, her green eyes wide with wonder.

He smiled at her, a bright, engaging smile that lit up his rugged face. "My species has a highly developed sense of echo location." After flapping his wings a few times, he refolded them into his back. Emitting a series of high-pitched squeaks, he appeared to listen acutely to sounds Mara and the others couldn't hear. "I believe the shuttle lies in that direction," he told Deke, giving an approximation of the distance.

"Hang on," Deke said, placing the earphones on his head.

Mara groaned. She was getting tired of the shuddering vibrations and her ears rang from the roaring of the engine. She couldn't wait until they reached the comfort of the *Celeste.*

The shuttle, still disguised as a boat, rocked gently on the water where they'd left it. No one was at the fueling station other than the owner when they arrived. Deke grinned broadly, expressing his relief. He'd half expected a welcoming committee. In his mind's eye, he pictured the two guards aiming their shooters at himself and Ebo back at the complex. In a movement too quick for the eye to catch, Ebo had elongated his arms, snatching the shooters from their opponent's hands before they realized what had happened. Then it had only been a matter of a few well-appointed kicks and punches to bring the guards down. As they headed back toward the entrance, their handiwork had been discovered and the pursuit had intensified.

Deke ordered his crew into the shuttle. Within moments, they'd lifted off and were soaring through the atmosphere toward their ship.

Every one of them uttered an exclamation of pleasure as they disembarked the shuttle and stepped out into the cargo bay of the *Celeste.*

He surveyed his scraggly team. They looked hot, bedraggled, and fatigued. Knowing they'd like nothing more than a hot shower and long rest, he grimly gave his orders.

"Set course for Revitt Lake City," he told Ebo.

Mara's eyes widened. "We're returning so soon?"

Deke observed the disappointment on her face. "We've just seen evidence that nasty chemicals are being produced in that plant. We didn't see any dead bodies, but the implications are that the Croags might be testing them on the Worts. We must talk to a representative of the Wort faction! If Fromoth Trun hasn't made arrangements, we'll seek them out on our own. Otherwise, I think it's best if we pretend ignorance at this point. If the Worts don't give us any satisfactory answers, I'll confront Fromoth Trun. I don't want to tip his hand yet when he might have Jallyn or know where she's being hidden."

Jallyn. Mara squeezed her eyes shut, a flood of anxiety overwhelming her. She felt Deke's hand on her arm, sensed his flow of compassion, and it strengthened her. Opening her eyes, she noticed that Wren and Hedy and Ebo had already taken the lift to the upper levels. She and Deke were alone.

"How is this going to end?" she whispered, anguished.

"I don't know," he said, his eyes darkening. "We'll find out the truth."

"Yes, the truth." Her stubborn defense of Fromoth Trun no longer seemed reasonable. Deke's arguments had been valid all along. She'd been too biased by her own sense of righteousness to be able to think clearly.

As though sensing her need for reassurance, Deke drew her into his arms. "Mara," he said, burying his face in her hair, "I'll make sure this turns out all right. We'll get Jallyn back."

She sank into the comfort of his strong embrace. His chest felt rock-hard against her soft breasts, his solid form like a tree trunk. She needed his strength and the security he offered. He shuddered as he held her, and she knew he was becoming aroused.

"I was so worried when you and Ebo didn't return right away," she murmured, tilting her neck so she could gaze up at him. His liquid brown eyes stared down at her, then meandered to her mouth.

Before she knew what was happening, she was in his viewpoint, gazing at her own pink lips, yearning to take her right there on the cargo bay floor.

"No," he said, abruptly releasing her and breaking the

spell. "Don't do this to me. Don't make me so crazy with desire for you that I can't think about anything else."

"Deke, I didn't mean to—"

"It still bothers me when you jump into my head without warning!"

"But I thought you liked it when we . . . when you . . . when we're together."

His expression softened. "I do, but everything I've been working toward my whole life dissolves into nothing when I'm with you. That's what scares me so much. Even this mission fades into insignificance when we're . . . linked. I'm losing it, Mara. I need to stay away from you to keep my sanity."

"You're just denying the inevitable. We're meant to be together."

His movements jerky, he jabbed the panel to summon the turbolift. "You keep saying that and I don't understand why. I'm not able to give you what you want."

"It's what you want too, Deke, don't you see that?"

"What I want is to be left alone! Now I'm going back to work. Please do me a favor and stay off the bridge."

"You're being unfair again. You're not giving us a chance." She looked at him woefully.

"I can't talk about it now!" And he straightened his back, effectively shutting her out and closing the conversation.

Chapter Fifteen

Deke agonized with himself as he stood on the bridge of the *Celeste* peering out the viewscreen during their approach to Revitt Lake City. Why was Mara so damn persistent? Any other woman would have backed off by now. Why did she keep bothering him? Stroking his jaw, he tried to understand what she hoped to gain. What if did agree to let their relationship work itself out? Maybe he'd eventually ask her to return to Eranus with him. If she stayed on his world, she'd have to give up her diplomatic career. Was she willing to sacrifice her life's work to be with him? Of course, they hadn't talked about it, nor was he even ready to consider the idea, but what did she intend to do with herself on Eranus?

He pursed his lips, mulling over the notion of bringing her home. Wouldn't his parents be surprised! They'd always expected him to settle down with a girl from one of the wealthier families on Eranus. How would they react to a woman like Mara? Her exotic beauty and unnatural ability would make her stand out in any population. Would they react with the same horror as Pietor's parents? Despite his wish to be free of her, he couldn't bear to see her hurt. Hopefully his father would be more tolerant. As leader of the planet, Jon mingled with people from different worlds at diplomatic functions and was used to socializing with aliens. So was Deke's mother, but Palomar would be disappointed he hadn't chosen a mate who could bolster the family fortune.

Deke realized he knew little about Mara's background other than the struggles she'd had throughout her childhood. Her parents must still be living. What kind of work did they do? If she had other relatives, how did they regard her? And why should he care? He wasn't seriously considering taking her home with him. What a ridiculous notion! How could he ever live with the woman, knowing she'd invade his privacy when he least expected it?

And yet the idea, once introduced, wouldn't disappear. It continued to nag at him, producing visions he didn't want to see: him showing her his favorite cavern by the Whispering Dunes; proudly introducing her to his colleagues at the institute; teaching her how to dive and exploring the wonders of Treasure Cove with her. Her sitting down with him to dinner and teasing him at his choice of seafood. Maybe she'd serve him an iced jelly, her sarong clinging tightly to her hips, her long raven hair cascading over the swell of her breasts as she sauntered toward him, a seductive gleam in her eyes. By the corona, he was tempted—

"We've received clearance for landing," Ebo said, breaking his reverie.

His attention reverted to his crew. "Proceed," he said, compressing his lips. He was letting his mind wander again. Would he ever be free from her influence? Satisfied that Ebo could handle the maneuvers, he glanced at Wren, hunched over his nav console, and wondered what was going through the Polluxite's head. Wren acted as though he enjoyed Hedy's attentions even though his manner of showing it was gruff. Striding over, Deke leaned forward, speaking in a low tone so their conversation wouldn't be overheard.

"What are you going to do when this is over?" he asked.

Wren looked up, startled. "Sir?"

"What are you going to do about Hedy?"

Wren's face colored, shadowing the rugged angles of his brow. "I haven't thought that far in advance, Commander."

"I don't know what I'll do about Mara. I suppose I can call on her when I visit Bimordus Two."

Wren raised a layered eyebrow. "And how often will that be?"

"Not too often if I win the chancellorship."

"What's that?" Wren's tone was sharp.

Deke realized he'd let slip his secret. Sighing, he decided to confess. "I'm only in the Defense League for two annums, Lieutenant. Are you familiar with the Institute for Marine Studies on Eranus? The chancellorship will be vacant several months from now. I'd like nothing more than to win the position." He grinned sheepishly. "I'm a marine biologist."

Wren's expression of shocked surprise was almost comical. "But your military exploits are well known, Commander. I've heard stories—"

"Those incidents occurred within the past annum and a half. Before that, I worked at the institute. My heart is there, Wren. That's why I joined the SEARCH force, so I could practice my diving skills while earning points with the selection committee. I'm a dedicated research scientist."

Wren's hazel eyes regarded him solemnly. "Mara knows about this, I assume?"

Plowing a hand through his unruly hair, he nodded.

"Have you asked her to return home with you?" Wren asked, performing a deft calculation on the nav computer as he listened.

"Why would I do that? I said I could call on her when I visit Bimordus Two."

"Which won't be very often. I don't think Mara is the type of female to abide that kind of relationship, Commander."

"No, I guess you're right. What about you and Hedy?" he said, changing the subject.

"She knows how I feel. Our relationship can come to nothing." Wren lifted his chin in the air, his gaze defiant.

"But you wish you could have her, don't you?"

"Aye, more than anything. She fires my blood so that all I can think about is when I'll see her next. Her sweet face dances before my eyes during every waking moment. Her lilting voice plays music in my ears. She drives me crazy but I cannot touch her!" He glared at Deke, his expression wild. "Have you ever known a woman could cause such distraction?"

Deke nodded, amused. "I have the opposite problem. Mara drives me crazy when I do touch her!" And here he was thinking of her again when he should be thinking of what to say to Fromoth Trun. Blast! That woman tormented him.

"There's no easy solution, is there, Wren? I think we were better off before we met the ladies."

Wren studied him, his demeanor serious. "Do you really believe so, Commander?"

Disconcerted, he shuffled his feet. "Maybe . . . I just don't know. I guess I'm confused, never having experienced feelings like this before."

"You know what that means, don't you?" Wren asked.

"What?"

"Being confused over a woman . . . so obsessed by her that you cannot think of anything else."

"What are you getting at?" he demanded curtly, anxious to return to duty.

"It's love, sir!"

Deke stared at him in astonishment. "Love!"

"I know that's how I feel toward Hedy. I love her!" Wren's voice was stricken with awe as though he were speaking of the Almighty. "It is a curse upon me that I cannot tell her, for that would be my undoing. But you, Commander, you can tell your woman. You can reveal your heart to her."

"You're unhinged, Wren. I'm not in love with Mara." And before Wren could contradict him, he whirled away, distraught and unsure of himself. Wren's vision is colored by his amorous inclinations, Deke thought. He's vastly mistaken about me. I want to bed Mara, not wed her.

Furiously pushing away such disturbing notions, he focused his thoughts on Fromoth Trun. It was much more comforting to think about his work than to analyze his feelings regarding one insistent and beautiful woman.

The Yanuran leader greeted Deke and his team in the spacedock landing bay. "Responding to the distress call did not take you very long, Commander," he said, his moist green skin darkening to a murky brownish color.

"It turned out to be a false alarm," Deke answered amiably. His hands tucked into his uniform pockets, he sauntered forward until he was within centimeters of Fromoth Trun's frog face. The fishy odor that assailed him made him suck in a sharp breath but he didn't let his reaction show on his face.

"Have you made the arrangements I requested?" he demanded.

The Yanuran fingered his voluminous robe nervously, his bulging amber eyes darting to the casements. Outside, the sun was just descending in a blazing crimson display. "I was waiting for your return, Commander. I didn't expect you back so soon."

Deke's mouth tightened. "We've packed our gear, since you said it was an arduous trip to the Alterland. We're ready to go. Just get us a guide."

"I have to contact the chief council who is leader of the Worts. He'll want to arrange for a proper reception."

"Forget the reception. I'd rather arrive unannounced. Now about the guide . . ."

Fromoth Trun glanced at Wren and the women who were waiting patiently behind Deke. They all wore insulated khaki treksuits. Deke had put on his uniform, replete with gold braid and service medals, believing it would make him appear more impressive.

"Perhaps if you would join us at our evening feast," Fromoth Trun began, his manner obsequious, "we can discuss this further. You've had a chance to scan the material regarding Vyclor, I assume?" At Deke's nod, he went on, rushing to get the words out before Deke interrupted. "Think how Vyclor would benefit everyone, Commander! Why don't you just make this easy and recommend approval of our application to the Admissions Committee?"

"I understand how the sale of Vyclor would benefit your people, Your Excellency. I'm not so sure how it would serve anyone else. I'd like to hear the Worts' opinion on the subject. They do take Vyclor, don't they? Didn't you say it's given to the population as a whole?"

Mara cleared her throat behind him and he wondered what emotions she was sensing in Fromoth Trun. The Croag leader was probably involved in that secret project in the swamp. Deke didn't need her psychic ability to realize it would be dangerous to reveal their knowledge. They still didn't know what that project signified, but the Worts might be able to tell them.

"Let us retire to the burrows, Commander," Fromoth Trun said, making a sweeping gesture toward the exit. "You can avail yourselves of our hospitality. Once you are comfortable, you may see things in a different light."

Deke squared his shoulders. "If you don't provide us with a guide, we'll proceed to the Alterland ourselves. I understand the terrain is difficult, so we can't fly our shuttle in, but we'll find a way. I would be grateful for your cooperation." His tone was edged in steel. He wanted it clearly understood that he'd recommend an immediate denial of Fromoth Trun's application if he wasn't obliged.

The Yanuran got the message. "Very well," he said with an air of resignation. "I have someone standing by to serve your needs."

An haura later they were transported by a winged pod to the Alterland, a tropical rain-forest habitat deep at the base of the highest mountain range on Yanura. Their driver deposited them at Camp Selva, a research site run by a pharmaceutical company. The property, basically a clearing in the jungle, consisted of about 20 bamboo cottages with thatched roofs. The main eatery, another thatched hut, sat by the banks of a murky river. It was connected to the cottages by a series of elevated boardwalks. Public lighting was conspicuously absent.

Of course, Mara thought as she survey their surroundings with a sinking sensation. The Yanurans can see in the dark. It's a good thing we brought a supply of flametorches. For an instant she envied Ebo. Deke had relegated his communications officer to duty on board the *Celeste,* ordering him to pull the ship into orbit and stand by. Ebo, none too eager for another land trek, had stretched his rubbery mouth into a broad grin. Admitting he hoped to catch up on reading the latest engineering manuals, he'd saluted as the landing party disembarked. Peering at a grotesque black insect scurrying across the clearing, she had a distinct wish to join him.

It wasn't going to be easy being in such close company with Deke over the next few days. After his latest rejection, she had no desire for any close contact between them. Her aspirations seemed hopeless. Even though she'd seen the cords binding them and they appeared to be strengthening, Deke's continual denial of his feelings was wearing her down. Was it worth the effort on her part to try to make him see the light? What was in it for her?

Simply put, she couldn't envision herself going through life without him. It wasn't only his physical presence that appealed to her; she felt linked to him on a higher level. She yearned to share his hopes and dreams, his fears and failures, to bring him comfort and to experience his joys. She'd touched the loneliness deep in his heart and knew he needed her, too. By the stars, if only her longing for him weren't so great! If only she could discard her feelings and get back to the way she was before they met. She'd been insulated against rejection then. Her defenses weren't working now, and every word he said had the ability to cut her.

Sighing, she figured she'd just have to make the best of the situation and let destiny run its course. Certainly in this location she should concentrate on her surroundings. Those creatures creeping along the ground made her skin crawl.

The air was dank and humid with the stench of rotting vegetation. As the sun rose, vapor misted through the thick tree canopy and lifted to the cloud-laden sky. Cicadas hummed in unison and strange birdcalls filled the air. She gazed around helplessly, wondering who they should approach for assistance. Most of the people seemed to have retired for the day.

Deke stalked over to the only Croag who wasn't in any hurry to retreat to his bungalow. The fellow lazed by the riverbank, holding a makeshift fishing pole that dangled in the water. He wore a wide-brimmed hat, a pair of baggy shorts, and a loose-fitting frock coat with threads that were coming unfringed.

"Mara," Deke called after his greeting in Jawani, the standard Coalition language, went unanswered.

She walked over, her boots sucking up mud along the way. Ignoring the rapid tempo of her pulse caused by Deke's proximity, she focused on the Yanuran.

"*Rogi Kwantro,*" she began and was gratified to get a curt nod in response. Trying the Croag dialect, she said: "We're supposed to meet a guide to take us into the interior. Can you direct us to the person in charge?"

With a laborious sigh, the fisherman laid his pole down and rose to face them. "'Tis me you seek," he replied. "I've been hired to take you inland. Folks in these parts call me Slime." He aimed his large vertical eyes in their direction. "How much?"

"I beg your pardon?"

"How much you payin'?"

She was taken aback. "I thought Fromoth Trun had set the terms."

"The only settlement he made was for me to be here. Now how much?"

"What's he want?" Deke demanded impatiently. Sweat trickled down the sides of his face and he didn't look very comfortable in his khaki treksuit. He'd changed out of his uniform but in this heat it wasn't any improvement. The suits were insulated but didn't shield their exposed skin from the elements.

"He wants to know how much we're paying him," she

explained, glancing at Hedy. Her friend was holding a whispered conference with Wren beside one of the cottages, making Mara wonder about their sleeping arrangements. She hoped she wouldn't have to bunk with Deke. It would only make their situation worse.

Deke cursed. "Fromoth Trun is trying to make this as difficult as possible, isn't he?"

"I wouldn't think so." She pursed her lips. "He wants us to approve his application."

"Well, he's sure going about it in an odd manner. Tell this frogface we'll pay him a hundred credits to take us to the nearest Wort village."

She translated, glad that her skills were proving useful.

The guide's features folded into a frown. "Not worth the effort," he said, lifting his fishing pole and casting the line into the water.

Deke's face reddened. "Offer him five hundred."

"Five thousand," Slime countered after Mara relayed his message.

"Two and a half."

"Three thousand and a crate of live torgus larvae."

Deke acquiesced, contacting Lixier Bryn via datalink to confirm the transfer of credits. "Your food will be flown in when we're picked up," he said, giving a smug smile. "How soon can we leave?"

Slime packed up his fishing supplies. "By first lunar light."

"Uh uh." Deke put out an arm to stop him. "We can't see at night like you can. We have to travel during the day."

Slime's complexion darkened. "You didn't say so before, human! That'll cost you extra."

"Agreed," Deke said wearily.

As soon as they'd gathered their equipment, Slime led the way down a dirt trail that wound into the jungle. Mara followed directly behind so she could translate whatever he said to the others, and Wren brought up the rear.

It rained briefly just as they were starting, a sudden torrential downpour that made their path more arduous. Mara slogged her way through the mud, wishing she had webbed feet like their guide. Exposed tree roots and rotting organic matter made the hike treacherous. Slime didn't have to worry about the sunlight drying out his moist green skin. A pale, diffuse light filtered through the dense jungle canopy which towered a hundred feet or higher. A multitude of insects presented him with ample meals, and his long tongue flicked out to catch treats along the way.

She shuddered, wishing for the comfort of the *Celeste*. This wasn't her idea of fun. We have to find Jallyn, she reminded herself. This trip is worth it if it leads us to her or sheds light on what's going on between the Croags and the Worts. The only thing that bothered her was Fromoth Trun's reaction if they did learn the answers, but it would be a waste of time to worry about that now. Being careful of her footing was more important.

She admired the ease with which Deke made his way through the dense foliage, as though he'd grown up in this type of environment instead of on a watery world. His Defense League training must have been thorough, she thought, glancing over her shoulder in his direction. He was hacking away with a machete, marking their route should they need to make a hasty retreat. Sweat poured down his face but he wasn't short of breath. His straining muscles seemed made for the exertion.

Thank the stars he'd ordered her and Hedy to work out in the physiolab! They'd never have been able to keep the pace if it weren't for those fitness sessions. The memory of her initial rebellion rose to bring an embarrassed flush to her face. Deke had been right again, she admitted. She was beginning to realize his counsel was wise on many subjects.

They spent part of the night in the shelter of their tents, but none of them slept much. Raucous cries of birds of prey and howls of wild animals kept them awake. Rising before dawn, Deke ordered them to move out by the light of their flametorches.

When not mired in muck, they had to watch their path for fallen tree branches and other debris. Slime warned them not to go near the huge brown blobs attached to nearby trunks. Swarms of biting insects lived inside and they wouldn't want to see the results of disturbing the nests.

"We're getting near Wort territory," he announced on the third day.

Mara breathed a sigh of relief. Exhausted and hungry, she was appreciating the advantages of working on Bimordus Two in an air-filtered office. What she wouldn't give for a blast of cool air right now! At least Hedy was holding up well. Her friend actually seemed to be enjoying the trek, but maybe that was because Wren was so solicitous to her comfort. In contrast, Deke was trying his best to ignore Mara, assisting her only when they had to cross a particularly treacherous tract of territory.

"That's odd," Slime said, abruptly coming to a halt.

She bumped into him, then leapt back, repulsed by the contact with his slimy skin. "What is it?" she asked, listening acutely. The sounds of humming insects met her ears.

"The path has changed." Slime's eyes were fixed on the ground. "See those markings? That was the usual way. There's dangerous bogs in that direction. Can't get too much farther without taking to the water, and folks who've tried get stopped by poison darts. I never went much beyond this point."

She frowned. "I don't understand."

"The brownskins use poison darts on folks who get too close to their territory. Won't get me going any further. Was goin' to take you to the pond but now the path's changed. I think this is where I'll split."

"Now wait a minute! We hired you to take us all the way," she protested.

"You follow that path, you'll get there." Slime crouched, prodding at the dirt. "They've been here, all right. *Rogi Kwantro,* humans." He straightened up, turning to leave.

"Where's he going?" Deke snarled. He'd been listening to the exchange, obviously not understanding a word from the scowl on his face.

"He's leaving us to our own resources. Says if we follow that path, it'll lead us to the Worts." Before she could elaborate, Slime pushed past, disappearing into the thickness of the jungle. She stared apprehensively at Deke. Now what?

A huge whoosh from behind made her whirl around with a cry of alarm. A grin spread across her face as she realized it was Wren flapping his wings.

"Whew!" Wren said. "I thought I'd never get the chance to stretch!"

"Stars, Wren!" Hedy squealed. Drained by the heat, she roused herself to watch him exercise, an enthralled look on her flushed face.

Deke rolled his eyes in Mara's direction and she grinned back. "Let's go, you two. It's getting dark," he said.

"Shouldn't we make camp here for the night?" Mara suggested hopefully. They could all use a rest.

He rubbed his unshaven jaw. "No, I'd like to reach the Wort village before it gets too late. Let's take a brief break, then continue on."

After a snack, they lifted their packs and trudged off down the new trail Slime had pointed out. A short distance later, Mara began to feel uneasy.

"You don't suppose there's any particular reason why Slime didn't want to go along with us, do you?" she asked, hustling to catch up to Deke, who'd taken the lead.

"Wait for us!" Hedy called as she and Wren scurried forward.

Mara caught the note of apprehension in her voice. She wasn't the only one feeling the jungle encroaching upon them as darkness descended. The wild cries seemed to have gotten louder and rustling noises brought shivers to her spine. Was it her imagination or were they being watched?

Deke stopped in his tracks. "Slime was telling us stories," he reassured them, picking a worm off his pants leg as easily as if it had been a speck of dust. "I don't believe the Worts would cause harm to friendly visitors. Do you?"

Before she could voice her opinion, the ground opened up beneath their feet and swallowed them.

The musty odor of mildew was the first sensation that snaked into Mara's mind as she rose through the levels of consciousness. A buzzing insect near her ear brought her fully awake. She blinked, swatting idly at it, and studied her surroundings.

Deke was out cold beside her. They lay on a bed of reeds on a wooden floor in some sort of hut. Daylight streamed in through an open doorway, beyond which she could make out the shapes of tall leafy trees. Hedy and Wren sprawled across a couple of woven mats in another corner.

Daylight? They'd been unconscious all night?

Crouching, she tested her limbs. Gratefully she noticed a lack of injuries from their fall. The pit hadn't been very deep but as soon as they'd landed, a pungent-smelling vapor had overwhelmed them.

Concerned about Deke, she checked the pulse at his throat. It felt strong and regular. Her gaze swept across his face to where a lock of hair had fallen across his forehead and she brushed it aside, letting her fingers linger on his skin. His lashes were thick and silken. Sparing a glance at his slack jawline shadowed by dark stubble, she rested her gaze on his mouth. His lips were curved with a permanent upward tilt that tantalized her.

He stirred, and she moved away quickly, afraid for him to find her hovering above him. Hoping to learn some answers by the time the others awoke, she crept toward the opening to peer outside.

By the Light! They were in a village set among the treetops far above the ground. Looking down made her reel dizzily. Entwined in the rain-forest canopy were dozens of huts like theirs with precarious ladder bridges swaying between the dwellings. The steamy humidity drenched her even as she knelt on a platform in the shade of overhanging branches. Insects were plentiful, and she swatted at a hungry mosquito, dismayed to find several welts already on her neck and bare arms. The repellent she'd applied earlier must have worn off. She hoped Deke had brought extra supplies, but that was the least of their concerns. How were they to get down? Their hut didn't possess any ladders that she could see. It was dreadfully hot and trickles of perspiration ran down the sides of her face as she leaned further over the platform's edge.

She sucked in a breath as she spotted a brown-skinned Wort who shimmied up a nearby tree trunk, clinging to the bark by thick disks on his fingers and toes. Glancing down again, she swallowed apprehensively. How had she and the others been brought here? What did the Worts plan to do with them? Would they listen to what she and Deke had to say, or did they already regard the intruders as enemies?

Peering in another direction, she noticed conveyances drawn by ropes and pulleys hauling goods to and from the structures and the ground. There were a few huts at ground level, but they appeared to be kitchens; smoke rose from chimneys in the thatched roofs. She caught a drift of the spicy aroma and decided she liked the smell. Doorways and casements were left open to the gentle breeze. From her perch, she watched her neighbor as his sticky tongue flicked out and caught a fly. Her stomach heaved and she wondered what they would be given to eat, if anything. Desperation took hold of her as she considered their plight. She was thirsty and had to use the sanitary but there weren't any facilities! Reluctantly she admitted they were being treated more like prisoners than guests and that realization heightened her fear.

A loud groan pierced her ears and she swung around to see Deke sitting up and rubbing his head.

"I feel like I've been run over by a roadbuilder," he griped. "What is this place?" His narrowed eyes surveyed their surroundings as he rose unsteadily to his feet. The top of his head touched the ceiling and he grunted his displeasure. Wren and Hedy were just beginning to stir in their corner and he spared a glance in their direction.

"Careful," Mara cautioned them as they stood, teetering confusedly. "We don't know how sturdy these wood planks are." Although the flooring seemed able to bear their weight, the Worts obviously were smaller than their burrow-dwelling cousins, the Croags. They certainly hadn't provided human visitors with any familiar amenities.

"That gas must have really knocked us out. Did you just wake up?" Deke asked her. At her nod, he scratched his head thoughtfully. "I wonder if Slime knew what was ahead. I should have taken more precautions. If I'd—"

"Deke," she interrupted before he could castigate himself further, "we're here. Accept it."

"This is a Wort village, I presume?" Deke stalked to the open platform outside and peered around. "How in Zor do we get down from here?"

She waved her arms in frustration. "We could shimmy down the tree," she joked.

To her surprise, Deke appeared to weight the option seriously, but then his steady gaze caught hers. "We've wanted to speak with the Worts."

"Yes, but not in this fashion!"

"You're right. I don't care for their methods," he said, a dangerous glint in his eye.

She put a hand on his arm. "Diplomacy might be prudent under the circumstances."

"The circumstances be damned! We could have been seriously hurt."

Hedy moved to join them. "I can't run a diagnostic on any of us. My equipment is gone."

Deke patted his pockets. "So are my datalink and my weapons."

Mara realized that the Worts had been thorough in their search. None of their knapsacks were evident in the tiny hut.

"I need to stretch my wings!" Wren said, pacing agitatedly back and forth, the top of his head brushing against the ceiling. "There's not enough room in here."

"And I need to use a sanitary," Mara confessed. "What are we going to do? We can't wait hauras until they decide to talk to us!"

"I don't think we'll have to," Deke said, his tone grim.

A movement of light outside made them all turn their heads. A lanky Wort swung through the open doorway on a vine and plunked himself down on the reed-strewn floor.

Chapter Sixteen

"*Rogi Kwantro,*" the brown-skinned male said, pounding his fist on his chest and bowing. A woven tunic and shorts covered his athletic body. "I am Onus Hahn, a member of the village council."

Mara was surprised that he spoke in standard Jawani. Following Deke's example, she extended a similar greeting.

"What's going on?" she demanded, grateful that the Wort exuded less of a fishy odor than his city-dwelling cousins. She supposed living so far from the sea might prove the discriminating factor in that regard, or the Croags might have a diet containing more fish. Whatever the reason, she was glad for the change. "Why have we been brought here in such a disagreeable manner?" Her eyes strayed to the pistol strapped at the Wort's belt and she swallowed convulsively.

Onus Hahn's keen tawny eyes regarded her. "You are the spokesperson for your group?"

She deferred to Deke. "Comdr. Sage is in charge of our expedition."

The tawny eyes glanced in Deke's direction, giving him a cursory appraisal. Mara tried to get a sensory reading but couldn't pick up any vibes, and the Wort's impassive expression told her nothing.

"For what reason do you intrude upon our land?" he asked her, eyeing her attire.

Since she was dressed identically to her teammates, she wondered at his close perusal. Someone must have searched them while they were helpless, she thought with a sudden shiver. He should know I wasn't armed.

As though sensing her discomfort, Deke sidled closer. His protective gesture strengthened her.

"We come as official representatives of the Coalition government," she said proudly. "It is imperative we discuss several issues important to us both. Our visit is friendly. There was no need for you to capture us."

"My apologies." The Wort bowed politely but his voice lacked any hint of regret. "We are not accustomed to having offworlders seek us out, and we must protect ourselves against . . . certain foes."

She wanted to question his statement, but her personal needs took precedence. "May we have the use of your, uh, private facilities?" Flushing embarrassedly, she hoped he'd get the message without further explanation.

Standing beside her, Deke clenched his fists, and she sensed he was angry at their predicament—or maybe at himself for allowing it to occur.

"It's damned hot up here. Isn't there a place on the ground where we can talk?" he gritted.

She shot him a look of reproach. His aggressive attitude wouldn't help their cause. Smiling sweetly at Onus Hahn, she tried to ameliorate the effect of Deke's demanding tone.

"Comdr. Sage wishes to meet with your council leaders. My name is Mara Hendricks. I'm his interpreter and a cultural attache in Interstellar Relations. Dr. Te'larr is our medic and Lt. Wren is . . . an administrative aide." She didn't want to name him as the ship's navigator. It might not be wise to imply they had a starship hovering in orbit. If the Worts thought they were siding with the Croags, revealing an armed presence could work against them. It was bad enough that Deke and Wren had been caught bearing arms, although trekking through the jungle presented its own hazards.

The Wort pursed his lips thoughtfully. "Let us go to the Council Hall. I will summon our leaders."

Stalking to the open doorway, he signaled for a conveyance slung on a rope. While helping them to step onto it, he darted his sticky pink tongue out to snare a gnat.

Lowered to the ground, Mara and the others followed Onus Hahn to a rectangular wood structure set on stilts in the center of the village. As they passed by various structures, the residents turned their heads in surprise. She was stunned that many of them bore arms, males and females alike. Were they engaged in warfare, and if so, with whom? Or was it mere precaution from the wild beasts that roamed the jungle?

Hedy poked her on the arm. "Mara," the brunette whispered, "their features are similar to the terrorists who fired upon us in town!"

Her eyes widened. She'd almost forgotten the incident in her eagerness to speak to the Worts about Yanuran politics. They could be among the very band of ruffians who tried to bomb Hedy and Wren! It certainly would account for the weapons if the Worts were waging their own brand of terrorism against the Croags. And if that were truly the case, how would they regard a group of Coalition representatives?

"This is the Council Hall," Onus Hahn intoned, leading them inside the rectangular building. He gestured at a conference table resting low to the floor. "Sanitary facilities are in the rear behind that partition. Make yourselves comfortable while I round up the others and arrange for refreshments."

While he was gone, they held a hushed conference.

"I don't trust them," Deke said, his expression grim. "This is the area where Larikk disappeared. You can see they don't take kindly to strangers." He glared at them as though trying to convince them he was right. "Be alert. We'll have to watch for a means of escape."

"The Worts were responsible for killing those people in town!" Hedy exclaimed. "They attacked me and Wren. What are they going to do with us now?"

Mara gave her a sympathetic glance. Hedy appeared wilted, drained of her usual energy. Even the sprightly medic was beginning to feel the result of the heat and anxiety. Laying a hand on her arm, she reassured her friend.

"Onus Hahn appears to be treating us with respect, so I wouldn't worry in that regard. As for the Worts attacking you, we only have Fromoth Trun's word on who was responsible. I think we should ask these people about it ourselves."

"Another thing," Wren cut in. They whipped their heads in his direction. Usually he preferred to listen silently, speaking only when he had something important to say. "Did you notice how there were no youngsters in the village?"

She gasped. "You're right! How very odd." An image of Jallyn came to mind, bringing with it the harsh reality of the situation. "By the Light, do you think they know where Jallyn is being held?"

"Ask them," Deke suggested, giving her a dark, sardonic look. "You seem so willing to believe in the goodness of other people's souls. See how much they're willing to tell you."

Challenged, she glared back. "And you're too eager to mistrust them. Try having an open mind, Commander. You might be able to deal with them more effectively if every word out of your mouth isn't laden with hostility."

"See if you can get our knapsacks returned," Hedy urged. "I'd like my medical equipment back." She took Mara's arm. "Let's go get washed. You said you needed to use the sanitary."

Inside the washroom, Mara finished her ablutions, then turned to Hedy. "He's as pigheaded as ever," she announced, retying her long hair into a low ponytail.

"Who is?" Hedy's green eyes regarded her innocently although a small smile played about her mouth. Tugging her treksuit into place, she smoothed it over her hips.

"Deke, that's who. He suspects these people of all sorts of dire doings."

Hedy snorted. "And you don't? Sweetheart, do you need an awakening! I hate to admit it, but I agree with your lover boy."

Her face flushed at the term. "How can you agree with him? We haven't even spoken to their council yet. The Worts may know nothing about Jallyn or Larikk or who attacked you and Wren the other day."

"Are you calling Fromoth Trun a liar? Because if you believe the Worts are innocent, then you're saying the Yanuran leader has been telling fibs."

She planted her hands on her hips. "I'm not saying they're innocent. Gods, you're just as blind as Deke! All I want is for both sides to get a fair evaluation."

Hedy gave a long sigh. "I swear, Mara, someday you'll wear me thin. You're just obsessed with fairness because you were never treated that way. Don't you have faith in your man? Deke is willing to listen to them. He's going into this with his eyes open, that's all."

"No, he's not. He views the Worts as murderers."

"I can understand why. Didn't you see the weapons they're carrying? And their manner of greeting visitors isn't exactly courtesy personified." Hedy began walking out.

"Wait!" she called, stricken that she might have offended her friend. "All right, I admit Deke might be correct. Is that what you want me to say?"

"No," Hedy said gently, "I just want you to be prepared."

Be prepared. Those were Deke's words. And hadn't he been right before? Maybe she should listen to his advice. Being too trusting was one of her faults, as he'd so readily pointed out to her. It wasn't always appropriate to give the other person the benefit of the doubt, especially when they were at a disadvantage.

Her senses alert, she strode into the meeting hall to take her seat next to Deke at the long table. Hedy joined Wren at the opposite side. They sat cross-legged on the wood-planked floor. A trio of Wort females had entered and were placing a selection of fruits and nuts and a pitcher of drinking water in front of them.

Mara grabbed a glass of water and drank greedily. She felt better after using the sanitary and splashing cold water on her face, but her treksuit stuck to her body in the humidity. The hall was open to the air, with ceiling fans lazily rotating overhead, providing a warm breeze. This is why I never cared for the tropics, she told herself. Heat, humidity, and bugs. She much preferred the temperate zone of her home on Tyberia, where the nights were cool and even in summer the temperature never soared to sweat levels.

She was surprised when Deke reached over and squeezed one of her hands. The warmth from his skin penetrated her, enervating her. She glanced at him, stunned at the look of tenderness on his face that was quickly hidden as Onus Hahn strode inside accompanied by four other males. The females who'd served them took places around the table, causing her to raise her eyebrows. Gender equality seemed to be the norm everywhere on Yanura and that part of their society she approved of vigorously.

Deke withdrew his hand from hers but then rested it on her thigh under the table where no one could see. She wondered if he sought reassurance by touching her, or if he was attempting to provide her with courage. Either way, the contact warmed her heart and made her soul yearn to break free and merge with his. It was all she could do to sit still and act composed with the Worts staring at them.

Onus Hahn began cleaning his teeth with a splinter of wood. "Explain your purpose in coming here," he ordered, directing his statement at her.

Deke responded before she could get in a word. "Fromoth Trun seeks membership in the Coalition of Sentient Planets. As planetary potentate, he represents the central authority. How much of a voice do you have in the government?"

One of the elder females replied. "I am Onus Laang and I sit on the Wort Elective Caucus, which is our main governing body. We agree with the Croags in the manner of government."

"Does that mean your vote is counted equally?" Deke persisted.

Onus Laang shifted in her seat. "It means we are satisfied with the status quo, Commander."

From the corner of her eye, Mara saw one of the younger females nervously drum her fingers on the table. Studying the council member, Mara saw she was fairly attractive, with large brown eyes and an upcurved mouth. Her dress was a pretty shade of rose enhanced by a white apron. For a moment it looked as though she would say something, but then her expression clouded and the moment was lost.

"How do your people feel about membership in the Coalition?" Mara asked, staring at the female. The Wort averted her eyes, focusing her gaze on the table.

"As a group, we have no objections to joining the Coalition as long as our privacy is respected," said one of the elder male members. "Our territorial integrity must be honored. The Croags seek to push us from our land by cutting down our trees."

"Fromoth Trun says the opposite," Deke countered, leaning forward. "He claims you're destroying the burrows by extending tree roots into the underground network."

Onus Hahn's face mottled as he cut into the conversation. "Not so! We can show you proof of the damage his people are causing our habitats."

"Fromoth Trun says a satellite survey would settle the boundary dispute."

The Worts cast surreptitious glances among themselves. "That is so," agreed Onus Laang. "If Coalition membership is granted, our dispute would be solved. We can arrange for a commlink, Commander, should you wish to contact Bimordus Two."

"I'd like my own datalink returned, thank you, and our other equipment."

"Of course." Nodding to the younger Wort, Onus Laang gave Deke a sly smile. "My apologies for the inconvenience. Since you came from Croag territory, we couldn't be sure of your loyalties. Your items will be returned at once." She watched the junior member scurry off.

Deke tightened his mouth, and from the pressure of his hand on her thigh, Mara could tell he wasn't satisfied with the flimsy excuse for their reception. Thankfully he let it go, changing the subject with his next statement.

"Fromoth Trun offers the drug Vyclor as an economic incentive so Yanura can be granted special trade status," Deke said, his mild tone disguising the tension radiating from his body.

"Of course," Onus Laang crooned, "otherwise we'd have to wait the standard probationary period before being granted trading privileges. We cannot afford the time. As Fromoth Trun says, the satellite survey is the definitive means to achieving peace."

Onus Hahn wasn't so polite. Leaning forward, he croaked, "Shall I show you where his people have destroyed our forest? The plant and animal life dependent upon the tall trees have perished in that area. It will be the fate of our entire habitat unless the Croags are stopped. They will only listen when the Coalition shares its advanced survey techniques."

"The Coalition will not grant approval when I tell them how our team was attacked by terrorists in Revitt Lake City," Deke countered. "Fromoth Trun claims your people were responsible. He says you wage a terrorist war in order to be granted extra land."

Onus Laang's eyes narrowed. "We are a nonviolent people! I know nothing of this attack. Fromoth Trun lies! He must have staged the act himself to prejudice you against us."

"Maybe there are those among you who take it upon themselves to—"

"No! My people would never resort to terrorist tactics." Her eyes darkened with fury. "It is not of us that he speaks. It is the—"

"*Golongus!*" screamed Onus Hahn in his native tongue.

Onus Laang's skin paled to light green. "Forgive me, Commander. I get upset over this situation."

The young female Wort returned with their supplies, interrupting the conversation. After piling the knapsacks in a corner, she resumed her seat and sat quietly, her eyes averted from Mara's probing stare.

Wren coughed, adjusting his position. He looked fidgety and uncomfortable and Mara wondered if he'd had a chance to spread his wings while she and Hedy were in the sanitary.

"What about your friend?" Wren asked Deke, giving him a pointed stare.

Deke nodded. "My friend Larikk, a researcher, vanished in the Alterland three annums ago. Have you any information about him that you can share?"

"An inquiry has already been completed," Onus Hahn snapped. "His death was ruled an accidental drowning."

"Did it occur near here?"

The Wort shrugged. "I am not familiar with the details."

Mara sensed prevarication, but then Hedy cut in, disrupting her train of thought.

"Where are the children?" the medic asked, her tone meek.

Mara suppressed a smile. Medical rounds were Hedy's forte, not matters of state. She had to be feeling disoriented by this entire situation, but at least Wren offered her some consolation.

"Pardon?" Onus Hahn said, his expression bewildered.

"The youngsters. How come we see only adults? Where do you house the children?" Mara clarified.

The young female Wort gave a choking sputter, abruptly cut off at a stern glance from Onus Laang.

The elder council member beamed widely, her smile expansive. "They stay in separate dwellings."

"May we visit them?" she asked eagerly.

"I'm afraid not. We don't want them exposed to outsiders. The contamination would be detrimental to our culture."

She got a distinct sense that Onus Laang was lying and wondered how much of the truth about anything had been spoken in this room. The young female exchanged a glance with her, then quickly lowered her eyes. It looked as though she'd speak if given the chance in private, she thought, but how to arrange it?

"What is your name?" she asked in a kindly tone.

"I am called Onus Laola, mistress." She darted a nervous glance at Onus Laang. "I am honored to be the newest council member, but I have much to learn."

"Thank you for fetching our belongings."

"I regret the necessity of taking them from you. It was our intention—"

"That's enough," Onus Hahn interrupted. "Would you like to see where our trees have been cut down by the Croags?" He addressed his offer to Deke. "It would be my pleasure to conduct you on a tour. Once you see the destruction, you'll agree it is imperative to relay approval of our admission status to your superiors."

Mara felt a twinge of annoyance at his insistence. He sounded like a parrot of Fromoth Trun. Both of them blamed each other's people for the border dispute but felt admittance into the Coalition would solve their problems. Or would it? What if they wanted to be granted special trade status for some other reason? What could they possibly hope to gain?

They'd reap huge profits from putting Vyclor on the market, she reminded herself. But how would they use the credits gained? Would they buy something that wasn't accessible through other means?

Seeing that Deke and the others were rising, she got up and stretched. It should be interesting to see the destruction Onus Hahn claimed was created by the Croags.

Accompanied by the village leader and a squad of hefty armed males, she and the others were taken via winged pod to a sector where whole tracts of trees had been ravaged, leaving nothing but loose soil easily dislodged by a strong wind. A wide swath of destruction was cut, brutal and devastating to the land. She was sickened.

"How could they do this?" she cried, sweeping her arm in the air. "Even if these trees weren't your home, how could anyone cause such massive rape of the land?"

"Talk to Fromoth Trun," Onus Hahn urged. "The Croags use the wood from our trees to make their furniture, which is widely prized throughout the land, but they destroy our environment in the process. Ask him why he's engaged in a purposeful annihilation of our homes. Now will you contact your base and recommend approval of our application? Use of the Coalition's resources is the only way we'll stop this massive destruction."

Deke's face darkened, and she feared he was going to blurt out something offensive.

"Can we return to Revitt Lake City from here?" she asked hastily.

"Traversing this terrain is hazardous. There are other routes that are . . . friendlier. Come, it is not wise to linger here."

She felt discomfited by the watchful stance of the armed guards who'd accompanied them. The escort reminded her of the security detachment Fromoth Trun had provided, and that in turn brought to mind a subject that troubled her. "If your people were not responsible for the terrorist attack on Hedy and Wren, then who was?" she queried, her brow furrowing in puzzlement.

Onus Hahn's skin mottled, emphasizing the ugly raised dark spots that dotted his brown exterior. "I wouldn't know, mistress. But I can tell you this is a border area, and I cannot vouch for your safety despite our precautions. Let us depart." His eyes darted about nervously as though expecting those same terrorists to pop out of the ground. "We can talk about your return voyage more comfortably in the village."

Deke gave her a questioning glance. She shrugged uncertainly and cocked her head, indicating they should comply. Besides, it wouldn't hurt to spend more time among the Worts. Perhaps she'd find the opportunity to talk to Onus Laola.

"We'd like to stay in your village for a few days," she said to Onus Hahn. "Would you mind?" Glancing anxiously at Deke, she was relieved when he gave her an answering nod of approval.

Flying in on the winged pod, Onus Hahn gave a loud croak to alert his fellow Worts of their approach. "We'd be honored," he replied, his tone guarded. She picked up on his hesitation but didn't have time to wonder what it meant because the thatched roofs of the tree dwellings were dead ahead.

The guest quarters they were given were much more luxurious than the hut in which they first awoke. Two bungalows high in the treetops were made available, accessible by a rope-and-pulley conveyance. The two lodgings were linked by a short log bridge. Twin beds that could be pushed together to form a wide lounger or separated to serve as couches made up the interior along with a wood bureau, a small table, and chairs. Electrical conveniences were noticeably absent.

"I could give you quarters on the ground but they're often visited by creatures of the night, which are tasty to our palate but disagreeable to you. Will these be suitable?" Onus Hahn showed them how to use the conveyance and pointed out the closest sanitary facility on the ground below. Running water was available from a spigot in a corner connected to a pipe leading outside to a central storage tank.

"Our manner of subsistence is simple but we prefer to live off the land," he explained. "Since the light is not strong in the forest, we accomplish our work during the late-afternoon hauras. Our rest time is between midnight and noon. While you're here I'll make sure flametorches are lit after dark. Please join us tonight for evening nourishment. In the meantime, if you need anything, blow this horn." He indicated a tubular object by the open-air entrance. "I'll have netting brought over to screen your casements and doorways." Grinning avariciously, he darted his tongue out to catch a fly. "You should find our meal to be . . . an interesting diversion."

"Yecch!" Hedy exclaimed as soon as he'd left. "I can just imagine what they'll give us to eat. Worms and roaches and other crawly critters if we're lucky."

"I think there's a pond nearby. Maybe they'll have freshwater snipes," Deke said with a teasing grin.

Mara felt her stomach heave. "I'm sure they'll have some fruits and nuts like they gave us before."

"Did you notice our weapons are missing, sir?" Wren asked, crouching on the floor and thumbing through his knapsack.

Deke frowned. "I'm not surprised. Something strikes me as odd about this place."

"Me too," Mara agreed, glad they'd found some common ground. She loosened her hair from its ponytail and shook it free, gratified to find Deke's eyes following her movements.

Hedy's gaze rested upon them thoughtfully. "Wren, let's go into our place," she urged, indicating he should grab his equipment and follow her to the other hut.

"*Huh?*" Mara and the two men asked in unison.

Hedy squeezed the Polluxite's arm. "We have things to discuss," she said, signaling him with her eyes.

Wren glanced from her to Deke and Mara and his visage reddened. "Oh . . . yes. I shall join you, Doctor." As an afterthought, he raised a layered eyebrow toward Deke. "With your permission, sir?"

Deke's mouth twisted wryly. "Go ahead, and enjoy yourselves."

Mara's jaw dropped. She hadn't expected him to approve! Watching with dismay as Hedy and Wren tramped across the short bridge and disappeared into the open doorway beyond, she swallowed apprehensively.

"Why?" she asked him, seeking clarification.

"Why what?" Deke busied himself unpacking his supplies. His broad back stretched the material of his treksuit taut, and she couldn't help focusing on the ripple of muscles displayed as he moved.

Licking her lips, which had suddenly gone dry, she said: "Why did you agree to share with me? I thought you preferred to avoid my company."

He straightened, giving a resigned sigh. "I can no more avoid you than I can avoid thinking. I'm just confused, Mara. You invade my mind even when you're not there, if you get the gist of my meaning."

His eyes burned into her and she looked away, flushing under his close scrutiny. "I've been trying not to push you."

"But I still feel the pressure. What if we let things go along, Mara? What then?"

Now she was confused. "I don't understand."

"Would you go back to Eranus with me?"

Hope flared within her. "Is that an invitation?" she asked.

"It's a matter of curiosity. If we decided to stay together, what were your plans?"

Deflated by his impersonal attitude, she mumbled her reply. "I . . . I hadn't thought that far ahead."

"Impulsive, aren't you?" he drawled. "Are you telling me that for all your claims that we're meant to be together, you've never considered what it means?"

She shrugged helplessly. "I never really thought that you would—"

"What?"

"Accept me," she finished lamely, her head lowered.

For a long moment he didn't answer; then he strode over and rested his hands on her shoulders. "Mara, look at me."

She lifted her face to gaze into his soul-searing brown eyes.

"If it were just you, I'd take you home in an instant. But it's more than that. You have a power that goes beyond my comprehension. It frightens me because I lose my focus when I'm with you."

"But I don't intend for you to lose anything. We can share our experiences, Deke. That's the joy of it. You don't have to be alone anymore."

"I'm used to being alone, to having my thoughts to myself. I don't like someone else being in my head."

"I can't read your thoughts," she reminded him gently.

"No, but you can sense what I'm feeling." His hand reached up to smooth her hair. "It's hard to resist when I'm with you. I don't mind the enhancement during sex, but—"

She pulled away. "That's not fair! You can't use me to heighten your pleasure and then cast me off."

He stepped closer, his eyes luminous with desire. "You can't deny that you like it, too."

"No, but I want more than that."

"I can't give you more."

"Can't, or won't?"

Pulling her into his arms, he buried his face in her hair. "Help me, Mara. I really don't know what I want anymore."

The moment was broken by the arrival of their mosquito netting, which made an effective privacy screen on the casements and entrance. When the Wort had left, she turned back to Deke, who was testing the mattress on one of the beds.

"I didn't bring anything to change into other than a clean treksuit," she said.

Deke grinned lasciviously. "That's all right. You don't have to wear anything to bed." His expression sobered. "I won't take advantage of you. It's your choice, Mara. You know my limits."

He'd certainly made them clear. He was still willing to have sex with her but nothing more. Depressed, she picked up her knapsack and began fumbling through the contents.

Deke glanced up. "Look, I'm sorry," he said, his voice earnest. "You're right, I'm not playing fair. I really don't understand what you want from me. What's in this for you? Why me?"

She gave a wan smile. "I can't help the way I feel." How could she explain the yearning to merge with him, to be as close to him as possible on all levels of their existence? Her need went beyond the physical realm.

Deke dashed a hand through his ruffled hair. "Gods, you drive me crazy. What am I going to do with you?" As soon as the words left his mouth, the idea of what he'd like to do showed in the fevered gleam in his eyes. "Hedy and Wren had the right idea," he said, sauntering toward her.

"Now just a minute. You said you wouldn't take advantage of me!" But even as she protested, her blood heated and her senses whirled dizzily.

"Did I tell you how much I love your hair?" he asked, halting in front of her and taking a few strands in his hand. "It feels like silk." He took some in his other hand and brought it forward, letting her hair flow over the rise of her breasts.

Her pulse quickened as he stared at her chest. His nearness weakened her knees and sent a flood of desire coursing through her. Her nipples strained through the fabric of her treksuit, aching for his touch.

As though he sensed her reaction, a slow smile curved his mouth. "You want this as much as I do, don't you?" he said huskily.

When his heavy-lidded gaze met hers, her resistance

melted. As though her body had a will of its own, she moved forward so that they were a hairbreadth apart. "Yes," she said, barely recognizing the passionate tone as her own. She couldn't help it. The temptation to merge with him was strong, and if he would accept her this way, so be it. Besides, he was right. Her nerves tingled with the anticipation of his touch.

Thrusting her breasts forward until they touched his massive chest, she wrapped her arms around him. "Kiss me," she demanded.

He took her mouth eagerly, lustily. Crushing her in his embrace, he plundered her sweetness without any trace of gentleness. She felt his hunger for her even as she parted her lips to receive his tongue. Their kiss mingled them until they became one, writhing against each other with need.

Still holding her against him, Deke edged her toward one of the beds. They fell upon it with their limbs entangled, mouth to mouth, unable to separate either physically or spiritually. Mara reveled in the feel of his hard body against hers but it wasn't enough. She craved contact with his naked flesh.

It took them a moment to shed their clothes and then they were back, entwined on the firm mattress, their mouths clamped together. Deke's hands roamed her body and she moaned from the sheer pleasure of it. Everywhere he touched, her senses flared and ripples of ecstasy radiated through her. She gripped his back, clutching at it, relishing the hard strength of his muscles as he moved against her. Her breasts pressed flat against his hairy chest and the feel of him aroused her beyond belief. Grinding against him, she felt his engorged manhood prod her thighs and she parted her legs, wanting him at once and yet wishing this would never end.

Her eyes closed, she concentrated on the sensations of his mouth on hers, his tongue exploring her depths. Merged with his psyche, she felt his pleasure from the contact between them, and his wish to prolong their delight as long as possible. With an iron will, he was restraining his powerful urge to thrust into her and to climax. Knowing that he wanted her to be satisfied hurled her further into the inferno of desire.

His hands found her breasts and she gasped with delight as he teased her nipples into taut, aching peaks. That he knew what to do to please her because he could feel her reactions increased her desire. She arched her back, thrusting her breasts more completely into his practiced hands. A sound of pleasure escaped her lips as he gently massaged her breasts, his thumbs stroking her nipples. The tingling sensations he provoked shot through her.

He shifted his position, moving his mouth to her nipple, suckling it with his swirling tongue. She thought she'd go mad with passion. Her head lolled back and she spread her legs, so intense was the ache between them. Deke's hand found her secret folds of flesh that yearned for his touch and obliged her, the circular strokes sending her into a spiral of ecstasy.

She grasped for him, taking his shaft into her hand, and was gratified to hear his sharp intake of breath. It was amazing how incredible it felt from his viewpoint, the pressure of her hand on his swollen tip. She caressed the petal-soft skin and didn't stop when his head raised and he gazed at her with passion-filled eyes.

"Mara, I don't ever want this to end," he rasped.

"Neither do I."

But she couldn't help raising herself over him, still holding on to his shaft. The temptation to impale herself was too great, her need to feel his fullness inside her too strong. She lowered herself onto him, smiling when his head fell back and he moaned in total abandonment. Slowly, she slid down the full length of him, reveling in the pleasure of their union.

"By the stars, Mara!" he exclaimed, his eyes squeezed shut. "I've never felt such wonder!"

She felt his wild need for gratification and began moving her hips, tantalizingly slow at first, then spiraling to a speed she couldn't control. Her own lust took hold of her, propelling her into a pool of hot, molten desire, and she cried out as it spurred her forward, rushing her down a river of passion toward a cataclysmic explosion. Her body jerked with tremors as her pleasure ignited into a fiery eruption, and she barely felt Deke's seed spurting into her.

Her body sweaty from lust, she rolled off him and lay exhausted on the bed beside him. Her mind took longer to separate. In the haze of her satiation, she couldn't tell which one of them was feeling what emotion. Contentment snared both of them and the web of their desire was merely loosened, not abated. Letting her spirit float free within him, she reveled in the joy of their union and knew he was sharing her pleasure.

His hand snaked over to grasp hers. "Gods, Mara, I don't want to let go of you," he murmured even as she sensed his response.

"It feels right, doesn't it?" she said, her voice trembling with emotion.

His eyes closed, he admitted his affirmation silently, and she picked up on it in his mind.

"Then why do you resist?" she whispered.

His lids flew open and she was thrust from his psyche. "Because I'd be tempted to stay in this village forever, to succumb to this life-style. You and me . . . in our own hut. Why should we leave?" His troubled gaze fell upon her. "I resist because this is the result. You make me forget my responsibilities, my identity. I have a duty to perform, and I can't do it when your presence drives me mad. Have you forgotten about Jallyn?"

His words brought her back to reality with an icy jolt. "Of course not. But there's no harm in—"

"Isn't there?" He sat up, rubbing his jaw. "Every time I'm with you, I lose my mind. You take over. How can I function like that? And even when we're not in the same room it happens. I can't go through life being so distracted."

"You're distracted because you can't accept what's happening between us. If you would, our merging would strengthen you. It doesn't have to take you from your duty." Even as she spoke, her heart sank. In the throes of passion, Deke wanted her. He shared in the pleasure of their joined souls when they made love. But when reality intervened he cast her aside like a pariah.

"I've got work to do," he said, his cold tone effectively shutting her out.

Swinging his legs over the side of the bed, he stood, but then as an afterthought, he turned to her, his eyes shining brightly. "I do care for you, Mara. At one time I wanted to bed you just because you were another desirable woman. But I don't feel that way now."

"Really?" she asked, her expression cool.

A mixture of emotions crossed his face: bewilderment, fear, longing, and regret. "I . . . I need time. I'm not sure—"

"Take all the time you want." She flipped herself off the other side of the bed and grabbed her clothes. "I'll try not to interfere."

"I'm really messing this up, aren't I?" he said.

"You do what you have to. Me, I know when I'm not wanted." Yanking her clothes on, she had just finished fastening the treksuit when someone lifted a corner of the screen netting and tossed an object inside the hut.

Chapter Seventeen

Deke's purposeful stride took him to the fallen object by the door. "It's a rock with a note tied around the middle," he said, a look of puzzlement on his face. Stooping down, he untied the piece of paper.

"Let me see!" Mara rushed over, watching as he straightened. "What does it say?" she asked eagerly.

He frowned as his eyes scanned the message. "Take a look for yourself."

She grabbed the paper from his outstretched palm. The words, scrawled by hand, jumped out at her:

Go back home! You make danger here.

"By the Light!" she whispered, her voice trembling with fear. "What can this mean?"

"I don't know," he said, "but you can be sure I'll find out soon." Hastily he pulled on his clothes. Taking the note from her, he tucked it into his treksuit pocket. "Let's go."

She stopped him with a hand on his arm. "Wait," she pleaded. "It might be better if we pretend we never got this message. I'd like to explore the village, and if we proceed normally we might find someone willing to talk to us. Aren't you curious as to why nearly everyone we've seen carries a weapon?"

For a long moment Deke stared at her, and she became aware of the heat radiating from his skin.

"You're right," he agreed, taking a step back. "It reminds me of Fromoth Trun's security detail guarding us in Revitt Lake City. You'd think these people were expecting an attack."

"Or maybe they're the ones instigating them."

"That's not what Onus Hahn told us. He said the Worts were not responsible for the terrorist incident. And if they weren't, where did those guerrillas originate?"

Shrugging, she said, "We're not going to find any answers waiting around here. Let's get Hedy and Wren and explore the village. I'm hoping for a chance to talk to the young Wort female who was in the council chamber. She seemed as though she'd be willing to talk if I could visit her in private."

Hedy and Wren seemed glad for the excuse to leave their hut. From the flustered look on the Polluxite's face, Mara surmised Hedy must have been giving Wren a hard time. She and her friend fell behind the men as they descended in the rickety rope-and-pulley contraption to the ground.

The scene that greeted their eyes was fascinating from Mara's viewpoint. While most of the Worts kept their residences up in the trees, their workplaces and kitchens were located at ground level. Across a dirt path, she spied an old female painting flowers on an intricately designed porcelain basket. She rushed over, eager to inspect the wares.

"These are lovely!" Mara exclaimed, running the tip of

her finger along the curved rim of a vase displayed on a shelf. The statuettes, vases, pitchers, and other items all bore an amazing creamy translucence and delicate structure. "I do sculpture work myself and I've never seen material like this before. How do you get this iridescent tint and the smooth texture?"

The old Wort's face crinkled with pleasure. "I use a special process to create this result. The white clay comes from the Lorn province to the north."

"It's wonderful," she said admiringly. With a series of well-placed questions, she encouraged the female to expound upon the skills of her comrades. Rope making, basket weaving, and making kalucha-nut jewelry were popular pastimes. As for industries, collecting gold lace and researching natural resources for the large pharmaceutical concerns were the main occupations.

"Gold lace?" Mara queried, scratching an itch on her neck. "What's that?"

The female's wizened face regarded her with interest. "It's a filament secreted by the walloie larvae. Harvesting it is delicate business; we don't want to harm the organism. Our trained guild members work the filament into lace."

"I see. So your businesses are organized into guilds."

"Aye, mistress. The master guilder is at the top of the guild. Below him are journeymen such as myself. We train through an apprentice system."

"Of course." She was familiar with other cultures that used similar practices. Still intrigued by the beautiful porcelain objects, she asked the woman about the glazing process.

As Mara conversed with the old Wort female, Deke watched from across the pathway. How easily Mara gets along with almost anyone, he thought admiringly. Charming the artisan seemed as commonplace to her as steering Fromoth Trun's flattery into meaningful dialogue. Whether she was with a planetary leader or an ordinary citizen, Mara's skills served her well in conducting interviews, and he realized how much he'd come to rely on her. Not only was she acting as his interpreter, but she complemented him by taking the edge off his bluntness with her diplomatic aplomb. Sometimes he lost patience with people like Fromoth Trun, and Mara was handy to have around in those instances. She reminded him to exercise tolerance, as she would fondly say. Like a ship on the stormy sea, her calm serenity offered a refuge. The temptation to seek harbor with her lingered in his consciousness, drawing him toward her like a diver in a whirlpool. The only thing that kept him from being sucked under was his fear that he wouldn't be able to surface. Yet beneath the depths awaited a sea of contentment such as he'd ever known and wouldn't ever discover with another woman.

Her arms moved in graceful arcs as she spoke to the Wort female. Seeing her so animated brought to mind her talent as a dancer and skill as a sculptress. Life with Mara would never be boring. Her varied interests and quick wit guaranteed she'd keep any man on his toes. A sense of jealousy swept him as he imagined her entertaining another man and with a shock he realized he'd already come to view her as his own.

"Commander!" Onus Laola's voice startled him out of his thoughts.

Deke whipped his head around and spied the young female council member hurrying toward him. Garbed in a bright yellow dress, her head was devoid of the fancy bonnet preferred by her city-dwelling cousins.

"*Rogi Kwantro,*" she greeted him, her smile warm and friendly. "If you and your comrades will follow me, we shall make for evening nourishment."

* * *

Mara disengaged herself from her conversation to join her companions. "The porcelain maker was telling me how she creates her lovely pieces," she said, smoothing a strand of hair off her face. "She received her training from the master sculptor beginning at age fifteen. Is that the norm for learning a craft?"

Onus Laola nodded in silent response as she and Mara strolled ahead of the others toward an unfamiliar section of the village. Rounding a bend, Mara was delighted to come upon a communal dining hall, a large open-air structure on stilts erected next to a kitchen hut. At Onus Laola's direction, she and her friends climbed a short flight of steps to enter and sat themselves around one of the long rectangular tables provided with carved wooden chairs. Other Worts began filing in as a loud gong clanged to announce the dinner haura. Onus Hahn, smiling broadly, introduced them as "Coalition visitors eager to learn about our culture."

Their attempts to ask pointed questions were skillfully parried, but she managed to coax Onus Hahn into talking about economics.

"Our gold lace, prized porcelain, and certain plant and animal products valued for their medicinal properties are sold to the Croags by members of our merchant guild. In return we buy sluer oil that fuels the few electrical devices we own, such as disposers and cleansing units."

"We see no need to invite the wildlife of the area to share our bounty by not disposing of our trash," broke in an attractive older female beside Mara. "And why not avail ourselves of mechanical labor-saving devices when it comes to washing clothes?"

"For that matter, why not use fabricators?" Deke asked.

Mara gave him a sideways glance. His hulking presence gave her a measure of security. She wouldn't have wanted to be the sole representative of the Coalition in a place like this. An undercurrent of restraint was shared by the Worts and she sensed they were purposefully steering the conversation in a direction more to their liking.

"Fresh, natural foods are more palatable than artificially synthesized molecules," the female told Mara. "We believe if a society relies too heavily on technology, it loses sight of its origins."

"I disagree," Deke said, hunching forward. "On Eranus, we use the most advanced technological tools available, but our laws protect the environment. We value our resources and seek to preserve them."

"But your laws are not all-encompassing, are they, Commander?" Onus Laang said from across the table. Slurping from a bowl of conkfish soup, she eyed him warily. "Isn't it a point of contention that your automated kelp harvesters destroy the crop in the process of cutting the stipes? Weren't you involved in an effort to modify this practice?"

Deke stiffened. "How do you know about that?" He shook his head when offered a second helping of pureed nog fungus.

"We try to stay informed." She smiled smugly. "An exchange of scientific data between our worlds could be beneficial to us both."

Mara glanced at Deke. Hadn't Fromoth Trun said something similar? From the way Deke's eyebrows arched, she realized he knew they were baiting him. But for what purpose? Averting her eyes, she studied the sly look on the older Wort's face.

Onus Laola commented from further down the table. "We have medicines other than Vyclor that your people would find helpful," she said in a shy tone, "and by-products of our plants are useful in commercial applications. Pharmaceutical research is our main industry, and we've made many discoveries."

Wren cleared his throat loudly. Having been engaged in conversation with a hefty male Wort at his side, he'd broken off his dialogue to listen to their exchange. Hedy was being unusually quiet and Mara had the feeling she was deliberating on how to get Wren into her bed when they were alone later.

Deke hadn't missed Wren's signal. "Speaking of pharmaceutical research," he said, "what happened to my friend Larikk? I want details!"

"An unfortunate accident," Onus Hahn crooned, dropping a live slug into his mouth. "He was last seen heading in the direction of Dead Wort's Marsh."

"Where's that?" Deke asked sharply.

Mara sat up straighter. This was the first concrete information they'd received regarding Larikk's fate.

Onus Hahn waved a hand in the air as though dismissing the subject. "It's a dangerous place. He was warned not to go, but his notebook was found beside one of the ponds. We assumed he leaned over too far to collect a specimen and toppled in. The stinger eels would have taken care of him."

"Stinger eels?" Deke said harshly. The look on his face was one of skepticism, and Mara didn't blame him. Why were they being given this information now?

"The eels live in the ponds and their sting is lethal. Our people avoid the area but your friend apparently didn't heed the warnings."

"What happened to his notebook?"

Deke's voice choked with emotion, and Mara closed her hand over his palm under the table, offering solace. She sensed how upset he felt over the painful memories of his friend and remembered that the first time she'd separated with him, she had sensed that he considered himself responsible for sending Larikk here.

"His research notes were sent to Seabase Pharmaceutical's central office. From what I understand, the work on the vaccine was completed."

"Why wasn't I notified? And why was this information being kept secret? Why are you telling me now?"

Onus Hahn's tongue flicked out and he caught a flying insect for his dessert. "The inquiry into Larikk's death was distressful to us, Commander. But I wish to demonstrate our good intentions to you, because we would benefit from Coalition technology as much as our Croag cousins. It would be unfortunate if a misunderstanding between our peoples colored your judgment."

He grinned broadly. "Now that there are no secrets between us, perhaps you'll be reasonable. I can set up a commlink so you can send an affirmative message to your superiors."

"I'll think about it," Deke replied tersely.

Under the table, Mara squeezed his hand. She sensed his inner surge of anger and felt they'd learned as much as they could during this discussion. A more subtle approach might earn them further rewards, but not now. There were still too many unanswered questions, such as how the Worts had access to information supposedly known only to the Croags. According to Fromoth Trun, the two races rarely communicated with each other, yet some of Onus Hahn's phrases seemed a duplicate of the Yanuran leader's convincing arguments. Frowning, she wondered why she felt they still weren't being told everything.

"Let us make for the Ceremonial Circle," Onus Laang suggested, rising abruptly. Her movement signaled an end to the meal. "We have a special entertainment planned for you tonight."

Onus Hahn gave a loud croak, his version of a belch. He fell into step behind Deke and Mara as they descended the stairs outside the hut. As the oppressive humidity hit her full force, Mara felt as though she could have sliced through the air with a knife. The sun had descended but the temperature was still warm and sweat beaded her brow. Night sounds of the jungle began to intrude into her consciousness. Whistles, howls, and whoops came from every direction, startling her so that she grabbed on to Deke's arm. Gratefully, she noticed that torches had been lit for their benefit, illuminating the paths around the village. Streaks of green light pulsated in the darkness of the jungle beyond where the black shapes of trees loomed like eerie shadows.

They followed Onus Laang to a large clearing where a series of cut logs were roughly arranged in a broad circle. Hedy and Wren were close behind. They were holding hands, and Hedy had a satisfied expression on her face. Mara wondered what had occurred between them to erase Hedy's glumness but didn't have time to ask. Their friends were guided to a perch on the opposite side of the circle to where she and Deke were seated. Onus Hahn flanked Deke while Onus Laang took her place at Mara's side.

"We celebrate our communion with nature in a series of ritual dances," Onus Laang said. "Our most talented performers are preparing a demonstration for you."

Mara's eyes lit up. "I love native dances! Perhaps I can learn a few steps." The idea of dancing in the sticky humidity brought to mind her need for a shower.

"Excuse me," she said embarrassedly, leaning toward Onus Laang so no one else could hear, "but where do your people go to wash? I used the sanitary but didn't see any shower facilities."

Onus Laang gave a warbling shout of laughter. "Forgive me, mistress, but your ignorance of our ways is most entertaining. When we wish to bathe, we swim in one of our natural pools. The rain forest is abundant with ponds and streams fed from the higher mountain areas."

"I didn't bring a swimsuit."

This statement brought forth another burst of uproarious laughter. Eyes turned in their direction and Mara felt Deke's questioning gaze boring into her. Blushing furiously, she gritted, "What's so funny?"

Onus Laang smiled at her. "We have no need for such modesty. Our mating urge comes only once an annum, unlike you humans who are constantly influenced by your hormones." Her speculative glance flickered to Deke. "If you like, I can have someone show you to one of the bathing pools in the morning."

"Thank you, I would appreciate that," Mara mumbled. A commotion from one of the nearby huts drew her attention and with relief she noticed a group of dancers emerge. It was time for the performance to begin.

Deke nudged her with his elbow. "What was that conversation all about?"

She gazed into his amused brown eyes. "I was just inquiring about the personal amenities."

"And?"

"They don't take showers. A swim in the local pond seems to be the norm."

"Sounds good to me." He grinned wickedly.

"Pay attention," she said, her cool tone belying the rising heat wave that assailed her senses. A staccato drumbeat reached her ears as a trio of Wort musicians struck up a tune. Shifting her attention to center stage, she was thrilled to count eight Worts in the dance troupe. Garbed in short-skirted tunic outfits in bright colors, they paired off into male-female combinations and gyrated to the blood-rushing beat of the music.

An elder Wort whom Mara hadn't met before sauntered up to her and Deke while they watched the performance. In his outstretched hand, he offered two ceramic goblets.

"Please accept this refreshment for your thirst," he said in a gravelly tone. "It is a precious drink from the nectar of anquilla blossoms. You may sniff their fragrance in the air. The petals open only at nightfall."

She had noticed the heavily perfumed air. During the day, a profusion of flowers was evident in the forest. Vibrant purple, white, bright red, and orange predominated. Many of the flowers grew as epiphytes, plants that depended upon other plants for their foundation. They could be found at all levels among the treetops. She'd been too preoccupied before to enjoy the beauty around her but after a few sips of the sweet anquilla drink, her senses heightened. Sounds of rushing water came from a distance and strands of bamboo creaked in the intervals between musical numbers. Closing her eyes, she expanded her awareness to the surrounding jungle until she felt at one with nature. It was a joyous, harmonious feeling and she regretted not having meditated more often on this trip.

"Mara, are you all right?" Deke's sharp tone broke her reverie.

She smiled at him, feeling somewhat tipsy. "I'm fine." It must be the rhythmic drumbeat that was vibrating her bones and stirring her senses, she thought. A peculiar lightness filled her limbs. In the center of the circle, the dancers whirled in a fast tempo, their feet prancing with lightning swiftness and their arms outstretched. Her pulse accelerated to match the beat of the drum.

"Come on!" she yelled to Deke, pulling him upright. "Let's join them!"

The Worts who were watching croaked their approval as she dragged Deke into the center. Flickering shadows created by the torches cast an eerie glow that excited her further. She looped her arm through Deke's in a manner that wouldn't allow him to escape, and laughed when his awkward shuffle made him stumble over his own feet.

"You can do better than that," she admonished. "Remember our duets on the *Celeste*?"

His eyes smoldered at the memory as he caught her around the waist. "No one else was watching us then."

"So pretend we're alone." In a daring move, she shimmied, pleased when his gaze dropped to the cleavage exposed through the unbuttoned top of her treksuit.

His lips tightened and his eyes shone with desire as he matched her movements with the grace of a panther.

"See, you're doing fine," she said, fluttering her eyelids provocatively as she'd observed Hedy do. Thinking of Hedy, she wondered what she and Wren were up to. She glanced around and saw them sitting on a log, leaning into each other's arms with glazed looks on their faces. What was wrong with them? They both appeared in a daze, as though a push from a feather would topple them over.

Deke grabbed her hand and twirled her around, spinning her senses so that she lost her ability to think rationally. Even his wild laugh sounded natural to her ears. Around and around the circle they went, whirling giddily to the insistent beat of the drum. The rush of water in the background grew louder, closer, until it became a pulsating roar. It took a moment for her to realize it was her blood throbbing in her temples, not the noise of a distant waterfall that was making her head feel so strange, but it didn't seem to matter. She laughed uninhibitedly, exulting when Deke pulled her into his arms to plant a firm kiss on her mouth in front of everyone.

"I believe you have enjoyed enough of the dance," Onus Hahn said, tapping Deke on the shoulder. "Follow me, Commander. I know you wish to express your appreciation for our hospitality and I have made arrangements for you to do so. Mistress, you may join your friends. They are retiring for the evening. You must be fatigued after such a long day."

Disengaging herself from Deke's side, she nodded numbly. She felt uncommonly tired and her head reeled dizzily.

"Go along," Deke said, the warmth of his voice penetrating her daze.

Giving him a wan smile, she trekked after Hedy and Wren, who were already stumbling down the path toward their tree house.

Deke watched her go, then turned to Onus Hahn, who was patiently waiting for his attention. "Where to?" he asked jauntily, vaguely aware of an odd ringing in his ears.

"This way." Onus Hahn led him through the flickering shadows of the village as dancers and audience dispersed. Leaves from the encroaching jungle brushed his face as they wound down a narrow path at the edge of the enclave. Strange birdcalls pierced the air and the hoot of an owl provided a soft background to the droning chorus of cicadas. He knew he should have wondered where the Wort was leading him but he couldn't seem to think straight. Conversely he started humming a tune as though he hadn't a care in the world.

Onus Hahn halted in front of a hut on stilts. "In here, Commander," he ordered, his tone bereft of its former friendliness.

Deke took a deep breath of the heavily scented air and then plunged into the interior. His eyes widened in surprise at the sight that greeted him. A sophisticated communications array was present, and a young Wort who'd apparently been on-line jumped up at their entrance.

"We've set up a link to Bimordus Two," Onus Hahn said, his frog face splitting into a broad grin. "I thought you'd like to tell your superiors how considerate we've been and that we are in full support of Fromoth Trun's application to join the Coalition." He handed a microphone to Deke.

"Why, sure!" he said, grabbing the device. His expansive mood made him want to share his pleasure but he couldn't remember who to ask for on the other end. "Uh, what do I say?"

"Ask for Deleth Goor on the Admissions Committee," Onus Hahn replied, his smile widening.

His frog face seemed uncannily large in the confines of the dimly lit hut. Deke's finger hesitated on the button that would transmit his voice message.

"Do it now, Commander!" the Wort croaked, his tone harsh.

Deke's hand began to shake. "I don't know." He wavered uncertainly, wanting to please his host, but a fraction of his mind was telling him to resist.

"Nahmrabi!" Onus Hahn muttered angrily in his native tongue. Stepping closer, he thumbed the control for Deke. "Speak, human."

Something snapped inside his head. "No . . . no, I won't." He shut down the link and dropped the microphone onto a counter.

Onus Hahn's eyes flashed furiously. "I expected you to be cooperative."

"Expected or planned?" A cloud seemed to lift from his consciousness but he hadn't the strength to pursue his renewed clarity of thought. "I'm finished here. It's time for me to join my friends."

Turning on his heel, he strode toward the door and weaved in an unsteady pattern down the steps. Surprisingly Onus Hahn didn't try to stop him. Wondering why he felt so strange, Deke wandered in the direction from which he'd thought they'd come. It wasn't until he came to a guard post at an unfamiliar section that he realized he was lost. One of the guards obligingly led him to the guest hut and saw that he was safely ensconced inside.

Mara was fast asleep, sprawled across her cot. Deke didn't even bother to check on Hedy or Wren. He collapsed onto his bed, falling into oblivion even before his head touched the pillow.

* * *

The softness of the pillow cradled Mara's head as she tossed restlessly in her sleep. Her dreams were nightmarish visions of Jallyn being guarded over by hostile Worts. They were dancing around her crib, their faces streaked with war paint, loud battle croaks warbling from their throats. And then she was dancing with Deke. They whirled round and round, laughing in each other's arms, oblivious to the Worts and to Jallyn's frenzied cries.

Jallyn! Mara bolted upright on her bed, her upper lip beaded in sweat. What was happening? Rays of sunlight pierced the interior of the hut. Bird songs filled the air and a heavy mist rose outside the open casement. It was morning, she realized. Her anxious glance rested on Deke's prostrate form. Fully dressed, he was sprawled on his lounger lying on his back. At least he'd returned safely. She'd meant to wait up for him but drowsiness had overwhelmed her and she'd collapsed on her bed, falling asleep instantly. She wondered what had transpired between him and Onus Hahn.

No matter. He'd tell her when he woke up. Not wishing to disturb him, she went to her knapsack and retrieved Jallyn's blanket. It was imperative to learn how the babe was faring when bad vibes from her dream still lingered in her head. Clutching the blanket in her hands, she sat on the edge of the cot and closed her eyes. An image of Sarina popped unbidden into her mind, and before she could focus her thoughts, she was zooming through astral space and jumping into her friend's viewpoint. Sarina's sleeping chamber met her inner eye. The lighting was lowered, so she assumed it must be night on Bimordus Two, but Sarina was awake, her eyes open. Giving a sigh of despair, she rolled onto her side and bumped into Teir.

Teir was home! Mara withdrew her essence, not wishing to intrude on their privacy. Thank goodness Sarina didn't have to bear her burden alone anymore. Glotaj, the supreme regent, was a friend but Sarina needed the closeness of family during a crisis such as this one.

Heaving a sigh of relief, she concentrated on receiving vibrations from the blanket held tightly in her hands. The infant's frequency attuned with her higher consciousness, drawing her nearer.

"How much longer do you intend to let this farce go on?" said a gruff male voice in the Wort dialect.

With a start, she realized she was in Jallyn's viewpoint, but the babe's face was turned toward a wall. She couldn't see the speaker but could sense the darkness of his presence. A shiver racked her spirit body. It was the same evil essence she'd encountered before.

Another male replied. "He hasn't given us an answer yet. I intend to wait as long as necessary."

"And I say kill the child now and be done with it!"

"Not while the Coalition team is on Yanura. They might find out about us."

"So what? If they do, we'll accomplish the same goal."

"I disagree! We'll lose our leverage. You'll follow my orders on this, Kromas."

Mara gasped. The males were arguing over Jallyn's very existence! One of them wanted to kill her. The other intended to keep her alive, but for what purpose?

The power of her thought tossed her out of Jallyn's consciousness and she hurtled through the astral plane back into her physical body.

"Deke, wake up!" She prodded him on the shoulder.

Deke didn't budge, so she shoved him again. "Wake up!" she cried, shaking him by the arm.

He mumbled something and rolled sideways.

She had rarely seen him sleep so soundly. Usually the slightest noise brought him fully alert. The only other time she remembered him out cold like this had been after they'd been gassed in the jungle pit on their way to the Wort village.

By the Light! Was that why she'd conked out so easily last night? A vague recollection of dancing wildly with Deke remained in her consciousness, but she'd attributed it to her dream. Now she recalled the dancers, musicians, and the syrupy nectar drink she'd gulped down in her thirst. Could the beverage have been laced with a drug that made them all woozy? It would account for her lack of inhibitions in front of the Worts, and now that she considered the idea, it would also be reason for Hedy and Wren's peculiar dazed behavior.

Now she was even more curious about why Deke had been singled out to go with Onus Hahn. How was she to rouse him? He was snoring lightly and she resisted the impulse to push him off the edge of the bed.

But she could touch him and enter his essence, although she ran the danger of succumbing to his state of sleepiness, or she could seduce him into wakefulness. She discarded almost immediately entering his space. He'd be angry at the invasion when he awoke and realized what she'd done. But the other option made her smile as she felt the irresistible urge to stretch out beside him, and smooth her fingers through his hair and breathe in his musky masculine scent.

Speaking of scents, he didn't smell so sweet and neither did she. Hadn't Onus Laang offered to send someone to show her the bathing pools this morning? Wrinkling her nose, she decided it was a necessary excursion.

A hand snaked around her waist and she drew in a sharp breath. Deke's dark, piercing gaze met hers.

"Morning," he said, his tone husky.

"Get up. I have something to tell you."

"In a minute." His eyes swept her face and trailed along

her hair hanging down her back. "Come closer." His arm tightened, pulling her lower.

She couldn't resist the hungry look on his face and bent to kiss him. He tasted so good she swung her legs up on the bed so she could lie beside him. And then she was in his arms, being kissed wildly and passionately. She wanted to preserve the moment, to enjoy the sensations he evoked in her. As she relaxed in his embrace, she willed herself to stay out of his head so she could savor the intensity of her response.

By the corona! Wasn't that how he felt? Whenever she joined his essence, he was forced to share his feelings, emotions he might want to keep to himself. It didn't matter that their union produced joy. She was still stealing his privacy. Wasn't he entitled to keep his reactions to himself?

Deke murmured her name, adjusting his position so he could reach her throat. He flicked his tongue out, stroking her neckline and making tiny nibbling motions that drove her wild with desire. She lost control, merging her psyche with his, her passion swirling into a haze of need. They tore each other's clothes off, grinding into a frenzy of naked flesh that burned from an insatiable fire.

Their lust satisfied, Mara slid to her side so Deke wouldn't see her confusion. Was that what it was like for him? Having his mind invaded, never knowing when his feelings would be vulnerable to her? No wonder he wanted to shut her out! She'd thought he would welcome her presence. No one truly wanted to be alone, and in their joined state, he'd never have to suffer loneliness. But perhaps she'd been wrong. This was the first time she hadn't wanted to merge with him right away and so she could finally understand his resistance. She had no right to intrude upon him against his will. Yet what could she do? Lacking control over her ability, she couldn't just cut herself off from him, nor did she want to. They were still bound on a spiritual level no matter how hard either one of them tried to deny it. It was their destiny to be together.

Shaking herself back to reality, she opened her mouth to tell Deke about her mental visit to Jallyn and her theory about a drugged drink, but before she uttered a word, a loud thud sounded from the platform outside their hut.

"Mistress, are you in there? It's Onus Laola. I've come to take you to the bathing pools this morning."

Jumping up, she snatched at her clothes. "Yes, I'll be right out," she cried, pulling on her underwear, conscious of Deke's eyes on her back. Risking a glance at his tall, naked body stretched out on the bed, she regretted it the instant her own body throbbed with renewed desire. "Do you want to join us?" she asked, her tone husky.

"No, thanks." Swinging his legs over the edge of the bed, he reached for his treksuit. "I need to contact Ebo for a report on the ship's status and I have to fill him in on what's been going on down here." He kept his voice low so Onus Laola wouldn't overhear. Rummaging in his sack, he pulled out his datalink. "You go on ahead. I'll find you later."

She hesitated. "Come now," she urged, unable to explain her sudden premonition that something threatening was about to happen to him.

"I'm not ready to leave yet."

"Please, Deke! Something . . . something bad might happen if you don't come."

"I said I'll join you later!" he snapped, irritated.

Afraid of angering him, she decided to drop it. As an afterthought, she retrieved a clean treksuit and a towel from her knapsack. "I'll ask Hedy and Wren if they want to go."

"Good idea," he said, fixing his warm brown gaze on

her. "Don't worry about me. I'll be along shortly."

"Right." She wondered how she and Hedy would cope with a communal bath. Unlike the Yanurans, they weren't used to coed bathing facilities.

Pushing aside the mosquito netting, she emerged onto the exterior platform. A light mist caressed her face and sounds of water dripping predominated over the ever-present birdcalls. It must have rained during the night, she concluded, noting the damp smell and moisture on overhanging branches.

"Morning," she said to Onus Laola. The Wort female appeared sprightly in a simple mauve gown overlapped with a white apron.

"*Rogi Kwantro,*" the Wort replied, giving a slight bow.

She flushed, embarrassed. She'd forgotten the standard greeting. "*Rogi Kwantro,*" she muttered, returning the courtesy. "I appreciate your coming to get me so early. Isn't this normally your sleeping period?"

"I don't require many hours of repose. It is better we go now, before the pools get crowded."

"Of course." How considerate, she thought, smiling gratefully. "Shall I ask my friends to join us?" She nodded toward Hedy's hut.

"Please do," Onus Laola said sweetly. "I would be honored by their company as I am by yours."

Mara experienced a moment's hesitation. She'd lose the advantage of being alone with Laola if her friends accepted the invitation. But there was also safety in numbers, and she didn't know how far they had to go to reach the pools.

As she crossed the log bridge, she heard sounds of arguing coming from within Hedy and Wren's hut. It didn't sound as though their relationship was going smoothly.

"Hello!" she called out. "I'm going to the pools. Anyone care to join me?"

"I will!" Hedy's voice yelled back, a petulant note evident in her tone.

"And I shall accompany you," Wren boomed.

The two charged out, colliding at the entrance as though they were so eager to depart from each other's company that they couldn't proceed properly.

Mara suppressed a grin. "Perhaps you'd like to bring towels and clean outfits," she suggested.

"Indeed!" Wren responded, glowering at Hedy. She went back inside and emerged a moment later carrying two folded bundles. Wren solicitously held the netting aside for her to pass.

What a contrasting pair! Mara thought, smiling. Hedy never failed to express her emotions, while Wren continued to deny his. She couldn't wait to get a report from her roommate on what they'd been fighting about.

For land's sake! Speaking of reports, she'd forgotten to ask Deke about his meeting with Onus Hahn last night. That man continually distracted her.

Right now, though, her objective was to get clean, she reminded herself, stepping onto the conveyor with her companions. The jungle was swathed in mist, and as they descended to the ground, a fresh earthen scent pervaded her nostrils.

The village was quiet, devoid of movement on the upper residential levels and without the pungent aroma of burning fuel from the kitchens. The wildlife made up for the stillness of the settlement. As they passed by a strand of creaky bamboo, Mara caught sight of a huge spider guarding a web which glistened with moisture. Catarrhines cheeped overhead as they leapt from branch to branch, and turtles crawled along dead logs. She saw a lizard sipping water from a cup created by a bright red bromeliad. A profusion of plants, flowers, and fruit trees surrounded them. Many of the species were unfamiliar, native only to Yanura.

"This is beautiful," Mara commented, glad their path through the foliage was defined by a dirt trail.

"Beautiful but not always safe," Onus Laola said. She took the lead, with Hedy and Wren trailing behind Mara single-file. "We maintain guard posts at various checkpoints to warn of attacks by . . . undesirable creatures."

"Is that why my friends and I fell into a pit on our way here? You have traps set, too?" She brushed away a vine that dangled from a figaras tree, a variety familiar to her from her studies. The vine was elastic and strong and could be woven into rope. Boulders became more prominent as they followed an incline toward the sound of rushing water.

Onus Laola ignored her question and continued to comment on the flora and fauna. As they climbed past a rock face on one side and a gigantic tree trunk on the other, Mara reached out and touched a spray of tiny pink flowers. What a beautiful place, she thought. The rush of water grew louder further along the trail and suddenly they came upon a river. A scarlet-beaked bird was rummaging for food among dead tree roots along the bank. Mist sprayed Mara's face with its cool caress. They followed the river until they came to a grotto with rocky cliffs on either side and a spectacular splashing waterfall. The water tumbled onto a series of fallen tree trunks and boulders. Sunlight dappling through the foliage glistened off the water, making it sparkle like thousands of diamella gemstones.

"Here we are," Onus Laola said. "Do you like it?"

"This is where we are to bathe?" Wren inquired gruffly.

Mara grinned at the look of dismay on his face. "I'll bet you expected a sanitary facility complete with sonic showers, didn't you?"

"Well," Wren sputtered, "I, er . . ."

"I'll betcha he did," Hedy said, laughing with delight. "Is the water cold?" she asked Onus Laola.

"It is cool for me," the Wort said. "I cannot spend much time in the water, but don't hurry on my account. I'll wait for you."

Onus Laola proceeded to strip in front of them.

Wren's face reddened and he spun on his heels, turning away.

"Come on, Wren," Hedy cooed. "Aren't you getting into the spirit of things? Look, I'm taking off my treksuit. What are you waiting for?" And Hedy very loudly proceeded to unfasten her garment.

Wren coughed. "I, er, need to make a call to nature," he stuttered, dashing off down the trail in the opposite direction.

"Don't be long," Hedy cried after him. Giggling, she turned to Mara. "Oh, isn't he the sexiest thing?"

Mara watched as Onus Laola plunged into the pool and quickly dove under the surface. Mara took a longer time in unfastening her treksuit than had Hedy, who stood before her stark naked. When she was undressed, she shivered despite the warm humidity.

"What's going on between you and Wren?" she said. She cast a surreptitious glance at their surroundings, hoping none of the Wort guards were nearby to observe them.

"Oh, Mara," Hedy sighed. "He just refuses to budge. I don't know what to do. I've tried everything I can think of and he still resists my offers."

"Tough, isn't it?" she said sarcastically. "Wren appears to be the first male who hasn't fallen at your feet. Perhaps that's why you're so infatuated with him."

"It's more than infatuation," Hedy said. "I can't get him out of my mind! I find myself looking at him all the time, wondering what he's thinking, trying to figure out how I can get his attention. I know he wants me, Mara, but I can't get him to admit it."

Mara gave her a solemn look. "You're trying too hard."

"Maybe you're right. I just don't know what to do anymore."

"Come on, let's jump in the water. I don't like standing around here so exposed."

"You first!" Hedy cried, grinning.

Mara descended to the water's edge and stuck her toe under the surface. "Not bad," she said, careful of her footing on the moss-covered rocks as she ventured further. The sound of rushing water was music to her ears. As a child, she'd liked to sit beside a waterfall and imagine herself as one with the drops of water cascading over the rocky backdrop. How free she would feel to tumble over the edge, soaring into space like her spirit body. Was that what it would be like for Wren if he could fly? Remembering Hedy's story about the ascension rites on his planet, she felt sad for Wren that he'd never achieved his goal. She wondered what Hedy could do to encourage him, but her own situation with Deke precluded her giving any advice. She certainly wasn't having much success on her own. With that glum thought, she stepped into deeper water and shrieked as the cool liquid surrounded her up to her neck.

"Come on, Hedy! It feels good once you're in," she yelled, flipping onto her stomach and beginning a series of strong strokes. The waterfall produced a huge spray of mist. She stood at a safe distance beside the cascade and scrubbed her hair as squeaky clean as she could get it. The water ran over her face and down her breasts and she imagined it was Deke's fingers smoothing over her body instead.

"Mara!" Hedy squealed. "Onus Laola is leaving!"

She opened her eyes and saw their guide trudging off down a path, their clothes in hand. Her moist brownish body gleamed with moisture.

"Onus Laola," she cried. "Where are you going?"

"I am taking your dirty suits to the laundry," Onus Laola

said, turning briefly. "You'll be all right: Wren should be along any moment. I'll return in a short while."

Getting up her courage to enter the water, Hedy swam toward Mara, her green eyes sparkling with mischief. "Have I got an idea," she said, once they were alone. "Listen." And against the background roar of the waterfall, she relayed her plan.

A few moments later, Mara was at the bank of the stream drying herself off with her towel. When she was done, she donned her clean set of underwear and new treksuit. She set off in the direction Wren had gone and it wasn't long before she found him leaning against a prickly tree trunk.

"Wren, come quickly!" she cried. "Hedy's in trouble; she needs you."

Instantly alert, Wren charged down the path, leaving Mara grinning behind him.

His heart thudding in his chest, Wren wondered what had happened. Was Hedy in trouble in the river? Could she have slipped on one of those slick rocks and injured her head? His breath caught in his throat as he imagined her lying unconscious and he realized how much he cared for her. She meant more to him than he could admit and it would crush him if any harm befell her. It would be his fault, he realized, for leaving her unattended. Never mind that their relationship wasn't a smooth one. It was still his responsibility to look after her.

"Wren!" Hedy screamed when he neared the riverbank.

He reached the water, took one look at her floundering in the deep current, and plunged in, clothes and all.

"Hang on, I'm coming!" he shouted, pushing through volumes of water with his powerful strokes. Swimming had been one of his favorite pastimes on Pollux; he'd hoped the exercise would stimulate his ability to fly.

"My foot's caught in a tangle of weeds!" she spluttered

as he neared. Her wet hair was plastered to her face and he thought her large eyes had never looked more beautiful. She was flailing her arms, desperately trying to stay afloat, but as he swam up to her, she stilled and swooned into his arms. The current rocked them and he clutched her tightly against his chest.

"By the moons of Agus Six!" he swore as his hands felt the soft flesh beneath his fingertips. She was naked! Unsuccessfully, he tried to suppress his own violent reaction. His awkward movements caused her to shudder but he dared not let go. Apparently she wasn't a strong swimmer and needed his help to reach the shore safely. But he was touching her in places he considered sacred. Were her moans expressions of fear or pleasure? And were her tremors from her trauma or his nearness? He couldn't tell and didn't want to know. Unable to keep his cry of need for her from escaping when his hands inadvertently smoothed over her belly, Wren cursed his weakness. He was mad for the woman. If only he was whole, he'd lay her on that bed of moss by the riverbank and—

His fantasy became reality when their feet touched bottom and Hedy twisted in his arms. Her mouth clamped on his as she pressed her nude body firmly against him.

"Take me, Wren. You've saved my life," she murmured against his lips, her hot breath teasing him into submission.

His hands followed a path of their own to her breasts. She thrust her chest forward, filling his palms with her soft flesh. As though he'd just been offered a gift from heaven, he stroked her nipples and plundered her mouth with his tongue. He must resist, he told himself. He hadn't earned the right to have her. And yet when she felt so good in his arms, how could he continue to deny them both the pleasure they craved?

She writhed against him and his battered willpower

drained further. He'd been able to refuse her in their hut when she kept finding excuses to touch him and pleaded with him to lie with her, but now he'd gone beyond the brink of reason and was in danger of drowning. If he went under, would any of his honor remain or would he have to live the rest of his days in shame?

She'd still want him, no matter what he did. She'd promised to stay by his side regardless of the circumstances. Would he be dishonoring her by his actions if he gave in to his desire? Yes, he would, he concluded, and Hedy was too good to be ruined by the taint of his sin.

A solution came to him as a yellow-feathered bird swooped over the water, plucking a fish from under the surface. He'd satisfy Hedy's need but withhold his own climax. Content with his decision, he lowered his hand, sliding his palm across the curve of her hip. Just the idea of where he was about to touch her made his pulse rate soar. Knee-deep in the water, the roar of the waterfall in the background and the music of his own passion thrummed in his ears.

"Wren!" Mara cried, and he and Hedy sprang apart. Mara was emerging from the path at a hard run. "It's Deke . . . I've just been pulled into his viewpoint." Halting, she gasped for breath. "He's in terrible danger!"

Chapter Eighteen

Deke contacted Ebo via datalink just after Mara and the others left for the pools. Alone in the hut, he exchanged status reports with his communications officer.

"We're in no immediate danger that I can discern," he said, "although I wouldn't trust these Worts beyond my nose. Have you been able to make sense out of their communications?"

"Not yet. I'm reading a high frequency of coded messages between various locations on Yanura, but the computer has been unable to decipher their meaning."

"Keep trying. You've still got a fix on our location, right?"

"Aye, sir. I've got a locator alert programmed in for all four of you."

"Good. Contact me if anything significant occurs. Sage out." He replaced the datalink in his knapsack, thinking he'd join Mara for a swim, when a loud crashing thud made him whirl toward the open doorway. Someone had hurled another rock inside the hut!

He dashed to the outdoor platform, hoping to catch the sender, but the village remained quiet and he didn't see so much as a moving shadow. Glancing up, he peered at the mist-enshrouded tree canopy and smiled grimly when a swinging vine caught his attention. Blasted frogfaces, he thought. They could maneuver through the trees like catarrhines.

Returning inside, he scooped up the rock and carefully untied the attached note. His eyes hastily scanned the scrawled message:

Come alone. I have vital information you want to hear.

Directions were enclosed.

Tossing the rock aside, he debated whether to bring his knapsack. His weapons were gone, but he could always summon his teammates with the datalink. No, he couldn't he amended. They'd left everything here. Just to be sure, he went over to Wren's hut and rummaged though his navigator's belongings. Sure enough, Wren had left his datalink behind. No one could activate them without their personal codes, but Deke deemed it wise to advise his crew not to leave without their equipment next time.

Figuring he could use the emergency backup link on his dive computer to call Ebo if necessary, Deke retrieved the conveyance from ground level and descended, feeling exposed, as though eyes were watching him. No one stirred in the sleepy village and he was grateful for the mist as he took off in the direction indicated. Later he'd insist their weaponry be returned. It was something he should have done before and he hoped he wouldn't pay for his negligence. The idea that this was a trap entered his head, and he grew increasingly uneasy as he wound along the jungle trails. The instructions were clear, using landmarks such as a huge banyan tree by the south edge of the communal dining hall, and dead logs crisscrossed at a 90-degree angle by the stream further on. He left the village proper and found himself on a muddy path cut through the thick foliage. The mist freshened his face with moisture and he sniffed in the moist, dank air that smelled from rotting vegetation. His boots squelched in the soggy earth and insects buzzed by his ears. Orchids, anthuriums, and other flowering plants he couldn't identify splashed bright colors against the greenery. A brilliant blue terin flashed by, stopping to hover over a large white blossom. The bird used its long bill to drink the nectar and he remembered the drink he'd been given the night before. He'd certainly behaved strangely, dancing with Mara in front of a bunch of natives and nearly acceding to Fromoth Trun's demands. Had there been something in that sickly sweet beverage that had affected them all?

"Aaarooo!" sounded a fierce noise from above.

Deke nearly jumped out of his boots. Grabbing a big stick from the ground, he glanced upward. Branches rattled and leaves and twigs rained down in an avalanche of debris. A giant somu nut crashed where he'd been standing a moment before. If it had hit him on the head, the impact of the weighted nut could have killed him.

A large male barrulu glared down at him from the somu nut tree. Shaking its shaggy mane and bearded face, the creature thrust out its lower jaw and bellowed threats at him.

He gave a tremulous sigh. He'd better steady his nerves, he told himself, continuing along the path. He broke out into a clearing where the ground was muddier, sucking at his boots, and soon he was curving around a wetland dotted with ponds. When he came to a huge kapok tree with cathedrallike buttresses, he halted at its base. This was the location given to him on the message.

"Commander," someone called out in standard Jawani.

He spun in the direction of the voice. An elder Wort female emerged from behind a cluster of tall reeds. The wild-growing grass had feathery flowerheads and straplike leaves. Sedges and rushes clogged the banks of the nearby pond and he could see how easy it was for the Wort to blend in with her surroundings. Her brown skin color and forest green tunic matched the colors of nature.

"Who are you?" he demanded.

She stopped beside him on the bank of the pond. Her expressive amber eyes inspected him warily. "You are alone? No one followed you here?"

He gave her a startled look. He'd assumed by being alone she meant bringing no companions. He hadn't thought the informant might be afraid of any Worts following him, but then she wouldn't care to be exposed, would she? "As far as I know, no one saw me leave the village," he said quietly.

Nodding, she lowered herself onto a fallen log. "Sit," she ordered.

He eyed a flat tree stump for bugs. Seeing none of immediate concern, he plopped onto the makeshift seat. "You said you had valuable information."

"I am Raisa, Onus Laola's grandmother. It is for her sake and the sake of her child that I speak to you."

"Her child?" He frowned in puzzlement.

"She had a male child six annums ago. As is our way, he was taken to be raised by the jakoon." Raisa leaned forward. "It is time for this sacrilege to end. Our children must be returned to our care."

"I don't understand. Who are the jakoon? Where are the children taken?"

"The jakoon are Croags who supervise the upbringing of our young. The children are kept until maturation, when they are sent home. If we were to resist, the Croags would cut off our supply of Vyclor. You can end the practice. Make it a condition of Yanura's acceptance into the Coalition."

Deke stiffened. "It always comes back to Fromoth Trun's application, doesn't it? Did someone put you up to this?"

Raisa stood abruptly, her eyes flashing. "I risked my life in coming here and you dare to insult me? I should have told the NARCs myself where to find you."

"NARCs?" He rose, squaring his shoulders. Now maybe he'd get some useful answers. "Who are they?"

The old Wort stared at a line of ants crawling on the ground. "The National Revolutionary Congress are activists who seek to end Croag dominance in our political affairs. They refuse to take Vyclor routinely as is administered to the rest of the population on Yanura. Their list of demands is threefold: Everyone should have freedom of choice regarding Vyclor; all factions should be allowed representation in the central government; and forced conscription of children must end.

"The NARCs have Jallyn and they're using her as a pawn to force Fromoth Trun to agree to their terms. If the Croag leader refuses, Jallyn will be killed and her death blamed on his people. The Coalition, informed of his treachery, would reject his application for admission."

He opened his mouth to ask a multitude of questions, but before he'd uttered a sound, a beam of red laser fire cut through the air, striking Raisa solidly in the chest. With a choked cry, she toppled over.

Frogfaces jumped out of the surrounding high grasses, flanking him on all sides. Desperately he glanced about for something to use as a weapon, but being outnumbered and outgunned, it was a moot point. The Worts bristled with shooters, laser rifles, and gas grenades, making him wonder who'd supplied them with armaments. Their style of dress differentiated them from the villagers. Woven tan tunics covered their bodies and all half-dozen were males.

"Your death will further our cause," the largest of the group snarled, stepping closer, his red eyes bulging ominously.

"Who are you?" he asked, his heart pounding against his ribs. At least they weren't about to kill him outright. Maybe he could buy some time, but time for what? None of his crew knew of his situation.

"The Coalition will be informed of your demise. They will reject Fromoth Trun's application."

One of the smaller assailants glanced at the leader. "What? I thought our orders were to capture the human, not kill him."

"I give the orders here," the red-eyed Wort said.

"Forgive me, Kromas, but our goals in the National Revolutionary Congress are to force the Croags to accede to our demands. If you murder this man and the girl child, you'll defeat our aims!"

Kromas's skin darkened, and he raised his weapon to fire before the smaller Wort had a chance to react. The trooper crumpled to the ground without a sound.

"You're next," the rebel leader said, swinging his shooter toward Deke. "Like your friend Larikk, you'll meet your end in Dead Wort's Marsh."

As his finger moved on the trigger, Deke used the only means available to save himself. He grabbed at an overhanging vine and swung upward, kicking the shooter out of Kromas's hand. Landing behind the big Wort, he whirled around and kicked him in the small of his back. The Wort grunted and doubled over, and Deke used the opportunity to land a chop on his thick neck. Immediately, the other Worts were upon him, punching and striking at his vulnerable areas. Utilizing the skills he learned in defense training, he tossed one of his assailants over his shoulder. The fellow landed with a loud splash in the pond. With a loud shriek, he disappeared beneath the surface. A hit on the jaw made Deke reel backward, right into the crushing embrace of Kromas. Kromas's arms tightened around his chest while three of his troopers approached with evil grins on their frog faces. Ignoring the painful vise squeezing his rib cage, Deke tensed his muscles, preparing to bend his knees and toss Kromas into the pond with his crony. Just as he was about to make his move, he felt an essence invade his mind. Mara's fear reached him and he froze, immobilized with the intensity of her emotion. His paralysis gave Kromas and his friends the advantage. The Worts closed in on him, and before he could fully recover, Kromas and his compatriots were edging him toward the pond.

"The eels will get you as they did Larikk. Join him!" Kromas said.

Deke's feet were lifted by the soldiers and they tossed him through the air.

As he toppled, he automatically activated a switch on the dive computer strapped to his wrist. He crashed through the surface of the water, which was covered with green algae slime and large round lily pads. Just before he went under, he sucked in a large breath of air.

When the cool liquid had swallowed him from view, Deke wheeled around, diving deep and veering in a direction opposite the bank he'd just left. He remembered seeing a thick cluster of tall reeds and made out their stems in the dimly lit underwater environment. Something slithered past his leg, about two feet long and fairly solid. Remembering that the villagers had warned him about stinger eels, he grinned. The dangerous inhabitants of Dead Wort's Marsh didn't threaten him. In fact, being tossed into the pond was his lucky move of the day. His dive computer contained a protective device that emitted an electromagnetic energy screen. It would shield him from any electrical impulses put out by dangerous predators.

Ignoring the slithering creatures that touched him as they

passed, he reached a cluster of reeds and grabbed one at its base, ripping it from its roots. Putting one end in his mouth, he gave a quick prayer to the Great Almighty and blew his remaining air through the hollow reed. At the other end, a flowerhead must have popped off, because when he tried to intake a breath of air, his lungs filled with ease. Using the reed as a snorkel device, he swam slowly away from the enemy. Hopefully, they would think he'd gone down like their comrade, never to surface again.

He could breathe through the hollow tube as long as necessary. The light was low down here, but he could make out large roots lying on the bottom, stems extending upward to the flat-leafed lily pads on top. Fish with whiskers swam past and he watched a crab crawl along the sandy bottom. Sitting on a large rock, he breathed evenly in and out of his tube. He couldn't keep his eyes open for long or they started burning, so he closed them. The water temperature was cool but it wasn't cold, and hypothermia shouldn't be a danger if he didn't stay down overly long. After a short while, he would surface and see if any NARC soldiers had been left to stand guard. Settling into position, Deke wondered how long he'd have to wait.

Undaunted by the position in which she'd discovered Hedy and Wren, Mara didn't wait for them to join her. Signaling for them to follow, she charged down the path toward the village, her heart pounding in fear as she wondered what had happened to Deke. She'd gotten a glimpse of brown Wort faces, a giant spreading tree, and the body of a village woman sprawled on the ground when she'd jumped into Deke's viewpoint, but what had alarmed her the most was sensing the same dark presence that she'd felt around Jallyn. Fear spurned her onward and she didn't even stop to answer Wren's bombardment of questions as he and Hedy caught up to her.

"Later!" she shouted.

When they reached the village, she ran into a kitchen hut where smoke billowed from a chimney, and she asked the old female for directions to the laundry. Onus Laola wasn't there so she got instructions to the female's residence. Her quick pace brought her to the ground below the tree house indicated.

"Mara, what's going on?" Hedy demanded in a huff. Still wet but properly attired, she patted her dripping hair with her towel. Wren had gone off to check the dwelling Mara shared with Deke to see if he'd left them a note.

Briefly Mara related what she'd seen; then she grabbed at a nearby rope ladder and began climbing.

Onus Laola's hut was empty of occupants. Built into a tree, several rooms rose on different levels. Mara felt guilty peeking into the private areas but she had to find Laola. She'd no idea where Deke had gone and the Wort female might be able to direct her. One room at an upper rise caught her attention and she entered. A small bed was properly laid out and a wood bureau held several small objects. What attracted her eye was the holographic photo of a young Wort male. The photo was propped next to a jagged white rock. A ripple of shock tore through her as she studied the picture. Did Onus Laola have a child, and if so, why hadn't she mentioned the boy? Where was he living?

She couldn't help but draw a parallel to the situation with the Croags. Where were all the Wort children? During their sojourn in the village, she hadn't noticed any youngsters. Where did they reside? Could Sarina's baby be with the Yanuran children?

She had so many questions but so few answers. She wasn't satisfied with the rationale given for Larikk's death. Deke believed data was being withheld about Vyclor. And what of that chemical plant? Could it be a facility for manufacturing sluer oil, which the Croags traded to the Worts for gold lace? If so, how did one account for the dead bodies on the data card Deke had been given?

Rubbing her hand over the jagged white rock, she puzzled over the mystery of it all. Even this rock seemed to ring a familiar bell but she couldn't remember its significance.

"Uh oh!" A piece broke off in her hand. Now what should she do? Flushing guiltily, she decided she didn't want the evidence of her visit to be so visible. Stuffing the broken edge in her pocket, she turned the rock so the rough surface faced away from the open portal. Wiping her sweaty palms on her treksuit, she turned to go.

Halfway down the ladder, she spotted Onus Laola marching in her direction, her arms laden with their clothes. From the ground, Hedy glanced at her anxiously.

"Onus Laola!" Mara cried, jumping down the last few meters. "I was looking for you!"

"And I have been searching for you. I did not expect you to return to the village by yourself."

"Deke is in trouble and we need to find him!"

Onus Laola thrust the bundle of neatly folded clothes at her. "Your suits are clean. Now what is this about Comdr. Sage?"

As Mara explained, the Wort female's expression turned thoughtful. "Did you see a wide pond before the spreading tree?" she asked.

Mara, reflecting upon her inner vision, nodded. "Do you know the place?"

"He's in Dead Wort's Marsh. We must hurry. Come, I'll show you the way. You may leave your clean laundry here."

Wren hustled toward them. "No messages," he gritted. "Here, Doctor, I've brought your medpack."

By the time they reached the wetland, Mara was perspiring and her treksuit stuck to her back. Luckily they all wore boots, or slogging through the mud would have proved tiresome. A sense of urgency compelled her to maintain a fast pace. What had happened to Deke? Was he all right? She berated herself for not keeping an item of his so she could do controlled separations. His intense emotion had drawn her into his life space before, but now when she wanted to reassure herself of his well-being, she wasn't able to do so. It was frustrating and she fumed at her helplessness.

They burst into the clearing and stopped in their tracks. A deceptively peaceful scene met their gaze: a stagnant pond, chirping birds, tall reeds and rushes swaying in a light breeze. And there was that huge spreading tree.

Mara spotted the body first and her heart leapt into her throat. With a stifled cry, she dashed forward. A wave of tremulous relief passed through her as she noted the female Wort's features. But where was Deke? Swiveling her head, she searched the vegetation but saw no sign of him.

"It appears as though the commander has been captured," Wren growled, coming up behind her and assessing the scene.

"By the grace of Mother Water!" Onus Laola cried, her face assuming an unhealthy pallor. "It is Raisa, my maternal grandmother!" Sinking down beside the old Wort, she covered her face with her hands.

"A weapon lies upon the ground," Wren said, loping over to retrieve a fallen rifle. "I thought your people avoided Dead Wort's Marsh."

Onus Laola looked at him with sorrowful eyes. "We do. Our villagers ply their trade in crafts, herb gathering, and fishing. We are not warriors. That weapon must have been dropped by a soldier in the National Revolutionary Congress, or NARC for short. They probably lured Comdr. Sage here and attacked him."

"What's the National Revolutionary Congress?" Mara

asked, her gaze focusing on the murky pond. A ripple creased its surface where a cluster of tall grasses bent in the breeze.

"NARC is an extremist splinter group made up of citizens who refuse to bow to Croag rule."

"Why the secrecy?" Hedy asked. She'd been running a diagnostic on Raisa, and now she straightened with a resigned look on her face. Switching off her medscan unit, she clipped it to her belt.

"NARC strategy involves using terrorist tactics in an attempt to force Fromoth Trun into agreeing to their demands," Onus Laola replied, a melancholy note in her voice. "They're probably responsible for the bombing attack at Revitt Lake City."

Mara nodded grimly. "And if we found out about the NARCs, Fromoth Trun realizes Deke would recommend a rejection of his application based on an assessment of political instability."

"Exactly," Onus Laola said. Her sad eyes roamed to Raisa's still form. "My grandmother hoped to help our people. She was always saying our children belonged at home."

"Where are they being held?" Mara's tone was unduly harsh, but it was tiring to keep repeating the same question. "And why didn't you mention you have a son?"

"I cannot give you any further information. It might endanger my child." Agitated, Onus Laola sprang from her seat.

"How can we reach Comdr. Sage?" Wren cut in. "Do you know where the NARC command base is located?"

Onus Laola pointed north toward the higher mountain ranges. "They come from Cloud Forest. It is a treacherous route by foot." Her expression turned pleading. "Please do not inform Onus Hahn or Onus Laang about my role in this. It is bad enough that Raisa was involved. I can tell you no more!" With a last fearful glance at her grandmother, Onus Laola scurried off.

A gloomy silence fell over Mara and her companions. Staring at the rippling pond, she screamed in surprise as a mountain of water erupted and a blackened creature reared its head from the depths.

"Mara!" exclaimed a familiar voice. "What are you doing here?"

"Deke?" She couldn't believe her eyes. The apparition washed the mud from its body and a dirty, sodden Deke emerged from the pond.

"Commander!" Wren rushed forward, accompanied by Hedy, who quickly scanned Deke with her medical device. "We thought you'd been captured!"

A rapid-fire volley of information ensued until each was updated on the other's activities.

"I knew something bad was going to happen to you," Mara said, her voice filled with concern.

Deke squatted on a log, peeling off his boots. Shaking one boot upside down, he grimaced as a pile of muck slid out.

"You should have come with us to the pools," she chided. "Now look at you! You're a mess." Relieved to find him unharmed, she hid her feelings behind a facade of teasing banter.

Deke glanced up, his eyes cool. "If you hadn't interfered, I'd have dispensed with those bastards myself. You distracted me again, blast it!" His mouth tightened into a thin white line. "If I knew you were going to jeopardize this mission with your lack of control, I'd have refused to bring you along. I can't tolerate another episode of your mind melding!"

Mortified, she stared at him. She'd thought he'd be happy to see her. Now he was blaming her for his predicament?

He squished his feet into his wet boots and stood,

glowering at them. Even Hedy and Wren had been struck speechless by his outburst. They stood mutely, stunned expressions on their faces.

"As you can see, I didn't need any help," Deke growled. "If Mara hadn't invaded my mind, I could have fought them off and hopefully kept one alive to question. Now the only information we have to go on is what Raisa told me."

"What do you mean, Mara invaded your mind?" Wren asked slowly. He seemed to be the only one unaware of Deke's meaning.

Deke shot her a venomous glance. "You know of her ability to separate? She does it to me, without warning. It can happen at any time or place. In this instance, her intrusion put me into a life-threatening situation."

His scorn hurt her deeply, and it was worse because he disparaged her in front of their friends. Moisture pricked her eyelashes, and she bit her lower lip so she wouldn't shame herself. Not that she could seem any more despicable in their eyes. Hedy averted her gaze but not before Mara saw her friend's pitying glance. Wren continued to study Deke with an obtuse expression.

"How about using your ability for our benefit?" Deke said with a sneer. "Where's that white rock you found in Laola's house? See if you can get a reading from it."

A reading . . . as though she were some smarmy ghost-chasing medium. "Very well." Casting aside her hurt, she focused on the importance of their mission and withdrew the rock from her pocket.

"By the Light!" she whispered when she'd landed at the other end of her astral journey. She was in a child's viewpoint, presumably Laola's son. He was swimming underwater, gathering specimens of similar white rocks. In his view, they appeared crystalline with a glittery surface. All around him swam other Yanuran children, Croags and Worts and unfamiliar races. They used some sort of tool to snip the stems of huge, stalklike plants with odd balloon-shaped protuberances.

"Those are the air-filled sacs that keep the merl afloat," Deke explained after she'd come out of her trance and given a report. "The youngsters must be harvesting the merl farms. But why the secrecy about the process? Every time I inquired about the harvesting techniques, I met a dead end."

He signaled to them to proceed to the village. As they trudged through the wetland, they discussed the problems facing them.

"If what Raisa said is true," Wren offered, "the children are being taken to work the farms against their parents' will, and the Worts are powerless to resist. They're afraid the Croags will cut off their supply of Vyclor."

"Do you think Jallyn is being held with the Yanuran children? It's likely the Croags have some sort of settlement where the youngsters live."

"The NARCs have Jallyn," Deke stated, his face grim. "I'd like to explore the merl beds on my own and search for the location of the young Yanurans, but our first priority is to rescue Sarina's child."

He glanced at Mara walking beside him. "You and I both overheard conversations indicating Jallyn's life is in danger. A moderate faction in the terrorist organization hopes to press Fromoth Trun into agreeing to their demands. But this Kromas character wants to kill her, ending any chance for conciliatory talks. We have to get to Jallyn before Kromas makes a move against her."

"Where did Larikk fit into this scheme of events?" she asked, risking Deke's displeasure by speaking. After his condemnation of her, she was afraid he'd disapprove of anything she said or did. If his opinion didn't matter so much, she'd try to shrug it off, but because she did care about him and her background made her particularly sensitive, it was impossible.

Deke's face was stony as he replied. "If you hadn't jumped into my head when you did, I might have found out more about what happened to Larikk. All I learned was that the NARCs were responsible for his disappearance. They did not indicate why they'd wanted him dead."

She compressed her lips as a sting of tears moistened her eyes. Why was his tone so accusatory? She couldn't help being pulled into his psyche. For land's sake, it was his strong emotion that summoned her essence, and the occasions were just as disruptive for her! If only she could hate him, but she couldn't.

Deke glimpsed the forlorn look on her face and tightened his jaw. He must steel himself against her influence! Knowing he was hurting her made him feel rotten, but it was the only way for him to maintain control over this mission. He hated himself for becoming distracted and allowing his attackers to get the upper hand. This wasn't the first time she'd interfered in his affairs, nor would it be the last unless he got rid of her. But they were stuck on this mission together and the thought of being without her left him bereft. What was a man to do? He couldn't stand the thought of living with her and yet life seemed bleak without her. Wasn't there some compromise they could reach?

Feeling guilty over the despicable way he was treating her, he cast her a sideways glance, marveling at how she could always look so beautifully composed even when upset. In some respects his feelings toward her were as ambivalent as the emotions he held about his own dual roles. Scientist or warrior, which was he? He tried to deny the fighting instinct that made him so good on commando raids. It reminded him of his father and the constant nagging he'd undergone as a child to engage in competitive sports. And yet now that Deke had a taste of combat, he could almost say he enjoyed it and that horrified him. As a scientist, he valued life and sought to study and preserve it. Was he becoming so like his father that he'd disregard his morals to make unethical compromises? Great suns, he hoped not! And yet what direction was he taking with Mara? Would he really be fit to assume the chancellorship should he get the position, or was it beyond his ability to reach a middle ground in disputes? The role required a diplomat as well as a scientist and leader, and maybe he just wasn't the right person for the job . . . alone.

That last thought struck him like a lightning bolt. Alone? Of course he couldn't do it alone! He needed someone like Mara who could steer him down the proper path, curb his aggressive tendencies, and help him manage an intergalactic community of hundreds. With her experience, she was perfectly qualified to advise him in negotiations and to mediate disagreements. But would the sacrifice to his own life be worth it?

He marched silently down the trail, glad she couldn't read his tumultuous thoughts. No conclusions came to him except that he had to apologize for his callousness. Her sad, drawn face wounded his heart, especially since he'd been the cause.

"We'll make preparations to leave for NARC territory. I don't think we'll tell anyone where we're going," he said once they reached the village. "There may be sympathizers among the villagers. I'll ask Onus Hahn for our weapons back and give him an excuse for our absence."

"I'll try bargaining with that old Wort by the cluster of berries," Wren said. "He's got a pile of ropes made from woody vines and they might come in handy."

"Speaking of berries, I'm starving," Deke remarked, feeling an empty gnawing in his stomach. "We'll need to eat before we go. Mara, you can arrange for us to have a meal. Doctor, I'm sure you'll need to recalibrate your instruments. Let's meet back here in an haura."

Deke split off from the others to find Onus Hahn, glad he didn't have to return to the hut he shared with Mara. He wasn't ready to face her alone yet because it meant confronting his own feelings. It was easier to remain distant and rattle off orders.

Onus Hahn believed his story that they were heading back to Revitt Lake City by land in order to collect valuable plant specimens. Deke knew he'd contact Fromoth Trun and didn't want the Yanuran leader to expect them too early. He refused Onus Hahn's offer of a winged pod for transport because their route would be traceable. They'd head up toward higher ground and then rely on Wren's unique navigational skills to guide them.

After a quick meal, he conferred with his crew and decided which trail they'd follow. Regretting that he hadn't been able to subdue a NARC rebel and force him into acting as their guide, he shook his head. Drop it, he told himself. What's done is done. You've lost the opportunity and there's no use brooding over it. Yet his regret made him morose, and so it was with a brusque gesture that he led his team onward.

Chapter Nineteen

The thick jungle closed around the landing party with an eerie stillness. Forced to proceed single-file on a trail roughened with rocks and tree roots, Deke took the lead. His backpack bulged, full of food and supplies he'd purloined from the Worts. He'd gotten enough to hold them for several days, but hopefully their journey wouldn't last so long.

As he trudged along the narrow path, brushing leafy branches and vines off his face, he mentally reviewed their stock: mosquito netting, protective sheeting, portable flametorches, dry socks and underwear and an extra treksuit each, a couple of machetes. Wren had his cans of high-calorie nutritional supplements in his sack, and Hedy had her medpack. Deke had recharged their shooters and felt prepared to meet whatever challenges lay ahead.

Somehow it no longer mattered if he was successful in distinguishing himself and getting the chancellorship. Saving Jallyn from harm was more important, and he recognized that his earlier goals might not have been valid. Blinded by his own need to succeed, he'd ignored the things that really made life worthwhile. Being with those he cared about and pursuing the research he loved were more meaningful. Troubled, he glanced over his shoulder at Mara, wondering what place she had in his future. He still wasn't sure where he wanted her, or even what role she hoped to play. He only knew that he couldn't contemplate a future without her.

As Mara's eyes adjusted to the dim light of the jungle, she glanced up to see ferns the size of trees rising like awnings above her head and vines twisting like gnarled ropes hanging from tree limbs. Mosses and epiphytic plants grew upon other plants, flowers providing brilliant displays of color among the greenery.

Feeling Deke's gaze on her face, she glanced at him, dismayed when he whipped his head forward and marched on. Challenged by his silence, she compared him to the trees. Like the tall signposts of the jungle, he was tall, firm, and unyielding. Only inside each tree trunk was a living core, giving oxygen even as it received sunlight and moisture through its leaves. How could she reach Deke's heart when he begrudged her even the slightest consideration? She gave him everything and he'd given back nothing in return.

No, that wasn't true. He'd shared his hopes and dreams, his yearnings and choices. It was possible she knew more about him than he did himself. But that didn't aid her cause. She didn't have the experience to break his barriers.

Practice your meditation! Master Keenan's words drifted into her mind like dust motes on dappled rays of sunshine. Of course, her anxiety was closing her off. She needed to expand her consciousness, to tighten the bonds between their chakras, and she could only accomplish that by becoming one with the universal energy force that flowed in and around all matter.

Concentrating on her footing, she didn't have the chance to meditate during their uphill hike along the increasingly mountainous trail. It was hot and windy and she felt like a steamy beast of burden when they rested at a lookout point where ridge after ridge of unbroken jungle met their gaze. Wiping the sweat from her brow, she turned to Hedy.

"I'm glad we had those fitness sessions on board the *Celeste* or I'd never make it!"

Hedy's chest heaved from the exertion. "Yes, you would. Your dancing keeps you in shape. I'd never have made it if Wren wasn't pulling me halfway up that hill!" Her infatuated glance fell upon the big Polluxite who was pacing back and forth, flapping his magnificent wings. He didn't even appear winded.

Neither did Deke. He stood off to the side, giving Ebo a report via datalink. Mara recognized the stiff set of his shoulders as representing the loneliness of command, the responsibility of decisions that were his alone, and she yearned to merge with him and offer support.

"Let's move on," Deke said curtly, terminating communications. "We'll make camp at nightfall. That should give us another two hauras."

She groaned. "I'm hungry! When do we eat?" Their meal of fruit and fish in the Wort village hadn't provided her with enough energy to go on.

"Very well. We'll eat now," he said, passing around a snack of bananas and nuts.

They refilled their canteens with fresh water from a gushing mountain stream. The cold liquid felt good sliding down Mara's throat. She was loath to budge but when Deke gave the signal, she gamely packed away the remnants of her repast and slung her backpack over her slim shoulders. Already her muscles ached and she knew it would only get worse. The soggy humidity added to the discomfort.

The path took them from a rocky incline to a tract along a river and then it diverged into a quagmire of greasy clay and mud. Water glistened on leaves, and dripping noises accompanied the chirping of birds and the cheep of catarrhines overhead. Once or twice she glanced back, thinking she sensed something watching, but the stillness of the jungle met her gaze. Plodding along, she did catch a glimpse of a furry gray animal peering at them from a thick cluster of reedy platwhacks. Then the trail took a downward curve. Up and down the hills they went, keeping a steady pace. One stretch hugged a slope and below they saw a rushing river boiling over a bed of boulders.

Deke called a halt when they came upon a dilapidated house constructed of roughly hewn boards. The wood sagged with rot and water ran in streams all around it. But the abandoned dwelling would provide shelter, so Deke ordered them to make camp.

Hedy passed around an igoob leaf. "I picked the leaves in the village. Chew on it. It'll keep the insects away," she advised.

Deke and Wren produced a meal of boiled elephant-ear roots. The plant food was starchy, tasting like potatoes with a nutty flavor. It filled their stomachs and left them satisfied, albeit sore and tired from exertion. Exhausted, they just had the energy remaining to wrap themselves in the environmental sheeting Deke supplied. Rain began to drum on the tin roof and insects buzzed outside the netting they'd strung across the open doorway. Wren stayed awake, taking the first watch, while Mara and the others drifted into sleep.

Mara awakened at the first hint of dawn. Rising, she saw Deke had fallen asleep at his post by the door. Poor thing, she thought, sparing a moment to gaze affectionately at the handsome angles of his face. His expression appeared peaceful. Not wishing to disturb him, she brushed past, lifting the netting out of her way. Beside a large tree, she relieved herself and cleansed her hands and face in a running stream. A flat rock beckoned to her and she sat, facing the forest. It had been a long time since she'd meditated like this, surrounded by the beauty of nature. She began a series of exercises, mental and physical, designed to open and charge the chakras. Her consciousness expanded as she experienced the connectedness of everything around her. The universal energy field flowed through her, penetrating her physical body, shining with radiance from her aura. Her vision clarified until she could see the shimmering vortices of her auric layers, pulsating with each breath she took.

A disturbance in the force attracted her attention. Glancing over her shoulder, she noticed Deke stumbling from the direction of the hut, a groggy look on his face.

"Mara?" he called.

"I'm over here." She brushed away a feeling of uneasiness and stood to watch him approach. With her heightened perception, the rose-colored arcs that sparked between their chakras were electrifyingly real. With pleasure she noticed they were thickening at the lower levels, meaning Deke was beginning to accept her. A leap of joy filled her heart and totally obliterated the ripple of darkness she'd sensed earlier.

Deke's auric bodies glowed with energy. As he approached, a finger of light reached out from his emotional layer, stretching toward her. Her astral being separated from her essence and she flew toward him, ready to envelop him with her love. Immediately his light was extinguished, and she was thrust back into her physical body.

I caused him to withdraw, she realized. He was still walking in her direction, unaware that anything other than a verbal exchange had passed between them. I must have been perceived as a threat. Again, my aura was about to invade his, my essence was out of control. That must be overwhelming to someone of his limited perception.

If only I could let him call the shots, she told herself. What if she tried? What if she reined in her responses, attempted to maintain tighter control over herself even during their lovemaking? Could she avoid the separations?

"What are you doing out here?" he asked, his tone gruff. "I got worried when I woke up and saw you weren't inside."

She thrilled at the concern implied by his words. His hair was unkempt, his jaw shadowed by stubble, and his treksuit rumpled, but for all his grime, she thought he looked spectacular. "I needed some time alone," she said softly.

His clear brown eyes caught and held hers. "I've been wanting to talk to you. I'm sorry about the way I acted yesterday. I was insufferably rude and thoughtless and I've no excuse other than I'm losing control over this situation and it bothers the hell out of me. I don't know how to deal with it . . . or you."

She reached out to trace her finger along his jawline. "It's my fault, too. I haven't been trying hard enough to control my separations. If I respond less intensely to events that affect you, perhaps that will help."

Deke caught her hand and kissed her palm. "I don't know if I like that idea." He stepped closer. "Your beauty stuns my senses, Mara. Even when I want to resist you, I can't. You're like a wood nymph come to tempt me. In your presence, my mind goes numb and my body reacts the only way a man can respond to a beautiful woman."

She shuddered at his sensual tone of voice. His mere presence had the power to weaken her knees and vaporize her ability to reason. Steeling herself against his allure, she closed her eyes when he bent his head to kiss her.

The pressure of his mouth on hers strengthened her desire, but she continued to resist the onslaught to her senses. If she limited her response, she might prevent another separation.

Deke's mouth hungered for hers. As he pressed his lips against her mouth, he pulled her close and reveled in the softness of her body. She was the Light personified: beauty, grace, compassion, and intelligence encased in a loveliness that had no parallel. His desire exploded and he moaned her name, scraping his fingers through her thick hair.

But what was this? Instead of her usual enthusiastic, almost wanton response, she was barely moving her mouth under his. Nor did her chest heave with excitement. Did she no longer find him desirable? Had he hurt her so badly that he'd killed her passion for him?

A wave of panic swept over him. So intense was it that he became frightened. Lifting his head, he gazed at her with a puzzled frown. "Mara, what's wrong?"

Her long lashes flicked open. Her eyes, wide and dark as an eclipsed sun, stared at him in confusion. "What do you mean?"

"You're not . . . I mean, you don't seem interested." He dropped his hands and moved back.

For a moment she didn't answer. Then a sympathetic smile curved her lips. "I was trying to be less responsive. I thought it might prevent me from separating if I exercised better self-control."

"But you said it was my strong emotions that drew you to me."

"That is so, but I can do my part to rein in my feelings. Perhaps you should try to restrain your reactions."

He stared at her. "Restrain my reactions? Are you crazy? Don't you know what being near you does to me?"

Mara merely shrugged. "It's your choice, Deke. I'm

offering you an option. You hate it when I jump into your head. If we both act more dispassionately, it may help avoid another occurrence."

"But . . . but . . ." He trailed off lamely. Speechless, he didn't know how to respond. What if she never entered his essence again? Wasn't that what he wanted? He thought long and hard while she kicked at a rotting log on the ground, and he reached the conclusion that he'd be unhappy either way. He couldn't abide her invading his mind but he didn't want to lose the incredible sensation of being united with her. Yet he couldn't have it both ways. Either he accepted her fully, sacrificing his right to mental privacy, or he'd have to reject her completely.

"I don't care for your option," he blurted angrily. "I like you the way you are when we make love. I don't want you to inhibit your response to me." He paused, struggling with his own confused feelings. "I'll try it your way. I'll let you into my mind . . . whenever you come." Not that he had any choice, but if he was willing to receive her, the experience might not be so intrusive when he wasn't expecting it.

Her keen eyes probed his. "You're not ready yet. I still sense reluctance and fear. You've got to be the one to take control, not me."

He didn't understand what she meant but he didn't care. Her feminine scent overwhelmed his senses. The sun had risen and a heavy mist was drifting into the valley. The meager sunlight caught the droplets of moisture and illuminated them in a luminescent glow behind her that made her look like a goddess with her hair streaming down. He felt a surge of blood rush to his groin. By the corona, if he was to be the one to take control, he wanted her, here and now!

"Mara, be mine!" he mumbled thickly, grasping her by the shoulders. Crushing her into his embrace, he lowered his mouth to hers. She must have sensed his wild need, his willingness to try to accept her, because this time her lips parted and her arms coiled around him.

Mara gave herself willingly to his embrace. Spiritually they were already connected, and now he was beginning to reach out to her on an elemental level. It was happening the way she'd hoped and she didn't want to do anything to disrupt the new status of their relationship. Accordingly, she decided to let him make all the first moves and tightened her resolve not to separate until he wished for it. Even if she found herself hovering in her astral body, she'd exert all her force of will not to enter his essence until he summoned her.

And he did summon her while his hands desperately roamed her back and his mouth plundered hers with a mad intensity that thrilled her.

"Mara . . ."

She could almost hear the unspoken words. They were like the wind, a whisper in her ear. The spiritual call broke her restraint and her aura floated upward through her crown, merging almost instantaneously with Deke's energy being. She felt his arousal and his state of abandonment and knew he wanted to give to her all that she'd given him and more. Her breath caught in her throat as he lowered her onto a carpet of moss. As the mist drifted over them, blotting out their surroundings, he slowly peeled off her treksuit and undergarments and discarded his own.

"Gods, you're exquisite," he said, kissing first one breast and then the other.

She writhed as he ministered to her aching nipples. When he drew one into his mouth and stroked the swollen tip with his tongue, she moaned his name. Clutching at his hair, she tangled her fingers in the soft waves as though they were a lifeline and she were drowning. He took his time, teasing each nipple into a taut peak and massaging her other breast with his hand. His tender touch drove her wild, more so when she shared his own excitement. From his viewpoint, stroking her heightened his pleasure, and that dual delight made her mad with passion.

He shifted his position and their mouths clamped together. Tasting his hot breath inflamed her senses and her desire skyrocketed. Splaying her hands across his broad back, she rocked her hips, pushing against his engorged manhood. She spread her legs, urging him in.

Now! Take me now! she pleaded silently.

As though he'd heard, Deke thrust into her in one hard motion. For a moment, he suspended movement, as if he were enjoying her tightness and experiencing the fullness he brought her at the same time. She could barely breathe, so taut was the knot of tension inside her. When he slid outward and inward again at an agonizingly slow pace, she dug her fingernails into his skin. The inferno that had been building inside her rushed toward the surface, and as he drove deeply inside her with a grunt of pure male glory, she reached her climax. Her shuddering spasms brought him over the edge and his hot, sticky seed spurted into her.

Yes! Mara thought. I am yours.

I know, Deke's mind responded. And I want you to be mine . . . only mine.

She couldn't read his thoughts but could sense his possessiveness and the pleasure he derived from her company. He wants me! she realized joyously. And he's finally recognizing how right it feels when we're together. At last! But now wasn't the time to count her blessings. They still had a job to do, and she didn't dare distract him any longer.

As soon as she'd broken their spiritual link, she rolled off him. "The daylight is dispersing the fog. We'd better move on."

Deke lingered to kiss her lightly on her tender lips. "We'll talk later . . . about us. I'm still not sure where I want this to go, but I know I can't risk losing you. We'll work something out."

Great suns, wasn't he going to ask her to go home with him? What did he mean by working something out? Troubled, she pulled on her clothes, casting a surreptitious glance at the forest surrounding them. Strange animal warbles and hoots accompanied the sound of dripping water. The air was fresh with the scent of rain. When the mist rose, it promised to be a lovely sunlit day.

So why did she have a sudden premonition of danger? Was it because of what Deke had said? A chill racked her body but she shrugged off her irrational fear, excusing it as anxiety over his remark. It wasn't a sense of real danger that bothered her; it was a fear of where their relationship was going. Deke still hadn't said he loved her, nor had he implied he wanted her as a permanent part of his life. A wave of depression hit her as she debated what he'd meant.

Striding toward the ramshackle house, she wondered if Hedy and Wren were awake. Deke walked quietly beside her, deep in thought. His mind is already focusing on the mission, she sensed, while I'm still thinking about him. If only I could cast him from my thoughts so easily! But given her serious disposition, that was impossible. Her problems preoccupied her to the exclusion of all else, and even Jallyn's precarious situation paled beside her yearning for Deke's acceptance. He was right: this was proving to be a distraction neither of them needed.

After breaking camp, Deke led the others along the trail up a rigorous incline. He should have been thinking about the upcoming confrontation with the NARC rebels but instead was replaying his lovemaking with Mara in his imagination. His loins stirred as he relieved the feel of her pliant body writhing under his. It was difficult to concentrate on their mission when all he could think of was when they'd lie together next.

Trudging along the mountainous path, he used the pretense of wanting to discuss a plan of action with Wren to move ahead of the women. His backpack felt heavier today, and even though the sunlight reaching the ground was dim, his body was bathed in sweat. The mist had lifted, leaving a heavy humidity that made breathing laborious on the rough path they followed.

"You're sure we're heading in the right direction?" Deke queried his navigator.

Wren appeared winded by the climb through rock-laden trails, or maybe it was the occasional glimpse of a precipice and a huge dropoff to the side that made his face pale and his breath come short. "I got a rebound echo from up there, sir," he said, pointing. "There must be many of them."

He nodded grimly. "The mountaintop must be crawling with rebels. We'll have to be careful. I wish we didn't have to bring the women along."

Wren glowered at him. "Don't let Mara hear you say that! She'd be sure to present an argument."

Deke gave him a sideways glance. "I still don't know what to do about her when this is over. Have you thought about you and Hedy?"

Wren's lips tightened. "I have no choice. I cannot pursue her."

"Mara told me how she caught you two in the bathing pool. She was sorry for the interruption." Mara had related the story yesterday during one of their rest breaks when Hedy and Wren sought a moment alone.

"I thought Dr. Te'larr was in distress," Wren explained, his face coloring. "When I came upon her under the waterfall, she was floundering in the lake and hollering for assistance."

"So you jumped in, clothes and all, while she was stark

naked!" He chuckled. "It was a come-on, you big oaf! And you fell for it."

"She was so incredibly alluring. I couldn't help myself."

"Maybe you need to lie with a woman to cure your problem. Have you considered that possibility?"

Wren shook his head vehemently. "I have not passed the ritual test. I cannot take a mate until I do."

"Well, in my opinion, you're wasting your life away."

They passed under a rocky overhang and Deke caught a glimpse of a small furred animal drinking from a pool of rainwater. The trail cut through a steep section of soggy forest and his boots squished through the muck. The fresh smell of green trees mixed with the scent of rainwashed soil and he found the trek rather pleasurable. In any event, the exercise helped to tamp his burning desire for Mara.

Mushrooms and molds sprouted on fallen logs and even the insects were coated with fungus, so damp was the forest in this area. Wren tramped beside him for a while, lost in silent thought. The women talked quietly behind them, keeping the pace.

The top of the mountain appeared unexpectedly. One minute they were enclosed by the lush jungle and the next they'd broken into an open area surrounded by trees barely higher than their heads. To the west, the shining reflective surface of an ocean as visible, and to the east were the dark green lowlands. A strong wind blew up, flapping their clothes and ruffling their hair.

"We'll stop along this ridge," Deke ordered, bringing his party to a halt. "Wren, do a weapons check. I'll notify Ebo of our progress." Pulling out his datalink, he conferred with his communications officer, informing him that they were about to enter unfriendly territory.

Wren took their shooters, checked the charges, and proceeded to clean off the moisture while Hedy knelt beside him on a nearby rise. They engaged in quiet conversation while Mara waited for Deke to finish his conversation with Ebo.

"I can't wait to see Jallyn!" she cried, her eyes shining with excitement.

"Do you wish to do a separation?" Deke asked, counting through his supplies.

"No, not now. Let's see what we're facing first. Wren said the rebels are stationed beyond that mountain pass." She ate a snack from their rations and drank her fill of water. Wiping her mouth with the back of her hand, she regarded him anxiously. "Do you really think we have a chance of rescuing Jallyn if she's there?"

"Of course. I've been on rescue missions before with heavy odds. We'll be successful."

She laid her hand on his arm. "I sense darkness on the path ahead."

He squinted in the bright sunlight. Huge boulders surrounded them where they sat on an exposed hilltop. At least they could see anyone approaching from their vantage point.

"Don't worry," he told her, patting her hand. "I won't let any harm come to you."

The reassuring words were barely out of his mouth when the sound of Hedy's shrill scream pierced the air.

Chapter Twenty

"Kill them!" Kromas snarled.

Mara's blood chilled at the words spoken in standard Jawani. She stood with her friends in the central hall of a huge stone fortress built into the mountainside, apparently the ancient lair of a tribal leader from Yanura's distant past. Hedy's scream had signaled an attack by hidden sentries who'd risen from what turned out to be artificially constructed boulders at the lookout point where they'd stopped to rest. Having been divested of their weapons and marched to the rebel stronghold, they were now the center of a heated argument. Armed insurgents surrounded them, and an uneasy grumbling pervaded the National Revolutionary Congress's command center as the leaders wrestled for power.

"We shall not harm them . . . yet," spoke a thin frogface with a yellowish tinge to his brown skin. He was called Ragger Minn, Mara had learned, and he appeared to represent a moderate stance while Kromas took a militant approach, advocating murdering them and destroying all ties with the Coalition.

"We can use them as a bargaining tool against Fromoth Trun," Ragger Minn urged his comrades.

Dressed in a short belted brown tunic with an animal fur thrown over his shoulders, he radiated an aura of command. She sensed he could be a formidable opponent even though he favored sparing their lives. Because her wrists were bound behind her back, she couldn't reach out to Deke for reassurance. He stood beside her, rigid with tension, and she guessed he was figuring the odds and trying to determine a means of escape. She'd prefer using diplomacy rather than violence and decided it was worth a try.

"Excuse me," she said, her voice ringing loud and clear in the cavernous hall. Dozens of bulging eyes shifted in her direction. "What exactly are your demands to Fromoth Trun? Perhaps we could help you obtain them."

Kromas's mouth split in a sneer. "Fromoth Trun doesn't listen to us. Why should he hear what you have to say?" He paced closer, eyeing her as though she'd make a tasty meal.

"He wants to be admitted into the Coalition," Deke ventured, glancing at her with a nod of approval. "Our welfare is important to him. If you tell us what it is you want, we can mediate between you."

"Yanura must not be accepted as a member of the Coalition!" Kromas shouted, spittle forming at the corner of his mouth. "Killing you and the infant will ensure that never happens!"

She caught her breath. "Is Jallyn here? Can I see her?"

Kromas stuck his face in front of hers and she sniffed his foul breath. "You'll be joining her soon enough." He swiveled his neck to regard Deke with unbridled hostility. "How did you escape the stinger eels in Dead Wort's Marsh? I'd thought we left you for dead."

Deke gave a cocky grin. "I scared them off."

Kromas stepped over and backhanded him. Stunned by the blow, Deke stumbled backward.

"No violence!" Ragger Minn cried. "Kromas, you are out of line. Do you wish to be forcibly removed from our council?"

Kromas's eyes narrowed as he slowly spun around. "Try it, *vermuchak*."

Ragger Minn met his gaze with a burning stare and seemed to grow in stature. "Don't upset my patience. Our demands on Fromoth Trun are valid. It is the reason why most of us are here. Are you saying you refute our goals?"

Tension cut through the air as thick as fog. Finally Kromas answered. "No," he said. "I just don't agree with your slow methods of achieving them, especially considering the current crisis."

"Will somebody please explain to us what's going on?" Mara demanded. Their lives were at stake and she still didn't understand why. "And can't our wrists be released? My fingers are going numb."

Ragger Minn nodded to an associate and their corded bonds were cut. Mara rubbed her chafed skin, wishing Hedy could apply a balm, but their knapsacks had been confiscated.

"Our demands to Fromoth Trun are threefold," Ragger Minn said, glaring at his prisoners. "Every Yanuran is routinely administered the drug Vyclor beginning at age twenty. After several initiating dosages, the drug must be continued for life. If stopped, the withdrawal symptoms can cause a painful death. Since the Croags control the merl beds and the processing centers, they control the supply of Vyclor. That means they rule over all of Yanura because no one dares oppose them for fear of getting their dose of Vyclor cut off. Taking Vyclor should be a choice of the people. Not everyone may want to extend their natural life span through artificial means, and certainly the Croags have too much power. That they use it to abuse our young is our strongest point of contention.

"Our children are taken from us shortly after birth, forced to live in underwater communities and harvest the merl. It is an arrangement that no one likes that goes back for ages, but who can protest it? The Croags allow no one else to participate in government. If other factions were represented, we'd make laws beneficial to us all, not just the Croag majority." His golden eyes glowed with fervor. "It is fairness we are demanding, and the right to make decisions that affect us. Is that wrong of us, human?" He directed his diatribe at Deke.

Deke's mouth tightened. "Then why did you abduct Sarina's child? You're trying to make us believe that your values are worthy, yet you are guilty of a heinous crime. How do you rationalize that action?"

Muttering off to the side with some of his cronies, Kromas suddenly straightened. "We are desperate to stop the Croags! Tell them about the missiles, Ragger Minn. See if they agree that our aims are just." An approving mumble sounded from the watching crowd.

Behind Mara, Wren grunted, and she wondered if he was uncomfortable. It had been several hauras since he'd opened his wings and he might be feeling the tension of the confinement in ways other than the rest of them. He'd be mortified if his wings erupted in front of their captors.

Ragger Minn strutted toward Deke and her attention reverted to him. The leader's face had gone solemn. "Our intelligence reported that the Croags had found a new use for their pharmaceutical research division. Their chemistry labs had produced a weapon of incalculable danger, and they were preparing missiles to launch an offensive against us. This is why our tactics turned desperate. We must stop them before a bloodbath ensues!"

Deke's eyes widened in shock. "What kind of weapon? And how far away are they from being able to launch it? Where did they get the technology to build missiles?"

Ragger Minn held up a hand. "You ask many questions, Commander. Perhaps when you learn the answers, you'll decide to join our cause." Scratching his ear disk, he went on. "The Croags have created a chemical weapon using genetic manipulation of the drug Vyclor. The destructive agent, when inhaled in droplet form, causes the reverse effect of the antiaging mechanism: the victim's metabolism accelerates and he dies of heart failure within minutes. Our spies have seen evidence of testing of this new chemical agent. They've used our captured comrades as test subjects. We've holophotos of their dead bodies to show you as proof."

Deke's jaw dropped in astonishment. So that was what those bodies on the data card had signified. Glancing at Mara, he saw understanding dawn in her expression. "Do you know the location where the Croags are experimenting with this stuff?" He had the feeling he knew even if the rebels hadn't a clue.

"Of course," Kromas growled, "how else could we have obtained our evidence? But the place is too remotely situated for us to plan an attack, and anyway, it's the missile site that concerns us more. The warheads are already locked in. All the Croags await is a detonation device which would become available to them if they had access to Coalition technology."

No wonder Fromoth Trun was in such a hurry to get special trade status, Deke thought. "The Coalition doesn't sell detonators or other war-making devices."

Ragger Minn made a dismissive gesture. "Once he earns enough credits from the sale of Vyclor, Fromoth Trun can buy them from the black market. Where do you think he got the missiles from? True, the things are rudimentary, but they'll serve the purpose. Fromoth Trun bought them from the Rakkians."

"Rakkians!" Deke was astounded, and so were Mara and the others from the looks on their faces. "It was two Rakkians who stole Jallyn from her nursery!"

"Joro and Pruet." Ragger Minn smirked. "You should know that the Rakkians are a stinking race who hire their services to anyone willing to pay the price. Their technology is also available but it's much more expensive. We hired the two assassins to steal the child for us. They hid her in a special sensor-reflective insulated cabin inside their ship at the spaceport on Bimordus Two. The Defense League was fooled into chasing after the three vessels that launched following the abduction. Two days later, the Rakkian ship lifted off without arousing suspicions, and they delivered her to us."

Deke nodded. "So Fromoth Trun didn't know anything at the time of his launch about the abduction." Mara cast him a triumphant glance and he grinned sheepishly.

"Correct," Kromas replied croaking malevolently, "but he found out about it soon enough when we told him we'd kill the child and place the blame on him if he didn't accede to our demands."

Hedy cleared her throat. "When he wouldn't listen, you attacked me and Wren in the city, didn't you?"

Ragger Minn glowered at her. "Your deaths would have impeded his relations with the Coalition. It was Kromas's idea, not mine. Having the baby is enough leverage to bring to bear."

"And it's not working!" Kromas shouted, and voices of approval joined his. "Fromoth Trun refuses to yield power. I say kill them all and notify the Coalition that Fromoth Trun is responsible. That'll put a halt to his grandiose plans."

Loud murmuring erupted, putting forth arguments for both sides.

"If you kill us," Deke cautioned, "you'll face Coalition retribution. They won't just target Fromoth Trun. The Defense League will wreak havoc on your entire planet. This jungle will be made uninhabitable for eons. Heed my warning."

"We are listening, human, but I fear you are not hearing us," Ragger Minn said, a resigned look on his thin frog face. "Take them below while we decide their fate," he ordered, and a troop immediately surrounded them.

"Please, may we see Jallyn?" Mara asked anxiously.

"You may assume responsibility for her care," Kromas growled. "The brat has been giving her Rakkian caretaker a headache ever since she arrived, and her squalling makes us all edgy. She's yours for as long as you are here. And if I have my way, that won't be for too many hauras."

Kromas's evil snorting laughter echoed in Mara's ears as they were led through twisting corridors into the depths of the fortress. The air grew cold and damp and she shivered. She felt grimy in her treksuit but that was the least of her concerns. What would happen to them? Where was Jallyn?

Something hit her with the force of a tidal wave and she stopped, stunned. It wasn't anything material; she'd sensed it in her mind. And now she was being tugged mentally in a forward direction. With faltering steps, she proceeded along. Deke steadied her by the elbow, giving her a sharp glance, their armed escort precluding any meaningful dialogue.

The chamber they were led into was small, with a vaulted ceiling, cold stone walls, and a casement high up on one side. She recognized it instantly. The baby's crib stood by a wall, and a basket heaped with supplies rested on the floor beside it. At their entrance, a woman with brown hair knotted into a low bun rose from her rocking chair. Her violet eyes regarded them with surprise.

A wailing began that made Mara and her companions cover their ears.

"Jallyn!" Mara cried, rushing forward even as she realized that the mental vibes were coming from the child. The baby girl howled in her crib. As soon as she peeked over the edge, the baby stopped crying and gurgled happily. Mara's mental tension eased and she sensed the child's acute relief at glimpsing a familiar, friendly face.

She scooped Jallyn into her arms and buried her face against the baby's soft cheek. "Oh, Jallyn! We've found you!" Tears stung her eyes. She couldn't believe it! At last Jallyn was safe.

Or was she?

Holding the infant, she glanced at the guards. The troop commandant was addressing the caretaker.

"Your duties are terminated. Transport back to Rakkia has been arranged. Gather your belongings and go see Ragger Minn for further instructions."

Beaming gratefully, the woman hastened into an adjoining chamber.

"You will remain here," he told them. "The infant is now your responsibility."

"What's going to happen to us?" Hedy asked, her voice cracking.

"Your disposition is being determined."

The caretaker returned carrying a large satchel. "I am ready," she announced, and the troop escorted her out.

A loud click signaled the latching of an electronic lock on the heavy wooden door. Shut in, Mara and the other three looked at each other.

Deke broke the silence. "How is she?" he asked, sauntering toward Mara.

Mara's eyes misted fondly as she stared disbelievingly

at Jallyn. "She's fine." Her senses picked up contentment and she realized that Jallyn's communion with the universal energy field must be strong. No wonder the caretaker had complained of constant headaches in her presence. Jallyn must have been bombarding her with hostile mental vibes.

Kissing the baby's forehead, she thought that she'd never felt such joy.

"Uh, what do we do with her?" Deke asked.

Out of the corner of her eye, she noticed Hedy and Wren disappearing into the adjacent chamber. "There's diapers and formula," she said, tilting her head to indicate the basket on the floor. "And I see a vapor unit and a synthesizer by that wall, so we can cleanse her cloth diapers and refill the bottles. All she needs is right here."

Hedy emerged in time to hear her last sentence. "I wish I had my medpack," she stated. "There's a lounger inside the other room, and a cooling unit with food and water."

A flapping noise told Mara that Wren was exercising his wings. "Wren needs his Cal beverage," she remarked.

"I can survive without it for several days," the Polluxite said, appearing in the doorway.

"What happens now?" Hedy asked, frowning.

"We wait." Deke glared at them as though being imprisoned were their fault.

Mara nuzzled the baby's neck as she sat on the rocker. "Jallyn," she murmured, tweaking her tiny fingers. At least Jallyn's footed sleeper kept her warm.

"We may have found her," Deke said curtly, "but that doesn't mean we're going to get out of here alive."

"What do you suggest?" Mara asked coolly, wishing she could accurately gauge his emotion. At first, she'd sensed strong affection, but now he seemed irritated. Could he be jealous of the attention she was showing the child? She wanted to laugh at the absurdity of that, but the look in his eye told her she might be on track.

"I don't know!" Deke cried, exasperated. Pacing the chamber, he avoided her gaze.

Hauras later, the first opportunity presented itself for the possibility of their breaking out. They'd slept fitfully through the night, snacking on the food in the cooler, and discussing different options for escape. Mara had packed the infant's supplies in a huge carryall they'd found in a closet. Now footsteps approached from outside and Deke straightened his shoulders, frowning. Mara enveloped Jallyn in her arms, and Hedy and Wren stood side by side, their faces wary.

The lock clicked and the door swung wide. Facing them was the same troop commandant and his escort. "You are to come with me. We have arranged for your transfer to Revitt Lake City. Bring the child," he added, nodding at Jallyn.

Deke felt a wave of relief. So Ragger Minn had won out, and they were being sent to Fromoth Trun to plead the case for the rebels. Of course, he'd have to recommend a denial of the Yanuran's application to join the Coalition based on the political instability of his government, but Deke would deal with the Yanuran leader once they were safely away from here.

But his relief was short-lived. As soon as they emerged from the fortress into the mist-enshrouded forest, Mara put her hand on his arm.

"Something is wrong," she whispered.

He adjusted the sack on his shoulder where he carried Jallyn's supplies. "What do you mean?"

She glanced fearfully at the encroaching jungle. "They haven't given us back any of our equipment, nor has Ragger Minn spoken to us. I don't like it." She bit her lower lip and Deke took her arm as they resumed their climb up the rocky incline. The raucous cries of birds and the occasional howl of a wild animal penetrated the heavy air. The mist swirled around them, morning sunlight barely penetrating the thick foliage. Deke felt Mara stumble as she clutched Jallyn tightly in her arms.

Suddenly the trail ended in a rocky precipice. Mara and he halted abruptly as did the guards escorting them. The troop stepped back, laser rifles drawn, barrels pointed at them. Hedy and Wren moved back-to-back with him and Mara.

"What is this?" he snarled, while Mara caught her breath in fear.

The commandant sneered. "I lied, Commander. Kromas has decreed that you are to die. It is for the good of the people." And he raised his arm to give the order to fire.

At that moment, a platoon of war-painted Worts jumped out from behind the surrounding trees, screeching battle cries. Fighting broke out and laser fire zinged back and forth as the attackers engaged the troop. An alarm sounded as the fortress was sieged and all around them a battle raged.

Mara screamed, and Deke pushed her to the ground, covering her body and Jallyn's with his.

"Hedy!" Wren yelled, charging after her as she ran from the melee.

Rocks and fallen logs obstructed his path but he agilely avoided them, his fear for Hedy heightening his perception. Running along a rocky promontory, he was heedless of the soldiers chasing after them. "Stop!" he shouted to her. "You don't know where you're going! This track is dangerous!"

One minute she was in his view, and the next moment, she was gone.

His jaw dropped in horror. Laser bolts singed his ears as the soldiers fired at him, but he didn't stop. Rushing forward, he shrieked in terror when he reached the edge of a precipice.

Glancing downward, he saw Hedy's body tumbling . . . and far, far below were jagged rocks. Without a thought, his wings erupted and he jumped off the cliff. If he couldn't fly to save her, then he'd die with her.

As soon as he began his freefall, a wondrous thing happened. His wings started flapping. Up and down in a series of powerful strokes, they beat rhythmically just as they did when he was exercising them. Instinctively, he furled them back, streamlining his body so that he was able to dive downward with startling speed. And then he was below Hedy, swooping her limp form into his strong arms. He soared upward, realizing she had fainted but glad she was safe. He broke out of the mist into the blinding sunlight just as her lids fluttered open and she regarded him with amazement.

"Wren!" she exclaimed dazedly. "You're flying!"

"Aye, so I am," he answered, his voice soft and tender. Gazing at her, he felt moisture in his eyes. "Because of you, Hedy Te'larr, I am a whole man. I would like nothing more than to demonstrate my deep appreciation for your devotion. However, I cannot abandon my friends. I shall put you down safely and then see what I can do to help them."

"Don't you dare leave me!" Hedy protested. "Mara's in trouble, and I'm coming along." She dug her fingernails into his back in such a way that he knew he'd have to bring her.

Wren landed a short distance away so no one could see him flying. He and Hedy closed in on foot, carefully assessing the situation from behind a clump of bushes. A contingent of Croags had arrived and taken charge. The Worts had routed the rebels and Deke, Mara, and Jallyn were unharmed. Deke appeared to be in a heated argument with the Croag officer in command, but no one was pointing shooters at him, so Wren assumed everything was under control.

"What's going on?" he asked after revealing his presence.

"Hedy!" Mara rushed to her friend's side. "Where have you been? I was so worried!"

Still clutching Jallyn in her arms, Mara appeared disheveled, her treksuit splattered with mud and her damp hair plastered to her face. It had rained in the short interval they'd been away, Wren noted.

Hedy gave a secretive smile. "We managed to avoid most of the battle."

"Apparently the Wort warriors from the village tailed us here," Deke explained to his navigator. "They notified the Croags of the location and both launched a joint attack. Will you look at this shuttle?" He gestured to a sleek metal vehicle. "It may be an older model, but I'd no idea the Croags had access to such stuff."

"Sir, if you don't mind," the Croag officer said, his orange eyes bulging ominously.

"He wants us to board the shuttle but won't explain where we're going," Deke told Wren.

"Fromoth Trun wishes a dialogue with you," the soldier commented.

"I'll bet he does." He drew his crew aside for a quick conference. "We know too much, and Fromoth Trun is a desperate character. I say let's head back to the *Celeste.* I should notify the Admissions Committee about this situation and ask for instructions."

Hesitating, he glanced at Mara. Seeing her holding the child brought a lump to his throat. "Do you agree?" he asked.

Flashing him a brilliant smile, she nodded her head.

A Wort ran up to them, delivering their knapsacks, which Deke had requested. A hasty check showed everything intact. The only items missing were their weapons and datalinks.

"Where's my datalink?" Deke demanded. "I need to contact my ship." He glanced up, straight into the barrel of a shooter pointed at his chest. The Croag officer had drawn his weapon. "What is this?" Deke snapped.

Instinctively Mara moved closer and he draped a protective arm around her shoulder. Hedy gasped as other Croags surrounded them, and Wren's string of expletives rang in the cool morning air.

"You are not permitted to make contact with your ship," the Croag said, his stance militant. "Board the shuttle now!" He lifted his shooter.

"Fromoth Trun will regret this," Deke promised, shouldering his knapsack on one side and the baby's carryall on the other.

The infant started squalling and Mara squeezed her close, murmuring reassuring words in her ear. But the child with the sign of the circle on her palm must have sensed danger, because she wouldn't let up. Deke cast Mara a sympathetic glance but was unable to help. Worried about how he'd get his team safely off planet, he marched in front of the others toward the waiting shuttle.

At least he still had his dive computer strapped to his wrist. He could use the backup datalink to call Ebo, but first it would be smart to see where they ended up. Maybe Mara could use her diplomatic skills to talk Fromoth Trun into freeing them, although Deke had a bad feeling that wherever they were going, it was a one-way trip.

"Move!" the Croag officer shouted, prodding him along by shoving the shooter into his back.

He grunted his displeasure, resisting the urge to turn around and punch the fellow. Getting beaten into submission wouldn't aid their cause. Gritting his teeth, he strode up the ramp into the shuttle, glancing back at Mara to make sure she didn't need his assistance. Taking the seat assigned him, he strapped on his safety restraint as the crew began flight procedures. Mara sat beside him, stretching the restraint to secure herself and the child. Hedy and Wren were situated behind them.

A jolting lurch initiated the journey while the sky tilted

outside the viewport. One minute they were soaring toward the heavens and in the next, they'd taken a sharp dive downward, vectoring away from the mountains toward a sparkling aqua sea.

As the hiss of pressurized air reached her ears, Mara's throat felt dry even though the humidity in the cabin was increasing along with the temperature. The sharp angle of descent made her queasy. A dank odor filled the air and it became almost too thick to breathe.

"I feel sick," she whispered to Deke.

He gave her an amused glance. "Hold your nose and blow. It'll equalize the pressure and you'll feel better."

The sea's surface loomed toward them and they plunged through the waves, the shuttle's vibrations altering with the fluid environment. Fish, strands of seaweed, and marine mammals swam past their viewport in a blur. Mara's jaw dropped in astonishment as they neared the seabed and a structure in the distance became visible. Built of a white material, it glistened in the reflected light from the shuttlecraft.

"By the Light, it's an undersea community!" she cried, staring at the habitat designed as an interlocking series of cylinders and spheres.

"Fascinating," Deke murmured, leaning forward as their vehicle approached a docking bay.

Mara saw Deke glance at his dive computer, and knew he was checking their distance from the surface.

The shuttle slowed, rocking side to side as the pilot lined it up with the connecting port.

A loud clanging signaled they had docked. Grating noises and a rush of water reverberated in the cabin as the locking mechanisms activated.

His maneuvers completed, the pilot glanced at the troop commandant. "What are my orders?" he asked.

"Return to Seabase One," the officer croaked. "Our

visitors won't be needing transportation for a while." Turning to Deke, he grinned maliciously. "Follow me."

Taking the lead from Deke, Mara unfastened her restraint and rose, stretching to ease a cramp in her leg. Jallyn had stopped crying, having worn herself out and fallen asleep in Mara's lap.

"Do you feel all right?" Deke asked her, a solicitous frown on his face.

Her mouth set determinedly, she nodded. She didn't speak as they were herded through a double hatchway to a service chamber that held a pneumatic platform.

Hedy touched her elbow from behind. "I don't like this place, Mara."

Mara clutched Jallyn tighter to her breast as they were prodded onto the platform. "I agree," she said, and their brief conversation halted as the troop leader pulled a lever.

Three levels down, the platform came to a slow stop, accompanied by a hissing sound. A familiar frogface stood waiting to greet them in another maintenance area.

"Rogi Kwantro," Fromoth Trun said, beating his chest with his fist and bowing elegantly as though they were on a diplomatic tour. "Welcome to Habitat Oceania."

"What is the meaning of this?" Deke demanded, stepping forward.

"Ludack, you may report to the duty station with your troops," Fromoth Trun addressed the officer. The Croag saluted and led his soldiers through a hatchway into another section.

"Comdr. Sage, you should be grateful we rescued you from the rebels. They planned to kill you and the child."

"You knew about Jallyn all along, didn't you?" Mara said, her voice tense with fury. Her arms were getting tired from holding the baby, but thank goodness she was quiet. Jallyn breathed softly through her tiny nose, her sweet scent making Mara want to scream in rage. How dare Fromoth Trun keep his knowledge from them! They could have used the *Celeste*'s resources to locate Jallyn a lot sooner.

"The National Revolutionary Congress contacted me shortly after Jallyn's arrival on Yanura," Fromoth Trun answered, his tone smooth. "I'd hoped to resolve the situation without having to concern you."

"How absurd. Why do you think we were sent here?" She glared at him. "Investigating your claims about Vyclor was only one reason. We were also searching for Jallyn!" She shifted her position. "By any chance, did your plans for resolving the situation include—"

"I'd like to return to my ship," Deke blurted. "Lt. Ebo has a fix on our current position," he told the Yanuran leader. "He'll take certain predetermined actions if I don't report in."

"You can contact him in a short while," Fromoth Trun said, a wily look on his frog face. "First, I'd like to show you around our undersea community. Coming from a water world, I'm sure you'll appreciate our unique life-style." The Croag gave Mara and the others a cursory glance, as though dismissing their importance. "Perhaps your friends would care to refresh themselves while we talk."

Miffed at Fromoth Trun's attitude, she tilted her chin stubbornly upward. "We'd be interested in a tour also, thank you. Which way shall we go?"

Fromoth Trun straightened his robe of office. "Follow me," and he proceeded through a series of compartments separated by hatchways.

Mara and the others trailed after him, Deke taking the lead beside the Yanuran potentate. She hung back, sensing hostility directed at the Coalition team, including Jallyn. It didn't bode well for their future, and she figured they'd be smart to consider a means of escape. Gods, to think she'd believed everything Fromoth Trun had told her on

Bimordus Two. What a naive fool! No wonder Deke had scorned her initial assessment of the Yanuran situation while on board the *Celeste.* She'd been right in Fromoth Trun's being innocent of Jallyn's abduction, but he'd been informed as soon as the NARCs received the baby from the Rakkians hired to capture her. He'd hidden the truth from them and even now was planning to launch missiles armed with chemical warheads at the rebels.

Her eyes widened. If Fromoth Trun learned how much they knew, he'd never let them go!

The Croag led them through the habitat, pointing out the sights as though they were welcome guests. They passed through a series of laboratories, data centers, a medical clinic, machine shops, and living quarters that covered all three levels. Finally, they came to a huge observation lounge with a floor-to-ceiling window.

Gaping at the view, Mara nudged Deke. "Look at those Yanurans swimming through that complex! They're . . . they're children!"

Deke turned a questioning glance on Fromoth Trun.

"Indeed, you are correct," the Yanuran leader bragged, gesturing them forward. "Our young are born with gills. Because they must breathe underwater, we bring them here. It is convenient to use them as a labor force to harvest the merl. At puberty, the young Yanurans develop lungs and are reunited with their mothers when they go to live on land."

Mara glowered at him. "The Wort villagers do not seem pleased with this way of life, nor are the NARCs. They claim you practice coercion to conscript the young of other races."

Fromoth Trun's skin mottled. "They do not see the benefit of what we do." He raised his arm in a sweeping gesture. "Look at what we provide for our young: an entire underwater city. We even bring teachers down from the surface to instruct them. Adults come in shifts, adjusting their life-styles in order to enter the underwater environment."

"How do you communicate?" Deke asked curiously. Beside him, Mara handed Jallyn over to Hedy. The baby stirred, making gurgling noises.

"The children have an inherent ability to communicate with each other underwater. As adults, we use a hydrophone device built into a face mask."

Deke nodded, that form of communication being familiar to him. A hydrophone sent out high-frequency sound waves. On Eranus, they used a headset that picked up mastoid bone sound transfers using a similar principle.

Gazing out the window, he studied the youngsters swimming around an open latticework where he could make out sleeping pods and work areas. The habitat he and the others stood in was filled with pressurized air. Adult Croags who came here to work with the young would have to adapt to a water environment before joining them. That meant there were air locks, an important factor he stored away for later use.

Fromoth Trun explained how the young labor force cut the merl stipes, loading the harvest onto platforms which rose to the surface. From there the cut stalks were transferred to a ship that went to a processing center. Communities like this one were stationed all around the globe at offshore regions rich with merl farms.

"The crystalline white rocks are used in the process for making Vyclor, aren't they?" Deke said.

Fromoth Trun nodded. "Our youngsters load the bits of rock into bins, which are then transferred to the surface." He gazed at Deke thoughtfully. "Your friend Larikk first introduced the idea of putting Vyclor on the intergalactic marketplace. When he learned about the drug, he offered to help get it approved in exchange for a cut of the profits. The

NARCs killed him, hoping to discourage other offworlders from visiting the planet and setting back any plans we had to market the drug to the Coalition."

"If Vyclor was put on the market, how would you use the profits?" Mara interceded.

"We'd buy harvester machines so our children wouldn't be forced to do this work. It would free them from the hardship so they could be raised with their mothers. That's why we're so anxious for early trade status. We wish to make reforms, Commander. We are not cruel on purpose. I shall set up a commlink so you can send a message to the Coalition approving our admissions status, and then you can all leave." He smiled broadly, expecting Deke's acquiescence.

Deke's eyes narrowed suspiciously. "I don't know that I'm ready to give approval. In fact, because of the situation with the National Revolutionary Congress, I just might have to recommend a rejection of your application."

Fromoth Trun bristled angrily. "But I just said we're willing to make reforms! Once we have the harvesters, we can sit down with the NARCs to discuss their complaints."

"The conscription of young is not the only issue," Mara stated. "They demand representation in the central government and an end to routine distribution of Vyclor. They say everyone should have freedom of choice regarding taking the drug."

The Yanuran leader scowled at her. "If they wish to die young, that is their business. It was decided long ago that the population as a whole would benefit from the treatment. But these are issues that can be discussed later, after we obtain the harvesters."

Deke was occupied in observing a group of youngsters working within clear view of the observation window, when Fromoth Trun whispered to Mara: "Breathing this atmosphere for any length of time could be harmful to

Jallyn. I suggest you use your time with us to convince Comdr. Sage of the sincerity of my request."

He grinned broadly, and she felt a wave of evil intent that belied the expansiveness of his smile. "Feel free to wander about on your own and explore the wonders of our community. Of course you have nowhere to go should you decide to leave."

His loud croaking laugh rang harshly in her ears. "Come," Fromoth Trun addressed the others, "I'll show you to your guest quarters. Your accommodations should be comfortable, and meals are available from a remote system. Order what you want and it will be delivered to your room. Are you set for the infant's supplies?"

"I think we have what we need," Mara said, her lips compressed. At this point she had the feeling Fromoth Trun wouldn't let any of them go unless Deke did what the Yanuran leader demanded. They weren't in any immediate danger, but they should use their time to formulate a plan of escape.

Deke agreed wholeheartedly when she voiced her concerns in the privacy of their sleeping quarters. It was a large room with dormitory-style beds, a table and chairs, softly cushioned loungers, and a music center. They sat around for a team conference. Mara ensconced herself on the lounger to feed Jallyn. Having helped Sarina enough times, she was familiar with infant care. Jallyn suckled happily on her bottle and Mara thought how fortunate Sarina was to have a child with such a sweet disposition.

Deke gazed at them with such a tender expression that her heart melted. "I don't believe Fromoth Trun," he said in response to her inquiry. "He wants those harvesters, but I'm not sure freeing the youngsters of their burden is the real reason for his request."

Hedy, standing beside Wren, perked up. "He didn't even

mention the satellite survey and the border dispute with the Worts."

"No," Deke mused, "and there's still that business about chemical warfare. I wonder what he's got up his sleeve."

"Detonators!" Wren's voice thundered. "I believe the rebels mentioned this is what is keeping the Croags from launching the missiles: they lack a detonator device. Does Fromoth Trun hope to buy them using the profits from Vyclor?"

Deke shook his head. "He'd have to purchase them on the black market. The price would be prohibitive."

"There used to be a farm near where I lived on Tyberia. If I recall, the land-based harvesting machines have an activator mechanism," Mara interjected.

"Of course! So do our kelp harvesters. By the stars, I'll bet you Fromoth Trun plans to convert the starter mechanisms into detonators. I know from my training and knowledge of machinery repairs that the electronics are similar.

"Fromoth Trun has everything in place," Deke said wonderingly. "The deadly chemical agent, missile silos, targets programmed in. Now all he needs is the detonator to make it work. Great suns, he really wants to join the Coalition so he can obtain the means to wipe out the opposition!"

Mara and the others stared at Deke and she knew they were all focused on one idea: total power. Fromoth Trun was a totalitarian leader who would stop at nothing to achieve his aims. No wonder the NARCs had kidnapped Jallyn. It was their last desperate hope to stop him.

"What do we do?" Hedy whispered, her eyes wide with fright.

The implications weren't good, Mara thought, her mood dismal. With their knowledge, Fromoth Trun could never let them leave. He'd force Deke to contact the Admissions

Committee and recommend approval status, then stage an accident and kill them . . . all except Jallyn, that is.

"He'll send Jallyn home," she told the others, her voice subdued. "He'll say her abduction was part of a Rakkian plot and he rescued Jallyn, but we were killed in the skirmish. Fromoth Trun will be regarded as a hero."

Deke's jaw tightened. "We have to stop him! He said we are free to roam about, thinking we have no means to escape. Well, he's wrong." Deke indicated his dive computer. "I can still contact Ebo, and we'll find a way out of here. Let's split up into pairs and explore. I want a detailed map of this place. Mara, will Jallyn nap long enough for you to come with me?"

She rose, putting the baby into a crib she'd fashioned on the floor using several blankets. "I think so. This place isn't that immense that we'll be gone for too long."

They prowled about with amazing freedom. The habitat personnel, advised that they were a visiting inspection team sent by the Coalition prior to being approved for admissions status, treated them to every courtesy and answered all their questions.

"What happens if there's an emergency and you need to evacuate?" Deke asked a worker monitoring the atmospheric systems in the main data control center.

Banks of video screens provided a 360-degree view of the habitat's surroundings. Outside, floodlights bathed the underwater environment in a yellowish-green iodide glow. A swirl of minute particles and marine organisms restricted visibility so that beyond the range of the lights, the scene tapered into murky darkness.

The worker glanced up. "A watertight transfer capsule is docked in Bay Two, available for emergencies." He tapped at a schematic diagram, showing a saucer-shaped vessel. "It holds thirty, but our capacity down here is generally around twenty-five personnel. Depressurization occurs automatically during the ascent. Most of us are here longer than forty-eight hauras, so we're at the same saturation level."

Deke pointed to a similar blip on the liquid crystal diagram. "Is that another capsule?"

"Aye, but the ballast system is damaged and we haven't gotten a repair crew down to fix it yet."

"What's the problem?" Deke's tone was casual but his heart thumped with excitement. Should the need arise, this might be their ticket out of there.

"There's an eight-inch tear in the hull. Also, the propulsion board short-circuited, so the capsule is stuck here until the electrical engineers arrive." He turned back to his duty. "The capsule slipped from its cable and hit a high ridge of rock," he added in explanation.

"I see. So normally you have one of these capsules standing by, but because of the damage, a second one was sent as a backup?"

The Croag nodded, his eyes intent on his work.

Deke raised his eyebrow, signaling to Mara that they should leave. "I'd like to get a closer look at the hole in the capsule," he told her, keeping his voice low as they passed a recreational center.

"Why?"

"In case we have to leave . . . fast."

His feeling about their imminent need to escape was confirmed when Fromoth Trun summoned him to his private suite.

"Commander, would you care for a beverage?" the wily Croag offered, still wearing his elaborate regalia.

"No, thanks." He stood nervously, wondering what the Yanuran leader wanted. Was he going to strike a bargain to let them all go?

"I have a comm panel in here with a link set up to Bimordus Two," Fromoth Trun said, gesturing toward a console by a wall. "You may notify your superiors of our gracious hospitality and extend your team's approval of our application."

Deke set his jaw determinedly. "I can't do that."

"Why not?" The Croag's face turned ugly and his hands clenched into fists.

Deke didn't want to reveal the extent of his knowledge regarding Fromoth Trun's plan to launch a chemical warfare offensive, because that would erase any pretense between them. If he hoped to be treated with civility and not clapped in irons, he'd better come up with a good reason for his delay.

"I, uh, was thinking about your previous offer," he said, meeting the Croag's bulging eyes. "You'd said our worlds—Eranus and Yanura—might benefit from a scientific exchange. You make a valid point. Not only does Eranus possess the harvesters you require, but we have other advancements that would benefit your people."

Noting an interested gleam in Fromoth Trun's eyes, Deke warmed to the subject, rattling off a list: speed thruster packs for underwater divers, a liquid breathing medium that prevented nitrogen narcosis, a prototype winged submersible for deep-sea exploration, ROVs—remotely operated vehicles—that performed difficult mechanical operations underwater.

"Besides our technology, we have our mining industry. Manganese nodules are only one of the rich mineral resources we can recover. On the other hand, you're ahead of us in pharmacological research and aquaculture."

Fromoth Trun stared at him. "I thought you said you have no authority on Eranus."

"Not now I don't . . . unless I win the chancellorship. But there's always my father. I'm sure I could convince him to listen. We still need Larikk's vaccine for Turtle Ravage disease, among other things you have to offer."

"Hmm. So you wish to make a private deal."

"You got it!" Deke said smugly. Sometimes it took a bit of crookedness to snare a crook, and it appeared as though Fromoth Trun might swallow his bait.

"I shall confer with my ministers. You are certain obtaining the harvesters from Eranus wouldn't be a problem? This would have to take place within the immediate future."

"I can arrange it."

"We'll still want to join the Coalition and reap the benefits of all the member worlds, but you and I may be able to reach an agreement." His skin mottled. "Of course, if you're bluffing, our medical researchers always have need for human subjects for their experiments. Your friends are expendable if you refuse to cooperate."

Deke felt his anger rise, but he forced a note of conciliation into his voice. "My offer is a better one. We can both benefit, and no one else needs to know."

He was escorted back to his room and he wondered if he'd be kept under guard, but the fellow departed and Deke figured Fromoth Trun realized he had nowhere to run.

"That's what he thinks," he muttered under his breath.

Mara sprang from her seat on the lounger where she was playing with Jallyn. "You're back! I was getting worried. What happened?"

"Where's Hedy and Wren?"

"They went to the rec room to watch a Katuba tournament. They should be returning soon."

She'd changed into one of the short, loose tunics provided by their hosts and his gaze drifted to her long legs. "I'll tell you about it when they get back," he said.

"In that case," she said, thrusting Jallyn into his arms, "you hold her for a while. I'm going to take a shower."

"What?" He nearly dropped the baby. "I don't know what to do with her!"

"I have confidence in your ability." And with those taunting words, she vanished inside the sanitary facility.

"Blast, now what?" He stared at the child's face. Her tiny mouth puckered and her eyes pinched and she began to wail. "Quiet!" he said, alarmed. Fumbling for a bottle in the supply bag, he jabbed the nipple at her mouth, but her howls grew louder.

"Drink!" he ordered, trying again. Her face reddened. Squirming, Jallyn opened her mouth wide and renewed her squalls with ear-piercing shrillness.

"Having a problem?"

Hedy's voice made him whirl around. She had returned with Wren and stood in the open doorway, grinning.

Relieved, he rushed forward. "She's all yours!" he cried, popping the wriggling infant into Hedy's outstretched arms. Winking at him, Hedy took the bottle and stroked the nipple against the baby's cheek. Immediately Jallyn's mouth grasped onto it and suckled noisily.

"Whew!" he said, glad for the silence.

"What's up?" Wren asked, his long stride carrying him inside. Going over to the cooler unit, he took one of his Cal drinks out and gulped down the contents.

Deke shut the door, swiping a weary hand over his face. "We've got trouble."

"So what else is new?" Wren raised a layered eyebrow.

Deke waited until Mara emerged, looking refreshed and exotically beautiful in a forest green belted tunic, her curves delineated by the soft fabric.

"Fromoth Trun has upped the stakes," he told them.

Relating their conversation, he concluded: "If I don't get him those harvesters, he's going to feed you to his medical researchers as test subjects. We may only have a few hauras before he sends for me again."

Tersely, he related his escape plan.

Chapter Twenty-one

"Deke, is this everything you need?" Mara asked.

"I hope so," he replied, a lock of his hair falling across his brow as he bent forward to examine their stash of supplies. Having discovered a vacant storage hangar, he had instructed his team to meet him there. His earlier inspection of the damage to the disabled transfer capsule showed what was required to fix it, so he'd assigned everyone a list of items to acquire and they'd split up. Using the excuse that the temperature in their guest quarters was too low, they'd received permission to construct a heating element and were granted certain materials to use in building the device. What they weren't given, they appropriated when no one was looking. The timing of their escape would be tricky. The entire plan depended upon how much Deke could achieve in the next few hauras.

He studied the heap of tools in front of him. Hopefully none of the Croags would have reason to visit this remote corner, but in case they did, he set Wren to work fashioning a miniature heater so they could show something for their efforts. He'd already sent Hedy back to their room to care for Jallyn and warn them if Fromoth Trun summoned him.

Squatting by the stash of supplies, he checked to see what his teammates had been able to obtain: cable cutters, pneumatic tools, couplings, fishnet, pressure lines, valves, foam sheeting, rubbery gum matrix, and assorted other odds and ends. Pilfered from various places such as the machine shop, science labs, data center, and systems maintenance, the items that were unauthorized shouldn't be missed for a while, and by that time Deke hoped he and his team would be gone.

Laying out the long-sleeved clothing Wren had received by complaining of the cold temperature, Deke melded the edges together into a one-piece suit and hood using Hedy's thermal tissue regenerator. Spraying the suit with the rubbery matrix made it waterproof. If his body temperature dropped, he'd lose dexterity, and with the delicate maneuvers he needed to perform during his splashdown, he couldn't afford to take extra risks. It was imperative he stay as warm as possible, because body heat dissipated much more rapidly in a watery environment than in air.

Instructing Mara to weld some hooks and snaps onto his belt, which he took off for her to work on, he examined the gas cylinders he'd confiscated from an emergency station along the way. They should be adequate, he thought optimistically. Using the pneumatic drill, he punched a hole in the two-foot-thick outer wall and threaded one of the hose lines through. The puncture was too small to cause a leak but would provide him with access to his air tanks once he connected the hose from the outside.

That part being assembled, he glanced at his chronometer. They should start back to their room soon.

"I'm finished, sir," Wren stated, holding up his miniature

heating device. "Shall I return to our chamber?"

"Go ahead. Mara and I will be along shortly."

Mara's eyes were round as saucers as she regarded him warily. "Isn't this awfully ambitious, Deke? What if something goes wrong?"

Relaxing on his heels, he stared at her. "What's our alternative? To wait until Fromoth Trun gets disgusted with my delays and kills us all? We don't have any options. If we don't make a break for it, we're dead."

"Can't Ebo do something?"

"He'll stage a diversion when we're ready to make our move, but he can't get to us until we surface."

"I'm afraid for you!" she cried, her voice laced with concern. "Your part is too dangerous."

"Don't do that to me, Mara," he said warningly.

She looked startled. "Don't do what?"

"Interfere. You acted like this before going to the pools with Onus Laola and I ended up getting attacked by terrorists."

"That wasn't my fault!"

"No, but you'll undermine my confidence if you sense bad things coming. I can't afford to be nervous. None of the rest of you can do my job. I've got to get you into the transfer capsule, plug the ballast hole, and fashion a buoyancy device to get you all to the surface. If I don't have total concentration, I'll fail."

His attitude softened when he saw the crestfallen look on her face. "I know you're concerned about me and I appreciate it, but please try to focus on your own job."

"Of course," Mara mumbled, wounded that he still couldn't accept her strong feelings for him. She'd been watching him work, amazed at how skillfully he welded materials together with a knowledge she couldn't begin to comprehend. Her admiration increased, but so did her dejection. Despite their team efforts, he wouldn't admit to needing anyone else . . . and her in particular.

"I'm about finished here. Help me pack these things and then we can go," he said, his tone curt.

She complied, wondering how Hedy and Wren were getting along. Ever since the conflict in the jungle, they'd been acting differently toward each other. It appeared as though their relationship was moving forward, while hers and Deke's just floundered in limbo.

Give it time, she told herself, but under their current circumstances, she feared time was running out.

In their room, Hedy was just putting Jallyn into her makeshift crib for a nap. She looked up to catch Wren gazing at her with an unfathomable expression.

"What is it?" she asked, wondering how he felt about her. He hadn't said anything intimate since they'd arrived here, and she hoped he still wanted her. Now that he regarded himself as a whole man, he might decide to pursue other females, perhaps those of his own native species.

"I was picturing how you will look holding *our* child," he responded, his tone gruff as he stepped forward. "Hedy Te'larr, would you do me the honor of becoming my mate?"

Her eyes widened and her heart caught in her throat. "I-I . . . yes!" she blurted, rushing into his arms.

Later, when he eased his desperate kisses to allow her a breath of air, she whispered mischievously but with barely suppressed desire, "How about getting a head start on creating that child of ours?"

The feverish gleam in his hazel eyes made her knees sag. "I wish to do it properly with you the first time," he said.

Her glance swept the bedding. "Why not—"

"Hush, this isn't how Polluxites initiate their coupling." And he whispered into her ear, telling her how his kind did it.

"My, that is worth waiting for, isn't it!" she exclaimed.

The door burst open and they sprang apart, flushing guiltily. Mara and Deke strode into the room.

Mara noticed the look Wren and Hedy exchanged, and her conviction grew that something significant had occurred between them. Could Hedy have broken Wren's cultural barriers? It was too bad that she and Deke couldn't have stayed away longer, but they had no time for such pursuits now. Deke was right; they needed to focus on their jobs if their escape plan was to succeed.

"How's Jallyn?" she asked, strolling forward.

"She's asleep." Hedy's color deepened. "Did, uh, you and Deke finish what you had to do?"

"Yes, we were intent on business," she said pointedly. "Do you have the baby's bag packed in case we have to move fast?"

"It's ready. How much time do you think we have?"

"No time," Deke said grimly, hearing footsteps in the corridor. A pair of armed Croags stopped at their door.

"Fromoth Trun wishes to see you and Mistress Mara."

Alarmed, he glanced at Mara. Why would the Yanuran leader request her presence? Did he need her to translate for him, or did he hope to use her mellowing influence to convince Deke to approve his admissions application? Was he going to discard Deke's offer of a private deal with Eranus?

Swallowing apprehensively, he followed Mara down the hallway.

The Yanuran leader dispensed with civilities and got right to the point. "I conferred with my ministers and we decided there isn't time for you to contact Eranus and make the arrangements we discussed. Getting Coalition approval is a speedier route. We must get those harvesters! Here, Commander." He thrust a microphone at Deke. "Give your affirmation of our admission status."

"I'm sorry," he said quietly, standing firm, "I cannot do that. Based on the political problems facing your government and the violations of Coalition law, I have to recommend a rejection."

From the way Fromoth Trun's skin changed colors, Deke feared a nasty reprisal was in store for them. *We haven't finished preparing for our escape, but now may be our only chance!* Pressing a knob on the side of his dive computer, he sent Ebo the signal to initiate their plan.

High-frequency sonic energy bombarded the habitat, affecting only the frog people with sensitive hearing. Fromoth Trun croaked and doubled over.

"Come on!" Deke yelled, knowing that a concentrated beam of goburon particles was going to be aimed at the ocean floor, disrupting the current and possibly shifting the habitat's foundation. They had to collect the others and reach the storage hangar before any of the watertight doors shut. Ebo was supposed to electronically jam communications, so the Croags couldn't send out an alert about their escape.

Grabbing Mara's hand, he pulled her toward the door.

"Emergency stations!" he ordered the armed troops standing guard outside. As he spoke, an explosion rocked the habitant and alarms started clanging. He rushed down the twisting corridors in the direction of his quarters.

"Let's go!" he told Hedy and Wren, who were expectantly holding Jallyn and their sacks of supplies.

They sped toward the storage hangar. Once inside, Deke gathered up his gear. "They'll expect us to be heading for the functioning transfer capsule. We've got to keep them busy while I'm making repairs to the other one."

Accordingly, he used his pneumatic tools to create havoc along the way. The Croags, hands held to their ear disks to block out the piercing sonic barrage, scurried about as compartments flooded and emergency teams responded. No one tried to stop them, but Deke figured that would change once Fromoth Trun regained control.

On their way to the air lock that would lead them into the disabled transfer capsule, they ran into their first snag. They had to descend to a lower level and the compartment below was flooded.

"I'll check it out," he said, donning his dive gear.

Mara held her breath as Deke submerged into the rippling water. He'd managed to find a portable light source which he had strapped onto his head as a lamp, and slabs of flexible plastic clipped onto his shoes made them into fins. His tools were strung onto his belt, providing easy access and weight. Covered in his manufactured wet suit with grease smeared on his face and body for added insulation, he appeared well outfitted, but she knew unknown hazards faced him and was terrified.

When his head popped up, she breathed a sigh of relief. With the tension they were experiencing, she feared she wouldn't be able to keep her separations under control. It would take a major effort on her part not to respond to Deke's strong emotional reactions.

The look he gave them was grim as he rose to the top rung of the ladder from the lower level and peered through his improvised face mask. "It's clear at the other end, but I'll have to get you through this portion. You'll be able to hold your breath until we're halfway; then we'll share my air."

He'd explained that his cylinders contained a travel mixture of gases that would allow him optimum bottom time. Mara gazed at him in panic. She'd have to swim through a flooded compartment? What if he lost his grip on her and she floated away?

Sensing her fear, Deke gave a reassuring grin.

She got a brief glimpse of his dimples and realized how

little he'd been smiling lately. How she missed those early sexy encounters on the ship before all this trouble started!

Gamely stepping forward, she cringed when the water covered her boots. "What about Jallyn?" she asked suddenly, glancing over her shoulder at Hedy, who cradled the infant in her arms.

"I'll encase her in a cocoon made from the spray-on rubbery matrix and fill it with air. Tying on these wrenches will give it weight. You go first; then I'll bring her to you."

Mara gasped from the cold temperature as she lowered herself further and the water soaked her clothes. Darkness enveloped her as she submerged, terrified. Deke guided her along and she held her breath until she thought her lungs would burst; then he gave her the mouthpiece. Unfamiliar with the equipment, she choked in several short bursts of air. Eventually slowing, she gestured for him to take it back and they alternated breaths, making it to a platform on the other side which stood clear of the water.

"This runs by hydraulics but they're not functioning," Deke said. "We'll have to raise ourselves manually. Wait here. I'll get Jallyn."

While Mara shook from the cold and her own fright, he vanished beneath the water's surface.

A short time later, they all stood on the platform, and Jallyn had been released from her makeshift cocoon. Wren helped Deke operate the manual cable system until they reached the upper level and faced a double hatchway.

"I figured they wouldn't post any guards here," Deke said, urging them forward.

No one obstructed their path as they cracked the hatch to the emergency escape vessel. The interior of the saucer-shaped capsule presented an array of dials, screens, and sensors: a searchlight, radio gear, an acoustic communications rig, compasses, a sonar monitor that revealed the surrounding terrain in three dimensional color, air-recycling controls. Deke ran a quick check on all systems. Battery power would sustain life support, but the propulsion system was dead.

The main problems he had to address were buoyancy and ballast in order to raise the capsule to the surface and send it down again. Their plan was for him to plug the hole in the ballast tank and then fashion a lift bag so the capsule could rise. Once on the surface, his crew would scuttle the transfer vehicle. Sinking back down, it would then provide transport for him. He didn't dare consider the risks involved. Rattling off a quick set of instructions, he exited to find an air lock that would lead him outside the city.

The haunted look in Mara's eyes as she had watched him leave touched Deke's soul. He'd never known anyone to care about him as much as she did and he flushed guiltily over the callous way he'd been treating her. He couldn't help it; every time he saw her holding Jallyn, it melted his heart and made him yearn for a life he couldn't afford to think about until they were safe.

If we get out of this, I'll think seriously about our relationship, he thought, locating a lockout chamber that would allow him to exit the habitat. Forcing aside his personal concerns, he focused his attention on the job at hand.

Swimming to the transfer capsule, he peered at the jagged hole in the bottom. Hopefully, his plan would work. Based on information one of the Croags had given him, he'd bolted together a piece of board with a lug-nut setup. Now he took the device and pushed the rod threaded through the center into the hole to plug it. On the outside, he fastened a wooden plate, sealing it off by turning the wings on the nut assembly. Now when Wren released the ballast from inside, his jury-rigged device should keep the water from gushing back in.

A shiver racked his body, reminding him that his time was limited. With stiff fingers, he took the fishnet that he'd stuffed with an expansive material, swam to the hose line he'd snaked outside, fitted on a connector, and filled the lift bag with air. Attaching it to a cable, he let it go. Like a tethered balloon, the lift bag rose to the surface along with the ascent line. Hooking a loop onto the transfer capsule, Deke attached the loop to the cable and thumped on the hull, signaling Wren to release the ballast so the vehicle could rise along the taut line. Now all he had to do was wait for his friends to send the capsule back down.

As he watched it ascend, he didn't pay attention to drift and a surge of current caught him unexpectedly, sweeping him away. Like a rag doll, his body was thrust against a section of exterior piping and a twisting cable pinned him in place. He felt a swell of icy water as scores of poisonous sea urchins living on the habitat's outer rim pierced his improvised wet suit with their spines. A burning pain lanced through his back as he fought to free himself from the tangled line.

Calm down! he told himself, panic threatening to overwhelm him. He'd lost sight of the ascent line, and even if he managed to free himself, he might not find it before his air ran out. He'd brought along backup cylinders, but even so his total bottom time ran to 20 minutes and he'd used up 15 doing the repairs. Gods, what was he to do?

His struggles caused the cable to pin him in place more securely and his hands, numb from the cold, couldn't wield the cable cutters hooked to his belt. His breaths came in choking gasps, but he couldn't help himself. He had to get free!

Mara . . . where are you when I need you? Where was her calming influence, the strength that would let him carry on? His spirit pleaded for her essence to reach him and guide him to safety. He couldn't make it without her . . . because she made life worth living. In a sudden burst of clarity, Deke understood what his soul had known all along: they were meant to be together. Like two halves of a whole, they complemented each other perfectly and he needed her to be complete.

By the stars, I love her, he realized with stunned comprehension. And if I don't get to the surface, I'll never be able to tell her. *Mara, help me! Come to me!*

The transfer capsule reached the surface and Wren cracked open the hatch. Inflating an emergency raft, he helped the women and Jallyn into it before turning back to flood the ballast. Shutting the hatch, he jumped into the raft just as the vehicle began to sink underwater along its cable. When Deke joined them, Ebo would pick them up. Using the *Celeste*'s cloaking mechanism, he'd already entered Yanuran airspace and was monitoring the sensor readings for their life-forms.

Wren's wings sprouted and he glanced at Hedy. "We're free!" he shouted, enjoying the warm blaze of sunlight on his face.

Hedy's eyes danced with glee. "We have a few minutes until Deke arrives. Do you want to, uh, you know?" She glanced toward the sky.

"Why not?" Turning to Mara, he asked: "You and Jallyn will be all right by yourselves for a few minutes while we leave?"

Mara's jaw slackened. "Leave? Where are you going?"

"To heaven!" Hedy called as Wren scooped her into his arms.

He took off with Hedy, flapping his powerful wings to gain height. As they soared higher in the sky, his wings folded over, enclosing them both in a feathery embrace.

Stunned speechless, Mara would have stared after them but something tugged at her consciousness.

Mara . . . help me.

Deke needed her! With a cry of dismay, she fastened her gaze on the sparkling azure sea. He's in trouble, she realized, and I'm helpless to assist him. What had gone wrong? Desperately she wished she'd retained an item he'd touched so she could separate at will, but now when she strained to stretch her awareness, her essence remained physically grounded.

Come to me!

By the Light, he was summoning her. Her astral body instantly flew toward the source and entered his essence. Joined with him, she understood his predicament and felt his comfort at her presence. Willing her strength to him, she prayed for his safety.

Deke felt her love flow into him and knew he couldn't fail her. Gripping the cable cutters in his hand, he snapped the line that had entrapped him and swam away. Groggy from the cold that had seeped into his bones, he gazed around confusedly for the transfer capsule. He couldn't see it and according to his dive computer, he'd used up his bottom time. But did he have the energy to make a controlled ascent?

You can do it.

Mara's faith warmed him and gave him the strength to think clearly. Grabbing a line reel from his utility belt, he tied off an end to a section of nearby piping and fed out the rest of the line so that it rose to the surface. He could follow this up without worrying about drift, and thus he began a slow ascent, working hand over hand. Stopping periodically to neutralize the nitrogen in his system, he saved his third tank for the longest decompression stop at 20 feet below the surface. By the time he broke through, over an haura had passed. When his head crested the waves, he was weak, dizzy, and shaking from pain, but his heart leapt in exultation. He'd done it! Now they'd all be safe! Jettisoning his air tanks, he treaded water while the *Celeste*'s shuttle veered in his direction.

He sensed it when Mara left his awareness, content at his survival. A feeling of emptiness assailed him, and he yearned to confess his newfound feelings to her. But when the shuttle hovered over his location, he had just enough energy to grasp the dangling ladder while he was hauled aboard. The last thing he felt was the solid floor of the ship's cargo bay beneath his aching back before darkness overwhelmed him and he passed out.

Chapter Twenty-two

"I've just discharged him from sick bay," Hedy said, standing in the doorway to Mara's cabin aboard the *Celeste.* "Deke said he was going to make a full report to Bimordus Two; then he needed to wash and change. He wants you to wait here for him."

Mara thrilled at her words. She'd visited Deke while he was healing, touching him mentally with her love. Using her expanded consciousness, she'd seen the strong bonds connecting them on every auric layer. When had this occurred? Had he finally recognized his need for her and was that why he'd summoned her essence? The cords between their chakras were thick and flashed with the rose color of love. Deke must have come to terms with his feelings for her, she figured. For the first time he'd exerted control over one of her separations. That had to mean he accepted her without reservations.

Once he had regained consciousness, he'd concentrated on completing a final task. He had ordered Ebo to search for and destroy the missile silos on Yanura before setting course for Bimordus Two. It was an action he'd have to rationalize to his Defense League superiors, but Mara would support him wholeheartedly. Her outlook had changed on this trip. She'd been hardened to reality and it wasn't a pleasant change, but perhaps now she'd be more effective in her diplomatic encounters by being less gullible.

"Jallyn is asleep," she told Hedy, who was studying her curiously. They'd devised a makeshift crib in Mara's sleeping chamber. "Sarina can't wait until we arrive."

"I know." Hedy had been with her when Mara had contacted Jallyn's mother.

"The baby's aura is strong. I can feel her power and sense she'll be able to do much more than heal people. She'll wield an awesome force when she matures."

"Sarina will guide her, and I'm sure you'll be willing to offer your advice." Hedy smiled radiantly, and Mara remembered that she still didn't understand what had occurred between Hedy and Wren on Yanura.

"Why don't you come in?" she urged her friend, smoothing her sarong-style dress over her hips. Tired of tailored clothes, she'd chosen her native-style garb to relax in. Her own report having been sent to her superiors, she was mainly responsible for Jallyn's welfare on the return trip.

Hedy shook her head, a secretive gleam in her eyes. "Wren is coming off duty in another half-haura. I want to get out of this tunic into something"—she eyed Mara's seductive emerald drape—"more suitable."

"How was it that he could fly, Hedy? And did you two do it? When he wrapped his wings around you—"

Hedy held up a hand. "The man is afraid of heights and that's what kept him from flying on his home planet. When I fell off a cliff during the skirmish in Cloud Forest, he flew to save me. He was spectacular, Mara!" Her eyes glistened dreamily. "As for your other question, well, they do it differently on Pollux." Grinning, she turned away.

"Wait!" Mara called, anxious for details, but Hedy had already vanished into her cabin across the corridor.

Heavy booted footsteps announced Deke's arrival into the crew's quarters. He planted himself in her open doorway, looking as rakishly handsome as the first time they'd met.

"Hi," he said, his appreciative glance warming her blood.

"How are you feeling?" she asked solicitously.

"I'm fine, thanks."

She studied him for any signs of illness, but he appeared fully recovered. Her gaze drifted to the lock of hair that fell enticingly across his forehead; then she let her glance roam over his alert brown eyes, freshly shaven jaw, and chiseled mouth. Her eyes inadvertently dropped to survey his muscular form encased in a crisp, clean uniform. Aware of her scrutiny, he smiled at her, showing his even, white teeth and those ravishing dimples. Her heart thudded against her ribs as she gestured for him to enter. His overpowering presence filled the sitting room as he stepped forward, holding a small dark box in his hand. She inhaled the spicy scent of his cologne and her knees weakened with desire.

"I brought something for you," he said, holding out the box.

Taking it, she turned it in her hands. "What is it?"

Shutting the door, he answered: "I contacted Fromoth Trun and made him an offer. Although his people will have to pay for their crimes, he's sincere in his wish to join the Coalition. While Vyclor won't be permitted on the marketplace for some time, the artisans on Yanura have other goods to offer in trade. I promised to put in a word in his favor for granting his people a restricted trade license in exchange for these products. I said if he sent samples, I could show them to the economic commission. This is a holoblock, but the real item should arrive within the month.

I've ordered it specifically for you."

He paused, his eyes glowing. "On Eranus, when we wish to ask a woman to become our lifemate, we offer her a gift that is symbolic of our future together. If she accepts the gift, it means she accepts the proposal."

Her eyes widening, she pushed a button on the side of the box and a holographic image sprang into view. The delicate porcelain sculpture could only have been created by the Wort artisan she'd met in the village. It was a statue depicting a mother and child gazing lovingly into each other's faces, their arms entwined.

Tears blinded her as she regarded Deke with radiant happiness. "I accept," she whispered, choking with joy.

With a crooked grin, he stepped forward and clasped her by the shoulders. "There's a land basin in Eranus with this marvelously pure white clay. I'll bet you could learn the technique for making these things . . . if you have free time as the wife to the chancellor of the Institute for Marine Studies."

Her mouth dropped open. "What? When did you find out?"

His smile broadened. "Just now when I called in to give my report. You don't mind, do you? Because if you did, I'd reject the position."

Taking the box from her hands, he set it on a table. Then he drew her into his arms. "You're more important to me than anything else. I realized that when I was trapped underwater. Survival mattered only so I could be with you."

Lifting her chin, he gazed into her eyes. "My life doesn't mean anything without you. I want to be a part of you as you're already a part of me. I want us to merge, to join together so we can be closer. Your gift is a special quality I'll always cherish."

"On Tyberia," she answered, heat sizzling through her

at his touch, "when a woman agrees to bond with a man, it is a done deed."

"Is that right?" he murmured.

His dimples deepened, and her willpower evaporated. She wanted nothing more than to lie with him and express her love.

Lowering his head, he brushed her lips with his. "I adore you," he said huskily. "Let me show you how much I want you." And he proceeded to kiss her senseless.

Their psyches merged and she thought she'd faint from the intensity of their emotions.

I love you. Deke's unsaid words reached her consciousness and ecstasy filled her heart.

I love you, too, she sent back, and then all rational thought dissolved in the rapture of their embrace.

When they reached Bimordus Two, events passed so quickly that time seemed to fly by in a blur.

Sarina was overwhelmed with joy to be reunited with Jallyn. Her tears of happiness were reflected on Mara's face as they rejoiced over the success of the mission. There was still time before the Elevation Ceremony, which made Supreme Regent Glotaj happy.

Yanura was denied admission to the Coalition. Because of the heinous crime of abducting Jallyn, they would not be eligible to reapply for five annums. During that time, they had to accomplish several reforms: Hostilities between the warring factions were to cease; the Croags had to allow for representation of all races in the central government; they were to give the people freedom of choice regarding Vyclor; and child labor laws had to be initiated with an end to forced conscription. The Croags had to accept the presence of inspection teams from the Defense League who would supervise dismantling of their chemical warfare apparatus.

If they followed Coalition law in these matters, they

would be allowed to resubmit their application at a future date. Restrictions on trade would apply to compensate the Coalition for Larikk's death.

Fromoth Trun agreed to start the peace process with the help of Coalition mediators. An arbiter from Circutia was assigned the task of paving the road toward progress.

Deke accepted the position of chancellor at the Institute for Marine Studies on Eranus. Mara was excited because working with him would give her the opportunity to promote cooperation among different alien races invited to participate in a joint scientific effort.

When the Elevation Ceremony for the Auranians began a few days later, Deke and Mara watched from the crowd. Sarina and Teir stood on an elevated platform, holding their baby between them. Suddenly a blinding light encircled them and radiated outward.

Mara felt an answering twinge within herself. Her consciousness expanded and she could see Jallyn's grown image shimmering before her eyes. It was more powerful than anything she'd ever seen. But the glowing form wasn't alone. Surrounding it were other beings, radiating warmth and love with the Light that permeated all of creation.

A joyous feeling filled her. Turning to Deke, she reached out to him with her psychic energy, infusing him with love. He shared her vision when another figure drifted into their view.

And they both knew it was their own child, a son.

Author's Note

Nancy Cane would love to hear from her readers. Please write to her at: P.O. Box 17756, Plantation, Florida, 33318. A self-addressed, stamped envelope would be appreciated for a personal reply.